# Hope for Fitzwilliam

## Hope Series Trilogy
### Book 2

## By Jeanna Ellsworth

Check out Jeanna Ellsworth Lake's blog and other books by Hey Lady
Publications: https://www.heyladypublications.com
Follow Jeanna Ellsworth Lake on Twitter: @ellsworthjeanna
Like her on Facebook:
https://www.facebook.com/Jeanna.Ellsworth
Like the book's Facebook page:
 www.facebook.com/PrideandPrejudice.HopeSeries
Connect by email: Jeanna.ellsworth@yahoo.com

# Dedication

I wrote *Hope for Fitzwilliam* a few years ago, while I was single, not even dating, and truly not looking for a companion. My daughters put up with my Darcy obsession year after year just as gracefully as I am sure many of your families do.

One day, my oldest daughter said to me, "Mom, I don't want you to marry someone like Darcy. I know you; you need someone different." And even though I love everything about the man from Pemberley, I agreed he wasn't a great fit for my personality.

I needed someone who was determined, fun, and social; someone who could teach me to have a sense of humor and to laugh every day. And considering that I write romances, I kind of wanted to live one too—don't we all?—so I also needed someone who was romantic and charming. But I didn't want to give up on my favorite Darcy trait either: passionate in every thought, conviction, and emotion.

Clearly everyone who told me I was being picky was mistaken. (Cue laughter.)

But truthfully, deep inside, I hoped for just one more little thing . . . I wanted someone who would *fight* for my heart, and break down the independently stubborn fortress around it. With my history of a few painful years, I had serious trust issues when it came to willingly offering my heart to another man. We all have fear, anger, sorrow, and insecurities, but hopefully they occur measurably less often than our joys. If I was going to trust someone with *all* my heart, he must not refuse to hold *all* the emotions that periodically dwell in it, and never give up fighting to keep my heart his.

So which "book-boyfriend" in the Jane Austen universe best represented my hopes for a future husband? I realized that I had very clearly described Colonel Fitzwilliam. Somehow I had defined the indefinable. Suddenly I knew what I wanted and needed. From that point on, I never gave up *Hope for Fitzwilliam* to enter my life.

And last year I found him, married him, and now I carry his last name.

So I dedicate this book to my new, and *last*, husband.

But, I will have to be honest, Arthur Lake, you do not make a very good book-boyfriend. You see, book-boyfriends are fictional. No one comments on the drastic transformation in your countenance or how much happier you are since you got your book-boyfriend. Nor do book-boyfriends smile when you kiss them or cause your stomach to flip flop with a simple flirtatious look. And I can't look at them from across the room and be overwhelmed with gratitude that they entered my life.

But, with you, Arthur, I can—and do.
You rule my kingdom, Arthur

## Love, Jeanna

# Acknowledgments

My heart refuses to claim any credit for this book without first acknowledging the real heroes—the servicemen and women who leave their homes and families to protect those who cannot protect themselves. I know many of you refuse to call it a sacrifice, and that it is really more of a privilege, but nevertheless, I acknowledge *you.*

You risk all to ensure that the Mr. Collinses and bullies of the world are humbled, even if you must do the dirty work of humbling them yourself. You possess a vibrant purity of heart, an intense courage, and not only a rock-solid loyalty to those who you love, but also to those who refuse to acknowledge the service you provide for them while zealously enjoying the benefits.

Nearly all of you come back injured. Some in obvious ways, others in ways not yet understood. Many of you feel like only half the person you once were. But to those of us who you protect, the fact that you willingly fought, makes you more of a man or woman than you could have ever been if you had not fought your battle. In truth, you fought *our* battle. So, I thank you.

*And I want to acknowledge the others*
*in the world who battle*
*against foes unseen;*
*KEEP UP THE FIGHT . . .*
*And when the sun rises on another*
*day, remind yourself that you won*
*yesterday's battle. Proceed to today's*
*foes armed with this knowledge:*

## You are a war hero.

# CHAPTER 1

The heat was not the problem; it was the humidity. A relentless summer heat wave gripped the coast of southern England, and East Sussex was no exception. The area was his most remote assignment yet. Not a village for miles. Quiet. And yet sleep would not come.

Colonel Fitzwilliam turned over on his cot and lit a candle and pulled the latest letter from his satchel. He really didn't need the light to read it anymore, for he knew it by heart; each snippet of information about her was caressed in his mind repeatedly. He once again thanked God that Georgiana was a faithful correspondent.

*24 July 1812*

*Dear Richard,*

*Greetings from the north! I hope you are well and your men well trained. I am pleased to report that all here at Pemberley are fit for duty—although that number still includes only Charlotte and I and the servants.*

*As you may have heard, William and Elizabeth have extended their wedding trip in Liverpool again. My brother states he has further business that requires his attention. His latest letter said not to count on him until early August, about six weeks before Charlotte's confinement ends. You would not recognize her anymore! Two months can really change a lady with child! She is growing out of her dresses by the day. I am missing the newlyweds very much, but Charlotte assures me that even if they were here, I would not see a great deal of them anyway.*

*The Gardiners and their daughter, Avelina, and Miss Catherine Bennet stopped by a week ago on their way back from the Lake District. Avelina is such a tenderhearted young woman. She showed me all of her drawings of the butterflies and birds she saw, and I was very impressed. We were able to surprise her with a birthday cake, for she is fifteen now! I even convinced them to come for Christmas. I do hope you will be able to come as well. By that time, Charlotte's baby will be three months old. We will have a beautiful baby boy or girl to hold and snuggle up to! Oh, please say you will come!*

*Charlotte complains that I am almost as anxious about the baby as she is. Mrs. Reynolds has been encouraging me to take up "a relaxing hobby"—I suppose to keep me from pacing the floor every day. Every time Charlotte makes the slightest sound, I jump up and wish to be of assistance. Then she laughs and says the baby just kicked her ribs. I read her all of your letters. She seems genuinely interested in your stories.*

*Speaking of which, do you really think you may have to go to the Americas? Why did they declare war on us? Certainly England did nothing to them. You mentioned they were upset about British insults and our preventing their trade with France. But war? Why do we even care if America trades with France? Can we truly battle Napoleon on the Continent <u>and</u> America across the sea? It makes me worried for our army—but for you in particular.*

*It seems I worry about everyone in my life now. I worry about William while he is away, even though it seems from his letters that he is enjoying himself. And I worry about Charlotte, who just bought another black dress, which I know she could ill afford. She said that it was necessary. She is certainly being very dutiful in her mourning. And I worry about her baby. And I worry a great deal about you. Please assure me you will not have to go to the Americas to fight.*

*I look forward to your next missive—or, better yet, a visit!*

*Sincerely,*

*Georgiana*

Colonel Fitzwilliam folded up the letter and slipped on his boots. There was no need to get dressed; in camp, a colonel always slept in his uniform. Exiting his tent, he turned north towards the campfire that was still blazing. It would have been nice to have more comfortable lodgings, but the tenuous nature of their assignment meant the colonel's unit had to be prepared for orders at any moment.

There were half a dozen or so soldiers there by the fire, a few playing instruments while the others sang out merrily. He took a moment and looked at all the men.

His men. Men he would die for. Men who had left their wives and children at home to fight under his command.

The weight of the responsibility was heavy tonight.

He suspected he would receive word any day now on whether or not they would be sent to war. They were ready. He had made sure of that, but some of them were so young! And he knew he was a young colonel himself, only one-and-thirty.

He left the music and campfire and headed towards the infirmary. It was a separate set of tents on the outskirts of camp. As he entered, Mr. Heather looked up at him.

"It is late, sir," he tsked, "and you have already checked on these men. Twice." Mr. Heather swept away his straight blond hair that was just long enough to interfere with his ability to see. He was due for another haircut.

"I know, doctor. I just want to make sure they have what they need."

"Is sleep evading you again?"

Like Colonel Fitzwilliam, Mr. Heather was young for his position, but he had a knack for seeing the sick men through their illnesses. He was indispensable, even more these last two months as he had become the colonel's confidant.

Colonel Fitzwilliam nodded. "It seems I am outmaneuvered every time I lay down. It must be this blasted humidity. If only we were not threatened with rain day in and day out! Do tell the heavens to drop their burdens and get it over with! I do not think I saw the sun once today, and yet, no rain. And this is supposed to be the *sunny* part of the country." The colonel sighed. "Between you and me, Heather, I'm sick to death of this peaceful valley."

"So, you still have no word on our orders?" Mr. Heather asked.

He sighed. "I suspect I will hear tomorrow. But I think the men know it in their bones. Soldiers have a sense about things like that. My guess is that we will be headed to Americas, after a few weeks of leave to allow for farewells to our families, of course."

"Ah, so now we get to the real heart of your insomnia! Come with me." Mr. Heather gave instructions to Adrian, his assistant, and announced that he would be back in less than an hour.

The doctor motioned for the colonel to follow him. Just outside the tent, Mr. Heather explained, "Let me see if we can do anything about your insomnia."

"But the remedy you usually give me is back in the infirmary."

"No need for that tonight. We are headed to see Chaplain Lisscord. You need the parable of the seed."

Colonel Fitzwilliam shook his head in disbelief. "That is all I need to put me to sleep—preaching!" Mr. Heather laughed only politely at the joke. "Why do you want me to see Chaplain Lisscord? I already listen to his sermons every Sunday."

"Sunday churchgoer, are you? What a title! No doubt you are even more proud of that than your rank as colonel."

"Do not mock me. I still outrank you," Colonel Fitzwilliam grumbled. They were walking quickly, more quickly than Colonel Fitzwilliam wanted. "Besides, I am still handy with my fives. And I am at least a head taller than you."

Mr. Heather laughed and said, "Yes, you are correct there. But I *avoid* the battlefield. After all, with me as the only surgeon, who would mend my wounds? I might have to talk you through the surgery! Ah, here we are. Looks like Chaplain Lisscord is still awake. Chaplain, may the colonel and I come in?"

They heard an affirmative answer, and they entered. Colonel Fitzwilliam was too tall for the tent, and so he hunched over slightly. Chaplain Lisscord was sitting on his cot and looked up at them. His slightly balding head, which was usually covered with a hat, glowed with perspiration. It seemed Fitzwilliam was not the only one suffering from the humidity. The chaplain's short graying beard was neatly trimmed into a thin line that traveled up his jawbone to his hairline. His Bible lay open on his lap, but he cheerfully closed it and motioned for them to seat themselves on the cot next to him. It was rare that a low-ranking officer, such as Lisscord, got his own accommodations, but considering the private nature of a chaplain's work, the colonel had made an exception for Chaplain Lisscord—one that probably would not continue when they left for war.

Mr. Heather announced, "Lisscord, our dear colonel is heartbroken and cannot sleep."

"I am not!"

"Forgive me. He is distraught over a lady—"

"Mr. Heather!"

"Colonel Fitzwilliam, I recommend complete honesty when speaking with a man of God. Now let me relate to the good chaplain what you have disclosed over the last few months." Mr. Heather turned back to Lisscord and continued, "He is in love with a woman he cannot have. Or at least he thinks he cannot have her. Mrs. Collins is a penniless widow who is still carrying her previous husband's child. She is currently a guest at his cousin's estate in Derbyshire for her confinement. From what the colonel has shared with me, I thought we should seek your counsel. He came to me seeking more tonic for his insomnia, but I think the parable of the seed would do him more good."

"Luke 8:5–18 is a very fine parable. I think I see why he needs to hear it." The man turned to the colonel and said, "Do you know why Christ taught in parables?"

"To be mysterious?" the colonel joked.

"No. Try again."

Colonel Fitzwilliam could tell his humor was somewhat inappropriate, and so he tried to give a serious answer. "I suppose because if he taught the truth, then people would condemn him for blasphemy."

"Yes, but that is not all. Why else?"

"I do not know. Perhaps he liked to tell stories."

Chaplain Lisscord scooted forward in obvious excitement.

*Obviously the things that excite men vary greatly from one person to another,* the colonel mused.

"Christ taught in parables so that his teaching could be understood on many levels depending on one's readiness to learn. I can see this will be true for you as well. Depending on your readiness to learn, you will take away many things from this parable. Think of a parable as an onion."

Colonel Fitzwilliam wrinkled up his brows and gave him a look he had learned from Darcy. "An onion?"

"Yes, there are many layers that can be peeled away one by one. I will help you peel the dry layers that are brown. Only then will you get a chance to really partake of what is at the heart of the onion. As you study this parable and apply it to your life, you will find a most delightful center—a gift that is most nutritious and offers the best flavor to life."

The colonel glanced at his friend Mr. Heather, who gave him an encouraging look. Fitzwilliam had never fully connected to the chaplain. Lisscord seemed passionate about the oddest things— like onions. "Very well, I am listening," Colonel Fitzwilliam replied.

"Do you know what a parable is?" Mr. Heather asked.

"Yes. It is like a metaphor with a moral lesson."

The old man nodded and continued, "The parable of the seed has several morals. And depending on your readiness to learn, you will taste of its enlightenment. Do you have a Bible with you?"

"Must have left it in my other breeches," Fitzwilliam said cheekily.

"It is no matter. You can borrow my second Bible."

*Two Bibles? Was one really not enough?* The colonel recommitted himself to listen closer to the peculiar man.

"The parable of the seed is found in the eighth chapter of Luke. I will summarize. There once was a sower who went out to sow his seeds, and some fell by the wayside. The seeds were trampled on, and the birds ate them. Some seeds fell onto rocks, but although they sprung up, they had no soil or water to sustain them, and they withered away. The next set of seeds fell in with thorns, and both the seeds and the thorns grew together, but the thorns choked the seeds. Even more seeds fell onto good ground and sprang up and flourished and produced much fruit. Do you know what the seed represents?"

"No," Colonel Fitzwilliam admitted.

The chaplain opened his bible and showed him. "Read verse eleven."

Fitzwilliam took the bible from him and read aloud, "The seed is the word of God."

"Exactly, now do you see?" Mr. Heather asked eagerly.

"So the seed is . . . the Bible? Colonel Fitzwilliam looked confused. "The Bible is the word of God, no?"

"Not exactly."

The colonel laughed. "I may only be a 'Sunday churchgoer', but I know blasphemy when I hear it."

Chaplain Lisscord took the bible back from him and held it up to the candle. "It is not the book itself that is the word of God. It is what is *inside* that is the word of God. Christ's teachings, His lessons, His parables, His miraculous healings, His admonitions, and His commandments. That is the seed. Not the paper and binding."

"Well, that is what I meant. I do understand the concept of books. It is what is in them that matters."

"And it is the same with parables. It is what is in them that matters. The only way we can peel away the layers of a metaphor and gain greater understanding from them is to open them up; apply them to our lives. Mr. Heather felt you needed to hear this parable in order to do what? To help you sleep?"

"I suppose so."

"Wrong," Mr. Heather called out.

"Then enlighten me, man," Fitzwilliam grumbled. "Talking in riddles will not help my eyes close peacefully."

Chaplain Lisscord replied, "I admit that Mr. Heather and I gossip like old wives. He has told me a great deal of your infatuation with Mrs. Collins, so I am better prepared than you may think to offer you advice. Mr. Heather even told me how instrumental the two of you were in getting Mr. and Mrs. Darcy together."

The colonel didn't know how he felt about his friend telling stories about him to the chaplain. Fitzwilliam cleared his throat and decided that he couldn't feel any worse, no matter how many people knew of his hopeless circumstances.

"Yes, we were quite instrumental. We knew Darcy and Miss Elizabeth loved each other, but it was a hopeless case. They were completely blind to each other's feelings. All Mrs. Collins and I did was to take off the blinders and offer them that hope. And it worked! Just six weeks later that they were married. But I do not see how this applies to me. I do indeed hold Mrs. Collins in great esteem, but I cannot marry her. She deserves much more than I have to offer."

Mr. Heather turned to Chaplain Lisscord, motioning with his head toward the Colonel said, "As I said."

Chaplain Lisscord nodded his head glumly. "Indeed, you are quite right about him."

"What?" Colonel Fitzwilliam asked. "What is he right about?"

"You, sir, are a hopeless case."

"I know. You do not have to tell me."

Mr. Heather put his hand on the Colonel's shoulder. "I think you mistake our meaning," the doctor said. "It is not that there *is* no hope for you, Colonel Fitzwilliam, it is that you *have* no hope."

"Precisely," Chaplain Lisscord replied. "You seem convinced that there is no hope for Fitzwilliam. Is there really no reason to hope that she holds you in some small regard?"

Colonel Fitzwilliam did not have to use much effort to recall his interactions with the lady, for every moment with her these last few months was permanently etched into his mind. "She has been the perfect example of what a woman in mourning should be. Once, I was escorting her and Mrs. Darcy's cousin back to the parsonage, and I offered her my arm. I certainly did not mean anything by it—it was getting dark, and I did not want her to take a misstep and injure herself. At first she took it, but then seconds later she dropped my arm and hurried on ahead of me. She folded her arms tightly across her chest. It was at that moment that I knew she did not look at me as a suitor. She could not even bear to take my arm."

"What about the time at the wedding, weeks later? You told me about sitting next to her at the wedding. Tell Chaplain Lisscord what she said."

Colonel Fitzwilliam rubbed his brow and tried not to show his discomfort. He didn't like showing his vulnerability to the chaplain, whom he admittedly didn't know well. He was getting fatigued, but he had reached a point over the last two months since the wedding where the special moment had kept him awake many hours some nights; offering him a bit of contentment—not hope, not peace, just contentment.

"It was the day of Mr. Darcy's wedding . . ." He began. Colonel Fitzwilliam was easily taken back to that moment in body, heart, and spirit.

*The garden was adorned with deep-green and rose-colored ribbons. Chairs had been set up in small groupings between the bushes in a very quaint and intimate way. He had to admit that Mrs. Reynolds and Mrs. Bennet had done a miraculous job in arranging just enough space for the guests to see the wedding. The potted plants had been positioned to create a botanical wall, making an even more private setting. The tree trunks on each side of the rose-colored path were wrapped with ribbons, and small bouquets of flowers hung in wicker baskets from the branches. The path had pink iris petals sprinkled on it, along with freshly picked tree leaves to accent their bold color. The sound of the creek behind them only made the moment even more magical.*

*His parents and Aunt Catherine sat on the right. On the left, Mr. and Mrs. Gardiner were chatting quietly to each other next to Mrs. Collins and Miss Gardiner. The latter two seemed eager to see the ceremony begin.*

*He hadn't intended to sit with them, only to offer greetings, but he had timed his entrance poorly. "Good morning, Mrs. Collins, Miss Gardiner. For such a short amount of planning time,*

*Mrs. Bennet and Mrs. Reynolds did a fabulous job at turning an already wonderful garden into a heavenly place." He looked at Mrs. Collins, and her eyes shined brightly in her dark lavender gown. She still wore a black lace shawl, but the black-veiled hat did not conceal her happiness.*

*She replied in her most musical voice, a voice he had not heard her use since the death of Mr. Collins: "I could not have said it better myself. Did Mr. Darcy explain why they chose Pemberley gardens for the wedding?"*

*"Yes. It seems Miss Elizabeth actually dreamed of this place during her illness, even though she had never seen it before. What a marvelous story!"*

*"It most definitely makes you believe in second chances." Then she broke eye contact and looked down at her hands, only to flick them back up at him momentarily.*

*He did not know what prompted him to do so, perhaps it was that the music was starting, perhaps it was that the crowd's conversations died down, perhaps it was something entirely different, but he sat down in the seat next to Mrs. Collins. She looked over at him, and a subtle look of surprise flashed in her eyes. She glanced at his parents' small grouping of chairs and then back again at him.*

*It was then that she smiled with her eyes. It was the same smile that lit up her face. He had missed that smile. It was a smile that said everything about her: genuine, honest, loyal, charitable, caring, courageous, and beautiful.*

*The wedding was that much sweeter as he remembered her smile.*

Colonel Fitzwilliam finished the story and sighed. "I was a guest at Pemberley for a week after the wedding, ostensibly to spend time with Georgiana. But Mrs. Collins was . . . distant. It was as if she had closed some imaginary door against me. I spoke to her several times, but I never saw that smile again. I was so sure that she desired me to sit next to her at the wedding, but I must have offended her in some way. All the ease and friendship we shared while we were in Kent, and even after her husband's funeral, simply vanished. So you see, there is no hope for me."

"Or it was veiled," Chaplain Lisscord suggested. "I suggest you take my bible and study that parable while pondering that moment when she smiled at you. Search your heart for its meaning. Remember, the seed is the word of God—His beliefs, His teachings, and His inner soul. It is the Bible, as you said. But you too have a Bible of sorts—your beliefs, your teachings, your inner soul. And if someone was interested enough, they could read it. What exactly is the word of Fitzwilliam? What would you like it to be?"

Colonel Fitzwilliam's head was beginning to spin under the weight of new information. He took a moment and pondered the chaplain's question, the discussion, the parable, and how it might apply to his situation. He simply could not puzzle it out.

After several minutes of patient silence, Mr. Heather asked, "What are your thoughts?"

"I am no simpleton, but I admit that I do not see a connection between my situation and the parable of the seed. Can you not enlighten me?"

Chaplain Lisscord smiled and shook his head. "Think of the seed in the parable as your Bible—all the acts of kindness you do for her, all these things you say to her, even if she seems distant toward you, she is reading your Bible. What kind of environment is Mrs. Collins in right now? Is she prepared to accept and nurture your advances? Or are you just throwing your seed along the roadside for the birds to eat? It comes down to sowing the seed in the proper place and time. She is in mourning, and will be . . . for how many more months?"

Without even thinking, he replied, "Just under nine."

Lisscord asked, "When would you say you started thinking of her the way you do now? I certainly hope it was not before her husband's death."

"No. We had a great friendship, and I respected her a great deal, but that was all. But when I saw how brave she was in the face of his death, my admiration blossomed rapidly."

"Ah, it 'blossomed'! A very apt word. I think you will understand the parable very soon. I believe she unknowingly sowed her own seeds in your fertile ground, and once the environment was right, they sprung forth and grew. She may not be ready to accept your advances, and if she is as loyal as you say, she may very well not be ready for nine months. A woman of strong character will guard her soil carefully and will not accept any of your kindnesses."

"Then there is no hope for nine months?"

"I would not say that. How much do you know about gardening?"

"Not much. Just a little about farming from working with my father's tenants."

"Consider farming then. How important it is to prepare the soil before planting?"

"Critical. I would say it is even more important than caring for the soil once the seeds are planted."

"Indeed. Ponder that along with the parable. Now if that is not enough of a hint, I might be tempted to call you bacon-brained. Think about the lesson. What do you wish for her to read from your bible and where are your seeds being sown."

Colonel Fitzwilliam stared at the two men who were anxiously looking at him to say something remarkable, but he had no idea what to say. It was a question that could not be answered in a single moment. It was a question that would keep him up for many more nights to come.

*What exactly do I wish to teach her? What do I want her to know about my thoughts, my passions, my inspiration?* Colonel Fitzwilliam unwillingly shuddered. He suddenly felt very exposed and vulnerable.

Was this how Darcy felt when he offered for Elizabeth? No wonder the man had very nearly been broken with sorrow at her refusal. Darcy had shown her his passions, his thoughts, his desires, and she had dismissed them heatedly.

That was a risk that Colonel Fitzwilliam may very well never be able to take. He then remembered the brightness in the Darcys' faces as they embraced each family member upon their departure for their wedding trip. Darcy had risked it all, twice, and Colonel Fitzwilliam was struggling to even risk it once. He had once called Darcy a prideful coward. He knew now who the real coward was.

He stood and bowed, taking the spare bible with him. There was so much risk ahead of him.

He absentmindedly pulled at his collar. The humidity was unbearable.

# CHAPTER 2

The colonel's hunch turned out to be correct. The very next day, early on the afternoon of the first of August, he received orders. He called a meeting with his officers to deliver the news.

"I know you men are anxious to hear what the express said. We are to report at Liverpool on the thirty-first of this month. It does not say whether we will depart for lower Canada directly from there, but I think we should prepare ourselves for that possibility. Officers and men are on leave until then. But before we all go our separate ways, I would like you to assess your men to ensure that their families will be well provided for while we are away.

"If we are ordered across the sea, it could be a full year or more before we return. Make sure the men talk to the quartermaster before they leave and arrange to have their monthly wages delivered to their families here in England while we are gone. You will be my eyes and ears, gentlemen. No wives or children will go hungry for any reason. I am adamant about that. Let me know details of any families that might need assistance, but I fully expect each man in this regiment to send home a full ninety percent of his wages. If that means less liquor and gambling, so be it. Do I make myself clear?"

Murmurs of consent were expressed, and the colonel stayed to answer individual questions. The general mood of the camp was quickly dampened by the news. He understood; no one wanted to risk life and limb on foreign soil thousands of miles from home.

Several of the men followed him around, as if doing so might somehow magically change the news. He finally turned to them and said, "Leavitt, Crawford, do you need assistance? You have several long days of travel if you are returning to London."

Leavitt asked, "Is that where you are going?"

The colonel hesitated, unsure of his answer. If he went to Pemberley, he could see Mrs. Collins again. But he would still have to report to Liverpool about a full month before the baby's arrival. "I have not decided. I may pay a call on my aunt in Kent first, after I finish my work here, of course. The colonel is the last to leave and the first to arrive, you know."

"Crawford and I, well, we jus' want to give our 'preciation to you. When we were under Colonel Smith's command, he never even knew our blasted names. It means a lot to us to know our families will be tak'n care of. I wouldn't want to go to war under any other man."

Colonel Fitzwilliam said, "Thank you, Leavitt. I admit I count you men as my family. When you get home, you kiss that baby of yours for me."

"A mighty nice thing of you t' say, sir."

Colonel Fitzwilliam excused himself and went to find Mr. Heather to tell him the news, since the doctor rarely left the men he cared for. Fitzwilliam found him cleaning his surgical tools.

"Did Everett need surgery after all?" Fitzwilliam asked with worry.

"Oh, no. He pulled through the fever without needing anything. He is doing splendid. I was just starting to pack up my things. I understand we will see each other again in Liverpool in a month?"

"Yes. I was just coming to tell you the news. Word is travelling quickly today. I have already witnessed many men taking down tents and loading them on the wagons. I believe some of them plan to depart straight away."

"And what about you? Where will you go?" Mr. Heather asked.

"Are you asking whether I plan to visit Pemberley?"

"That was not my exact question, but I would like to hear your answer."

Colonel Fitzwilliam raked his hands through his hair. "May I be frank? Your words last evening—the parable, the advice . . . I know you have my best interest at heart, but honestly, I am more confused than ever. Should I leave her alone until after her period of mourning? Or should I plant seeds of friendship?" Fitzwilliam sighed. "Besides, even if I do choose to pursue her, what good will it bring me? What might *she* see from it, for that matter? I have no money, no home, and no title. And with two wars going on, I may very well be offering her nothing more than another chance at widowhood."

Mr. Heather put down his tools and peered at his friend. "Colonel, when I am presented with a sick patient, I have several treatment options at my disposal. But it mostly boils down to two very simple methods: act or react. I can be proactive and treat the symptoms to the best of my abilities, or I can wait. Good care at the beginning often prevents a disaster later.

"But there is a benefit to the wait-and-see approach as well. Sometimes my own actions create further complications. Take Everett over there. With his fever and chills, I had a choice to leave him be or to put him under the knife and amputate his hand. Given enough time, he pulled through on his own. I suspect that is how it will be with Mrs. Collins."

"You think if I give her enough time, she will pull through on her own?"

"Indeed. Surely you see the options before you. You can either act or react. She showed some resistance after the Darcys' wedding, for who knows what reason. Now you have a choice whether to act or react. Take a moment and evaluate how you have behaved toward her since the wedding. Have you acted or reacted?"

Colonel Fitzwilliam pondered that a moment. He remembered breakfast on his last day at Pemberley. Georgiana had not come down yet, so it had just been Mrs. Collins and himself breaking their fast. The longer she stayed silent, the more resolved he was to keep the silence as well. When she finally spoke and politely asked what the weather would be like for his travels, he started speaking as if a dam had broken. But when Georgiana came in, Mrs. Collins quickly looked away. The colonel noticed how her behavior had changed back to the uncomfortable silence again, and he simply retreated.

He answered the doctor's question. "I have let her dictate how I behave. I have most definitely reacted, not acted." He felt a rise in his mood suddenly. "Look at me. I am a good two hundred miles from her, and yet she affects my sleep. I have memorized every interaction she and I have had and have mentally examined what I could have done to make her so altered. But I think you may be right. I need to act. I have never been passive or hesitant before, but look at me now. I am about to go to war and I am fretting over whether or not I can offer her a home."

"Hold on, Colonel. Do not get too far ahead of yourself."

He could feel his excitement growing with the awareness that he was feeling. "I have been as broody as Darcy, Heather! When have I been afraid of a woman, or anything for that matter? Why, I have danced all night long at every ball and soiree in London without want for a female partner! The time to act is now! She needs to know I care for her! I cannot be afraid or anxious one day longer."

"Colonel, hear me out a moment. I fear you misunderstood a key point. Sometimes when we choose to act, we risk even greater problems. If I had not waited to see if Everett could pull through the infection by himself, he would have been left with only one hand. A man's life would forever be altered."

"Be assured, my friend, I have no intention of attempting an amputation," Fitzwilliam chuckled.

"But there are risks and a ripple effect with every choice. Do not to be brash in your pursuit. She is still a widow in mourning."

Colonel Fitzwilliam was only half-heartedly listening. He was planning his next move. Strategy was something he was good at. "I am glad we had this talk, Heather. As I must make my way to Liverpool, I see no reason not to stop by Derbyshire on the way. I intend to spend a good deal of time sowing my seeds, if you understand my meaning. Oh dear, that sounded somewhat ungentlemanly . . . well, you know what I meant. Ha! And to think I did not understand the metaphor!"

Colonel Fitzwilliam turned on his heel and entirely missed Mr. Heather's warning as the doctor called out after him: "I worry that you still do not!"

*****

Georgiana looked out of the carriage window and declared, "Oh, Charlotte, you will love Darcy House! It has been in the family for five generations." Georgiana turned her head back to

Charlotte and saw that her friend had her hand on her protuberant stomach. "Is the baby kicking again?"

"No, it is not that. I am so sorry, but I find myself in need of a necessary room again. Something about the jostle of the carriage and not being free to move around makes it feel quite urgent. Oh, this is so embarrassing! I am afraid you have had to learn a great deal about being with child well before you should have."

"I do not mind, Charlotte. It is rather exciting for me! I feel like every day there is something new. You seem to be growing larger every minute. Oh, dear! Not that you are *large*. Forgive me. I should not have said that. Oh, I am so sorry." Georgiana looked at her hands, and her shoulders drooped.

Charlotte felt sorry for the dear girl. They had become quite close these last weeks—nearly three months now—while Elizabeth and Mr. Darcy were on their wedding trip. They stayed up several nights a week talking. Charlotte had repeatedly dodged all questions about her marriage to Mr. Collins, and eventually Georgiana had stopped asking. The young woman probably thought that Charlotte was uncomfortable or still grieving the death of her husband, which suited Charlotte's purposes well.

Indeed it did. How does one talk about a man who was, at best, insipid, but behind closed doors . . . behind closed doors he was . . . she would not think about that anymore. No, not anymore.

Charlotte reached a hand out to Georgiana, "Sweet Georgiana, I am not sensitive about my size any more than I am sensitive about my plainness."

"You are not plain!"

Charlotte smiled at her companion's innocence. She was used to having friends who were younger than her. Even Elizabeth seemed to forget that Charlotte was seven years her senior. Charlotte could recall the day Elizabeth had been born, and even the day Jane had been born. Before she married Mr. Collins, even in all her twenty-and-seven years, she had never had a suitor. Not one. Not until William Collins. She knew why.

So when Mr. Collins had appeared in Lucas Lodge in a huff that day, shouting out tirades against the Bennets and then unexpectedly asking for her hand, she had not given any thought to the consequences of marrying him. She knew it was likely to be her only chance at marriage—her one opportunity to run a house of her own and secure her future and have a family.

She deftly steered the conversation to something else. "There is no point in debating an issue that we will never agree upon, Georgiana. I thought we settled that when we tried to choose baby names. And for the record, I will *never* name any child of mine Bernard. I simply cannot do it."

This made Georgiana's face brighten. "I only offered it teasingly because you would not consider William. If it is a boy, why not name him after his father? I still do not understand."

*And you never will.*

"William is a fine name, but I feel strongly that the baby is a girl." This was her usual method of steering Georgiana away from baby boy names.

As expected, the young woman giggled and the conversation naturally moved to safer avenues.

"I have heard of old wives' tales that will tell you whether the baby will be a girl or a boy," Georgiana replied. "Put your wedding band on your necklace and hold it in your hand over the stomach, and then let the ring drop and watch how it swings. If it swings back and forth, it is a girl. If it swings in a circle, it is a boy. Or maybe it is the other way around. Have you heard of that?"

Charlotte laughed and said, "We shall try that very thing when we return to Pemberley. My wedding ring is in my treasure box. How much longer until we reach Darcy House?" She was relieved that she had again dodged questions about Mr. Collins. The baby kicked her hard, which made it all the more urgent to reach the house.

"Ten minutes. We are at Gunther Street now, so it should be only about a mile. Do you need to stop again?" Georgiana asked with concern.

"No, I can wait ten more minutes. But I will certainly be quite *relieved* upon our arrival." She laughed at her own joke; the laughter helped her mind to settle. Any moment where she did not focus on her current situation as a pregnant widow was always a welcome relief. It had been months since the constriction in her chest had abated for any length of time. The last time she had felt anything close to peace was when Colonel Fitzwilliam had found her weeping in the kitchen at the funeral luncheon.

She closed her eyes and remembered that moment. She had held up well with all the neighbors and parishioners who came to give their condolences for Mr. Collin's death until she was greeted by a beautiful young brunette named May Goodwin. May had taken her hand, squeezed it, and looked into her eyes with a piercing look. Then tears began to fall from May's face. Charlotte let her hold her hand as the silence grew between them. The woman had continued to squeeze her hand and look deep into her eyes. Charlotte had begun to feel awkward under the woman's intense gaze. It was like she was looking into her soul and reading her very thoughts. But then May lowered the shawl from around her shoulders, ever so slightly, and Charlotte could see several bruises in different stages of healing. May quickly returned her shawl to her shoulder and put a hand on Charlotte's face.

There was never a word spoken between the two, but so much was said in that moment.

It was then that Charlotte lost all control and excused herself. She retreated to the kitchen and discretely ordered the staff out, so she could have a moment to herself. She had thought that was what she wanted as she wept in private.

But then he came. The colonel's voice was so kind and gentle. He approached her ever so slowly. She remembered how differently Mr. Collins had always approached her, the sound of his heavy boots tramping through the house to find her. She still had the handkerchief the colonel had offered her, but more treasured was the feeling of friendship and companionship he had given her that day, suddenly making her know that she was not alone. She knew then she would always be able to count him as a friend.

She had not realized how long she had been thinking on the moment; suddenly the carriage slowed, and Georgiana started packing her things.

Charlotte looked out the window and saw a beautiful white house with Roman pillars on each side of a handcrafted set of double French doors. "Is that your home?"

"Yes and no." Georgiana's voice had a slight hint of humor in it, and it brought Charlotte's attention back to her. There was a mischievous grin on her face. "Charlotte, this is *your* home! You are not a guest. You are very nearly my sister, if not the closest friend I have. And if you call Pemberley your home, then you must call Darcy House your home as well. I dearly hope that you will feel welcomed and find everything you need."

Charlotte felt the pinpricks of tears forming, and she blinked them back as the door was being opened by the footman. "Thank you, Georgiana," she said quietly. "You are too kind. I am sure," she paused as they were handed out by the footman, and then continued once her feet touched the ground, "I am sure I will find exactly what I need at Darcy House."

She looked up to thank the servant, only to realize he was not a footman.

"Colonel Fitzwilliam!" Charlotte's head began to spin, and she suddenly felt light headed. The last thing she remembered was him bowing and kissing her hand.

*****

Just as Georgiana realized what was happening and cried out, Richard's quick reflexes caught Charlotte just in time, easily lifting her into his arms. Georgiana had not realized she was crying until her vision failed her and she had to wipe away tears. She hurried to the front door and the footman, who had been standing to the side, opened it immediately.

Once inside, she found the butler, Franklin, polishing silver. He was immediately on his feet, removing the polishing gloves in an instant.

"Mrs. Collins fainted," Richard explained, carrying her inside. "Open the door for the Blue Parlor."

Georgiana followed the men and Mrs. Collins to the chaise. Richard turned to Mr. Franklin and said, "Fetch Mrs. Franklin, and tell her we need a cool washcloth."

The butler left to do his bidding and Georgiana followed him. Mrs. Franklin, like Mrs. Reynolds at Pemberley, had mothered and cared for Georgiana for many years; both housekeepers held a special place in her heart. Georgiana raced to the housekeeper's private office off of the kitchen and was relieved to find her there, mending some article of clothing.

"Mrs. Franklin, Charlotte has fainted! And she is with child but has two months to go still! She is in the Blue Parlor."

"Oh dear!" Mrs. Franklin put down her sewing and stood up. "How long has it been since she last ate?"

"Let me think . . . we stopped several times, but she has not eaten since luncheon at the inn. And even then she only picked at her food. She said she felt ill from the ride and could not eat."

"I will be there shortly. I must fetch a few things."

But Georgiana, after years of being dependent on one of the many substitute mother figures, simply followed the housekeeper. Mrs. Franklin walked into the kitchen and ordered the cook to send cucumber sandwiches and fresh fruit to the Blue Parlor. Then Mrs. Franklin took a clean washcloth and a pitcher of water and set off.

Georgiana could hardly keep up with Mrs. Franklin's brisk walk. As they entered into the room, she saw Richard kneeling at Charlotte's side brushing the curls away from her face, his face much too close for propriety. It was as if they had interrupted a private moment between them, yet Charlotte was not even conscious.

Georgiana had never seen such tenderness, except between her brother and Elizabeth. It struck her rather odd to have Richard touch Charlotte in a way that spoke of affection, especially without her consent.

He was quickly ushered aside by Mrs. Franklin, and Georgiana felt a sudden desire to speak with her cousin.

"Richard? May I have a word with you?"

He didn't even glance her way when he responded. "Not now, Georgiana. Mrs. Collins needs me." The last part was said with true concern, yet almost like a caress.

She wasn't the only one who noticed the inappropriateness of not only the comment, but the tone as well. Mr. Franklin looked briefly from Charlotte to Richard and then looked away.

Charlotte's eyes started to flutter open, and Richard took a step closer, but Mrs. Franklin firmly stood her ground between them. "There now, Mrs. Collins," she whispered. "Everything is well." She wiped her face with the wet washcloth, and Charlotte moaned and reached a hand to her head.

Charlotte opened her eyes and looked around. "Georgiana?"

Georgiana came to her side and said, "You fainted, dear. Are you well?"

She started to sit up, but her protuberant abdomen made it difficult, and Richard quickly stepped forward to assist her shoulders, holding her a bit too close. The puzzled look Charlotte gave Richard mirrored exactly what Georgiana felt. Her cousin had always been kind and loving to Georgiana. He had never held back his welcoming embrace with her, but he was her guardian. Richard had always been very cognizant of where the line between being a ladies' man and showing preference resided. But if Georgiana didn't know better, she just witnessed that line being crossed.

*But with Charlotte? Could he have feelings for Charlotte?* If he did, that was certainly concerning. She would love to see Charlotte happy, of course, but she was not about to let Richard get her hopes up for nothing.

Charlotte sat up straighter and put her hand on her belly and looked at Georgiana with a look of desperation. Georgiana knew that look. It had occurred frequently in their three days of travel. The baby was kicking again, and she needed to find some privacy soon.

"Mrs. Franklin," Georgiana began, "I believe Mrs. Collins would like to refresh herself upstairs. Will you help her find her rooms and assist her in anything she will need? Richard and I will redirect the food to her room."

Mrs. Franklin nodded and helped Mrs. Collins stand. When Richard moved to start following them, Georgiana quickly took his elbow and guided him to the window. Mr. Franklin followed after the ladies, leaving Richard and Georgiana alone.

"Perhaps I should help them up the stairs," Richard suggested, looking at the door they had just exited.

Georgiana pulled harder on Richard's elbow until he turned his gaze on her. Georgiana then put her hands on her hips and said, "What are you about?"

Richard's brows furrowed in confusion. "What is wrong, Georgie? I have never seen you look so cross at me."

"I have never needed to protect my friend from you!"

"Protect her from me?"

"Yes. Charlotte is my closest friend besides Lady Jane, and I will not have you treat her as if you had real *feelings* for her. I know how you are, Richard. You like to flirt with any beautiful lady, but I will not allow you to get her hopes up, not when I know the kind of man you are. You may think you can—"

Richard interrupted her, "—woo her and make her fall in love with me only to abandon her? Georgiana, what exactly have I done to deserve such a decidedly low opinion from you?"

"Richard, do not trifle with her. She has been through too much. She still cries at night at least once a week for her husband. I hear her calling out his name."

Richard paused and said, "Poppet, I . . ."

"Do not call me 'Poppet'. I am nearing seventeen, and I will not allow you to treat her this way simply for your own amusement."

"Very well, then. Perhaps we can come to an agreement. I promise not pay her any attentions that are not sincere and intentional."

Georgiana looked at Richard in the eyes and saw a little bit of something that she had never seen before. He was very sad, even slightly gray around the temples. He looked as if he had not slept well in months. His usual jovial self was dampened. It was this lost look in his eyes that made her concede. "Very well, I shall take you at your word. Nothing but sincerity and intentional behavior. Richard, are you well?"

"As well as can be expected."

"Oh dear, I did not even pause to take a moment to ask you why you are in London! Are you on leave, or did you get your orders?" Fear shook her insides hard, and she felt the nausea come as it always did when she thought of her favorite cousin going off to war.

She had lost both of her parents when she was so young. She never even knew her mother's voice, as the poor woman had never recovered from childbed fever. Her father had lived until she was twelve, but he been heartbroken at her mother's death; Her brother had said he was left a shell of the man he had once been. He had been a dutiful and affectionate father, but, at times, his private sorrow made him distant. Georgiana worried his sorrow was compounded by her presence, since her birth had caused her mother's death.

And now she saw a bit of that same distant sorrow in Richard's eyes. "Richard? You did not answer me. Are you going to war?"

She heard someone at the door, and Charlotte stood with her hands supporting her back. "You are going to war, Colonel Fitzwilliam?"

Her cousin noticed her first. "Mrs. Collins! Please sit down!"

She did so, and then repeated her question.

He stepped away, bowed, and said, "Perhaps. All I know is that I am to report to Liverpool with my regiment in three weeks. Did you get a chance to eat something?"

"I am not hungry, thank you."

Georgiana went to her side and said as firmly as was possible, "I am going to have to insist that you have some fruit at least. Women do not simply faint for no reason."

Charlotte said, "When they are with child, they do, dearest. I am sorry I worried you. It must have been the long carriage ride."

Colonel Fitzwilliam stood silently in the corner and then blurted out, "I stopped by Darcy House last night on my way to Pemberley and was told of your imminent arrival and decided to delay my departure and escort you all home. What are you doing traveling in your condition? It seems very unwise."

"We only plan to stay in town two days and then return thereafter," Georgiana explained. She had been the one who suggested going to the city. Charlotte had seemed so distracted; she thought she needed a change of scenery. "Charlotte still needs to purchase a few things before the babe comes, so I suggested a trip to London."

Richard slapped his knee and said, "Splendid! I have a bit of shopping to do as well. There are a few items I have had my eye on at the bookshop. I shall accompany you tomorrow. It is not wise for a young lady and a beautiful woman to go unescorted to town without the proper escort. I shall be delighted to offer my services."

"Thank you, Richard." Georgiana saw a flash of light cross Richard's face and wondered at its import. Had he not just declared that he would only be sincere with his attentions? Yet he just offered to take two beautiful ladies shopping. *No, that is not what he said.* He said he would take a young lady and a beautiful woman . . . She looked at him further, but he did not see her inspection of him because he was entirely engrossed with Charlotte.

Could it possibly be? Could Richard have tender feelings for Charlotte? She looked at Charlotte for her reaction to his kindness. She was looking at her clasped hands resting on the top of her belly.

Georgiana watched as Charlotte took a deep breath and looked up, avoiding Richard's eyes, and said, "Yes, thank you for your offer."

# CHAPTER 3

Charlotte felt short of breath most of the time now, but she had never struggled like this to choke out her words. When Colonel Fitzwilliam offered to take her and Georgiana shopping, she forced herself to respond. It felt as if the words gathered in her throat like a beaver's dam, yet somehow she managed to accept his invitation. In that brief moment before answering, she had contemplated several scenarios.

He could be offering to accompany them out of pity. In that case, she should have answered, "No, thank you." Just because she was a widow did not mean she intended to let people shower her with sympathy nor pity. That was one of the things she loved most about her new friendship with Georgiana. Charlotte's young friend did not pity her.

Another possibility was that the colonel felt a duty to maintain their friendship. Her standing in society had plummeted from the reasonably respectable position of a rector's wife to a penniless widow, entirely dependent on her dear friend, Elizabeth Darcy, for the very food in front of her. Who could possibly still wish to associate with her? The idea that he was being kind to her only out of obligation somehow choked her heart.

But another problem quickly came to mind that drove away her careful consideration of his motives. She could not be seen on the arm of an eligible bachelor! Not with her obvious black mourning gown and protuberant abdomen! The gossip would be unbearable. He would be tainted by association. Rumors would spread faster than the cats fleeing Lucas Lodge whenever her sister Maria started to sing. No. She could not, and would not, allow his reputation to be damaged by her condition. He would be far wiser to shun her and forget any obligation he felt toward her. The second she had this thought, her head had dropped and she very nearly declined.

But then reason sprang, and Charlotte allowed that perhaps she had been too hasty in all her other pervious assumptions—for what could be more natural than for the colonel to wish to ensure the safety of his niece, to which he had guardianship. Perhaps he felt it was his duty to accompany his young ward in the bustling metropolis. And he had mentioned he had needed to go to the bookshop—although that was most likely an excuse to discreetly supervise Georgiana without her realizing she warranted supervision. If anything were to happen while they were out shopping, Charlotte reasoned, Mr. Darcy would hold the colonel responsible if he had known what they were about yet had not offered to escort them. And she knew the colonel too would never forgive himself.

Indeed, accompanying Georgiana might be the only way for the colonel to keep his head from Pemberley's gallows that would be made expressly for him if he failed Darcy. Yes, this must have been why he offered to take them.

Duty was a strange and unavoidable master at times. Oh, how she knew the shackles of duty.

*****

The rest of the afternoon was spent planning the next day's shopping. The three of them, Georgiana, Charlotte, and Richard, were huddled in the library discussing the last-minute needs of the baby when Franklin announced that they had visitors.

"Mrs. Gardiner and Miss Gardiner," Franklin said.

Georgiana giggled in delight. "Come in! I am so glad you were able to come! I was afraid our hasty and nonsensically short stay in London might mean we would not see each other. Avelina, look at you! I think you are almost as tall as I am now!"

Avelina smiled sweetly and hurried to Georgiana and kissed her cheek. "That cannot be true. You saw me only a few weeks ago. And turning fifteen did not increase my height, even if you did stuff me full of delicious strawberry cake."

Richard had stood and bowed at the guests when they came in. "Ah, but Miss Gardiner, I have not seen you in nearly three months! Not since that beautiful May wedding at Pemberley. Let me see you." He strutted over to her and took obvious glances up and down while he walked in a circle around her. He pressed his hand to his chin and then folded his arms in front of him. "Hmmm," he added pensively, which made a bright flush appear in her cheeks.

*Richard could be so insufferable!* Georgiana quickly pulled Richard away from Avelina. "Ignore my cousin, Avelina," she instructed. "Do not let him see your pink cheeks, for it only adds fuel to the flame. The man has no scruples when it comes to winning a lady's affection. He cares not who or how many; the goal is simply to capture and conquer. And I have seen many ladies fall victim. But have no fear; I will let you in on a secret that will assist any lady to resist his unwelcomed advances." She sent a sly look to her cousin.

"Is that so? And what secret could possibly have such an unmanageable effect?" the colonel countered.

Georgiana tried not to giggle as she said, "Dear Richard, if you understood the basic definition of a secret, then you would know better than to ask. There is no getting it out of me. You think your charms, generous smiles, and flirtations will work on anyone; but I happen to know they do not." Richard seemed to flinch slightly at her comment, but she couldn't back down from her threat now. "Sorry, Cousin. We may share a bloodline, but my loyalty lies with Miss Gardiner."

When he seemed to have recovered from the verbal spar, Richard made an exaggerated grimace. "What? Are all such family loyalties so easily broken? Dear Georgiana! You wound me!" Then turning to Charlotte and looking intently at her, he added, "No matter. I shall prevail. If I want the attention of a beautiful lady, I can get it, with or without my nearly-seventeen-year-old cousin's help." Richard then bowed deeply to Charlotte. "Now, if you ladies will excuse me, I feel the need to explore my masculine side before our shopping spree tomorrow." He turned back to the Gardiners and said, "I do hope you plan to stay for dinner."

Mrs. Gardiner giggled, "We would be delighted, thank you. My husband will arrive in an hour, and I have no doubt that he will be most eager to join you with your quest for gentlemanly pursuits."

"Splendid! You may tell Mr. Gardiner that I await him in Darcy's study. I will begin my mission there, by partaking of a very *manly* brandy." Richard looked once more at Charlotte, and then he paraded out with a flirtatious flip of his coattails.

As soon as he left the room, the ladies burst into giggles.

Avelina spoke first: "It is just the same with butterflies, you know. The male butterfly has more colorful markings than the female."

Georgiana laughed. "Really?"

"Oh yes," Avelina assured her, feigning a serious tone. "The male butterfly's coloring is so vivid that the female is nearly drugged by the sight of him." She stifled another giggle before continuing, "But of course, male butterflies do have one advantage over the gentlemen of our species: they possess no verbal form of communication. Fortunately, most gentlemen know that they should keep their mouths shut if they wish to receive the attention of a female."

Georgiana laughed and said, "Why, Avelina! I did not even need to tell you my secret!"

*****

Colonel Fitzwilliam let out his breath as he left the library. That had been *exhausting*—a sensation that was becoming all too familiar. He rubbed his eyes and quickly shook his head. He hadn't slept well in weeks now, perhaps months. He could sense that Georgiana was worried about him. He had seen his face in the mirror enough times to see the new lines there himself, and he most certainly knew the effort it took to smile when there was so much to worry about. But he was determined to put all of his energy into convincing Georgiana—and Mrs. Collins—that he was his usual, charming self.

He felt confident that his display in the library had done some good. He had managed to compliment Mrs. Collins on her beauty—for the second time today—and she couldn't have missed the way he had looked at her when he said it. His attentions must be affecting Charlotte—no, *Mrs. Collins.*

*Watch it man! Do not start talking as if you are on such familiar terms. No matter how suave and debonair you present yourself, she has not given you leave to call her by her Christian name.*

It was going to be a very long three weeks until he reported to Liverpool. He sighed, and the familiar sense of exhaustion returned.

He poured himself some brandy and then smelled it. Although the aroma had not changed, the appeal to drink had vanished. He put it down and rang the bell. When the servant came in, he ordered coffee and sat down in the high-back chair. Fatigue overcame him, and he let his head fall back against the chair.

*Were* his attentions affecting her? He admitted his demonstration in the library felt forced and even awkward, but surely she had received his covert message, no? Admittedly, he might have presented himself a little rakishly, but Miss Gardiner was nearly family. She was Elizabeth's cousin, so that would make Avelina his . . . well, they were related somehow.

The coffee came, and he poured himself a cup and sipped it, letting the deep-roasted liquid fill him while he savored its warmth. But this only led him to wonder why he felt so cold inside. What exactly had been Mrs. Collins's response to his peacock of a display? He had gazed straight at her and remarked about "a beautiful lady", and yet she had only stared back blankly at him with the subtlest nod of agreement. He could not identify that strange look of confusion and desperation in her eyes. She hadn't said anything. Not the entire time.

She did understand that he was trying to flirt with her, not Miss Gardiner, did she not? Goodness, Miss Gardiner was half his age!

Fitzwilliam grimaced and closed his eyes tight. "Oh, Lord!" he said, but it came out more of a sigh.

More confused than ever, he put down his cup and told himself that she was a smart lady who read people very well. She *must* have understood his meaning.

She simply was too much of a lady to acknowledge his attentions.

*Yes, surely that was it.*

\*\*\*\*\*

Charlotte heard a knock on her door that could only be one person. "Come in, Georgiana."

The door creaked open, and Georgiana peeked her head in. "May we come in?"

For a brief moment Charlotte felt herself stiffen. "We?"

"Avelina and I. Who else did you imagine?"

Relief flooded her, and she offered a smile. "Of course. I was just reviewing the list of what I still need to purchase."

Charlotte turned her head back down at the list and looked it over. There was not enough money to get anything more than the essentials. The christening dress would be necessary, and she would have to pick up the two black dresses she had ordered a few weeks ago that would allow her to suckle the baby. She would have preferred to order three, but that was not as important as purchasing a family Bible. How a rector had neglected to purchase a family Bible was mind boggling; she needed one right away. Mr. Collin's oversized Bible would not do. Upon realizing the impossibility of packing it in her trunks, Charlotte had donated it to the parish.

She had kept only a few of his personal effects. There was a gold watch that bore an inscription in some foreign language. She had been told it said something about making one's own luck. She planned to save it for her child if it was a son.

Then there were the handkerchiefs that she had embroidered his initials on, and the parson's collar that she made sure to wash vigorously since it still held his scent—an unpleasant mixture of sweat and licorice—as well as his wedding gift to her: a used copy of *Fordyce's Sermons*.

She saved the lace shawl she had crocheted in the first few months of her married life, and of course she kept the embroidered cross she had nearly finished when Elizabeth, and then Mr. Collins, took ill. She still had not finished it, but there would be plenty of time to do so later. It would be a gift to her daughter to remember her father by if it was a girl.

She had also held on to the three letters Mr. Collins had sent her before they were married, since they held her most pleasant memories of him. Those letters had seen her through the difficult first few months of marriage, offering the slightest bit of hope that he could be gentle and kind.

She was faintly aware that Georgiana had come in and was looking over her shoulder at the list that Charlotte was no longer examining; her thoughts had led her down much darker paths.

Georgiana said, "But why have you crossed so many things off the list, Charlotte? You will certainly need more than *two* dresses. That is exactly why my brother left you with an allowance. He told me to ensure that you purchase whatever you require."

"I know he did. But I am a guest and not a ward of his. He does not need to provide for me and my child. I do have a little money. Colonel Fitzwilliam was able to balance the ledger from the parish in Kent, and Mr. Darcy—"

"He has told you to call him William many times."

"And I have told him many times that I prefer not to. How would it look for a widowed woman to refer to a man of no relation so casually? Especially when I live in his home? If you know me at all, you know that I feel most comfortable when propriety is being maintained. I do not wish for anything to appear amiss or cause any more talk than there already is."

"But he is not even here. He would not care."

"I am. And I care."

"Very well, *Mrs. Collins*."

Charlotte knew Georgiana was trying to tease her out of her mood, but the banter fell on deaf ears. Mrs. Collins sighed and started to fold the list and busied her hands adjusting the combs and brushes on her table.

Georgiana's hands rested on top of hers until Charlotte looked up in the mirror at her. They were kind eyes. And it did to her what it always did. It reminded her of all those months she had begged for kind eyes from Mr. Collins.

Georgiana squeezed her hand and said, "If you never allow yourself to cry, it will always hurt this badly."

Charlotte remembered that Avelina was in the room. She was standing quietly by the door, respectfully looking away, trying to give them some privacy. Just then the dinner bell sounded, and it was time to put on a show. People needed to see the Charlotte she used to be, before William Collins entered her life. Before he left her penniless. Before he had robbed her of hope. At least back then she had her dignity.

She could pull it together again, she had to. *Minute by minute. Hour by hour*. And with the chime of the second bell she said to herself, *dinner by dinner*. The show must go on.

*****

As she descended the stairs, Charlotte didn't realize she was looking for Colonel Fitzwilliam. But as soon as she saw his beaming face at the base, she looked away. His gray eyes were bright tonight, almost blue, and his chestnut hair had been neatly swept back in the latest fashion. She could tell he had asked for a fresh shave since his cheeks and chin were still slightly pink from the blade. Or was he flushed for some reason? Either way he was grinning at them.

She adjusted her black shawl and lifted her chin. It wouldn't be appropriate to return his kindness. Mr. Collins had only been dead since the end of April.

But she couldn't help but offer a warm smile when he turned his kind attentions to Georgiana and embraced her. He was an affectionate cousin. She had to admit that.

Mr. and Mrs. Gardiner and Avelina entered the vestibule as well, deep in discussion.

Colonel Fitzwilliam chuckled and then turned falsely serious. "Georgiana, I have quite the predicament. Three ladies need to be escorted into the dining room, and I only have two arms. Would you be a dear and hold onto my leg like you did when you were a little girl? I will make sure to give you quite the ride!"

Charlotte understood in an instant that she was the odd lady out. He was trying to be kind, but she would not accept pity in any form.

Before Georgiana could even respond, Charlotte replied, "No need, sir. The doorway would become jammed if I took your arm in my condition." She gave him a polite curtsy that was as graceful as a lady in the middle of her seventh month could possibly be, and she motioned with her hand for them to lead the way.

His teasing look turned to something serious, he took her outstretched hand and wrapped it around his own; he clearly had misunderstood her gesture. She had merely been motioning to him to lead the way! Now, it seemed, he was escorting her to dinner. She glanced back and caught a slight frown on Georgiana's face. Mr. and Mrs. Gardiner were looking perplexed as well. Though they were all so kind to her, she knew what they must be thinking. A widow in mourning certainly would not be the first choice for a bachelor to escort to dinner.

*Why must every moment be so difficult!* She squeezed her eyes shut as she walked.

"Do you enjoy walking blind?" His voice was soft next to her, like warm caramel; sweet and thick with emotion, comforting her in an indefinable way.

She found herself licking her lips, quite hungry for some reason. She pooled all her self-control and replied nonchalantly, "It is just a small headache."

"I do hope it is not the beginning of something more serious."

"No, sir." She rallied her composure and dignity once again. How weak she felt to have let down her guard so quickly.

She was a strong woman. And the only thing required of her was to get through dinner. She smiled up at him and answered, "I believe it is nearly gone. Thank you for asking, sir."

This seemed to appease him a bit, and he grinned and patted her arm. "I do not think you need to call me 'sir' anymore. Certainly the friendship we have allows for less formality."

Mr. Gardiner interrupted at the perfect time as to render answering unnecessary.

# CHAPTER 4

Dinner had gone nearly as badly as a green recruit's first day of training. Colonel Fitzwilliam had been hammered with questions from Mr. Gardiner about the war, about his orders, and about the likelihood of him going across the pond. Colonel Fitzwilliam couldn't exactly be flirtatious and jovial with these topics, but he had tried to at least sound intelligent and knowledgeable. Ladies liked a man who was intelligent. He even threw in a few brave statements, full of confidence about how the war would be over in no time. But Mrs. Collins had been seated at the other end of the table. Georgiana's idea, no doubt. So the colonel had been unable to discern Charlotte's reactions to any of his attempts to impress her.

But now wasn't any time to contemplate last night's defeat. A more pressing onslaught was at hand.

Georgiana, Mrs. Collins, and the colonel were in the midst of their shopping expedition, and both ladies were disappointingly cool to him in displeasure. Georgiana peered at him every time he gave the slightest attention to Mrs. Collins.

But she needn't have bothered, as Mrs. Collins seemed intent on completely ignoring him. Every effort he made to offer his arm, or hand her into the carriage, was met with brevity and curtness. Whenever he tried to engage Mrs. Collins in conversation, Georgiana eagerly interrupted him while Mrs. Collins suddenly turned deaf. He was no match for their united front. After several hours of such maneuvers, he admitted defeat.

Late in the afternoon, the three of them walked down the street in a companionable stalemate. Georgiana was on the colonel's right and Mrs. Collins on his left, all three trying to appreciate the late-summer sunshine. Georgiana's companion, Mrs. Annesley, who had insisted on accompanying her charge, trailed behind. It was hardly the romantic, private outing with Charlotte that the colonel had hoped for. And just when it seemed the day could not get much worse, the colonel understood that it just might do that.

Coming their way was Lady Atkinson and her daughter, two people he did not much care for. More than once he had found himself alone in Miss Atkinson's company, in dire need of a chaperone, and he had no doubt that Lady Atkinson was the mastermind behind the schemes. Someone needed to remind them that he was only the second son of an earl, and, unless his brother died, he held no claim to the title.

Lady Atkinson stopped in front of them and looked at each of the ladies on his arms. "Miss Darcy, how nice it is to see you in town!" she said. "Colonel Fitzwilliam, you remember my daughter, Miss Gwendolyn Atkinson, do you not?"

"That I do. Some of my memories of your daughter are difficult to forget. Lady Atkinson, Miss Atkinson, allow me introduce my friend, Mrs. Collins. She is a dear friend of Mrs. Darcy and has been staying at Pemberley. And Miss Darcy's companion, Mrs. Annesley."

Lady Atkinson looked at Mrs. Collins with such finality in her assessment that even he was embarrassed for Mrs. Collins. So it did not surprise him in the least when Mrs. Collins stiffened and dropped his arm.

Mrs. Collins said politely, "It is a pleasure to meet you. If you will excuse me, I must see to my dress order." She curtsied and turned towards the shop.

He hurried after Mrs. Collins and held the door open for her, giving her a smile he had perfected over his bachelor years. No lady could resist that smile. But she gave only the slightest hint of awareness and quickly entered the shop without meeting his gaze.

The whole day was truly frustrating.

As he returned to the other ladies, he announced, hoping to extricate himself from their presence as quickly as possible, "Ladies, I fear I must leave you in Georgiana's capable hands, for I have a bit of shopping to do myself."

Just then Miss Atkinson seemed to have missed her footing and screamed in an exaggerated descent. Fitzwilliam reflexively reached out to steady her shoulder.

*A little dramatic*, he mused.

He righted her and stepped away from her grip and tipped his hat. "Careful now. There may not be a gentleman to catch you next time you fall."

He left Miss Atkinson simmering at her near miss. Obviously she had hoped to capture him in some sort of public embrace, which would have forced him to offer for her. He was halfway across the street when he felt a chill run down his spine and glanced back to see the fire in Lady Atkinson's eyes. He watched her take hold of her daughter's elbow and head into the dress shop.

*Women!* They would be vicious on the battlefield! One could never know who was friend and who was foe with their false words and conniving ways.

He had a strange feeling in the pit of his stomach, and he knew he had to listen to it. He turned back towards the dress shop and entered quietly, only to find exactly what he was afraid of.

*****

Charlotte lifted her chin and tried to respond to the questions that were being fired at her like a twenty-one gun salute. But she knew that this public interview was in no way a salute to her. She barely drew breath before the next question was fired.

The merchants and shoppers all stopped to hear what Lady Atkinson asked so loudly. "Who did you say you are?"

"Mrs. Charlotte Collins."

"And where are you from?"

"I grew up in Hertfordshire but am lately from Kent."

"Where is Mr. Collins?"

"As you can see from my mourning dress, he is no longer here."

Their eyes narrowed. "How long have you known Colonel Fitzwilliam?"

"Only since March. My late husband was the rector of Hunsford, in service of the colonel's aunt, Lady Catherine de Bourgh."

"And you are with child?"

It was quite obvious that she was, but she held her tongue, regardless of the ill-mannered question. No stranger would ever directly ask such a thing, certainly not a gently-bred lady. "Yes, my lady, I am."

There was a brief pause in the questioning, which only meant they did not know how to ask the next question. She offered the answer before they had a chance. She put her hand on her abdomen and said, "Mr. Collins died three months ago, leaving me with only his child to remember him by." She felt, rather than saw, Georgiana step closer to her in support.

Lady Atkinson looked down her nose in complete pity and announced, "Come, Gwendolyn. The colonel would never marry a penniless widow. She is harmless. Obviously you have no need to worry."

The insult hurt her deeply, not only because of the words themselves, but because the man Lady Atkinson spoke of was standing right behind her. Mrs. Collins was mortified by the realization that he had heard every bit of the rapid spit-fire drilling.

As the Atkinsons turned around to leave, Colonel Fitzwilliam looked directly at them and—without even a nod in acknowledgement of their presence—he stepped around them and gave them the cut direct.

It seemed the whole shop stood stock still, and Charlotte found she was under the scrutiny of more than just the Atkinsons. There was not a single eye that had not witnessed the looks of displeasure, the disparaging remark, nor the colonel's cut. They were eyes of vultures.

All but one set. His. His eyes didn't have green flecks of envy like the Atkinsons, or pity like everyone else in the shop. His were the gray of something else, something less carnivorous. She could not quite describe it . . . shame?

The vultures she could withstand; his disappointment she could not. She brushed off his hand as it reached out to comfort her and left, passing the shocked faces of the Atkinsons.

*****

"Richard, leave her be," Georgiana urged quietly. Colonel Fitzwilliam saw Georgiana motion for Mrs. Annesley to follow after Charlotte so she would not be on the London streets alone.

He knew he could not go after her, but he also knew his heart would not let this go. He mumbled to Georgiana, "It seems I have neglected my own shopping. I must be off. I will leave the carriage for you ladies."

He gave no consideration to the Atkinsons as he passed them. He glanced down the street and spied Mrs. Collins walking south, which served his purposes nicely since he needed to go north.

Colonel Fitzwilliam's lengthened stride had purpose. It helped to burn off the energy and anger that flooded his body. It felt much like the never-ending march he had been sent on when he first enlisted. At the time, he had thought his colonel wanted to break him under his command. But he hadn't broken. Instead that march had strengthened him and built him into the soldier he was now. His first colonel had known what he was doing.

He knew that resistance, which at first breaks down the muscle and causes pain, making you feel like giving up, eventually builds your capacity to handle more. It only makes one stronger. When he started that march, he had thought that with his broad shoulders and toned chest and abdomen, he had the physique to be a soldier. But he had soon learned that the moderate demands of riding a horse or fencing a few hours a week will never build anything. A soldier must be pushed to his brink. Pushed until he can take no more.

He realized years later, as he continued marching with his own regiment, that the lesson was quite adaptable into every aspect of his life. Through resistance, we build character and strength that allow us to flourish in our tomorrows. In short, the trials of yesterday paved the way for today's success.

He saw that success in the mirror now. Those trials forced him to rise to the challenges placed in front of him. Now he was not just broad shouldered but thick-chested and sculpted. By putting one foot in front of another, he had trained the recruits to fight for what they wanted. Then when the true battles came, a good soldier was prepared to do more than fight; he was ready to completely overpower any enemy.

*This was just another march*, he told himself. *Today's pain will only bring on stronger tomorrows.*

With such a short distance until he would reach the bookshop, he turned left and decided a walk around the block would be good for him. One lap turned into two, which turned into four.

What exactly had happened in there? Obviously Lady Atkinson had felt her daughter's chance of a marriage proposal was at risk, but what had led her to be so vile? She had very nearly accused Mrs. Collins of carrying his child with her pointed questions. And poor Mrs. Collins! To be measured and found wanting in such an offensive way would put any woman in tears.

But not his Charlotte. She was made of sturdier stock. Her courage and loyalty bore no bounds. Once again she had shown just how brave she could be. There were few in the *ton* whom he feared more than Lady Atkinson. He only prayed that the cut direct of an earl's second son held some weight.

Eventually, his legs started to protest at the pace he had been keeping. He was also beginning to feel strange looks burrow into his back from his timely and predictable appearance as he rounded the corner of the block for the innumerable time. The sun was lower in the sky. He realized he must have been marching for several hours. He had best get his shopping done.

He turned around and returned to Harland Row and entered the bookshop that he knew would still be open.

The bell rang, alerting the shopkeeper to his arrival.

The middle-aged man had his hands full with a recent shipment but kindly said, "Good afternoon. May I help you find something or are you just browsing?"

"Good afternoon to you too. I am in need of a Bible."

"My goodness! You are the second person in the last half hour looking for one! I dare wonder if I should buy one myself! Why, I am the sort that if I saw Noah building an ark, I would have pitched right in. A man willing to put that much work into something, has got to have inside knowledge from the Big Man Himself. Dare I ask, is the world coming to an end soon?" He chuckled slightly, "Forgive me. At the end of the workday, I become all talk and no work! To the right, third row from the end. You will find them on the top shelf. If you need anything else, let me know."

He thanked the man, followed his instructions, and found what he was looking for.

There she was.

In the third row, her prominent belly pressed into the shelf below, delicately balancing on her tippy toes to return a book to the top shelf. He had never liked the color black on a woman until he saw Charlotte Collins in it. Her bonnet must have just slipped off her head. Her dark chestnut hair was pulled up in nothing more than a tight bun, not a hair out of place as usual.

Simple but elegant. Yes, that was Charlotte. He corrected himself in his mind once again—*She is Mrs. Collins, not Charlotte.* But he knew it was a battle he would soon surrender, if he hadn't already. If only his heart would stop racing whenever she was near, he might have enough blood flow to his brain to direct it more appropriately. But for now, she was Charlotte. Beautiful, courageous, loyal Charlotte, who was still attempting to place that book on the shelf.

He suddenly snapped out of his distracted state and took the last few steps in her direction. He took the book from her and placed it on the shelf. "Allow me."

She definitely looked surprised to see him. She blushed brightly and returned her hands to her side and said, "Thank you, Colonel. I admit I have been struggling with it for some time." She looked away and then up at the shelf as if she was still reading the titles.

"Are you looking for a particular book?" he asked.

"Indeed, but I cannot make up my mind."

He followed her gaze to the books she was looking at. It was a shelf with five or six sizes of bibles in various shades of leather. "A bible?"

"I am afraid so. I need a family bible to write my babe's birth in. It is the last thing on my list. You must have seen the carriage outside. I told Georgiana I wanted to do this on my own, but as you can see, I am having some difficulty."

He leaned his shoulder against the shelf, crossed a foot behind the other, and tucked his thumb into his vest pocket giving her a grin. He waited until she looked at him to speak. "How is it that we have come to the same bookshop looking for the same book?"

Her brows furrowed. "You are looking for a bible?"

"Indeed. I have been counseled by the chaplain to carry one and have even been given a particular section to study. I do not particularly like the man, but I must respect that he has several years of maturity on me, with life experiences to boot, and he is a man of the cloth. I suppose it would be prudent to heed his counsel."

She seemed uncomfortable for a moment before saying, "Yes, men of the cloth often merit respect," she said dryly.

He suddenly felt like he had put his boot in his mouth. He stood upright and said, "I apologize. I had not meant to remind you of your late husband."

She took a slightly deeper breath before she looked at him and said, "What kind of bible do you need? Perhaps we can assist each other."

Colonel Fitzwilliam smiled at how Charlotte had just maneuvered around the topic of her grief. What a strong woman. He remained businesslike and said, "A small one."

"That is all?"

"Small is all I need."

She returned her gaze to the shelf and said, "I believe you will be in luck. There are two small ones to choose from."

He turned and started examining the bibles and took the smallest one and flipped through it. It was what he needed. It could fit into his satchel without it weighing him down too much. "Perfect. And what kind of bible do you need?"

"I would like a nice one that has a strong sturdy binding. The darker leather one is pushed just far enough back that I could not reach it. Do you mind?"

"Certainly." He easily reached and pulled it down, handing it to her.

She took it and flipped through it a bit. Then she opened to the front binding and examined the blank pages before the title page. "This will do for me."

"Splendid. If I may, I will buy your bible for you. It is the least I can do after subjecting you to Lady Atkinson's horrid performance back there."

Charlotte lifted her chin and seemed to deliberate momentarily, but then handed the bible to him. He reached for it, but she held it for a moment making him look down at it, then back up at her. In hushed tones, she said, "As a friend, Colonel Fitzwilliam, I will tell you this only once. I do not need your pity nor your sympathy."

He took the book from her hands and said, "And as your friend, I promise that you shall never see pity in my eyes when I look at you."

*What an infuriatingly stubborn and, God grant her, courageous woman!*

# CHAPTER 5

With all of the shopping complete, Charlotte suggested they depart the next morning for Pemberley. But despite everything she had to do to prepare for the departure, she was quite distracted by his words in the bookshop. They seemed to echo in her head. *As your friend, I promise that you shall never see pity in my eyes when I look at you.* If it wasn't pity, then what was it she saw in those deep-gray, nearly blue eyes?

She found she was in need of a friend. Not, of course, to discuss the colonel's eyes, but because it had been a trying day. But just as she opened her door to seek out Georgiana, she discovered the young woman already standing there, ready to knock.

"Oh!" Charlotte cried in surprise. "I was just coming to see you!"

"May I come in?"

"Of course you may. I was just thinking how nice it would be to talk with you."

Georgiana embraced her and said, "I am so sorry for everything that happened today. Please know that Richard and I consider you a dear friend. Indeed, I feel like I should apologize for that woman. You were so brave! I am so lucky to have you as a friend and confidant. I have never had a better friend than you, other than Lady Jane, of course."

Charlotte definitely did not want to talk about what had happened in the dress shop. It would only bring his eyes to her mind again. She smiled and asked, "Who is Lady Jane? And if she is so close to you, why do you address her so formally?"

"It is her father's preference. He is very strict about propriety. I have to address her as Lady Jane in all our letters. She and I send each other our latest ladies' novel recommendations.

We have so much fun writing creative reviews on them! She has even sent a few of her polished reviews to the *London Times*. But they are unwilling to print a lady's writing, so she has decided to adopt a pen name and pretend she is a gentleman! She is so clever!"

"She does sound intelligent. A lady in today's world needs to be resourceful. I should know." Charlotte motioned for her to come in.

They both sat down on the bed. Georgiana put her hand on Charlotte's and asked gently, "Is it terribly scary to think that you will soon have a mouth to feed, but no husband?"

She had to think about her answer. At the moment, no one besides May Goodwin from the funeral suspected the truth about Mr. Collins.

And Charlotte was determined to keep it that way.

If she thought people pitied her now, just wait until they learned that he had raised his hand to her every night. That he was provoked into a rage at the slightest annoyance.

It had come as a shock the first time he hit her. Her hair had fallen out of her bun while she was working in the garden one day. She quickly learned to keep herself presentable. Appearances were vital: a lesson that only needed to be covered once. Later, when she splurged on a piece of roast beef for his birthday, she learned that he preferred to choose what they ate. With every breath she took for the next month, each inhalation sending pain to her broken rib, she was reminded that he was to be consulted on all matters of finance. The only moments of peaceful sleep during those five months of marriage were when he was sent out of town by Lady Catherine.

She didn't want to burden Georgiana with her troubles. The girl was strong, but fate had dealt Georgiana troubles of her own—both her parents had died and she had endured an unhappy year at a school for ladies. Georgiana had also confessed that there was a time she had fancied herself in love and almost eloped at fifteen. Charlotte knew that if a girl could be manipulated into eloping, she had an element of naivety that Charlotte never had.

Well, that wasn't entirely correct. Charlotte had naively underestimated the importance of selecting a compatible spouse. Marriage had not turned out to be what she imagined, and it had put an end to nearly all her other relationships. It took a great deal to convince Mr. Collins to allow Elizabeth and Charlotte's sister, Maria, to visit the parsonage last spring. Mr. Collins finally agreed to the visit so that "Elizabeth could see what she had passed on." Another lesson learned: validate his importance to others. There were simply too many lessons learned in such a short amount of time.

She thought it was high time she stopped reviewing the past and answer Georgiana's question. "I admit I am nervous about having another mouth to feed, but as strange as this sounds, I do not fear doing it alone."

Charlotte saw the perplexed look on Georgiana's face and knew she would have to explain herself, before the young woman returned to the topic of her dead husband again. Discussing Mr. Collins with Georgiana was growing increasingly difficult. She would have to tread carefully.

"I have spent a great deal of time evaluating my future. In doing so, I have had to look at my past. I know you are under the impression that I loved Mr. Collins, but the truth was, I did not. I never believed in love. I suppose I still do not. My marriage was what many term, a marriage of convenience. I am sure you know what I mean. Neither of us had any great fortune to share with each other, nor were either of us gaining titles or connections by marrying. But I gained the status of wife. Before that, I was nearly resolved to accept the title of spinster."

"Oh, do not say that!"

"Let me finish. I was seven-and-twenty and had no suitors until William Collins came to Meryton. He was perhaps a little socially inept and certainly verbose, but he held a respectable position of rector for your aunt, Lady Catherine de Bourgh. He had a home, a living, and—you may not know this—but he had just been refused by Elizabeth."

"Yes, she mentioned that your husband had offered for her once. From what I gather, his proposal had much to be improved upon."

"So I understand, although Elizabeth and I have not spoken much of it. After she had refused him, Mr. Collins came to my parent's home, Lucas Lodge, rather worked up, and . . . Well, it took me only a moment to realize that this was a man who could offer me what Elizabeth had just refused. I do not deny that I did all I could to encourage him in those few days he visited with us. In fact, I gave it a considerable amount of thought. I knew that if I gave him some encouragement, I could gain the only three things I thought I ever wanted. Do you know what they were?"

Georgiana only shook her head, intently listening.

"A home, security, and independence."

Georgiana said rather flatly, "But not love."

"No. I admit I did not think that was necessary. I thought as long as I respected Mr. Collins, then a home, security, and independence were all I wanted. I received the offer of marriage, and a few weeks later we were married. It was not long until I realized that I did not gain all three—a home, yes; security, perhaps; but not independence. I was not mistress of my home any more than Mrs. Reynolds is mistress of Pemberley. Your brother owns it and makes all the decisions. Perhaps she makes suggestions on what to serve at dinner or the colors of your room, but in the end, it is not her house.

"The parsonage was a home in the sense that it offered shelter. But without love, there was no warmth, and therefore there was no security. And now, I am left a penniless widow, with neither security nor home. But I have something that I vow I will never give up again."

"What is that?"

"Independence. Never again will I be dependent on a man to put bread on my table or to validate my worth as a wife and mother."

Tears had begun to form in Georgiana's eyes, and they finally dropped. "Oh, Charlotte, how can you say such a thing? It sounds like you have given up on love!"

"It sounds like that because it is true. I admit that seeing Mr. Darcy and Elizabeth's happiness sometimes makes me question my beliefs about love. When I see their selfless relationship, I wonder if there is a good man out there who might love and cherish me. But even if there is, I have nothing to entice him with. I have no fortune, no connections, and now my status is lower than before I married. I have yet to come up with an idea of how to place the bread in front of my child, but I have a year to come up with something."

"You know Elizabeth has offered you a permanent place at Pemberley as long as you need it."

"I know, but do you not see? She too has offered me a home and security, but yet she is unable to offer me independence. I still must do as she or Mr. Darcy directs."

Georgiana shook her head. "To hear you talk makes me worry whether I have any chance of finding my own love match next season when I come out."

Charlotte had not considered how Georgiana might have internalized her speech. "Oh dear, please understand that my views are mine alone. As I said, I have nothing to entice men. You, however, have a handsome dowry, a beautiful face, and you are a Darcy! There will be suitors lined up to meet you! I have no doubt of that. And like I said, I see what Elizabeth and your brother have together. The way he treats her is so considerate and kind. Every time he looks at her it makes me blush!"

This seemed to brighten Georgiana a bit. "Me as well! Their love is almost palpable. I am so thrilled to see them again. We should expect them home any day now. Oh, Charlotte, I am so sorry to know that your marriage was not a love match, but no one would have ever known. You speak so well of Mr. Collins, at least the few times you have discussed him with me. In fact, I was worried that you were nearly crippled with grief. I hope this does not sound heartless, but I am glad you are not melancholy over his death."

"Georgiana, what I have told you, I have told you in confidence. I hold no secrets from Elizabeth,"—*well, perhaps a few*—"but please continue to help me pay proper respect to Mr. Collins. I feel very strongly that he deserves to be properly mourned, even if our marriage was not a love match. It will say more about *me* and *my* character if I wear this black and behave as a proper widow should. I want people to look at me and see a strong woman who is devoted and loyal. For that is who I am."

The next part took some inner strength to say, but Georgiana needed reassuring, so Charlotte continued. "Being married was different than I expected, but not worse than I had hoped." Oh, how she hated to lie! "And now, I can be my own woman and not hope for any man to bring me a home, security, or independence. I feel that as smart as I am, I will be able to supply all three for myself and my daughter."

Georgiana giggled slightly. "Do you really think it will be a daughter?"

Charlotte was relieved that once again the distraction worked.

"I do. Let us talk about names again." And so they did. The conversation had been draining, but, in a way, it felt good to put to words all that she had been feeling. She would find a way to be her own master.

And with a slight flicker of doubt, her heart deviously told her never to give up hope on love.

Unbidden, a deep-gray set of eyes came to mind.

*****

A few days later, Mr. Darcy reached to hand his wife out of the carriage at Pemberley. He loved the sparkle that came to her eyes when he kissed her, and the enticement was simply too great. He took her face in both hands and held her to his lips regardless of having numerous servants standing as witnesses. He did not care. The whole world could watch if it wished to.

"Dearest Elizabeth, welcome home."

"Will, you are incorrigible." He could see the corners of her mouth turn up, and he kissed her again.

In one quick movement, he swept her off her feet, chuckling at her squeals of laughter. He teased, "Do not think for one moment I would let you come home to Pemberley without being carried over the threshold of our home." He walked by Mr. Reynolds, the butler, who was holding the door for him. "Thank you, Reynolds. Is there any chance we can hold off the news of our arrival while Mrs. Darcy and I refresh ourselves; perhaps until dinner?"

Elizabeth giggled and said, "Dearest, I am afraid it is too late for that!"

He heard a familiar male voice behind him. "I say, Darcy, stop manhandling your wife, and say hello to your cousin and sister whom you have not seen for three months. Georgiana, is this what we have to look forward to? Is this what we have rushed home to see?"

Darcy grinned and carefully placed Elizabeth on her feet and turned around to find that Georgiana was running to him with open arms. Charlotte stood next to Richard somewhat stiffly while he was leaning into her and whispering something. From Richard's laugh afterwards, Darcy suspected it was a bit of teasing; however, Charlotte didn't seem to appreciate the remark.

Darcy embraced Georgiana, and she then embraced his wife. He walked to Charlotte and greeted her. "Charlotte! I see we returned with little time to spare! I am terribly sorry for the delay."

She smiled at him and said, "I still have a few weeks to go yet, probably over a month and a half. Although we missed you and Elizabeth, it was wonderful to get to know your sweet sister while you were away, Mr. Darcy."

"William or Will. I have told you many times to call me William like all the rest of my family does."

"I remember, sir." Her unwillingness to do so immediately told him that she still was not ready.

Richard interrupted, "He prefers 'Little Willy', Mrs. Collins. It is a nickname his mother gave him when he was two, and I am afraid being two years older, it simply stuck with me. Oh, but do not call him Fitz. He truly hates it. Which is why I do it."

Darcy declared, "Richard Allen Fitzwilliam, I shall never tire of your humor! Although I have, on occasion, tired of your presence. But now is not that occasion. Come here, man!" He took his hand and pulled him in and slapped him on the back.

"Well, Darcy, I have never seen you so . . ." He turned to Charlotte. "Help me, Mrs. Collins. What is the word I am looking for?"

"Animated?" she offered, which made both men chuckle.

Georgiana spoke up from behind and said, "Dilly-headed?"

By now the game had started, and Elizabeth joined in. "Jolly-bopped?"

"Dandified?" Charlotte's face finally gave way to a genuine smile as she added another comment.

"Walloped and horsewhipped!" Georgiana yelled out.

Darcy said, "I am none of those things!"

"I daresay, Mrs. Collins, if he is not animated, dilly-brained, jolly-bopped, dandified, walloped or horsewhipped, what is he?"

His wife came and took his hand and brought it to her lips. "He is in love."

He looked down at her face and resisted the urge to kiss her smartly.

Richard stepped a little closer and whispered, "Keep it in check, Fitz."

Darcy suddenly remembered the proximity of his younger sister and knew Richard was right. "How has Pemberley been without us?" he asked.

Georgiana said, "We do not rightly know! We just arrived from London."

Darcy's brows furrowed, and he looked at Richard. "Why were you in London? Where is your regiment?"

"Go refresh yourself first; we have a few weeks to talk of my plans."

"A few weeks?" Elizabeth asked, her voice unnaturally high. "Richard, are you going to war?"

Darcy glanced over at Charlotte to see her reaction, but her face was expressionless. Richard then said, "I am afraid so. At least we have been asked to gather in Liverpool in just over two weeks."

He caught Elizabeth glancing at Charlotte too. When his wife turned to him, he saw the same concern in her eyes. How were they to get Charlotte and Richard together if he was going off to war?

Always ready with a joke, Richard said, "For king and country! These next two weeks will have to be memorable!"

Something about his effort to sound jovial, seemed forced. Darcy made a note to have a private talk with him a bit later.

"Yes, we will talk about it later. Come, Elizabeth, let us refresh ourselves."

*****

Once their bedroom door was closed, Elizabeth was lovingly attacked from behind, and she felt him snuggle into her neck. He started to unpin her hair, and she turned to him and said, "Will, did anything seem amiss downstairs? I mean, between Charlotte and Richard." He stopped snuggling her and allowed her to turn around and look at him.

"I am glad I was not the only one who noticed."

"What was wrong with Richard? He seemed different. And Charlotte seemed uneasy with his attentions."

"I am not sure what to make of it, love. Not a one of his letters to me in Liverpool even mentioned Charlotte. Perhaps his time away from her has tempered his affection. I think it is too early to tell. Though I do agree with you that we should not tell him all we have found out about Mr. Collins, the ledger, and the ships. I think if we are careful, we can appease Richard for two more weeks until he departs with his regiment. That will buy us plenty of time to work things out with Mr. Pastel."

Elizabeth remembered finding the mysterious ledger in Mr. Collins's room on the day of the funeral. She had never told Charlotte about the ledger, and she wasn't quite sure why she hadn't. Maybe she hesitated because she didn't want to get Charlotte's hopes up that she might have a small fortune. Charlotte had asked Darcy to balance all the household ledgers, and so it seemed only natural to give him this ledger too. But the last balance recorded was over eleven thousand pounds!

Nor had they told Charlotte of the letter in it from a mysterious C. W. Pastel. Darcy had raced about London trying to discover the correspondent's identity before their wedding, and it was one of the main reasons they kept extending their stay in Liverpool on their wedding trip. When they finally connected with Mr. Pastel in Liverpool, Elizabeth's mouth had nearly dropped to the floor with what they had learned. Although Pastel wasn't entirely forthright, what he told them would have a significant impact on Charlotte's future, and possibly Richard's too.

Elizabeth wasn't so sure it was wise to keep the information from Charlotte. But, now that there was some discord between Charlotte and Richard, the idea didn't totally lack merit. And how could Richard's feelings be tempered?

They had found out a great deal in Liverpool, not much of which was comforting. But there was so much they did not know about the ledger, the ships, or the fortune.

It was possible Charlotte might not be a penniless widow after all. But surely the only thing that could be worse than being a penniless widow was for Charlotte to believe that her situation might soon change, only to have all those hopes dashed. Elizabeth could not let that happen.

# CHAPTER 6

Richard was enjoying another cup of coffee after dinner when Darcy silently poured himself a cup as well. The two just stared at each other while drinking.

The parting of sexes seemed like such a strange custom when both men wanted to spend time with the ladies they loved. At least Richard assumed Darcy wanted to spend time with Elizabeth. But it was clear enough that Darcy had something to discuss, hence Darcy's insistence on parting after dinner.

Richard finally broke the silence. "So . . . you are happy." It wasn't a question.

"I am. Elizabeth and I are entirely happy. I was so blind in Hertfordshire."

"And she is completely recovered from the near-death experience?"

"Yes, thank God. Her illness turned out to be such a blessing. It allowed her to see me for who I am. It gave her a second chance to fall in love with me—delusional as she was—in spite of my pride and prejudice. How she ever got around to hoping for another proposal from me, I do not know."

"But you did gather your courage to ask again." Richard wanted to get a feel for how Darcy felt about the original refusal. He could not imagine offering once, let alone twice, but knew he had to gather the courage eventually. He had made his decision to act and not react to Charlotte. He had to find a way to somehow let her know that when her mourning time was over and when he returned from war, he would be there for her—always. He felt pressured to declare his admiration, and, if possible, know what her opinion was of him.

He had been getting so many mixed signals. One moment he would get nothing but short answers to direct questions; the next, he caught her looking at him. Not just looking at him, but really studying him. She had pulled back significantly since Darcy and Elizabeth's wedding, and he did not know why. She had once seemed to enjoy his companionship. They had always been comfortable in each other's presence. But the smile that she had given him when he sat down next to her at the wedding made its appearance only rarely now.

Darcy seemed to know what Richard was thinking of. Never one to mince words, he pointedly asked, "I was under the impression that you admired Charlotte. Is that still the case?"

"I do not know," the colonel sighed. "I know I thought of little but her while I was in Sussex. Sometimes I wonder if I made the men march a little longer simply because I was too distracted to blow the whistle. I think I love her, Darcy. In fact, I know I do. But what good does that do? I have nothing to offer her but another chance at widowhood. Father has bequeathed me a small country home, but what would we live off of? A man needs to provide for his wife."

"Sounds like you are thinking with your head."

Richard laughed. "Is there any other way to think?"

"Yes, there is. As a man about to go to war and risk his life and limb, you might try thinking with your heart for a change. You do not need to have all of the answers at once. Do you remember what the blind curate, Mr. Cress, said at Mr. Collins's funeral?"

"Heavens! Are you going to give me another parable to look up?"

Darcy looked confused. "Another parable? What are you talking about?"

Richard took a breath. "It is something that someone said to me in Sussex." Darcy patiently waited for his cousin to explain. "Well, I confess I have not been sleeping well since your wedding. My mind simply will not be at peace. I lie down and close my eyes, and there she is in my head. Her eyes, her smile—everything about her—haunts me. While I was in Sussex, I became rather dependent on the doctor, Mr. Heather, to give me sleeping powders. While we waited every night for the powders to work, we would talk. It felt safe to discuss her with someone who did not know her and who understood the life of a soldier. Night after night I would find myself talking to him about her.

"The night before we received orders to go to Liverpool, Mr. Heather rather unscrupulously betrayed the innermost secrets of my heart to the chaplain, Mr. Lisscord. Lisscord is the kind of preacher who can see directly into your soul. It is quite unnerving. He has a way of discerning things that you do not intend others to know. Well, Mr. Lisscord sympathized with me and shared with me a passage in Luke called the parable of the seed. Do you have a bible in here?"

Darcy stood and put down his coffee cup. He walked to the corner wall of books. It only took him a minute to find it and bring it back. Richard opened up to the scripture and read it aloud.

*Luke 8*

*5 A sower went out to sow his seed: and as he sowed, some fell by the way side; and it was trodden down, and the fowls of the air devoured it.*

*6 And some fell upon a rock; and as soon as it was sprung up, it withered away, because it lacked moisture.*

*7 And some fell among the thorns; and the thorns sprang up with it, and choked it.*

*8 And the other fell on good ground, and sprang up, and bare fruit an hundredfold. And when he had said these things, he cried, He that hath ears to hear, let him hear.*

Darcy looked at him and seemed to be thinking on how to respond. He finally asked, "And Mr. Lisscord called it the parable of the *seed*?"

"Yes, why?"

"I believe it is actually called the parable of the *sower*."

"Truly? Why would he call it something else?"

"I do not know," Darcy confessed. "Why would they direct you to a parable about missionary work?"

"Missionary work? Ah, yes, because the seed is the word of God. Now I understand . . . Well, then again, no. Actually, I am more confused. They said that each of us has our own Bible, the sum of all our words and actions and deeds, which is the seed. According to them, if I want to pursue a relationship with Mrs.

Collins, I should encourage her to read my Bible. You know, let her see my passions."

Darcy furrowed his brows. "And you have done this? Shown your preference for her? Your passions? While she is in mourning?"

"Well, I have tried! I have blatantly flirted, smiled, and complimented. I have even escorted her on a shopping trip in London, and you know how much I loathe shopping. I would much rather have taken a stick in the eye. That did not go over so well either."

"What happened?"

"We ran into Lady Atkinson and Miss Atkinson and the whole 'show her my passions' blew up in my face. Lady Atkinson nearly ate Charlotte for lunch, presumably because she felt her daughter's chances with me were threatened." He went into detail about all the questions that were fired at Charlotte and how admirably she had held her ground. He was proud to tell Darcy about his direct cut but then expressed his frustration at Charlotte's hasty departure.

There was a long moment, and silence filled the room. Richard knew that the cut he gave to Lady Atkinson would be frowned upon by his mother, and he was preparing for a similar tongue-lashing from Darcy. But Darcy surprised him and said something he was totally unprepared for.

"It sounds to me like you have just described the first part of the parable of the sower."

"What do you mean?"

"I mean you, a sower, sowed seeds, in other words showed preference to Charlotte, and not only did they not spring up, but they were trodden down and devoured—"

Richard finished his sentence, "—by fowls of the air. Gads, Darcy! When did you become so wise? The look on Lady Atkinson's face was exactly that of a vulture's."

"And I mean no offence," Darcy continued, "but the effort you have put into showing preference, or at least what I saw tonight, seemed forced and, well, insincere. Take dinner for example. I have never seen you behave so much like a dandy. You flirted with her so shamelessly that I felt embarrassed for her. You nearly pushed me out of the way as I offered to escort her into dinner so that you could have that honor. And you boasted about your regiment going bravely to war. I think you are trying too hard. You are forcing yourself on her. And, if I may be so bold as to say, now is the wrong time. Her husband died in April, and it is barely the third week in August. That is not even a full four months. She is still carrying his child."

Richard felt the truth of his words and leaned forward and put his head in his hands. "Then what am I to do? What if I go to war and come home to find she has remarried and never knew how I felt for her?"

"I am not saying do not tell her how you feel. By all means, tell her. If I had listened to my heart back in Hertfordshire and talked with Elizabeth about my growing attraction, I may have saved both of us a great deal of heartache. But stop playing the flirtatious dandy. Show her your genuine, kind, and loyal heart. I am not going to say it will bring forth fruit, but you can at least plant the seed."

Be himself. Talk about his feelings. Plant the seed and pray it brings forth fruit. As if on the verge of waiting for the trumpet to sound at the beginning of a battle, his heart began to race in both fear and anticipation.

Could he do it? And did he have enough time before he had to leave for Liverpool?

*****

Charlotte was beginning to feel more relaxed in Colonel Fitzwilliam's presence. He was behaving more like the same sensitive man she knew from Kent. He had volunteered to move the furniture around in the nursery for her a few days ago, and he had made her laugh with his jokes. She had to admit that he could always make her laugh.

He had been a good sport too. Every time she asked him to move a piece of furniture somewhere else, he had bowed slightly saying, "Yes, ma'am. I am *your* humble servant," with the slightest emphasis on "your". Charlotte couldn't help but change her mind a few extra times just to hear him say it.

She felt a moment of true happiness each time he gave her one of his quirky genuine smiles. He spoke very little of his imminent departure in four days' time, nor did he talk about going to war. She feared he was more worried than he let on. When she asked him about it after Sunday services, the only thing he said was, "I am only a tool in the Master's hand. He does his part to keep me sharp and humble, and I do my part by staying strong. If the King asks this of me, I cannot let him down." She had a sneaking suspicion he did not mean King George III.

She had always thought the colonel to be a "gentleman of the world"—quite comfortable with the flexibility of morality. But now she wasn't quite so sure. Lately she had seen a whole new depth to him, and her thoughts were often pulled in his direction.

Little things came up in conversation that made her reassess her view of him. The few times they had spoken of spiritual matters, she had been surprised and impressed by his humble beliefs. It was becoming clear that he had a simple and very private faith. She would not have thought it of him, but then again, he did buy a bible to take to the battlefield. She had come across him numerous times, alone in a room reading the tiny book. She couldn't think of a single time that she had seen Mr. Collins studying the bible like that. And yet he had been a rector. The colonel was a mysterious man, for sure.

He had also escorted Georgiana on several horse rides across Pemberley. Georgiana was always brighter afterwards. He seemed to be an affectionate and attentive cousin as well, committed and genuine.

*Why am I sizing up the colonel?* She focused her mind back on her embroidery, but it held no allure for her. She had been planning to finish the prayer pillow embroidery for months now so she could give it to her daughter. She had started the embroidery back when Elizabeth was visiting the parsonage. She had made a good deal of progress on it while Elizabeth was feverish and deathly ill. But once Elizabeth regained her health and left for London, Charlotte's problems only compounded when Mr. Collins took ill. Charlotte had not seen the similarities of their illnesses until it was too late or she would have taken more aggressive action when he took ill. Ever since, it had been a chore to work on the embroidery.

She looked down at the four-toned brown cross that she had finally finished and debated whether or not to start the decorative wreath and flowers at its base.

For some reason, she felt self-conscious that she had been pondering the changes in Colonel Fitzwilliam while still mourning Mr. Collins.

She didn't mean to let out an exasperated breath, but the others in the room seemed to have noticed.

Elizabeth looked at her and asked, "Charlotte, are you and the baby well?"

Georgiana seemed to be alerted as well and said, "Can I get you anything?"

"No, thank you. I fear I just need to move a bit. I have been sitting in one attitude for too long."

The colonel's deep voice was kind as he offered, "Georgiana and I can take a turn in the garden with you, if you like. I believe the sun will be setting shortly, and there is nothing like a sunset at Pemberley."

"I think I should like that very much," Charlotte said.

"I am *your* humble servant." His reference to their time in the nursery made her smile, and the colonel smiled handsomely in return.

Elizabeth stood too and said, "Come, Will. Sunset in the gardens of Pemberley is a sight I shall never forget nor tire of."

Charlotte smiled again, because she knew very well what the sunset in Pemberley gardens meant to Elizabeth and Mr. Darcy. While she was deathly ill, Elizabeth had seen a vision of herself walking in a beautiful garden with Mr. Darcy, who at the time, Charlotte thought she despised. Elizabeth had told her how loving and tender Mr. Darcy had been in the vision. Elizabeth called the garden her "own kind of heaven" and often referred to it as such. It had been mind-boggling when she learned that the garden she had seen only in her delusional state was not only real, but was to be her future home.

The gardens of Pemberley truly were beautiful, but knowing that such a miracle had occurred gave them a magical and angelic atmosphere. Mr. Darcy and Elizabeth always mysteriously disappeared when it was time for the sun to set, but they were fooling no one. Everyone knew it was their special moment together, and no one bothered them. So for them to desire company at sunset was truly monumental.

Georgiana said, "I fear I am fatigued from riding today. If you do not mind, I will stay here. I will have tea ready for your return."

"Very well," Darcy agreed. "We shall see you shortly."

They each gathered their things at the door, and while Mr. Darcy lovingly wrapped the shawl around his wife's arms, Charlotte watched him steal a kiss. It was a sweet kiss. Each time Charlotte caught them in an embrace or stealing a caress, or flashing flirtatious smiles at each other, it knocked another brick from the fortress around her heart.

It had always been that way with Mr. Darcy and Elizabeth. Somehow their love was so real and powerful that even the worst skeptics—and she counted herself as one of them—felt their doubts slipping. Maybe love really did exist. Here were two people who were vastly different and yet so perfectly matched.

Charlotte watched Elizabeth place her hand on her husband's jaw and whisper her thanks. Charlotte looked away in embarrassment. Another brick knocked down.

The colonel was standing ready with her own shawl and waiting for her to turn around. She did so immediately, and he carefully placed it on her shoulders. She looked up at him and said, "Thank you."

He offered a small smile and then winked. "I am *your* humble servant, my lady. I fear ours will be a lonely walk if we do not commit to keep each other company. Those two lovebirds over there are already in their own world."

Charlotte smiled and said. "I believe you are right." He offered her his arm in a polite and gentlemanly manner. As she placed her hand on his arm he patted it momentarily before retracting his arm behind his back.

As they walked towards the gardens, she saw the colors of the sky flash brilliant yellow tones that she knew would give way to orange and then red and eventually the deep purples and blues of nightfall.

They walked quietly for a few minutes. Charlotte sensed that Colonel Fitzwilliam was deliberating about something important. He had been there for her in a very trying time, and she wished to be the kind of friend that he had been to her.

She cleared her throat and said, "Is there something on your mind, Colonel?"

He looked down at her, and for a brief moment, she saw what he must have looked like in his youth. In his gray eyes was a flash of pure kindness and innocence. He then said, "I see that we have lost our chaperones. Do you think the Darcys will mind if we leave them alone a bit longer? I admit there is something on my mind, but I fear this soldier's courage is faltering."

"Are you afraid to go to war? Is that what bothers you?"

"Always. Any honest soldier must admit to that. But no, that is not what is on my mind tonight, nor is it what has occupied my thoughts for some time." They turned away from the path and headed towards the roses, which held brilliant red and yellow blooms. She reached for one and leaned in to smell it, which was not necessary since their fragrance filled the air.

Colonel Fitzwilliam gently dropped her am, freeing it to cup the rose in her hands and breathe in the scent of it.

He asked, "They smell lovely, do they not?"

She murmured her agreement. From the corner of her eye she saw him bend over and pull a knife, still in its leather case, from his boot. She looked at him suspiciously and said, "You carry a knife in your boot?"

He raised an eyebrow at her and said, "A soldier, remember? Now allow me to cut one for you. Which one would you like?"

"Ooooh, I do not know. This one is the tallest and has outgrown all of the others."

He unsheathed his knife, reached for the base of the stem, and with one flick of the knife, the flower was free. "My lady." He handed it to her, looking at her with darker-than-usual eyes. She thought the sun behind him might be playing tricks on her, but then he suddenly looked away.

They continued in their walk, and she asked again, "What is on your mind?"

He took a deep breath, and she waited for him to begin.

When he did not speak right away, she added, "I do not wish to pry, but I have always counted you as a friend and wish to be the same for you."

He stopped walking and planted his feet while looking at her. He folded both arms behind his back and in that moment she got a good view of his handsome frame. He was not just tall, but he was broad shouldered and his chest muscles seemed to fight his waistcoat for notice. She was a bit ashamed to admit it, but the muscles won. A bright flush fused her cheeks, and she looked away.

"Mrs. Collins, if I may, I have pondered and strategized how best to go about this, and I admit I am still at a loss. You would think a man who has been among the finest ladies of the *ton* would know how to speak to a lady. Let me start by saying that I see in you a finer specimen of genteel womanhood than any of my acquaintance. I have always been able to speak with whomever I please. No matter where I am, I can find something to converse on. But now, as I try to speak with the one lady whose good opinion I desire most, I find myself speechless."

What was he getting at? *Finer specimen of genteel womanhood?* "Colonel, you certainly have my good opinion," she assured him. "You need not seek it with false flattery. I have always admired you and do not think ill of you in any way."

"Truly?"

"Indeed, is that what troubles you? You fear that I do not enjoy your company? Colonel—"

"Please call me Richard."

"I prefer not to, sir," she said a bit too briskly. A brief look of confusion crossed his face. There was no small amount of pain as well.

She tried to explain. "Propriety is very important to me. I do not even call Mr. Darcy by his Christian name, yet I reside in his home. Do not take offence that I do not call you by yours. I very much consider you one of my closest friends."

"I really would prefer you to call me Richard. You said you liked being in my company. I thought that meant you thought of me the same way I do of you."

What a strange conversation they were having! "Colonel, of course I think of you the same way."

As soon as she said it, his gray eyes lit up, and he took great strides to her and took her shoulders in his strong hands and kissed her on the lips. The shock sent tingles from her lips to the top of her head. His lips were soft and gentle, but what in the world had made him do that?

She pushed him away firmly, and suddenly memories of Mr. Collins forcing himself on her sent shudders up and down her spine.

She turned away and started walking back towards the house, but the colonel was calling after her. Her heart began to race uncontrollably, and it seemed her feet were keeping time with its beat. She felt an insatiable impulse to run for safety. Her rational mind knew it had nothing to do with the colonel, but she needed to outrun something, or someone . . .

He caught up to her, reached a restraining arm out to her, and she whipped around and shook off his hand. Her rational mind shrunk into the shadows. "Do not ever, ever, do that again!" she hissed. "Do not kiss me! Do not grab my arm! I am my own woman. I may be a widow but I have my pride. How dare you think you can take liberties! How dare you play on our friendship for your entertainment!"

"Whoa, hold back the forces, Charlotte. Clearly there has been some kind of misunderstanding. You might as well be speaking Chinese for all I comprehend of what just happened. Now see here, I apologize for kissing you. I should have asked. But I thought you . . . I thought you loved me the way I love you, and I wanted to seize the moment. Look around us! It could not have been a more romantic setting! Is it not every lady's dream to be kissed by her future husband?"

Her eyes grew wider as he talked.

*Husband?*

The word alone was vile.

She had to get away.

Her mind was searching for somewhere to hide, somewhere safe.

On instinct, she turned to leave, and the colonel reached out for her arm again. Suddenly the memory of a man grabbing her elbow painfully engulfed her.

She turned around quickly, too quickly; her emotions roiling. Surprise, fear, confusion, a sense of danger, anger, unabashed fire, protectiveness . . . they were all there, each battling for dominance.

She vaguely perceived that Colonel Fitzwilliam put his hands up in surrender—a peace offering—showing he meant no harm. But what she sensed was much different.

Dirty, grimy hands holding her so tightly that her fingers turned numb. She no longer smelled the roses, only the vile stench of sweat and licorice of Mr. Collins. She closed her eyes hoping the memory would be forced out. When that did not help, she put her hand to her eyes and rubbed them furiously.

But even that did not stop the memory from coming. She sank to her knees.

\*\*\*\*\*

*Her face still stung, but he was raising his arm once again.*

*"You will do as I say. Get on your knees." His voice was harsher than she had ever heard him use. She was confused why he was being so harsh.*

*"William, what have I done?" Her voice broke with the tears that flooded and stung her burning cheeks.*

*"Do not call me William! I am your husband, and you shall give me the respect I deserve. What have you done? Look at yourself! Your hair looks like you have rolled around the hayloft. Is that what you have done? Is it guilt that drives your cheeky answer? Who have you been with?" His words were punctuated with an open palm to her face.*

*Fear took over, and she stepped away from him. The fire in his eyes spoke of danger. He took a menacing step towards her, and he gripped her arm so tight that she could once again feel it go numb as each of his fingers dug into her arm. His grip forced her to do as he commanded, and she got on her knees. He raised his arm once again, but seeing it was not an open palm this time, she closed her eyes and prepared for the blow. She couldn't help but scream.*

\*\*\*\*\*

Colonel Fitzwilliam watched as Charlotte crumped to the gravel pathway, screaming, with her hands shielding her face. Colonel Fitzwilliam's heart broke at the hopeless piercing tone of her painful cry.

"Charlotte! What is wrong?" She flinched away from his touch, shrieking even louder. "Are you all right? I am so sorry I kissed you! Please stop!"

As her hysterics intensified, he looked up to see Darcy and Elizabeth running toward them.

Her screams pierced his heart in every way. She was no longer on her knees but was curled up in a tiny ball—well, as tiny as any woman so far in her condition could be.

Her screams continued. "No! William! William!" she cried.

Darcy arrived first and knelt down next to Charlotte. "Are you all right, Mrs. Collins?" he asked gently, touching her shoulder. She made no reply. Darcy flashed Fitzwilliam a look of confusion.

The colonel raised his hands in surrender and exclaimed, "I kissed her and . . . When I put my hands up to try to calm her, she started screaming. I did not lay a hand on her, I swear!"

Elizabeth had caught up by this point. She knelt beside Charlotte, whispering in a quiet reassuring voice, "It is going to be all right, Charlotte. You are safe. No one is going to hurt you anymore. Take a deep breath and open your eyes. Look at me. It is Elizabeth. No one else is here but Mr. Darcy and me."

Charlotte screams died down. "William?" she gasped.

Mr. Darcy looked briefly at the colonel, hesitated, then said, "Yes, I am here."

She took a deep breath and looked around. Elizabeth helped her sit up, and as quickly as it had begun, she was drying her tears and looking mortified. "Mr. Darcy, forgive me. I must have fainted."

*That was no damn faint!*

But Colonel Fitzwilliam held his tongue.

He stayed back and watched Elizabeth and Darcy pick her up from the ground. Charlotte hurriedly started brushing off the garden debris that had attached itself. Her hands were racing against some foe that was nowhere in sight. He was tempted to look around as if there was a foe he did not know was there.

She kept muttering under her breath, "I am sorry. I am sorry."

After many minutes of trying to make herself presentable, she stood up straight and lifted her chin. She took a few breaths and clasped her shaking hands in front of her. She turned to Colonel Fitzwilliam and yet failed to look directly at him.

"Forgive me. I feel I must retire. Perhaps we can continue our discussion when I have the strength."

Elizabeth spoke for him, for which he was grateful, as he had no words for what he had just witnessed. "Come, Charlotte," she murmured, "let us return."

The two ladies turned to leave, but Colonel Fitzwilliam stopped Darcy. Darcy gave him a look that said he knew more than he let on. "A word, Darcy?"

Darcy nodded. The two men turned and walked pensively away from the house. They took long strides. Once Richard was sure the ladies were out of earshot, he ordered, "Speak."

"I cannot."

"Is that all the explanation I am to expect?"

Darcy looked away and said, "It is not my explanation to give. I am sorry. Some battles can only be fought alone."

Colonel Fitzwilliam gave him a most dissatisfied look. "She called out your name."

Darcy then took a step towards him and very purposefully looked directly into his eyes.

They were nose to nose. "Did she?"

# CHAPTER 7

Colonel Fitzwilliam was fairly confident Charlotte was avoiding him. It had been two days since the episode—or whatever it was—in the garden. She had taken most of her meals in her room. Even Darcy and Elizabeth seemed to be avoiding him. At least Georgiana had not lost her appetite for his company. He stood at his bedchamber window looking at the deep purple night skies. He had been doing it most of the night. In an hour or two, he would see them give way to pale lavender and then spread to the brightest of yellows as the sun rose, but for now the skies whispered his own deep, dark thoughts.

Charlotte had said that she felt the same way about him as he did about her. But she certainly had not welcomed his kiss. It was painfully clear that she did not love him. She thought of him only as a friend. And he had taken advantage of her. He felt like the worst rake he could think of. George Wickham's face came to mind, and he bowed his head to think he was in a class with Wickham.

A gentleman does not kiss a lady before she accepts his offer! Of course, in the last two days of pondering, he had realized another critical error—he had never actually offered for her. Blinded by his own exuberance, he had assumed she loved him and assumed her acceptance. He hadn't even managed explaining that, of course, they would have to wait until her mourning was over and until he returned from war.

The sounds of the household were picking up with the hustle and bustle of servants' feet hurrying to light fires and prepare the house for their masters. Sleep had once again evaded him, and he wished he had Mr. Heather to talk to. Or at least a bit of his sleeping powders. Soon enough he would. For, this time tomorrow he would be saddled and riding to Liverpool.

He heard a faint female moan from down the hall and wondered if a servant had run into something in the dark.

He continued to ponder what to do about Charlotte. He surely could not leave Pemberley without apologizing and explaining himself. He heard hurried footsteps pass his room, which surprised him since his fire had not been lit yet. *No matter. No fire could warm me at the moment.*

A minute later he heard Darcy's distinct gait coming down the hall, and it was definitely quickened. Colonel Fitzwilliam left the window and opened his door. Darcy and Elizabeth were both in their wrappers, and Elizabeth was leading the way to Charlotte's room.

Darcy stopped outside her door and whispered to Elizabeth, "I will wait here."

Colonel Fitzwilliam had been dressed for some time. In fact, with all the rest he received, he might as well have stayed dressed all night. "Darcy, what is wrong? Is Charlotte well?"

"I do not know yet. Elizabeth is checking on her. It seems her time might be upon her. The servant just now informed us."

"But it is too early! She is only eight months along." Darcy furrowed his brows but made no reply. "What can I do?"

"Since you are already dressed, I may send you for the doctor. You know these grounds as well as any other and without the light of sun—"

"Of course I will go."

They waited in silence for what felt like an eternity until Elizabeth came out. "It is time," she said. "She has been having pains for the last two days, but they did not become regular until a few hours ago. She is in a great deal of pain but doing well. If you will excuse me, I need to prepare myself to assist her."

Darcy looked at the colonel and said, "Fitzwilliam will fetch the doctor, and I will tell Mrs. Reynolds. What else can we do?"

"I am afraid that I am as new to this as you are," Elizabeth stammered. "Do whatever men do during this time."

"Right then," Darcy replied. "We will stay out of the way."

If Colonel Fitzwilliam had not been so worried about Charlotte, he would have laughed at Darcy's comment.

*****

Darcy and Richard took turns pacing the halls downstairs. Every time a servant bustled out of Charlotte's room, they asked for an update, desperate for information.

"She is doing wonderfully."

One said, "Mrs. Collins is such a fighter."

Another servant commented, "Ain't none been so brave as her!" Darcy looked at Richard and saw the worry etch deeper with the comment.

Morning gave way to mid-afternoon, and Mrs. Reynolds took pity on them. "Oh, sirs, do try to get some rest. That babe wants out in the worst way. It cannot be much longer."

A few minutes later the doctor came down wiping his brow and confirming Mrs. Reynold's assessment. "Not long now, sir."

Darcy didn't know why he was so nervous. It wasn't *his* wife that was up there delivering, but he knew all too well that things can go wrong very quickly. Darcy's own mother, Lady Anne Darcy, had died of childbed fever after Georgiana's birth when he was just twelve years old. And he knew, or at least hoped, that Elizabeth would soon become with child. If he was this worked up for Charlotte, he could only imagine what it would be like for him when it was the love of his life having the babe.

Richard finally spoke. "The upstairs has gotten entirely too quiet. Why does she not scream or moan? We have not had an update for over an hour. Maybe you should go enquire about her, Darcy."

"Me?"

"I bloody well cannot go up there! She has not even spoken to me since that night in the garden."

Darcy suddenly felt deeply sorry for his cousin. He had been so preoccupied with his own anxiety that he had not thought to consider what Richard was experiencing; that *was* the love of his life delivering the babe. "If Mrs. Reynolds hears you using that kind of language, she will wash your mouth out with lye soap like she did when you were eight."

"Really, Darcy? You are going to chastise me for my language at a time like this?"

"Forgive me. I can only imagine what you are going through. Why do we not go to my study and have a drink? Pacing the vestibule like this will do nothing, but a few fingers of brandy might help."

Richard turned to leave and Darcy followed. As they passed the front hall, Richard said, "Reynolds, please have coffee delivered."

"Right away, sir."

Darcy went to the sideboard and started pouring two drinks. He handed one to Richard, who took it and then set it on the table.

Darcy asked, "You do not want a drink?"

Richard shook his head. "I cannot stand the stuff lately."

Darcy raised his eyebrow at him. "Since when?"

"I am not sure. It just smells wrong. No doubt your brandy is as rich and fine as ever, but I find I enjoy coffee a bit better these days."

"I take it you are worried about Charlotte."

"And the babe. It seems too early. Charlotte was not expecting this for another month. Babies born early struggle a great deal. It is heartbreaking to see."

Darcy remembered talk of Fitzwilliam's little sister, Elena. She had come nearly two months early when Fitzwilliam was six years old. The tiny child didn't survive. Darcy felt he had to offer some sort of support. "Charlotte's baby will do just fine. Just you wait and see."

"I suppose if anyone's baby can survive hardship, it will be Charlotte's. Tenacity will be in its blood."

There hung a stinging silence in the air for a moment where neither man seemed to know what to say. There was a very real possibility that either Charlotte or the baby or both would not survive.

A bit later there was a knock on the door. Both men turned abruptly, and Darcy called out, "Enter." But it was not the doctor; it was only the tray of coffee.

Richard grumbled as the servant left the room, "They know I like it black. I do not know why they feel the need to put sugar and cream on the blasted tray."

Darcy could tell Fitzwilliam was deeply worried. Even in the presence of his fellow soldiers, Richard usually held a tight rein on his cursing. This was obviously a trying time. Darcy decided that the only thing he could do for him was distract him. Darcy had wanted to tell Fitzwilliam what happened in Liverpool ever since returning home, but it never felt like the right time. And now, time was running out. Fitzwilliam would be leaving for Liverpool tomorrow morning.

To be honest, Darcy realized he may have neglected Fitzwilliam and Georgiana these past few weeks. They had both been left to their own devices a bit. Perhaps more than a bit.

It was different being married to Elizabeth. She occupied his every thought. He thought of every possible way to spend his time with her. Each day, she patiently read in his study while he worked with his steward, or he took his business into the drawing room where she sat and played the pianoforte. He followed her everywhere he could. But now was not the time to think about Elizabeth. Right now he needed to be the friend Richard needed him to be.

Darcy put down his drink and said, "You have not asked me about Liverpool."

"I assumed you would tell me if there was anything to tell."

"Elizabeth and I enjoyed our wedding trip, of course, but we also worked on tracking down an associate of Mr. Collins. Elizabeth found something in a ledger about a gentleman with offices in both London and Liverpool. At first it was like a wild goose chase. We were told he would be in town in a few days, but when we checked back, we were told that we had missed him. Another time we set up an appointment with his partner, and when we arrived at the office, the doors were locked.

"I finally sent a note stating that I was helping Mrs. Charlotte Collins with William Collins's death. I stated that one of his ledgers indicated that Mr. Collins had done business with the man I was seeking. I left a forwarding address at our lodgings, and weeks went by without so much as a note. Then on the same day I get two. One from Aunt Catherine stating that there a solicitor had called on her, asking about Mr. Collins's death. The same afternoon, the second note arrived from the very man himself. He wished to speak with me immediately.

"As Elizabeth and I sat down in front of the huge mahogany desk, we were offered nothing by way of nourishment or tea. It was all business. He introduced himself and said he had worked with Mr. Collins for over four years. He pulled out nearly an entire tome of legal documents that showed their relationship. He then drilled me with questions about Mrs. Collins and what had become of her. So I shared with him that she was anticipating the birth of her child quite soon and was staying with us at Pemberley. He seemed genuinely interested in the fact that she was with child. Apparently Mr. Collins had a bit of money put away. The solicitor would not tell me how much, but he claimed that Mr. Collins's will stipulated that the entire sum could only be distributed at a future date if specific unnamed requirements are met."

Darcy could see instantly that his efforts to distract his cousin had worked. Fitzwilliam asked, "What kind of requirements?"

"I cannot say."

"You will not say or you cannot say?"

"*Cannot* say. He would not divulge the requirements or the 'future' date, but he left me with his card and said he would be in touch. He then asked one more time about Mrs. Collins and very pointedly said a rather bizarre comment. He said, 'I assume Mrs. Collins is mourning her husband properly. Please let her know I intend to pay a call or two in the next year. I would like to see her for myself.'" Darcy waited to see if Richard understood the importance of the comment.

"This man, and I am not oblivious to the fact that you have purposely omitted his name as you told me this story, seems to be concerned a great deal with Mrs. Collins and her period of mourning. Do you think there is something in the will that withholds the money if she does not properly mourn Mr. Collins?"

"Elizabeth and I feel that can be the only explanation for his questions. He would not show me the will, nor would he describe the nature of the stipulations, but I believe he was trying to warn us. And thereby warn Charlotte."

"Warn her?"

"Yes. Elizabeth and I both felt that it was said as a warning. So, it may be more important than ever that you let her mourn her husband properly and step back a bit. You may very well be going to war. By the time you return, she will be out of mourning. And perhaps she will have a bit of money from Mr. Collins."

Richard drank the last in his cup, set it down, and turned his head to Darcy. "I have never hidden the fact that, as a second son, I must marry into wealth. But if she were to inherit, it would be all the more reason for someone else to snatch her up while I am gone. Hardly a reassuring prospect, Darcy."

"Richard, I only—" Luckily they were interrupted by Georgiana who burst in the door with news.

"It is a boy! A healthy baby boy!" Georgiana looked directly at Richard and said, "I came as soon as I could, Richard. She is fine. She had a bit of trouble at the end, but she will be fine. She is resting now." As quickly as she came, she left, closing the door behind her.

Darcy asked, "Does Georgiana know you admire Charlotte?"

"Apparently. Am I that transparent?"

"For a man who makes his living deceiving the enemy, it is surprisingly evident that your heart has surrendered." Darcy was relieved to see Richard's worry give way to a smile.

# CHAPTER 8

Charlotte looked at the clock. It was just after 3:00 a.m. Her son had only fed an hour ago, but she couldn't help but go and check on him. Charlotte had agreed to Mr. Darcy's request that a housemaid sleep in the nursery on only one condition: Sally was to wake her at any time, day or night. The maid was young and had never had a babe of her own, but she was the oldest of five children. Charlotte put on her wrapper and house slippers and tried not to groan at how sore her body was. It had only been twelve hours since she had given birth to her son.

She remembered having her son placed in her arms for the first time like it was yesterday. She smiled. It *had* been yesterday. That sounded like something the colonel would have said to make her smile.

He was good at that; making her smile.

Her son was born with a mop of huge brown curls on top of his head that made him look so much older. Why did she keep calling him "her son"? Why could she not find a name for him? She reminded herself that the question of his name did not have to be settled at 3:00 a.m. People would certainly understand if she took a day or two to decide.

She tiptoed down the hall, and just before she got to the door, she heard her son squeak like he did when he was stretching. She had almost entered the room when she heard Colonel Fitzwilliam start to speak.

"There now, General. You must be quiet just a bit longer. Your dear momma is sleeping, and I only have this short period of time to discuss our plan of attack."

Charlotte peeked around the doorframe and saw that Colonel Fitzwilliam was sitting in the rocking chair. He was turned from her, seated near the window, and the moonlight lit up his face like a silhouette, showing just how defined his jaw was. He had one leg bent and was resting the ankle on the opposite knee. Her son was cradled in that little space between his legs. The baby stretched again and grabbed Colonel Fitzwilliam's finger.

He chuckled. "I see you have a grip on things already."

She was so mortified by her reaction to the kiss in the garden that she hadn't been able to bring herself to face him again. What must he think of her? What kind of woman did he declare himself to? She had gone over it again and again, and the only thing that could account for it was that Colonel Fitzwilliam had grown to truly admire her. When she realized this, it made it all the more difficult to imagine being in his presence again. But surely after seeing her screaming on the ground in such a way, he had changed his mind.

He knew now that she was damaged goods.

"What a strong man you are, General Collins!"

Charlotte smiled at the nickname he must have come up with for her nameless son. She watched a little longer. "I am very pleased to see that you are healthy and strong, regardless of how early you were," the colonel continued. "No doubt you will slay many foes in your lifetime. You are the man of the house now, General. Charlotte will need someone to look after her. That is an order that came directly from King George III. He allowed me to read the missive before delivering it to you.

"Since you are much too busy squeaking and trying to wake the entire house, I shall paraphrase. It said, 'General Collins, you are hereby commanded to love and obey your mother. Protect her at all costs and surrender control of her heart to no one while Colonel Fitzwilliam is away. She has built a rock-solid fortress around her to withstand any advances, but I know I can trust you to direct the day-to-day dealings of her heart. Defend her by any means necessary. Sincerely, King George III.'"

Charlotte had to smile. Her son's eyes opened, and he seemed to be looking at the colonel while he spoke.

She looked down at the base of the rocking chair and saw that Colonel Fitzwilliam's satchel was packed and ready to go. Her heart lurched for a moment to think that he was going to leave without saying goodbye. She reminded herself that she had not exactly given him any opportunity to say goodbye. She had, in fact, avoided him for several days now. And yet here he was. Her thoughts were interrupted by his voice again.

"I am told that she has not picked out a name for you. But I cannot go to war without knowing your name. What soldier does not know his commanding officer? You know, with your strong chin and enormous thick curls, you remind me of someone I met once: General Isaac Brock. He is a great man, tall and robust like you. He rose quickly through the ranks, without any kind of political connections, because he was wise and hard-working. Some say he was blessed with a bit of luck too.

"General Isaac Brock's promotions occurred in a time of peace. He was his own man. He fought hard and made a name for himself, in spite of very humble beginnings. I suspect that will be the same for you, general. I am told by Sally that you are a good little eater, and I am not at all surprised at your success so early. Speaking of Sally, she will be coming back shortly, so I must hurry along.

"Did you know that I may be going to the Canadian colonies soon? General Brock was sent there once. He had to deal with a problem that had plagued the British in that area: desertion. Yes, I know that is a big word for a little man like you. It means having a change of heart, but let me assure you of something. It will not happen to me; I am not leaving for good. I will be back. But you must keep your little momma's heart from deserting. Do I make myself clear, General Collins? Help her to remember where her loyalties lie.

"She may not believe it yet, but I love her. I will do anything to be with her. She needs all the encouragement you can give her. You must talk of me often and remind her of those times that we shared. Like that moment in the parsonage kitchen where I saw her deep pain turn into hope as we watched Darcy and Elizabeth through the window. Or that moment when she smiled at me in the garden at their wedding. I still firmly maintain that she wanted me to sit with her. And a man has to do what a lady directs. That is your first lesson as a gentleman—listen to the lady. I made an unfortunate mistake a few nights ago by not following this counsel. And now I must go to war without clarifying things with her."

He seemed to pause a bit, as if remembering that moment. What she was expecting, was a softer voice, one that was half in another world, but instead, he spoke with firm confidence. "When I look at your mother, I see a strong, confident, independent, and courageous woman. I had hoped she felt the same way as me, but now I see I was quite blind." Then his voice dropped slightly. "She sees me only as a friend."

Charlotte wiped her tears away and stepped away from the doorway. She leaned against the wall, letting her head fall back so her gaze was toward the ceiling, and felt her heart and mind battle. She had accused him of taking liberties with her for his own entertainment. But she hadn't really meant those words. She had been angry and thoughtless. It was becoming clear that he actually loved her. He respected her and thought she was courageous. He did not see someone to pity, he saw a strong woman. A woman who was independent!

She saw Sally coming down the hall, and she put her finger to her mouth and silently shushed her away. Sally looked confused for a moment but then retreated. Charlotte returned her attention back to the nursery conversation.

Her son had started to squirm and grunt, and Colonel Fitzwilliam placed him gently up on his shoulder and rubbed his back in circular motions. "Yes, of course, you are right, General. I have less than an hour before I must depart, so I should finish the story about General Isaac Brock in the Canadian colonies. Well, one night, while in Montreal, seven soldiers mutinied and stole a boat and escaped across the border to the United States. The general did not hesitate to follow them onto American soil and he pursued them until all seven men were captured. So you see, General Collins, he insisted on capturing his men, even if their loyalties wavered. But, have no fear, *my* heart will never waver.

"I will always love Charlotte. I will never desert her. But you must remember your orders too; under no circumstances are you to allow another man to break down the fortress she has around her heart. That is a task that I have volunteered for, and I am very confident I do not need reinforcements. So take care of her while I am away. Keep her safe. Speak of me often. Do I have your word, General?" Her son made a screeching sound and then let out a small cry.

Colonel Fitzwilliam started rocking him. "I will take that as a yes. Very good. Now we are partners in this endeavor. You and I will be the only men in her life. We must pray for her heart to change toward me. I may not have a fortune to offer her, but perhaps she does not need a fancy home like Pemberley. Maybe all she needs is love. You tell her that for me, you hear? Tell her she deserves to be loved by a man. But not just any man—this man. Tell her to wait for me. Brag about me if you must, but tell her to hope for Fitzwilliam—a man who went to fight for England but came back only to win the one thing that is worth fighting for: a lady's heart."

He seemed to sigh a bit and then whispered so quietly that Charlotte had to strain to hear. "You are the only hope for me, General. Keep this hope alive for your colonel. Indeed, that hope may very well be the only thing that keeps me alive."

Her son began to cry in earnest, but Charlotte had not regained her composure yet. She wiped her eyes and took a few breaths. His last words had hit her like a ton of bricks. Just like the tenderness she so often saw between Mr. Darcy and Elizabeth, Colonel Fitzwilliam's words were sending giant cracks in the fortress around her heart.

"Let us keep this between you and me for now. Repeat after me: I solemnly swear an oath of brotherhood that we will fight for the same thing. That is, to keep her heart from deserting to any other man. Good. Now that I have your cooperation, I will sign this peace treaty with a kiss." She saw him kiss her son's cheek. "Now we are comrades in arms with the same purpose; to love your mother. There now. Go to sleep. I must be going."

Charlotte's heart could not possibly beat any faster than it was beating at that moment. Not only because of the tenderness in his voice and the words she heard, but because she was about to be found listening, and she didn't know how she felt about that. She took a step away and tried to clear her throat loudly. Pulling the wrapper completely closed, she waited a moment longer before she entered the nursery.

She tried to act surprised. "Oh, Colonel! Forgive me. I heard my son cry and thought Sally had forgotten to wake me."

He stood and smiled at her, still oblivious to the fact that she had listened to his speech. He was kind enough to ignore the fact that she was wearing only her nightdress and wrapper, but a blush still came to her face. "No need," he said kindly. "The general and I have been having a heart-to-heart. I believe we have come to an understanding, he and I."

"Is that so?" She felt her blush deepen, if that was possible.

"Indeed. He has taken upon himself the mantle of responsibility to love you so fiercely with all of his heart that you will never doubt his loyalty. I believe we even sealed it with a kiss. Is that not so, General?" Colonel Fitzwilliam lifted her son up and kissed his cheek again. He then turned a dashing smile on Charlotte.

She was very grateful for only a bit of moonlight, because the blush on her face would have given her away completely. "Why do you call him 'general'?"

The colonel chuckled, and the sound was so comforting to her ears. "I suppose I could not keep calling him 'baby Collins' like everyone else does. I hope you do not mind that I do it. If it is offensive—"

"It is not. I rather like it." Now she was sure her blush could be seen.

He seemed to be studying her a bit, and then he took her son and handed him to her. As if saying it like a caress with hidden meanings, he said, "Here is your soldier, Mrs. Collins."

She felt his arms brush against hers gently, sending goose bumps up and down her spine. She took in a deep breath to steady her heart. His clothes had a leathery-spicy scent with a touch of cloves, and the delicious scent nearly overwhelmed her. Once the exchange had been done, he turned to reach for his satchel on the floor.

She was running out of time. "Colonel?"

He swung the bag over his shoulder and asked, "Yes?"

"Promise me you will be safe."

He looked blankly at her, and then his smile slowly made its appearance. "Only because you have asked, my lady; I am *your* humble servant, after all."

He could always make her smile. There was so much that needed to be said, but she could not find the strength to say it. They stood staring at each other for a few minutes until her son started squeaking, which soon turned into a full angry cry. She looked down at her son and said, "My thoughts exactly, General Collins. But he must go. When a soldier makes an oath, there is no turning back. Is that not so, Colonel?" Charlotte felt goose bumps again when she remembered his oath—not the one to King George, but to her. *I will always love Charlotte. I will never desert her.*

She rocked her son close to her, swaying from side to side. Her son seemed to calm a bit with the motion. She looked back at the colonel when he spoke.

"Indeed," he agreed. "And Mrs. Collins? I must tell you how sorry I am for kissing you. I am not that kind of man. I never meant any disrespect. In fact, I have the utmost respect for you. I admit I like flirting—however inept I seem to be of late—but my intentions were honorable and always will be. I know it may be hard for you to believe, but I . . . what I am trying to say is I am not some womanizing rake."

A combination of holding her newborn son and the tenderness and honesty in his words brought fresh tears to her eyes. She looked away briefly and said, "And I am not the woman you saw in the garden."

Out of the corner of her eye, she saw him bow deeply. Then, as softly as possibly, he whispered, "I know. Deep down, I know. Thank you."

And without a final goodbye, he left the nursery.

# CHAPTER 9

As he walked out of the dim nursery, Colonel Fitzwilliam's heart flooded with many feelings. But as overwhelmed as he had been by the sight of Charlotte holding her baby, gratitude was the most prevalent sensation. They were not parting with ill feelings. He had found his chance to apologize. For that, he was grateful beyond words.

And he was grateful to have seen her beautiful face once more. Her high cheekbones and that adorable dimple that appeared whenever she smiled. And she *had* smiled. That same magnificent smile. The one that rocked him every time, making his heart start marching to an entirely different drum.

Her hair had been swept to the side, over her right shoulder, and braided with a single white ribbon at the end. He had never seen her like that before, never seen her hair in anything other than a tight bun. Considering it was so early in the morning, a little dishevelment was understandable. Tiny wisps of hair had escaped, and she had casually tucked them behind her ear. He wasn't sure he would ever forget the sight of her rocking General Collins from side to side, nor did he wish to. It was unlike anything he had ever experienced in all his one-and-thirty years. She was glorious.

He stopped back in his room for a few minutes to take one last inventory of his satchel and to make sure his bible was in there. He took a moment to kneel down and offer a prayer.

He prayed first for Charlotte and General Collins. Then he prayed God would keep his family and friends safe while he was away. He made sure to express his gratitude for the sliver of hope he felt inside. Then, selfishly, he promised that if God would just grant him the chance to return and court Charlotte properly, he would do anything that He asked, no matter how hard.

And then he went downstairs and quietly slipped out the servants' door. Looking over his shoulder at Pemberley, he very nearly skipped towards the stable in the predawn darkness. There had been something there in that nursery between them, something to hope for; he had felt it in all the things she had said, and the things she had left unsaid. Yes, this soldier might just have something to come home to. She had blushed at least three times, smiled even more times, and although she had been careful not to say anything directly, she had asked him to be safe; no, she had made him *promise* to be safe. He had much to be thankful for.

He reached his horse and saw that it was already saddled. "Good man, Charles. He looks ready to go."

But it wasn't the stable hand, Charles, that replied. "So, you thought you could run off without saying goodbye?" a deep voice teased.

Colonel Fitzwilliam nearly came to tears. There, behind his horse, were three of his favorite people. "Darcy! Georgiana! Elizabeth! You did not have to get up this early to see me off! The dawn has not even broken the horizon. We said our goodbyes last night."

The tears Georgiana had been struggling to hold back now began to fall onto her cheeks. Colonel Fitzwilliam stepped forward and gathered her into his arms. "There now, no need for that. I will come back. I promised a certain someone that I would be safe. Even said a prayer or two." He patted his satchel and said, "And I have the Good Book with me. I will be back. You just wait and see."

Georgiana stepped back and wiped her red eyes. "You must promise me too. Be safe and come back. I know you are an honest man, so you have to keep your promises."

"I promise. And do not let Darcy hear you call me honest. He thinks I bend the truth to meet whatever passing need I have."

Elizabeth came and embraced him and gave him a kiss on the cheek. "Every soldier needs a goodbye kiss."

"Well then, here is a kiss back from me!" he chuckled and kissed Elizabeth's cheek. "But best not to tell that jealous husband of yours."

Darcy was hardly less emotional. Colonel Fitzwilliam could see his cousin was trying to hold back his feelings. Colonel

Fitzwilliam offered his hand and when Darcy took it, Richard pulled his cousin hard into an embrace and pounded him on his back, squeezing a bit. Then he whispered pleadingly, "You will look after her for me?"

"I will. I will. As if she were my wife."

"Not that closely, if you please! I see the *attentions* you bestow on Elizabeth! And I would hate to come home from battle unharmed only to fight my own cousin in a duel."

The four of them laughed for a moment. When the sound died down, the silence was entirely too much to bear. "Well then, I am off. I shall write from Liverpool when I have further orders."

He turned to go, and Darcy held out his hand once more. He shook it again, wondering why Darcy was being so ninny-pipped. Seeing his cousin being a bit emotional was not making it easy to keep his own composure.

Their hands grasped each other and then he realized that Darcy was discreetly handing him something. He concealed the piece of paper in his hand and mounted up. After one final wave, he nudged the horse on. As soon as he was no longer in sight of Pemberley, he slowed his horse and pulled out the note. What was so important that Darcy couldn't have, at some point in the last two weeks at Pemberley, found a way to give it to him?

*****

Charlotte cradled her baby, the General, as she looked out her bedroom window. She watched the red coat as long as she could before it disappeared out of sight. She finally returned to bed and fed her son. She sighed. She couldn't very well keep calling him "her son". Apparently the whole household was calling him, "baby Collins". That wouldn't do either. Her mind drifted back again to what she had overheard at the nursery door.

*"No doubt you will slay many foes in your lifetime. You are the man of the house now, General. Charlotte will need someone to look after her. That is an order!"* How someone could speak with authority but soothe a baby at the same time was a feat she was sure that only the colonel was capable of.

She smiled as she remembered the orders from King George. *"General Collins, you are hereby commanded to love and obey your mother. Protect her at all costs and surrender control of her heart to no one while Colonel Fitzwilliam is away."*

She thought of how he compared her son to General Brock. Her grandfather's name had been Isaac. It was a good strong biblical name. Isaac was the only child of Abraham and Sarah; a beloved son who was willing to put his life on the altar in obedience. She had certainly sacrificed a great deal to get him here safely. She looked down at her son, Isaac, and knew that it was the perfect name. He would grow up knowing the Bible stories. He would be obedient, like the biblical Isaac. And with such humble beginnings, he would have to make a name for himself, like General Isaac Brock. Yes, Isaac was a good name.

She still felt a twinge of guilt that she was not honoring Mr. Collins in some way so she started rolling several names around her head. Her late husband's full name was William Nathaniel Collins. *No,* she corrected herself, *Byron William Nathaniel Collins*. But he had hated the name Byron. He was so enraged by her thoughtless mention of it one time that she had never dared repeat the name aloud again. Once had been enough to learn that lesson. She had even left it off his tombstone.

Isaac Nathaniel Collins. *No, too biblical.*

Isaac William Collins. *Too much like his father's name. It would not do to have bile rise up in my throat every time I call out his name.*

Isaac Byron Collins.

It was perfect. Byron could be the name passed down to the next generation, instead of William, and everyone would still assume she had named him after his father. But she would know the truth. Every time she thought of the name, she would think of a tall robust man cradling her son on his lap in the wee hours of the morning, telling him stories of a faithful general. She hoped that her son would share some of his traits. For a moment, she wondered which man she meant. Colonel Fitzwilliam? Or General Isaac Brock?

Charlotte laid her son down on the bed and went and found the bible the colonel had purchased for her. She carefully wrote in her son's name on the inside of the cover.

Isaac Byron Collins

Son of Byron William Nathaniel Collins and
Charlotte Emmalee Collins nee Lucas
Born 28 August 1812

She frowned, unconsciously realizing that her son had been born on the four-month anniversary of Mr. Collins's death. But knowing what to call him seemed to lift a great burden.

As she looked at her baby sleeping on her bed, she couldn't help but think further on the colonel's words.

*"When I look at your mother, I see a strong, confident, independent, and courageous woman."* Did he really see her that way? Did he see the woman she was before William Collins entered into her life? A woman who was respected and appreciated; did he see that woman? And if so, how? After what happened in the garden a few nights ago, how could he see her as anything but weak? She knew the truth. She was like a battered, weathered pitchfork, not even fit for shoveling manure, lest she crumple into pieces. His good opinion of her was baffling.

Colonel Fitzwilliam had spoken to Isaac like he was a grown man, fully expecting more of a response than a squeak or cry. He had said, *"Desertion. Yes. I know that is a big word for a little man like you. It means having a change of heart, but let me assure you that will not happen to me; I am not leaving for good. I will be back. But you must keep your little momma's heart from deserting. Do I make myself clear, General Collins? Help her to remember where her loyalties lie."*

Her eyes involuntarily wandered across the room to her wardrobe full of black mourning dresses; she was painfully aware of where her loyalties lay for the next eight months.

But *he* seemed afraid only that he would come home from war to find *her* married again. She found the prospect . . . incomprehensible. Yet Charlotte wasn't the Colonel's second choice or the most convenient choice, not like she had been with Mr. Collins. She was Colonel Fitzwilliam's *first* choice. What a comforting, yet bewildering thought! Thoughts began to swim through her mind in a confusing swirl.

His final words echoed in her heart repeatedly, sending it dancing out of control: *"Now we are comrades in arms with the same purpose; to love your mother."*

Did she deserve the love of a man like Colonel Fitzwilliam?

\*\*\*\*\*

Colonel Fitzwilliam put the letter away for the third time since stopping at the resting post. But less than a minute later, as if it was burning a hole in his uniform, he found himself taking it out to read again. What had Collins been up to?

*12 August 1808*
*P&S*
*London*

*Mr. Collins,*

*As per your instructions, £4,000 has been applied to your account. The funds are immediately available. All remaining funds were spent refinishing the deck of the* Horizon's Challenge, *just as Captain Blackhurst suggested.*

*We have addressed your concerns regarding Captain Dixon, and are confident it has been dealt with to your liking. I have placed an advertisement in the* London Times *for potential candidates and have several very promising prospects. Enclosed are Captain Conrad Jersey and Captain Frank Farthington's credentials.*

*I, myself, would recommend Captain Jersey, as he seems to have the most experience with vessels of this size. Although a little older than most, I think he is capable of running the crew. I will confer with Captain Blackhurst on the matter as soon as the* Winter's Night *returns to port and will forward his opinion as well as any other available news.*

*I would like to thank you for your business. My brother and I appreciate working with such a fine man. If you have any other needs, please do not hesitate to ask. We are at your bidding.*

*C. W. Pastel*

The letter had clearly been the subject of intense scrutiny and study. The names of Captain Blackhurst and Captain Farthington were underlined. And *Winter's Night* and *Horizon's Challenge* were crossed out, with similar names written above them in Darcy's handwriting: *Summer's Night* and *Eastern Challenge*. Next to the *C* in C. W. Pastel was the name "Clyde". Then there were two addresses penciled at the bottom. One was simply a street in London, known for its solicitors' offices. The other address was underlined.

> *214 Dale Street*
> *Liverpool, England*
> *Leaves every Sunday afternoon for tea at the Chipped Kettle at 2:45*
> *From there goes to harbor and does not return until Wednesday morning*
> *Ships still operating? Type of cargo?*
> *Keep Mr. Collins's involvement confidential*

*What the devil was Mr. Collins doing directing captains and ships?* At the bottom Darcy had scribbled a few last words: "Be careful and good luck."

Colonel Fitzwilliam paid his bill and set off, leaving behind half a bowl of watered-down venison stew, even though he knew it was better than most of what he would be served in the next few months.

It was Saturday. If he kept a good pace, he might be able to observe Clyde Pastel tomorrow in Liverpool for himself. He stirred the horse and directed it towards the road, energy filling his soul.

*****

Elizabeth looked up from her book and studied her husband, who was still diligently reviewing an estate ledger. He was such a hard worker, and she loved him so much. They had been married since the end of May, and she had hoped to have some special news to share with him this month, but her courses had come again.

She kept telling herself that it had only been three months. These things took time. But Charlotte had become with child immediately.

This returned her thoughts to Charlotte again. She considered bringing up the topic that she and her husband had been avoiding.

"Will?"

He looked up at her with a smile, but upon seeing her serious countenance, his face took on a look of concern. "Yes, love? Is there something wrong?"

She took a deep breath and tried to put words to her thoughts. "It has been four days since Charlotte's incident in the garden with Richard."

"Yes, I know," he replied. "I have thought about it much as well. Has she spoken to you about it yet?"

"No. When I saw her like that, I . . . I reacted without thought. I consoled her, forgetting that she does not know what *we* know about Mr. Collins. But she is astute, and the things I said to comfort her . . . well, I fear it is fairly evident now that I know the truth about Mr. Collins."

Darcy started passing his pencil from finger to finger and back again, a habit which exhibited itself when he was deep in thought. The seconds ticked by as he pondered what to say. "I worry about that as well," he admitted. "When she called out 'William', I knew she was not calling out for me. I only answered to conceal the truth from Richard. Yet he suspects something. He asked me about it."

"How did you respond?"

Darcy sighed. "Something about how it is not my secret to share. Especially since Charlotte does not know that *we* know. I feel guilty about all this secrecy, but I do not know what else I could have done. We cannot expose her. Charlotte is a very proud woman."

"Indeed she is."

Darcy went on, "Her response to Richard's touch was quite a shock. I confess I did not expect it. What a tortured life she must have led with that odious man!" he scowled. "Was there really no evidence of it while you were a guest at the parsonage?"

Elizabeth considered the question. "She was certainly altered by marriage, yes," she answered. "She seemed excessively eager to please her husband and was most definitely anxious, sometimes extremely so. But it was not until the day of the funeral when I overheard the servants' whispers about bruises and screams that I realized the truth. Looking back, I remember that whenever I embraced her, she seemed to flinch slightly. She offered no excuses for her reaction. I suppose the signs were there all along. Perhaps I was too naïve to consider that a man would ever strike his wife," she sighed.

Darcy stood up from his desk and came over to the chair where she was sitting. He kissed her cheek and squeezed her hand. "Do not blame yourself, dear. None of us considered that possibility."

She smiled back at him. "What should we do now?" she asked him.

"Nothing, not until she brings it up herself. Although I fear her secret may already be out. Richard is a smart man. He saw too much to truly be ignorant of what she must have gone through. I think he knows that Mr. Collins was worse than insipid."

*Clearly much worse than insipid.* Elizabeth leaned against William's shoulder and listened to his steady breaths. She felt his strong arms. The idea of him raising one of them against her was so foreign to her. Tears filled her eyes.

How had she not seen the truth about her cousin? She remembered once looking out a parsonage window and seeing the rector of Rosings Park being very firm with a plow horse. Apparently the creature had shied away from a snake in the field. With a riding crop seized tightly in his hand, Mr. Collins had struck the mare more than once as it stood helpless and terrified in the plow harness. *"It is true. Mr. Collins would hit her until she begged him to stop. I heard her screams night after night . . ."* Elizabeth involuntarily shuddered remembering the parsonage servants' words.

"What is it, my love?" Darcy asked her.

Elizabeth's remorseful tears began to spill over onto her cheeks. "I just . . . I . . . I do not know why Charlotte did not say something. Why did she not confide in me? Or her father? Sir William is a good man; he would have taken her in." She took a shuddered breath. "How could she have stayed with such an awful, spiteful man? Why did I not see it sooner?"

Darcy wrapped his arms around his wife and pulled her onto his lap. He gently wiped the tears from her eyes and cheeks. "Shhh, my love. You cannot blame yourself. And we must not blame Charlotte for not leaving. This world offers few opportunities to women in her situation." Darcy softly stroked her back for a few moments while they sat in silence.

"Did you know I once tried to help a tenant's wife escape from her abusive husband?" he asked her.

Elizabeth looked up at him in surprise. "Truly?"

"Indeed. It was a few years ago. I was in the process of evicting the couple when I learned of the abuse. The woman's name was Alma. I offered her a position at a country estate in Scotland. It would have meant long hours but anonymity and a fresh start. Alma declined my offer."

"Declined it? But why?"

"I think she had come to expect the abuse. She believed that she deserved it. Alma even said that the periods when he did not abuse her were almost worse than the abuse itself. The anticipation and dread of the moment when he finally snapped were miserable.

"She said the abuse was a cycle, and predictable in its own way. There would be short periods of happiness, an armistice of sorts, like a dawn that makes the world seems so magical and fresh. She explained that these periods were when things were good and there was no tension. She felt happy during this time. She said she could not imagine leaving him. He was a good husband on those days."

Darcy idly picked up the pencil from the desk and began passing it from finger to finger and back again. "But just as predictably as the sun moving from dawn to mid-day, his tension would start to build. Often she did not even know the reason why. She said it felt like walking on eggshells, or like watching horrible storm clouds roll in and not knowing how much time she had before everything fell into chaos. She said this was the worst part of the cycle. She had to meticulously think through every little thing she did and said. Her words broke my heart. She said, 'The effort it takes to please him is so excruciating, that sometimes I beg God to make him hit me and get it over with.'"

Fresh tears fell from Elizabeth's eyes. "How could she pray for such a thing?"

"I do not know, my love. And then after the tension was the actual abuse. She claimed it was 'not so hard to bear.' Sometimes he would just slap her or kick her. Although he occasionally burned her with the fire poker, which, to me, seems *quite* hard to bear. Then came the final part of the cycle; the moment her husband showed his remorse for what he did."

"Remorse? You mean he would actually hit his wife and then apologize for it?"

"Precisely. And then they were happy together again. She said those were the times that she actually saw the man that she had fallen in love with. He would bind up her wounds and kiss her tenderly and even cry in his apology. And then the cycle would start all over again: the armistice, the tension build-up, the abuse, and finally the apology. So even though I could barely stomach my disgust for her husband, Alma was shocked when I urged her to leave him. She seemed to think there was no problem with their relationship. She liked the routine, the predictability of it. She had come to expect the abuse. To even think that she deserved it."

Elizabeth considered William's story. "It was ingrained in her."

"Precisely."

"Whatever happened to them?" Elizabeth asked.

"Well, I told her she would always have a position with the Darcys, but I continued with the process of evicting him. She followed him. It nearly killed me to see it. But there was nothing else I could have done. I could not force her to leave him. I could not help her see her own value. I could not erase her fear of abandoning the life she had learned to expect. I have not heard from Alma since then. I do not know where they went or how she is doing."

Elizabeth pondered all she had heard. She wondered if Charlotte blamed herself for the abuse as Alma did. Maybe that was why she held on to her rules of propriety so dearly, to avoid any punishable misdeeds. "Dear, I think you should stop asking her to call you William."

"Why? I want her to feel like I am family."

"I know, but in light of what we just discussed, I think Mr. Collins's rules of propriety have been ingrained into Charlotte's very being. She just spent five months obeying them under threat of violence. She will not be easily persuaded to discard them." Elizabeth thought for a moment before adding, "And remember, her husband's name was William. Surely you see she is desperately trying to avoid that name for her son?"

"As usual, it seems you are right, my dear," Darcy teased. "I will no longer correct her. So, she has decided on Isaac?"

"Yes, she said it was her grandfather's name. But she keeps calling him 'the General'. She said it was the colonel's nickname for the baby, and she thought it was fitting."

Her husband looked over at Elizabeth. He had that look in his eyes. "Nicknames do have a tendency to stick, my love, my life, the love of my life."

"Mr. Darcy, you had best be careful. It is mid-afternoon, and there is much that needs to be done before dinner."

"Right again, my dear. There is indeed *much* that needs to be done. So much that I think we might find ourselves quite occupied until dinner."

"You wicked man!" she laughed. But she gave no resistance as he gently pulled her towards the door of his study, and they snuck up to their chambers.

*****

Some time later Elizabeth's husband snuggled his face into her neck and kissed the tender flesh. He murmured something that she couldn't understand.

"What is that?"

He pulled his face from her and said, "I am afraid that there is no getting around it now. Mr. Bingley is aware that we are home from Liverpool. He has written that he would be delighted to bring his new wife to Pemberley in October."

She nearly screamed with anticipation. "Jane is coming? How delightful! You did not even tell me that you had invited her!"

Will laughed and said, "You mean to tell me, Mrs. Darcy, that you have not already invited her? You write to her weekly. Did not the thought occur to you?"

She blushed brightly. "I may have casually asked if she was still in a condition amenable to travel." Jane had confided that she was. Elizabeth felt a little comfort in the fact that she was not the only bride who still did not have news for her husband, but she instantly regretted such a thought. "She seemed rather eager at the idea of leaving Hertfordshire," Elizabeth continued. "In Jane's own kind way, she has admitted some difficulty at being located so near our mother. Though she writes that both Lydia and Kitty have matured some, the latter more than the former."

"Well, should we make a party of it? Invite the whole family?"

"Even my mother? Dear, you are too good."

"Then it is done. I will issue the invitation for mid-October. That should give me plenty of time to prepare. Do you think your father will require anything other than a four-poster bed in the middle of the library?"

They both laughed. "Careful now," she warned, "or I may stop calling you Will and call you a wit instead!"

"I am only trying to keep up with you, dear."

# CHAPTER 10

It was just before 3:00 p.m. on Sunday afternoon, and sure enough, an average-sized young man using a cane as nothing more than a fashion accessory walked out of the building on Dale Street with an excessively tall beaver hat. His attire was impeccable. It had to be the mystery man in Darcy's letter. Colonel Fitzwilliam kept a distance and watched. Three blocks later the man turned into the Chipped Kettle. Colonel Fitzwilliam waited ten minutes before following him in.

As he entered the pub, the colonel saw a wide variety of patrons with an equally wide variety of drinks: everything from pints of ale to tea. There were even a few with nearly empty whiskey bottles in front of them. He spied the mystery man sitting alone at a table with a cup of tea.

Colonel Fitzwilliam had assessed all the available clues. The man was near his own age. His walk and manners indicated he had been raised among the genteel society. Perhaps he was not a landowner himself, but the man undoubtedly did business with those who were.

The colonel timed his approach perfectly and knocked another man, who was quite foxed, into the mystery man just as he raised the teacup to his lips. Just as Fitzwilliam had hoped, the drunkard spilled the man's tea and knocked over a kettle. The colonel grabbed the drunkard and said, "Watch it, man! You have run into this fine gentleman!"

Then he turned towards the mystery man and offered a handkerchief as the man started dabbing at the tea stains on his cravat. "I am terribly sorry," the colonel continued. "I cannot understand those who drink in the middle of the day. I was hoping this establishment was more fitting for gentlemen like ourselves."

"It is quite all right," the nameless man said.

The colonel looked at the man's face and feigned awareness. "Well, if it is not the man himself! I have not seen you since university!" It was a gamble, but he hoped the man had been schooled.

The man looked confused for a moment and then politely masked it. "A fellow Cambridge man, are you? You obviously know me, but I am afraid that your name eludes me."

*Drat!* Fitzwilliam knew the man was somehow connected to Mr. Collins and the office on Dale Street, but nothing else. "Know you? How could I forget the man with the finest knack for numbers I have ever seen? Couple that with a solid appreciation for getting around those old-fashioned laws and, well, you are unforgettable."

A buxom barmaid came and started cleaning up the spilled tea on the table. "There be anythin' else, Mr. Pastel?" she asked.

He could have kissed that woman!

Mr. Pastel said, "Just bring us another kettle and cup for me and Mr. . . . ."

"I realize it has been a while, but we were chums! You can call me Richard, no need for that ridiculous 'Mister' formality. May I call you Clyde?" He prayed this was Clyde. The letter had alluded to another brother, but his name was still unknown.

The man replied, "Ah, now I see why I do not remember you. I am Benjamin Pastel. Clyde is my younger brother. He lives in London now. When we were young, we looked a great deal alike."

It looked like getting information was going to be easy. The man had evolved from perturbed to confused, then flattered, relieved, and, finally, confident. And it was always the confident man who slipped on the ice. "Forgive me," the colonel replied. "Yes, you do look a great deal alike, but now I can see the subtle differences. Your jaw is more defined, I believe. So did you both become solicitors then, like your father? The three of you are in business together?" The letter had mentioned a brother and father.

"Yes and no. My brother and I are both solicitors, but I am afraid that my father has left this life."

"I am terribly sorry. He must be very proud of you though. What exactly is your specialty? Law? Estate planning?"

"I dabble in a great deal of things, but mostly I manage trade businesses."

Now he was getting somewhere. "Really! How fascinating. I suspect being in Liverpool with its growing port, you must dabble in a bit in shipping."

The man laughed. "It is a growing metropolis, to be sure. In fact, I am on my way to oversee a shipment in a few minutes. Please sit down and join me for tea, unless you want something stronger."

"I would love tea, Mr. Pastel." Colonel Fitzwilliam took his seat just as the new tea was being brought out.

Benjamin Pastel motioned for Colonel Fitzwilliam to fill his cup. Perhaps flattery would keep his tongue wagging. "Do tell me, are you as quick with numbers as Clyde was? That man could whip me with his calculating mind. I spent several study sessions in his chambers, more than I care to admit."

"Well, I have been doing it longer than he has, so experience counts for something. I cannot say, exactly, that I am *better* at it, but perhaps I have a stronger work ethic. Maybe I judge him too harshly. I am free to live out my life here in Liverpool, while he is forced to constantly travel back and forth between the offices. But I cannot say he is unhappy with the arrangement. He has always enjoyed the . . . ah, freedoms offered in a large city like London."

"Yes, the man always knew how to have fun." *At least I hope he did.*

"Too true. I, for one, do not see the value of risking so much money at the races only to lose it all."

Colonel Fitzwilliam was taking a risk pretending to know Clyde, but he was eager to keep Benjamin Pastel talking. He sensed some bad feelings between the two brothers. Benjamin seemed to resent that he had a great deal of work to do whereas Clyde wasted his time traveling and gambling. "I am sorry to hear that he has failed to keep his gaming under control. With his mathematical mind, he was the finest card sharp I have ever come across."

"He still is when he limits his drink, if you know what I mean."

"Of course. It has always been that way with him. If it helps any, he spoke well of you. Always said he wished he had your study habits."

A pensive look came across Mr. Pastel's face. "That is good to hear. Truth be told, Clyde and I have grown apart a bit over the last few years. I find that our extracurricular habits tend to bring in varying clients."

"How so? Surely he does not bring in his friends from the tables."

"It seems so. There have been more than a few shady players in my office."

"Anyone I would know from Cambridge?"

The man laughed outright. "No, a Cambridge man is the kind of client *I* bring in. I am slowly weeding out his clients. There are still a few that cause me trouble though."

Colonel Fitzwilliam felt Mr. Pastel was starting to clam up with all the questioning. It was time to take his leave before Mr. Pastel got suspicious. He looked at his pocket watch and said, "Oh dear, you will have to forgive my poor manners. My regiment is expecting me to address them within the hour. May I be so bold as to say I have thoroughly enjoyed getting to know you? Do you think we could meet again sometime?"

"Of course. Come to 214 Dale Street Tuesday afternoon, and I will show you what a simple tradesman can do for himself. I do not like to boast, but I think I have done well."

"Indeed you have. I shall do that very thing. What a pleasure it was to meet you! But before I go, I must say that I have not been completely forthright with you." *No, certainly not.* But he had to build a certain amount of trust with the man.

Pastel raised one eyebrow slightly before schooling his features. "How so?"

"I used to have a gambling problem. With a great deal of work, I have mastered it. But I can no longer associate with gamblers. You know how it is. They are always throwing out wagers and bets, and the temptation is too great. After what you said of Clyde . . . well, would you mind not mentioning our meeting to him? Reconnecting after all these years could lead me into trouble."

The man stood, smiled, and shook his hand. "You have just earned my respect, good sir. But I could not help but notice that you offered only your first name." It wasn't a statement; it was a question.

*I hope I am choosing correctly here.* This man seemed like a smart, honest hardworking person. But Fitzwilliam was such an uncommon name. If he told the truth, there would be nowhere left to hide. After a moment's hesitation, the colonel decided he had bent the truth too much already, a skill Darcy always credited him with. "Fitzwilliam. Colonel Richard Fitzwilliam. You may have heard of my father, Lord Matlock."

"Fitzwilliam? Yes, that does sound familiar. I look forward to Tuesday. Good luck with your regiment. There have been many ships departing with soldiers for across the pond lately. Will you be among them?"

"Very likely. We are awaiting further instructions. Good day, Mr. Pastel. I apologize again for mistaking you for your brother. It was a pleasure to make your acquaintance."

"For me as well."

The colonel bowed and left.

*Well, that went much better than expected.* As he walked back to camp, he tried to piece things together. Benjamin was a solicitor, along with his crooked younger brother, Clyde. He took a great deal of pride in his work. Clyde brought in shady clients that Benjamin did not approve of. The very topic caused a great deal of discomfort. They dealt mainly with exports and imports, which would explain them assisting Mr. Collins with decisions about his ships. But the big mystery was how and why did Collins own two ships, and what exactly were they carrying?

*****

It was Monday morning, and soldiers were trickling in by the hour. He had nearly accounted for every able-bodied man. Just then, a quite unexpected soldier marched in.

"Everett, what are you doing here?" Fitzwilliam asked. Colonel Fitzwilliam was very surprised to see him. Everett, the soldier Mr. Heather had pulled through the infection without amputating his hand, and had rightly been given medical leave, waved the very hand that almost took his life.

"Colonel, do you really think I could let my brothers go to war without me at their flank?"

He had felt a positive and almost tangible energy in camp over the weekend. His men were ready and anxious to serve their country. It caused no small amount of pride.

"Of course you would want to be with us. I am glad to have you. There is no better swordsman in the regiment. How is your left hand?"

"I will not be a weak link, if that is what you are asking, sir. After a month of recovery, I am ready to fight. I promise you I will be an asset to the regiment."

"No doubt you will. Find your tent. Once you are settled, check in with Mr. Heather so he can give you a clean bill of health. I will go tell him now to expect you."

"I shall, sir, thank you," Everett said.

Fitzwilliam turned to head towards the makeshift infirmary but was hailed by a man from behind, calling his name. He turned and saw him waving a letter of some sort. "Colonel, you have an express!"

He had not been the only one to hear the news.

Like pigeons flocking around someone throwing stale bread, soldiers suddenly migrated towards him. He took the letter. Seeing it was from Pemberley, he shooed them away. "Just some personal correspondence, gentlemen. Go back to work."

He walked to a tree, leaned against it, and opened his letter.

*30 August 1812*
*Pemberley*


*Fitzwilliam,*

*I apologize for sending this as an express, but I was worried it would not reach you before your orders. I hope you have made progress on the letter I gave you. No doubt you have pieced together far more in the last few days than I did in two months. Of course, you must concede that I was on my wedding trip and therefore preoccupied.*

*Speaking of which, I apologize again for downright ignoring you while you were here. Even my mild-mannered steward, Kelsey, has complained about my recent lack of attention. Apparently I have not learned to balance married life yet, as grand as it is.*

*Here is what I have concluded so far: I believe Mr. Collins owned both the* Eastern Challenge *and* Winter's Night. *I assume the names were altered for secrecy. And I believe the business—whatever it is—is still operating under the Pastels' management.*

*The brief interview I had with the eldest of the Pastel brothers provided no additional information. The man seemed to be respectable, though somewhat indifferent to Mrs. Collins's current state of poverty. I gathered that he does not think well of us, which is understandable in light of our connection to Collins. (Indeed, I can hardly blame him.)*

*I know you have a great deal on your mind as you prepare to go to war, but I pray you will be careful in your research. I did not perceive Mr. Pastel as dangerous, but he did warn us about the necessity of Mrs. Collins properly mourning her husband.*

*Speaking of which, you will be happy to hear that the General now has a name: Isaac Byron Collins. She named him after her grandfather, Isaac, as well as Mr. Collins, whose first name was actually Byron. I have not seen Mrs. Collins myself as she is not yet well enough to leave her chambers, but apparently she was very insistent that I write at once to tell you of the baby's name.*

*Rest assured that the doctor reports both mother and baby are healthy. And Elizabeth reports that she seems very happy. Isaac has apparently brought something to life in Mrs. Collins that was dormant a long time. She says Mrs. Collins seems brighter and more cheerful, more along the lines of Charlotte Lucas that she knew in Hertfordshire.*

*Do keep us up to date with your orders. If you will be in Liverpool for several weeks, I would like to come and visit. I feel terrible that I offered nothing more than a letter to assist you in your quest.*

*Elizabeth reports that Charlotte has asked if we have heard word from you yet. I hope that offers you peace at this time.*

*Sincerely,*
*F. D.*

Colonel Fitzwilliam's heart beat wildly in his chest. She had named her son Isaac! The letter said she had named him after her grandfather, but he could not help but wonder . . . Had she overheard him talk to the General about Isaac Brock? He quickly reviewed all he had confided to the baby that night. Although his monologue had been an honest expression of his feelings, he never intended for Charlotte to hear it. He didn't mind her knowing of his feelings. In fact, quite the contrary. But Darcy had counseled him not to pursue her while she was in mourning. If she responded that dramatically to his unwanted kiss, what must she have felt upon hearing how deeply he admired her?

A familiar voice recalled him to his surroundings. "Why the long face?" Mr. Heather asked.

"Mr. Heather, I am glad to see you have arrived! How was your journey?"

"Splendid, if you count sharing a post chaise with a young couple and their crying baby as pleasant. It took me all of ten minutes to discern that the baby's ears were pained, most likely infected. I encouraged the mother to suckle the babe, and she looked at me aghast, as if I had suggested she dance stark naked in the village green. I tried to explain that I was a physician and promised to divert my eyes, but she would not hear of it. She was offended beyond words. Between the baby's cries and the mother's indignation, I am afraid I have quite the headache now. But you did not answer my question; why the long face?"

"A letter from Darcy. Come, join me in my barracks, and we shall get reacquainted. How is your wife? Was it difficult to part ways for an unknown amount of time?"

As they walked from the infirmary, the conversation touched lightly on the superficial greetings that close friends exchange after being apart. But when they finally were in the seclusion of Fitzwilliam's room, Mr. Heather announced, "I see sleep still evades you." It wasn't a question.

"I am afraid so. I am looking forward to a bit of your sleeping powders tonight."

"And how is Mrs. Collins? I assume you saw her?"

"Yes I did. But I am not sure how to answer your inquiry. At first, she was cool and indifferent to me. I made repeated attempts to plant the seed of friendship to no avail. Then Darcy counseled me to be more myself rather than play the ladies' man. We both relaxed a bit then, and I saw more of the lady I have known all along. She seemed to enjoy my company."

"That is good news," Heather said encouragingly.

"Ah, but, a few days ago, I may have bungled things irrevocably. With the looming deadline of departure approaching, I seized the opportunity to declare myself. It was the hardest thing anyone has ever asked of me."

The doctor looked confused. "She asked you to declare yourself?"

Fitzwilliam laughed. "No, quite the opposite. It seems I have been blind. Not only did she not welcome my feelings of admiration, but she quite plainly stated that I am never to ever kiss her again."

The look on Mr. Heather's face was telling of his disapproval. His voice was low, "Please tell me you did not kiss her." After Colonel Fitzwilliam sheepishly held his silence, Mr. Heather said, "Good God! What were you thinking?"

"It was really just a misunderstanding. She said—"

He interrupted him before he could explain. "Oh flummery! No gentleman would blame his ill manners on the lady. Pardon my forwardness, but I am deeply disappointed in you."

The colonel could not have agreed more. "I am too, I assure you. But I have not even told you her reaction to the kiss—"

"You said that she told you never to kiss her again! What more does anyone need to know?"

"Actually there is quite a bit more to the story. After I kissed her, she stormed off, so I naturally followed after. I reached for her arm to try to explain and apologize, then saw how unwanted it was, so I removed it immediately. I started backing away with my arms in the air to show her I wanted peace, and suddenly she started screaming—"

"Yes, I think I would be screaming too in her position."

"No," Fitzwilliam explained. "This was different. She did not sound angry this time, she sounded . . . terrified, like she was in danger. When I tried to help her, she shrank away from my touch and screamed even louder. Darcy and Elizabeth came to her aid and ushered her off to her room. I only saw her one time after that day."

Richard took a deep breath. Remembering Charlotte like that brought a fresh ache into his heart. "Heather, I have never seen anything like it. She was lying on the ground in front of me, hysterical and completely undone. Each scream ripped a lesion in my heart. I do not understand . . ."

The emotion of the situation started to overwhelm him again. He had not gotten a chance to really discuss the situation with anyone, not even Darcy.

Mr. Heather came over to him and placed his hand on his arm. "I do not know what to say," he said quietly. "I am so sorry."

Fitzwilliam nodded. "I have considered the episode a great deal since then, and I have come to a conclusion: I sowed my seeds among thorns."

"Thorns?"

"Yes. Like in the parable. Something else was in the garden that night. Something that is choking out our friendship. Obviously, I acted unpardonably. I should have been clearer. I should have explained that I would wait until her period of mourning was over. I should have made her a proper offer of marriage. Instead, I rushed on, brash and impulsive like an eager lad who hopes for his first kiss behind a barn. Or worse, a rake of the worst form."

Heather shook his head slowly. "You are too hard on yourself, Fitzwilliam. You are not a rake. Your sympathy for Charlotte is surely evidence of that fact." He slapped Fitzwilliam on the back encouragingly. "Tell me more about your theory about the thorns."

Colonel Fitzwilliam pulled out the small bible he carried with him, but before he could open it, Mr. Heather started chuckling. "You now carry a bible with you now? In your uniform?" he teased.

"Of course," Fitzwilliam replied with a twinkle in his eye. He patted his left vest pocket. "Right over my heart. Makes me look more muscular, no? Although, admittedly, rather lopsided. Nevertheless, several of the local ladies have already tripped over themselves in their efforts to catch my eye."

They both laughed at the absurdity of such a thing. "I see," Mr. Heather replied after catching his breath. "I suppose I find it humorous that a self-proclaimed Sunday-churchgoer could be so altered in such a short amount of time."

"Ah, but I must correct you, dear friend. It was you who gave me that title. I believe in God and pray a great deal, I simply do not wear my faith on my sleeve like a badge of honor. My faith is very personal."

"Indeed. *So* personal that it has never come up in any of our discussions."

"Well, we spend so much time discussing Charlotte that there is little room for any other topics."

"Ah, so you are calling her 'Charlotte' now?" the doctor joked.

Fitzwilliam blushed and tried to feign a look of shocked offense, which Heather saw right through at once.

"Very well, since your ears seem to be *smoking*, I will take pity on you. We can revisit the topic of your usage of Mrs. Collin's Christian name at a future date. Tell me more about the thorns you spoke of."

Colonel Fitzwilliam opened his bible to the fourth chapter of Mark. "In verse seven, it reads: 'And some fell among thorns; and the thorns sprang up with it, and choked it.'" The merriment of a few moments ago quickly dissipated in the thick silence. This was hard to say. He looked out of the barracks to the green fields beyond. "That day in the garden with Charlotte . . . She was furious with me, obviously, but when I touched her, she flinched as if a thorn had pricked her. And then everything changed in an instant. Her screams . . . it was as if she thought I was going to . . ."

He looked back at his friend and saw Heather staring intently at him. "As if she thought you were going to what?"

Fitzwilliam hesitated to put his fears into words; in doing so, would it make it true? "I think her late husband might have been worse than a blabbering idiot. I think he might have had an evil side to him; a side that only a wife would know."

If the silence had been thick before, it nearly choked him now. Saying it out loud was indescribably painful. If he was right, that meant that Charlotte had endured moments that no woman ever should have to endure. It meant her husband had made a mockery of his vow to love, comfort, and honor her. And it meant that she might never trust another man again. The thought made his knees weak just thinking about it. How her heart must have ached for kindness! She should have been loved and cherished, like a rare antique of infinite worth, but instead she had been saddled with a man who showed her only cruelty and indifference.

Mr. Heather finally asked, "How does this make you feel?"

"Besides wanting to dig up the man and choke the life out of him again?" Fitzwilliam growled. "Helpless. I feel completely helpless. There is nothing I can do. There is no one to fight. And yet the foe is still there. He has left a mark so powerful and deep that I know not how to battle it. Her heart is so ensnarled by his thorns that my advances cause her only pain. All my seeds are being choked out. How can I get her to trust me—or any man for that matter—when she has been taught by a sinister man to be suspicious of love?"

"I admit I do not know." Heather replied. "But tread lightly, my friend. If you have any doubts whatsoever about your love, if you are not absolutely sure, it may be time to withdraw your troops and retreat."

If it were possible to feel one's backbone harden, Colonel Fitzwilliam felt it do so at that moment.

"Never."

# CHAPTER 11

*1 September 1812*
*Liverpool*

*Darcy,*

*Thank you for your express. Alas, I have nothing new to report in regards to my orders. All but a handful of my men are assembled here. There are rumors that a regiment has never waited longer than two weeks to depart from Liverpool, so I fully expect to hear from General Fredrickson soon. The men's spirits are high. If we wait much longer, I will need to invent something to occupy them before they start making mischief in town. They seem just as anxious as I am to be under way.*

*However, I have made good use of my time here in Liverpool. With my natural wit and charm, I have made the acquaintance of Mr. Benjamin Pastel, the elder of the two Pastel sons. I have discovered that Pastel and Sons are solicitors that deal mainly with the shipping of goods between Liverpool and London. Benjamin is an honest, hardworking man, but, from his own confession, his brother Clyde is rather less so. I believe it was Clyde who brought Mr. Collins into the office. Benjamin seems to prefer his own clients and is eager to be rid of Clyde's.*

*With my impressive skill at bending the truth—the very same expertise which you so despise yet so often avail yourself of—I feigned an interest in the import-and-export business and garnered an invitation to watch the loading of ships in the docks on Friday. Pastel manages six ships which run cargo between Liverpool and London. As luck would have it, one of the ships we will be watching is the* Eastern Challenge. *I can hardly believe my good fortune! I shall use all of my charm to discover what kind of cargo it carries and how Mr. Collins was involved.*

*Today I was invited to the office. I am pleased to report that the door has a simple pin-and-tumbler lock—almost identical to the lock on Mother's candy cupboard back at home, which, as you know, I have a good deal of experience with. But, do not fret, I only mention it in case of future need. I am being very careful, in case you ask. Besides, there has been no need to resort to such tactics, since my absurdly proficient conversational skills have been so well received thus far. (No wonder your efforts were in vain, my dear taciturn Cousin.)*

*On a more personal note, thank you for relaying the news that Charlotte and Isaac are doing well. I have considered the situation at length, and I feel strongly that I should pull back a bit. My feelings for her have not changed—very much the opposite—but she needs something right now that I cannot give her. Please do me this favor, however: keep calling her son the General. Forgive me for not explaining further, but I hope this will remind her of me while I am away. I once felt anxious about being sent off to war when all I really wanted to do was be with her, but now, after much thought on the topic, I am glad that she will be without a man in her life for some time.*

*I have done it all wrong, Darcy. I have sowed my seeds in the wrong way and at the wrong time. I know you know more than you have told me, and I understand why you could not betray her confidence. But suffice it say that I now realize our aunt's former rector exhibited a darker side in the privacy of his own home.*

*I am not asking you to confirm my suspicions. I understand now that Charlotte needs to find strength inside herself. I fear my actions have only added to her confusion. She does not know it, but it is clear that she wants to be loved and appreciated. More importantly, she wants to be respected. These needs are so basic. It is what make humans stand apart from mere animals. Even wild beasts will fight among themselves for power and dominance, but it is only humans that desire respect, love, and honor. (And I firmly believe that Collins had instincts more along that of the wild beast, perhaps a donkey's backside.)*

*If my suspicions are correct, her heart is still plagued with his thorns and my advances are only deepening her pain. She has been whittled away to a fragment of the woman she once was. Which makes her all the more impressive, because the only Charlotte I ever knew was Mr. Collins's wife, and yet, I still fell madly in love with her. She is most loyal. I only wish I could show her how prized a jewel she is.*

*Forgive the length of this epistle. Ironically, I started writing because I could not sleep, but composing this letter has brought me some respite from the inner turmoil that has plagued me for several months. Perhaps I might find sleep tonight after all. I must count my blessings, no matter how they come.*

*I have enclosed a letter for Georgiana and a brief one for the General. Please ask Charlotte to read it to him and beg her forgiveness for the presumption.*

*There is no need to apologize for being married, you poor, poor thing. How miserably happy you must be. Even if your wretchedness were*

*to make you more broody, I will always be your
faithful friend.*

*Colonel Fitzwilliam*


He folded the letter and set it aside. Somehow putting words to his feelings lifted a burden that had occupied far too many nights. It was the right choice to give Charlotte time to heal. If she had overheard his conversation with Isaac in the nursery, her reaction had been encouraging. But he could not rush her. She would have to find strength inside herself first.

It all made sense now. And he was now surprisingly grateful for the distance between them. In her presence, it was hard to think of anything but his needs and feelings. But here, miles away from her, he could see how much she was hurting and suffering. Now that he knew the truth, everything he loved about her was accentuated. His urge to pursue her was stronger than ever. But she needed time.

Hopefully being a continent away would allow her to thrive and find her dormant intrinsic power. Hopefully seeing Darcy and Elizabeth together would show her that a man could be gentle and loving to his wife. He finally saw the wisdom in the tradition of mourning a spouse for an entire year.

But even if they had to be apart, he did not want her to forget that he cared. He still wanted her to remember him. And that was all he needed from her at the moment; it was selfish of him to ask even that much of her. No more ridiculous fighting for her attention or flattering her with compliments that made her cringe. And no more reminders that men have an unfortunate habit of trying to manipulate the world around them if it suits their own needs. Real love was not like that. He cringed at the memory of all his mistakes. Hopefully she would remember only the good parts.

He took out two fresh sheets of paper and wrote a brief letter to Georgiana. Then, before writing a very important letter to the General, he took a moment and prayed. When he finished, the words came to him easily, peace filling his soul. He couldn't help but seal it with a kiss. General Isaac Byron Collins was his only link to her now.

He sealed all the letters together, and suddenly his fatigue was overpowering. He blew out the candle, collapsed on his cot, and, for the first time in months, his mind was saturated with peace. The comfort from the last hour of introspection had worked even better than Mr. Heather's sleeping draughts.

He loved her enough to let her go.

*****

"For me?" Charlotte asked, surprised.

"No," Mr. Darcy explained. "The letter specifically said it was for the General, but you are to read it to him."

Charlotte took the letter and eyed it suspiciously. Why had Colonel Fitzwilliam written to her son? Sure enough, there was his full name scripted in a neat hand, General Isaac Byron Collins.

She stood and said, "Excuse me please."

She dismissed the young maid as she entered the nursery. "You may go now, Sally. I will ring for you later." But as Sally turned to leave, Charlotte felt an urge to say more. She took a deep breath and reached a hand out to the young woman. "And, Sally? Thank you for all that you do. Your efforts and devotion to my son are not overlooked. I have heard how you stood your ground; it was you who persuaded Mr. Darcy to let me leave my chambers. I am not used to being confined to my bed, and I cannot tell you how restless I was, even though it has only been a week since Isaac's birth."

Sally smiled brightly and curtsied. Charlotte, once again, was glad beyond words Mr. Darcy had suggested Sally as Isaac's nursery maid. Charlotte had resisted the idea of a nursery maid at first and had insisted on diligently interviewing the young woman before leaving Isaac in her care. What she discovered was impressive. Although young, Sally had been in service for quite a while. For many years, Sally had supported her younger siblings, and now that her parents were too old to work, she supported them instead. The young woman was loving and selfless.

"Yes, ma'am," Sally replied. "I ain't never seen anyone leave their childbed so soon, but I saw the determination in yer eyes. Any lady who will fight for her right to make her own decisions is mighty right in my book. I shall come back in a bit to check on ya."

"Thank you."

The rocking chair next to the crib was positioned just close enough to watch the rise and fall of her swaddled baby's breaths. Isaac had the fullest set of curls she had ever seen on a newborn. She picked him up carefully and sat back down in the rocker. It did something to her to hold her child. His every little movement felt like a caress. Each time she patted his back to ease his stomach after nursing, it was like he was telling her how grateful he was for her.

She was needed. She was wanted. And she was capable of supplying all of his needs, from the basic eating and sleeping needs, to the more complex needs of loving and teaching him. She had an entire lifetime to be called "Mother", and it was as if her title of widow no longer applied. She wasn't defined by the black dress or the lace shawl anymore. She was a mother. What greater title could there be?

After a few moments, her curiosity got the better of her and she decided to read her letter, or rather her son's letter. Soon she was laughing out loud, struggling not to startle the baby in her arms. The man was so ridiculous sometimes!

She was preparing to read it out loud to the General when Elizabeth and Georgiana came in.

"It is so nice to hear you laugh," Elizabeth said. "It has been far too long."

Georgiana asked, "What did the colonel have to tell the General? My letter said much the same as William's: only that they have not received their orders yet."

Charlotte smiled and waved them in. "I will read it to you," Charlotte offered. "The man is as much as he ever was. He writes,

*Dear General,*

*I must inform you that I have not yet heard from the command center. But have no fear, King George III is a faithful correspondent. He and I once reached for the same lemon tart at a masquerade ball, and we struck up the liveliest conversation about the sweet-and-sour nature of*

*the treat. If anyone overheard us, they would never have guessed that we were having a covert discussion on Napoleon's abnormally short stature. It was difficult to stay in character—me disguised as an intimidatingly dashing, painfully handsome pirate; him dressed as a rooster. His costume was even fitted with a wattle attached to his chin which, I solemnly promise, wobbled when he talked. Very distracting, let me tell you.*

*As usual, I am keeping my men occupied. I sent them to the churchyard yesterday to scrub the moss off the headstones. Surely you do not imagine I would force them to do something as mundane and ordinary as march around town? Well, truth be told, I did that as well. I would prefer to task them with cleaning cobblestones, but with so many regiments in Liverpool right now, there is not a dirty cobblestone to be found in the entire metropolis.*

*Tomorrow I believe I will make them all do a bit of sea bathing, as some of them seem to have forgotten to bathe at all since I last saw them. Their stench alone is enough to compel me to do it. Of course, I will need to invent some surreptitious purpose. Perhaps I shall make the most odoriferous of them bring me the 'best' sea water from the rocks 100 yards out from the coast.*

*It saddens me that I was forced to step away from you so soon, but perhaps you can ask about that ridiculous man who told you stories when you were less than a day old. I am sure Mr. Darcy will have plenty of stories. Georgiana as well.*

*But if they tell you one that involved a certain goose who honked all night and a slingshot, do not listen to him. And do not let them even start the story about the kitten named Princess Le Grande Fiona—she meant nothing to me, and I certainly did not dress her up in doll clothes and try to smuggle her in my coat all the way from Derbyshire to London against my mother's wishes. Do make Darcy tell you about the first time I gave him a nosebleed. It was for a perfectly good reason, I assure you.*

*Well, General, I continue to await orders and, until then, we must remember to press on and enforce our previous orders. You do remember the orders that King 'Rooster' George III gave you? I am sure you do. His words can be very cryptic but his message is clear: do not let anyone take the last lemon tart. It is too sweet to pass up.*

*Your comrade in arms,*
*Colonel Fitzwilliam*

Charlotte folded the letter and laughed again.

"Those stories sound quite intriguing," Elizabeth giggled. "I might have to make Will tell me the one about the kitten."

"Oh, I have heard it many times!" Georgiana replied. "Princess Le Grande Fiona!"

"Quite a long name for a tiny kitten," Charlotte mused.

"Well, the name was inspired by Fiona, his childhood sweetheart, daughter of a marquis."

"And when was this?" Charlotte asked.

"Oh, long before I can remember. I think Richard must have been fourteen or fifteen. Anyway, Fiona was apparently beautiful, with hair as black as night. But she was nineteen and, unsurprisingly, she wanted nothing to do with a lanky young Richard. So, Richard's broken heart took solace in a kitten with a jet-black coat. He used to purloin my doll clothes to dress it. Once, Darcy spied him kissing it on the whiskers and vowing to marry her someday, even though he was just a second son, heir to nothing. 'Surely love alone is enough for us to live on, my dear!' he promised."

Elizabeth said, "Aw, how sweet!"

"Yes. He was completely besotted. He could not bear to leave the kitten behind at Pemberley, but Richard's mother refused to admit an animal, not matter how beloved, into her carriage. Besides which, the kitten was not old enough to leave its mother. So Richard gave the kitten a final kiss and pretended to say goodbye, but instead he wrapped the tiny thing in his coat! He snuck her all the way to London, and his parents had no idea!"

"But how did the kitten survive without its mother's milk?" Charlotte queried.

"Richard fed her," Georgiana explained. "Every two hours, day and night, for weeks. I am told he was quite devoted and never missed a feeding. He kept that cat for years and years. As Princess grew older, Richard ended up caring for her just like in the beginning, once again waking every two hours to give her warm milk and letting her sleep on his bed with him. Once William found the two of them asleep together like that, the old cat resting in Richard's arms, no longer black, but frosted with gray from age, wrapped in one of Richard's shirtsleeves like a baby. When Princess finally died five years ago, it broke Richard's heart."

As Charlotte listened, her mind wandered slightly. It was a sweet story, one that seemed to show how deeply his heart loved. She was so grateful to know a man like him. But she tried not to think on the conversation he had with the General in those wee hours of the morning in the nursery. It was still difficult to remember his deeply loving words.

It felt safer to think about Georgiana and Elizabeth. Charlotte felt extremely close to them. She had always been close to Elizabeth, but there was something about Georgiana's innocence and deep belief in true love that was contagious. It was as if she still believed the fairy tales about knights in shining armor that rode in upon white steeds to rescue fair maidens.

Even now, it seemed strange to Charlotte that she herself had helped bring Elizabeth and Mr. Darcy together, that *she* had been the one to encourage her friend not to give up on love. She had never seen a love match up close before. Certainly neither her parents nor the Bennets had love matches. They seemed to have found their place in the world without love. They proved that life and marriage could be tolerable without it. So, she had never experienced or desired romance for herself.

But something began to change when she saw Mr. Darcy's kindness and tenderness, when she watched him cradle Elizabeth's terribly ill body. The things that he whispered were completely improper—Charlotte could still remember the heat on her cheeks as she had looked away in embarrassment—yet she began to crave their interactions. She began to need to see them together again. It had sparked something inside her. Something deep inside which whispered that love mattered and was worth overcoming any obstacle.

116

Now, seeing them blissfully happy together, she craved it even more. The stolen kisses and caresses that they shared when they hoped no one could see them made it even more meaningful; they loved each other when no one was watching. These moments were not false outward *demonstrations* of love, intended to create the perception of love, they were impulsive and natural *expressions* of love. She had experienced only the former with Mr. Collins.

After five days of resting in her childbed, she had felt a void in her life. At first, she had thought it was because she missed the colonel's jokes, which was true to some extent. But it was more than that. She had missed seeing Mr. Darcy tuck a stray curl behind Elizabeth's ear. She had missed seeing Elizabeth flash him a brilliant smile that made him grin. She had missed seeing her cup his jaw when they neared an argument and seeing how his tension seemed to evaporate at her touch. It was the absence of these tender moments that made her insist on leaving her chambers so soon.

And now, hearing Georgiana speak so lovingly about her cousin's devotion to a kitten made her longing and aching for love even stronger. She wasn't ready yet, but she could see that the fortress around her heart had cracks in its foundation. How could it not? She was surrounded by kind, considerate people who treated her so lovingly. Georgiana had checked in on her every few hours, day and night, since Isaac's birth, quietly tiptoeing past her door so as not to wake her if she were sleeping. And Elizabeth had done the same. They had been so solicitous. Elizabeth had told her how concerned Mr. Darcy had been for her during the delivery— "Nerves as flighty as sails in a storm, Charlotte. He put my dear mother to shame," she had confessed.

Even the Master of Pemberley loved her, it seems. She was family. She knew it now. And somewhere in the back of her carefully guarded heart, she wondered if the colonel was one of those people who loved her too. She shook off the thought. It was too dangerous to consider it a possibility.

Charlotte smiled as Georgiana finished the story. "Well, General," Charlotte declared, "Would you like to hear more of these stories about Colonel Fitzwilliam?" Isaac let out his squeak, and everyone giggled. "I believe that is a 'Yes, ma'am!'" They all laughed again.

Their musical tones of true happiness sent further cracks into the walls around her heart. If these women loved her so much, did that mean that she was worthy of love?

# CHAPTER 12

The following Friday, upon returning from his visit to the *Eastern Challenge* with Benjamin Pastel, an express was waiting for Colonel Fitzwilliam. It seemed the orders had come at last. Mr. Heather and half of the regiment were patiently gathered outside his barracks.

Fitzwilliam opened the express and read it quickly, doubling back to note the details before looking up at his beloved men's expectant faces. "Well, gentlemen, it should come as no surprise that we have received our orders. We are to board and load the *Meridian's Promise* on Monday. We depart for the Canadian colonies at dawn on Tuesday. I happen to have seen this ship myself not an hour ago, and she is a fine vessel.

"When we arrive in the Canadian Colonies we will be serving under General Isaac Brock, a man I have met and respect a great deal. The travel will take just under a month, so eat all of the fruit and vegetables you can. After the first week, we will have nothing but floured drop scones and fish soup. Mr. Heather, here, will instruct you on how to fight off illness on the long voyage. As we have only one doctor among us, I will need each of you to do your part in preventing disease. Mr. Heather, if you please."

Colonel Fitzwilliam walked away as Mr. Heather started to explain the importance of cleanliness. Colonel Fitzwilliam made his way through the crowd of men, where an assortment of anxiety, hope, courage, and pride were reflected in their faces, along with relief at finally knowing their orders.

All were quite normal feelings, and all were feelings he felt himself. At least now he knew.

There was much to be done. While the men were occupied, he quickly penned a note to Darcy.

*5 September 1812*
*Liverpool*

*Darcy,*

*I shall depart on September 8 for the Canadian Colonies. I do not know how long I will be gone. I will be serving under General Isaac Brock, whom I have known since I enlisted. I have not seen him for years, as he has been stationed overseas, but I look forward to working with him again. The voyage will likely take me a month and any correspondence afterwards will be sparse, so I must tell you all of what I have learned here.*

*I am confident that Mr. Collins indeed is, or shall I say, was, the owner of the* Eastern Challenge. *It is being managed now entirely by Benjamin Pastel's office, which is encouraging.*

*He mentioned that he might sell both of the ships in eight months or so, which, coincidentally, is the end of Charlotte's mourning period. I am beginning to agree with your suspicion that her inheritance is somehow linked to her mourning period observance.*

*When I questioned him about the ships' previous owner, he became very nervous. All he said was that the owner had directed them from afar and was no longer capable of doing so. I imagine being six feet under the ground severely limited his capabilities.*

*Its current cargo includes bolts of fabric and lace from Italy and India as well as the occasional historic artifact that the ship has been commissioned to transport to the recently restored Hampton Court Palace in London. They are hoping to make a museum of some sort eventually. A slow process, to be sure, but it has to start sometime.*

*I believe the ship is in excellent condition, and I even met the captain, Captain Blackhurst. But I must admit he made a very poor impression on me. He bears a very worrisome similarity to Collins. When I shared my poor opinion of Captain Blackhurst with Benjamin, he confided that he is hoping to replace him soon, as he is not particularly fond of him either. Are you acquainted with any captains that need a ship? I jest only slightly. Blackhurst sent shivers up my spine. Clearly Mr. Pastel was uncomfortable as well.*

*This is all I have to report. May God bless you and your family. Kiss the General, Georgiana, and Elizabeth for me. I need not say the next part.*

*Help her to remember me, and show her how loving a husband can be. It gives me hope to know that she has you and Elizabeth as her exemplars as she heals. And as I tell any soldier who is afraid to go to war, a man is nothing without hope.*

*Colonel Fitzwilliam*

\*\*\*\*\*

Elizabeth watched Charlotte closely while Will shared parts of the Fitzwilliam's recent letter. Elizabeth had already read it and discussed it with her husband. Charlotte always seemed to hover when the post arrived, and Elizabeth suspected she was eager to hear from Colonel Fitzwilliam.

Will cleared his throat. "He states he has received his orders and is probably loading the ship as we speak. They are due to leave port tomorrow morning. I had hoped he would have more than a few days' warning, but he and his men have known the most likely outcome for some time now. They are ready. He will surely be missed. His lightheartedness and jovial nature are a special kind of balm."

Elizabeth watched Charlotte look down at her hands and fidget slightly. Will continued, "I am to give Elizabeth, Georgiana, and the General all kisses and hugs. But he sends his love and he specifically wanted me to let you all know his spirits are hopeful."

Georgiana sounded a bit disappointed, "Is that all?"

"It was not a long letter. I am sure he was very busy and had several others letters to write to his parents and his brother."

"And there are no additional letters for any of us?" Georgiana asked, looking briefly at Charlotte.

"I am afraid not. Most of the letter was directing me in a matter of business that I was looking into in Liverpool while on my wedding trip. I believe he would have written more if he could. But like I said, he was hopeful and his men were ready for this directive."

Georgiana was not the only one who had small tears forming in her eyes. Charlotte stood and excused herself and walked out of the room. Elizabeth looked to her husband, and Darcy motioned for her to go after her.

Elizabeth followed Charlotte and took her arm as they went upstairs; no doubt the nursery was the destination. They walked in silence together, Elizabeth gently rubbing Charlotte's arm. She heard a few sniffles, but Charlotte held her head high even though her glossy eyes threatening to betray her.

They stopped outside the nursery, and Sally stood to leave. It was a routine that had become commonplace. Charlotte often relieved Sally for several hours to be with her son. Elizabeth did not know a more stubborn woman. She had refused to stay in bed after the baby was born. She said that walking helped her aches. The doctor, although wary of his patient being so active the first two weeks after childbirth, admitted that it was unlikely to do any harm. Elizabeth certainly understood Charlotte's need to walk out her anxieties.

Charlotte finally spoke. "I hope . . . I have a great deal of hope for Fitzwilliam. I believe he will be safe. He is a smart man and quite strong. And he is not inexperienced. I know he has been to battle before, but never for so long. It is likely to be a year or more before he returns."

"Yes, more than likely. But he will not be alone. He spoke to me many times of his men. He was quite fond of them and of Mr. Heather, the surgeon."

Charlotte looked at Elizabeth with pained eyes. "I know. But he will not be *here*. He will not be with . . . with us." Elizabeth got the distinct feeling that Charlotte had wanted to say "with me" but had caught herself at the last second.

"Do you want to talk about it?" Elizabeth offered. Charlotte shook her head. "Can I do anything for you?"

"No, Elizabeth, I am doing quite well. You have been such a good friend. I know I have been distant and moody lately. Things have not been the same over the last few months, but I am trying to do the best I can. Everyone assumes my silence is because I am grieving Mr. Collins. But I am not, not inside, that is. On the outside I am." Charlotte paused, fingering her black mourning dress while considering how to express her feelings. "Your neighbors who dined with us the other night, the Birminghams—their son seemed to take a fancy to Georgiana."

"I noticed. He was quite forward with his flattery. Georgiana could hardly respond to him before he made some other obsequious comment. "

"It made me nauseous," Charlotte replied flatly. "He reminded me of Mr. Collins. What kind of wife does it make me that I cringe every time someone reminds me of my dead husband?"

Elizabeth did not know how to respond. Was Charlotte about to reveal the abuse she endured? Elizabeth waited a bit longer before responding. "I think that makes you the kind of wife who has been through too much in a short amount of time. No one blamed you for excusing yourself early that night. You really should not even be out of bed yet. But I know how important it is for you to join us, and I respect you for your resolve."

"Truly? I mean, you respect me?"

"Indeed I do. You are paving the road for me. Do you think for one minute that I will be capable of staying in bed either? The fact that you are doing it with such glorious success only means that I will be able to follow your lead. You are a wonderful example of tenacity."

Charlotte smiled. "I told myself when I married Mr. Collins that there would be times that would demand a great deal of endurance. But I did not know how true that would be. I certainly do have tenacity, as you say. But do not judge my bleak opinions of Mr. Collins too harshly. Ours was not a love match of course. Even Georgiana now understands."

"Then why do you look so sad?"

"I do not feel as sad as I look, I assure you. In a way, I feel much the same way as Colonel Fitzwilliam does. I feel hopeful. I have a long road ahead of me, and no real answers yet. But someday I will not be dependent on you or Mr. Darcy to place food in front of me. I will find a way to be my own woman."

"I am sure you will." Elizabeth wished she could share the news about the two ships that Charlotte would probably very soon inherit. Will had brought her into his study as soon as the last letter arrived and shared what Richard had written. It was very likely that Charlotte would soon have a great deal of money to her name as well as a source of income. She remembered the brief conversation.

*Will had watched her read the letter and then had said, "So, it seems Charlotte will be awarded the ships and the eleven thousand pounds in the ledger once her mourning period ends. I think Benjamin Pastel might be willing to continue to manage the ships if the right captain can be found. Do you remember Captain Conrad Jersey?"*

*"The man who tried to kill you in London?" Elizabeth answered with a smile. "Yes, I remember. I have an excellent memory for stories where someone draws a sword on you, Will."*

*"Well, yes, he did do that. But it was all a misunderstanding of course. He was the captain who withdrew his application for the captaincy of the* Eastern Challenge *years ago because his instinct told him that there was something shady about it. I admire him a great deal. I think I should invite him to Pemberley and approach him about asking for the position again. No swords this time."*

*Elizabeth laughed. "Well, as long as he leaves his sword at home, why not invite him and his family to the house party with the Bingleys and my family? It would be easy to include them. Does he have any grown children? I remember you saying he was older than most captains."*

*"He does have two sons. I think that would be a fine idea. I am sure your sisters would appreciate more gentlemen around the house. As soon as I share the news with Georgiana and Charlotte, I will write him at once. The party is not for a month and a half. That gives us plenty of time to contact him."*

Elizabeth realized Isaac had started to fuss. She followed Charlotte into her chambers and said, "I hope you do not mind, but Mr. Darcy and I have discussed inviting some guests in mid-October. We would like to expand the list a bit. How would you feel if it was a real house party? It might lift your spirits a great deal."

"Could you invite Anne?" Charlotte rubbed her son's back, and he calmed down again.

"Mr. Darcy's cousin?"

"Yes. We were quite comfortable together when I lived at the parsonage, and we have written a few letters."

"Are you sure you want us to invite Lady Catherine de Bourgh?"

Charlotte looked sheepish. "I will admit I was only thinking of Miss de Bourgh, but if her presence necessitates her mother as well, so be it. I have no qualms about that. But it is your home; you may invite anyone you choose."

Elizabeth put her hand on Charlotte's and said, "No, Charlotte, it is your home too. I will not do anything that you do not wish."

When Charlotte didn't say anything, Elizabeth continued, "Both of them would probably appreciate the invitation. I shall let Will decide. Although I, for one, could do without the running criticism that tends to flow from Lady Catherine's mouth in my direction. I was grateful to avoid her almost entirely when she came for the wedding."

Charlotte stiffened almost imperceptibly and a blush covered her face. "She does express herself quite clearly."

Elizabeth was confused by Charlotte's reaction. "Did Lady Catherine say something to you at the wedding?"

"It was nothing really."

"Charlotte, what did she say?"

Charlotte seemed to hesitate for a moment, and then she let out a breath. "She implied that I was disrespecting Mr. Collins's memory by flirting with Colonel Fitzwilliam. I . . . well, perhaps I enjoyed the colonel's company a little too much that day. He did sit next to me at the wedding, and he was so kind and charming . . ." Charlotte's voice had become reverent and nostalgic, then she seemed to collect herself. "Well, perhaps her warning was a good reminder."

"What exactly did she say?" Elizabeth pressed.

Charlotte frowned and looked away from Elizabeth. "I believe her words were, 'A widow in black who courts suitors courts only ruin. Besides, my nephew must marry an heiress. He flirts with every lady. Pay him no mind.'"

"Oh, Charlotte, what an awful thing to say!"

"No, she was right," Charlotte insisted. "After that, I tried to keep a respectful distance between myself and the colonel."

"I must tell you that Colonel Fitzwilliam noticed the change in your behavior. He worried he had somehow offended you at the wedding. He missed your friendship greatly."

"That is unfortunate, but it hardly matters," Charlotte continued. "The colonel and I can never be anything but friends, regardless of my mourning period. He flirts with every woman he meets. Surely I am no different from any of his other conquests. Even Georgiana warned me what a flirt he is. She told me once, 'The man has no scruples when it comes to winning a lady's affection. He cares not who or how many; the goal is simply to capture and conquer.'"

Now Elizabeth knew she had to say something. If Charlotte and Richard had not stepped in and pushed Elizabeth and Darcy past their difficulties, would they ever have found the happiness they enjoyed now? She could not stand by and leave this misunderstanding unchecked. "Do you remember when we talked when I was ill? About how hopeless I felt that Mr. Darcy had left me?"

"Yes."

"And you came up with a plan?"

"Of course."

"You wrote to Colonel Fitzwilliam and enlisted his help, and together you both restored Mr. Darcy's hope. And do you remember how Mr. Darcy came to see me at the Gardiners' that very afternoon? That was the day I began to hope again."

"Yes, but what does this have to do with me?"

"Hope for Fitzwilliam, Charlotte. He may be talented at flirting, but he has never, ever sought any lady's heart except one. Yours. He cares a great deal for you. So much so that he has made himself look quite ridiculous lately. His obnoxious flirting and boasting at Darcy House was more of the rooster he pretends to be than the kitten he actually is. I think you know that deep down. He admires you a great deal, more than any woman of his acquaintance."

Charlotte hesitated before making her reply. "But there is still the problem of him needing to marry an heiress."

*But you are an heiress, Charlotte!* How Elizabeth wished she could tell Charlotte about the ships and the ledger! But Mr. Pastel's warning left no doubt that Charlotte's inheritance was not final. It was painful to keep the information from her friend. "Well, we may not know all the answers, but if you appreciated his friendship so well before, why let something Lady Catherine said, no doubt with a great deal of malice, affect you? You both deserve better. And you are stronger than that, my dear."

Fresh tears came to Charlotte's eyes. "I am," she replied with newfound confidence—a trait that Elizabeth hadn't seen in her dear friend's countenance for such a long time. "I *am* stronger than that. But he has gone to war now. It might be too late."

Elizabeth put her fingers on Charlotte's trembling chin and turned her face to look at her. "My dear Charlotte, a wise woman once taught me something. As long as there is hope, it is never too late for love."

# CHAPTER 13

All of September and the first half of October were consumed in a whirlwind of events. Isaac Byron Collins was christened just over three weeks after his birth. Charlotte wrote the date in her Bible just under his birth. It was a special day for her. As a parson's wife, she had been to many christenings, but hearing her own son's name, the name she had painstakingly decided upon, announced and blessed for all to hear was magnificent. At that moment, she knew in her heart that she had chosen the right name for him. It lifted a weight that she did not know she was carrying. That seemed to be happening a great deal lately.

During that time, Georgiana was frequently singled out by the Darcy's neighbor, Frank Birmingham. The process involved several dinners at the Birmingham estate on the other side of Lambton, as well as return invitations to hear music and play games. Though frequent blushes could be spied on her cheeks—as so often occurred when Georgiana interacted with anyone other than family—the youngest Darcy seemed to enjoy the attention. The same could not be said of the eldest Darcy. Her brother became more and more reserved, and some argued downright irritable, each time the Birminghams visited.

Meanwhile, Elizabeth was fully swept up in arranging the upcoming house party, which boasted a guest list to rival that of the entire Meryton Assembly.

There were to be all three of Elizabeth's unmarried sisters, Mary, Catherine, and Lydia, as well as her parents, Mr. and Mrs. Bennet. Charlotte's sister, Maria, and their parents, Sir William Lucas and Lady Lucas, were invited, and, according to the last letter, were well pleased to be staying at Pemberley. Then there was Colonel Fitzwilliam's parents, Lord and Lady Matlock; Mr. Darcy's aunt, Lady Catherine de Bourgh, and her daughter, Anne;

and of course Anne's companion, Mrs. Jenkins. Elizabeth's sister Jane and her husband, Mr. Bingley, had been the inspiration for the party in the first place, so of course they would be in attendance. Luckily, Mr. Bingley did not inform his sisters, Caroline and Louisa; had they known he had been invited to Pemberley, they would have insisted on an invitation as well. Avelina Gardiner and her parents had agreed to return for a visit with only the slightest encouragement.

Then there were guests that Charlotte was not acquainted with. There was to be a Captain Jersey and his two sons, the names of which Charlotte did not care to remember. Elizabeth invited the Birminghams for the evening festivities, much to the chagrin of Mr. Darcy. And Georgiana had invited her dearest friend, Lady Jane Andrews. The lady's father had insisted that he and her oldest brother accompany her. Colonel Fitzwilliam's brother and his wife had written at the last minute to say that they both had caught the grippe and did not wish to be in the cool Derbyshire weather.

All in all, including Georgiana, Elizabeth, Mr. Darcy, and herself, Charlotte counted a dazzling thirty-one people. Eight unmarried ladies, four unmarried gentlemen, seven couples, two widows, and one widower, the latter being Captain Jersey, would all be sharing a roof for a full three weeks.

Charlotte watched as Elizabeth planned and re-planned the festivities and dinner parties until Mr. Darcy came up to Elizabeth from behind and started twirling the ringlets at the base of her neck. Elizabeth's shoulders noticeably relaxed with his touch. It was such a private moment, but Charlotte could not exactly leave the room at the moment since she was helping Georgiana pick out the music she was to play for the music night. Georgiana was terribly distressed to have been asked to perform, but Elizabeth had begged her to provide some of the entertainment. While Charlotte half-heartedly gave input to Georgiana about which pieces would both put her at ease as well and help her shine, Charlotte watched Elizabeth and Mr. Darcy.

It was impossible not to hear the exchange between the two. Mr. Darcy whispered, "They will start arriving within the hour, my love. You have already made such marvelous arrangements. Try to relax."

Elizabeth sighed. "I will try. But this is my first opportunity to present myself as the Mistress of Pemberley. Your family will be here, my family will be here, your friends and neighbors will be here—I am sure they will all be watching to see if I can live up to your mother's reputation."

"And I have no doubt you shall exceed their expectations. Would you like me to rub your neck and shoulders again?"

"You are far too busy to do that."

"Elizabeth, do not deny me the chance to show you that you are the most important person in my life. You are my love, my life, the love of my life. I cannot even consider attempting another task if I know you are distressed."

"Oh, Will, you are too good to me. It is just a mild headache. You do not know how many times I have thanked God that He brought you to Hertfordshire. And that you had the courage to follow your heart, not once, but twice. I shall never lament my tasks as mistress if I know you will be by my side through it all. But I will say that you have far too much faith in my abilities to handle a party of this size."

"There was once a time when we agreed that we should never lose hope, for hope is the precursor to faith. You once had hope for Mr. Darcy; I now have hope for Mrs. Darcy. Just as you have done with everything that stands in your way, you will lift your head up and rise to the challenge." He lightened his tone. "Besides which, Mrs. Reynolds has assured me that she has substitute plans for your substitute plans."

Charlotte watched as Elizabeth lovingly swatted at Mr. Darcy. "You wicked man!"

He then leaned into her and whispered what Charlotte thought was something like, "You know, we have an hour or so to prove just how wicked I am."

Charlotte blushed deeply and tried to ignore what she overheard. She looked away and saw that Georgiana had been watching them too. Georgiana voice was barely audible, "I do not think I will get used to seeing him so relaxed. But I shall never tire of it. He is so happy now, thanks to Elizabeth."

"Indeed, I could not agree more. But let us pick out the music and make ourselves scarce before my ears start burning." Charlotte took one last look in their direction to see a single chaste kiss being placed on her forehead and Elizabeth's head leaning hungrily towards him to receive it.

She couldn't help but sigh.

*****

All of the guests soon arrived except for Lady Catherine and Anne, who had written that they would be arriving the following day. Elizabeth ushered them in marvelously, personally escorting everyone to their previously assigned chambers. Darcy felt proud, knowing she would far surpass everyone's expectations as Mistress of Pemberley. But after an hour or so of her darting off every few minutes to attend to a guest, Darcy started to question the wisdom of having any guests at all. She hardly stayed by his side more than ten minutes altogether.

Most of the guests were now assembled in the music room. Georgiana was huddled in a corner with Mary, Catherine, and Lydia Bennet and was introducing them to her friend, Lady Jane.

He overheard them eagerly discussing Georgiana and Lady Jane's coming out next season. The very thought of it made him cringe. His baby sister was now seventeen. He had only a year until her curtsy before the Queen. He was already beginning to feel the strain of worrying about her. How naïve she had been just a year and a half earlier when George Wickham's conniving ways had convinced her to elope. With Darcy's intervention, they had only narrowly diverted disaster before it was too late.

He watched as Frank Birmingham approached the group of five ladies. The young man's smooth manners begin to charm even Mary Bennet, who had never seemed to pay notice to any gentlemen before.

Captain Jersey came up next to him and teased, "Do not frown so much at her, Mr. Darcy. It gives away your thoughts."

"I do not know how a father does it," Darcy scowled. "How am I to help her find a suitable match? Someone with all the right qualities? And what if I am wrong in my choice? She would then live with that mistake for the rest of her life."

"I had similar thoughts before my oldest daughter's coming out. But the good and bad news is that, in the end, I hardly had any say in the matter."

Darcy groaned. "But I would much rather arrange a safe match than see her heart broken. She is so young yet."

"That she is, but she has a great example to follow. You and Mrs. Darcy obviously have a love match. I very much doubt your sister will settle for anything less for herself."

"Forgive us. I had not realized we were so transparent."

Captain Jersey chuckled, "I am aware of that. One can see that you are trying to hide your affection, but the looks exchanged between the two of you make it obvious. My late wife, Olivia, and I were like that. Do not try so hard to hide it. There are a great number of people who never know love like ours."

"How did you cope when she passed?"

Captain Jersey paused. "It has been a full ten years since Olivia died. It is never easy, but the pain lessens with time." Jersey paused and looked at Darcy intently. "May I ask you a question, Mr. Darcy?"

"Of course."

"What was the purport of inviting me here? I have thus far been introduced to your wife's parents, her sisters, her aunt and uncle, and what seems to be the entire Bennet clan. I must admit I feel somewhat out of place."

Mr. Darcy hadn't intended to broach this topic so soon, but Jersey's candid questions deserved an honest answer. "Captain Jersey, may I say how much I appreciate the friendship we have maintained since our first, nearly murderous, introduction?"

Captain Jersey chuckled. "Yes," he replied, "I believe I introduced myself with the tip of my sword to your chest. Forgive me for that. I do not take kindly to being followed around the seedier part of London. The docks are no place for a gentleman. You were quite out of your element."

"No apology needed. As I told you in our correspondence since then, I admire your integrity and honor. I have two purposes in inviting you, and I am afraid they are as different as night and day. I gathered from the way you spoke of your late wife, that you are a man who appreciates the genteel nature of a good woman."

He raised his eyebrow. "You mean to tell me that you have a lady in mind? I do not wish to offend, but I am nearly six-and-fifty, well past my prime. I am of the age of putting my affairs in order, not starting a new life."

Mr. Darcy did not know how else to say it, but he spoke softly so that no one else could hear. "Perhaps that is what makes you so uniquely qualified for *this* particular lady."

"Very well, every impulse says to run, but you are an honorable man and must have your reasons." He drew an open palm directing Darcy's view across the room. "Who might you have picked to be my next wife? Surely not young Miss Lydia—I am older than her father. Charming to be sure, but too energetic for me. I would most definitely bore her. And Lady Jane is far too intelligent to fall for someone who has one foot in the grave. Mrs. Collins—"

"No, it is none of them," Darcy promised. "It is my cousin Anne. She will arrive tomorrow. She assisted me with a delicate family matter when I wished to marry Elizabeth, and I owe her a great deal. I would be pleased if you would simply get to know her. Her mother, Lady Catherine, can be quite interfering. But Anne and I have spoken several times about what she wants in a husband, and I believe you could be quite compatible with her. I admit that I would like to return the favor she once did for me."

"I cannot say that I have much experience with ladies of late. Nearly none, in fact. However, I will certainly offer her friendship. You said there were two reasons you invited me here. What is the other one?"

Mr. Darcy looked around and motioned with his head for Jersey to follow him. As they left the music room with all of the hustle and bustle of family and friends welcoming each other and new friendships being formed, Darcy seemed to let out a breath of relief. He did not particularly enjoy social affairs. But hosting one in his own home had its benefits, especially when there were so many people that his guests could not notice his escape.

Darcy ushered him into his study and went directly to his desk. He motioned for Captain Jersey to have a seat.

"I take it the other reason is a delicate matter."

Darcy took out the last letter from Colonel Fitzwilliam and handed it to Captain Jersey. As he read, Darcy leaned back in his chair.

After a few moments, the captain looked up. "I do not understand how this all relates to me. What are you asking me to do, Darcy?"

"I have a second request to make of you, Captain. Let me start by telling you that my wife's best friend, Charlotte Collins, is the widow of Mr. Collins, who owned of the *Eastern Challenge* and *Winter's Night*. The ships have been managed by the firm of Pastel & Sons."

"I met Clyde Pastel several years ago regarding the position of captain of one of the ships. But I have no interest in working with Pastel & Sons, Darcy, and I told you why."

"Hear me out, Jersey. It was right of you to be suspicious of Clyde Pastel, and of the cargo and the secrecy that was asked of you. I think it admirable that you showed your integrity and turned the job down."

"However . . .?"

"Yes, there is more. The ships are now being managed by Clyde Pastel's brother, Benjamin Pastel. My cousin Colonel Fitzwilliam has met him several times. He states Benjamin Pastel is a good man, and that he is trying to clean up the shady nature of his brother's business. He has already secured new cargo for the ships. And now Benjamin is interested in securing a new captain for them."

"So now we get to the bottom of the request. I take it you wish me to apply for the job."

"Yes, but it is more delicate than that. Mr. Collins died in April. Mrs. Collins is probably the new owner of the ships, but we are being kept in the dark regarding the details. We suspect Mr. Collins stipulated a certain amount of time must pass before his will is to be read. But as of right now, Mrs. Collins is oblivious to the existence of the ships, so much so that she believes she is penniless. I must request that you not mention this conversation to her or to any of the other guests. We are told that she will be visited soon by Benjamin Pastel, and we hope to be better informed at that time."

"But in the meantime, you wish me to keep you informed about the ships?"

Darcy nodded. "I would feel better knowing they were captained by a good man with an honest crew."

Captain Jersey contemplated the idea for a moment. Finally he said, "You do know I was hoping to step down soon."

"I do. If you were to manage the ship just until the will is read, it would put my mind greatly at ease."

"As a widower myself, I am sympathetic to Mrs. Collins's plight," Jersey began. "I would certainly need to investigate it a bit before applying."

"Certainly," Darcy agreed. "I would expect nothing less."

"Very well. If you think this would help, then I will look into it. Provide me with the details, and I will start making inquiries."

Darcy felt relieved. "Thank you," he said. "I hope you enjoy Pemberley. If you need anything at all, do not hesitate to ask. My staff is anxious to show what they can do for a group this size."

"I will, thank you."

They then returned to the music room where Mrs. Bennet was soliciting Elizabeth for a tour. He caught Elizabeth's gaze from across the room and winked at her. She then smiled brightly, and he heard her say, "Mamma, what a fine idea! I am sure Mr. Darcy would love to show you around!"

Darcy cringed slightly. He heard Elizabeth's teasing laugh as she added, "But, I must tell you, there is someone else who knows even more about the estate than Mr. Darcy. The housekeeper, Mrs. Reynolds. And she has already prepared a tour for you."

"The housekeeper?" Mrs. Bennet asked with a frown. "Is she suitable for such a task?"

"Most definitely, Mamma. She once took me on a tour of Pemberley that was nothing short of life-changing. I will ring for her now."

After passing her mother into Mrs. Reynolds's capable hands, Elizabeth walked over to Mr. Darcy.

"Was I really that transparent?" Darcy asked. "You know I would have taken her on the tour if would ease your burdens."

"Yes, I know. But there is no need, dearest. And I would much rather have you by my side than occupied with the histories of the estate and how many can fit in the ballroom."

They didn't realize that Lydia had walked up beside them until she said, "A ballroom? Oh, do tell me that we shall have dancing! There is nothing better than dancing! Mr. Bingley thinks so too, is that not so, Mr. Bingley?"

Mr. Bingley cheerfully said, "Of course! And I believe that if we were to pose the idea of a ball in just the right manner, we could convince Mr. Darcy to host an All Hallows' Eve masquerade."

"I very much doubt that," Darcy replied.

Lydia whined, "But, Mr. Darcy, surely we could have at least one little ball!"

Bingley said, "Miss Lydia, I said we had to propose it in the *right* manner. Mr. Darcy is a new husband."

Jane gave a subtle wink to Bingley that Darcy just barely caught before she said, "Yes, of course. No doubt he always makes sure that his wife's every wish is fulfilled."

Georgiana cleared her throat loudly and added, "And we know how much his wife would love a ball."

Lady Matlock had caught the tone as well. "And how solicitous he is to her. Why, she loves tradition! And Pemberley used to host a Harvest Ball every year."

Mr. Bennet grumbled, "Will someone just say it already? Lizzybell, my dear, tell your husband you wish to host a ball. He will say yes only to you, and we all know how much you want a ball at Pemberley. Pity your dear papa, child. For although I detest dancing of all sorts, your sisters and young cousin will sulk for the next three weeks straight if there is to be no ball."

"Yes!" Mrs. Bennet shrieked. "Lizzy, I simply cannot fathom why you have not hosted a ball yet! You must be properly shown off to the neighborhood! Be introduced! Goodness, you have waited long enough, I say!"

Darcy took Elizabeth's hand and asked, "Is that so? Do you feel I have not properly shown off my wife?"

Elizabeth's cheeks turned pink as she said, "Mr. Darcy, I would never say such a thing."

"But you wish to host a ball?"

The room quieted for a moment, and Elizabeth hesitated. Then she raised an eyebrow and said, "Well, I have always enjoyed dancing when there are tolerable partners."

He smiled at her effort to lighten his mood. He took her hand and kissed it. "Why did you not tell me?"

"I was not sure you wished for a ball. Mrs. Reynolds says you have never hosted one. I . . . I was not sure it would fit with Pemberley's traditions."

Darcy could not quite deduce what she meant. Did she think he didn't like dancing? Surely all that talk about "every savage can dance" was far behind them now. Surely she knew he enjoyed dancing with her—they had danced privately in his chambers a few nights ago. Or was it that she felt she had no say in what traditions they could create? He felt very confused and knew every eye was on him.

He had counseled Richard that communication is vital in any marriage. So he reached up and caressed Elizabeth's cheek with the back of his hand. "I would love to dance with my wife at a ball. You are as much a part of Pemberley now as I am, my dear. Therefore, you have just as much say in Pemberley's traditions. You may not have grown up here, but you shall live out the rest of your life, with me by your side, right here. Furthermore, as Pemberley's mistress, this is your decision. I could never deny you anything."

Elizabeth smiled back at him sweetly as Avelina loudly called out, "Say yes, Elizabeth! Oh, please! We all want a ball! Do we not?"

Elizabeth nodded, and cheers and shouts of affirmations abounded through the room.

Lydia cheered the loudest and then seemed to check herself, smoothing her skirts and taking a deep breath. Mr. Darcy had to admit that she was certainly trying to be better-behaved, but it was the spark in Georgiana's eyes that finally solidified his decision.

"We shall have an All Hallows' Eve masquerade two weeks from today!" he declared. "Georgiana, will you help me make a list of our neighbors and tenants who might wish to come?"

"Thank you," she cried as she rushed over to him. She stopped just as she was preparing to throw her arms around his neck and then very properly kissed his cheek instead. The brightness in her eyes turned to tears as she told him, "It will be just like before Papa died."

"No, Georgie, it will be even better—I will not have a twelve-year old holding onto my coattails, pestering me about who would be my next dance partner."

"Did I really do that?"

"Only for the first two hours. After that, you were sent to bed."

Georgiana giggled and said, "I hope you do not plan to send me to bed this time, Brother, for I wish to dance all night!"

Darcy squeezed her hand and was about to turn to Elizabeth when he noticed that Spencer Jersey, Captain Jersey's oldest son, was in the process of asking Georgiana for the first set. Behind Spencer was Frank Birmingham, who seemed a bit perturbed by his opponent's quick thinking. Darcy pretended to watch the others in the room start discussing costumes and music, but he kept a close eye on Georgiana. She blushed brightly at the request and then shyly looked away. It was no surprise when Frank Birmingham reserved the next set.

Elizabeth gently pulled him away from the scene and said, "Do not forget to breathe, darling. It is really the only way to put your face back to normal. She is growing up, Will."

Darcy frowned again. Georgiana was not the only young lady being asked. Lady Jane was nearly scarlet with Lloyd Jersey's request for the first set. "Those two young ladies will have a very successful coming out next season," Elizabeth hinted. "And my advice to you is to start letting go. Now, would you be so kind as to make sure Charlotte plans to attend?"

It was clear that his wife was trying to distract him. "Yes, of course, Elizabeth. But before I go, you should know I plan to dance the first set, the supper set, and the last set with my beautiful wife; society rules be hanged. It is my ball, after all."

"I would not have it any other way, Will. Now go talk to Charlotte. She looks as if she is about to escape to the nursery."

Seeing that the rest of the room was distracted by the news of the ball, Darcy quickly kissed his wife's cheek and whispered, "I love you." He was ecstatic that she turned a bright shade of pink. He hoped to always have the ability to make her blush in a crowded room. *I really am a wicked man.*

He couldn't help but smile as he walked towards Charlotte. She indeed was standing to leave. He stopped her before she could flee. "Charlotte, I am afraid that I have been waylaid by my entire family into hosting a ball. You have known me long enough to understand that it can be a daunting task for me to dance with someone that I do not know well, so I wonder if you would be so kind as to accompany me to the punch table during the second set so we may decorate the walls together. If I have someone standing beside me, it may actually look like I am enjoying myself. And truthfully, it may be the only way I enjoy myself, given that as host, Elizabeth will be quite occupied."

Charlotte smiled kindly, but said, "Mr. Darcy, I own nothing but black mourning dresses at this time."

"Then masquerade yourself as a black swan," Darcy offered.

He worried she was about to refuse. But then she put her hand on his arm and said, "I shall look forward to it. Thank you for your kind invitation. I will be delighted to see Elizabeth honored at her first ball as Mrs. Darcy. How could I pass up such an opportunity?" Charlotte paused, clearly deliberating how much to say. "You may not know it, Mr. Darcy but I watch you a great deal. I see how much you respect and honor Elizabeth. You two have given me something that I did not know I even wanted."

"What is that?"

"You have taught me it may not be such a dangerous thing to hope . . . to hope for . . . love." Charlotte then suddenly burst into tears and rushed from the room.

Elizabeth came and took his arm. "What was that about?" she whispered.

Darcy whispered back, "I believe she finally has hope for Fitzwilliam."

# CHAPTER 14

"Colonel Fitzwilliam, General Brock wishes to speak with you immediately."

"Thank you, Everett." Colonel Fitzwilliam headed towards Brock's command center. They were stationed on the British side of the Niagara River, and the whole camp could sense the rebels were getting ready to move. The Yanks had been anxious to prove their superiority ever since General Brock captured Detroit. The British were feeling quite proud of that victory.

The colonel's regiment had finally arrived at Queenston late yesterday afternoon. Fitzwilliam had meetings nearly every hour with General Brock, who was being referred to as the "Savior of Upper Canada" and rightly so. His capture of Detroit was likely to earn him a knighthood.

The air had turned frigid, especially cold for the twelfth of October. There had been evidence of the winter ahead all along their journey to Queenston. Abandoned supply wagons stuck in the mud were now frozen in place until spring. It was an ominous sign of what was in store.

Colonel Fitzwilliam entered the cabin and saw a group of officers huddled over a map. He stepped in and listened to the conversation that had begun without him.

"It is confirmed," General Brock announced. "The Americans were preparing to attack yesterday, but something changed their plans at the last minute. We do not know what. It might very well have been a diversion, simply an attempt to make us concentrate our troops on our right while they attack from the left. Evans, tell them what you learned yesterday."

Major Thomas Evans reported, "I was ordered to petition the Americans to exchange prisoners yesterday. Their colonel was apparently ill and refused to see me. He sent his secretary instead, and when I proposed a prisoner exchange, I was told very directly, 'Not until the day after tomorrow.' I thought it was an interesting turn of phrase, and yet he repeated the exact same wording again. On my return to Queenston, I noted several American boats hidden along the shore under the bushes. I believe we will have an imminent attack upon us."

A colonel, someone whom Colonel Fitzwilliam had not yet been introduced to, laughed outright. "Do not be absurd, Major!" he replied. "That is little more than speculation. Of course they would hide their boats so that we do not see how many they have. They still were willing to exchange prisoners, no? They just want to dictate the date of the exchange. No doubt those filthy Americans are starving our soldiers and offering no mercy."

But Colonel Fitzwilliam watched as the general nodded knowingly at Evan's report. "I agree with the major," General Brock announced. "We must prepare ourselves for their advance. I want men at Queenston, Chippawa, and Fort Erie. With the slope above the river, the Americans will not have an easy time climbing to Queenston Heights, but there is certainly enough brush to make the climb possible."

The same colonel who laughed earlier argued, "I must protest, General. The river is nearly two hundred yards wide, and, at this time of year, it would be treacherous to cross. I think we are safe from any invasion on that front."

"Skilled oarsmen could cross it," Brock replied. "And if it is possible to cross, we must be prepared. Now, men, I am stationing several lookouts to watch for the invasion. I want the 49th Regiment with me and Colonel Fitzwilliam's regiment as well."

Captain John Williams, the head of the 49th regiment, spoke up, "Of course. The 49th never backs down from a fight, and the men will be happy to serve under you again, general. We will locate ourselves at the top of the slope and keep watch all night."

Another man whom Colonel Fitzwilliam did not know complained, "General, we cannot afford to spread our men thin by defending the river against an impossible crossing. The Americans have at least two thousand militia as it is."

"Our latest estimate is closer to three thousand, counting the regulars," General Brock replied, "which is why we need to be prepared. If those boats get across the river, it will be a massacre. I must defend it. I have no intention to sit back and wait for the Americans to spring a trap. Major Evans, how many boats do you think you saw?"

"At least a dozen, each able to carry thirty to forty men, but they have larger boats as well, ones that are too big to hide. Those can carry up to eighty."

Colonel Fitzwilliam did the math in his head. The initial attack could be as strong as six hundred enemy soldiers. Together, his regiment and the 49th numbered all of three hundred. If the Americans did come tonight, his men would be outnumbered two to one. "My regiment will position the 18-pounder gun and a mortar as high up on Queenston Heights as possible. If we see them crossing, we will open fire and try to prevent the boats from reaching the shore."

General Brock turned to Captain Williams and said, "Ready the 49th at once. If the invasion does not happen, I will have the 2nd Regiment relieve you in the morning. We will be ready, men. A man prepared is a man who can count his successes. That is all, gentlemen. Go direct your regiments. I would bet my own life that the Americans will attack tonight or tomorrow."

Colonel Fitzwilliam turned with the others to follow his orders, but General Brock called after him. "Colonel Fitzwilliam, do you have a moment?"

"Certainly."

After all the others left, General Brock reached out his hand and said, "Welcome to Queenston. I realize it has been many years, but I could not have been more pleased when I was informed you would be joining our ranks. Even from this side of the Atlantic, I have followed your career closely."

"And I yours, General. May I congratulate you on the capture of Detroit?"

"Thank you. But I am not one to rest on my laurels, Colonel. I fear there are still many, many more battles ahead in this conflict. Which is why I need good men at my side. A good man on your flank is irreplaceable. Did you know I specifically requested you here?"

"Thank you, sir. My men will serve you bravely."

"Yes, I am sure they will. I have noticed your rapport with them. You have eighty soldiers, and they are all devoted to you. Tell me, if you had to pick any of them to be at your side, who would it be?"

"Everett, to be sure. He has the sharpest mind, and no one is quicker or more powerful with a sword."

"Then you and Everett are to flank me on each side tonight. The Americans will attack. I feel it in my gut. Prepare your men."

"I appreciate the confidence you have in me. I shall not let you down. And while I am here, General, may I ask how you earned that God-awful sash?"

Brock fingered the piece of cloth draped over his shoulder. "This bright-yellow thing? It was given to me by Tecumseh, the Shawnee confederate leader, after Detroit. I am quite proud of it. Why do you ask? Do you not like it?"

"Yes, of course, sir. Only it seems rather flagrant, especially against your red uniform. An enemy sharpshooter could train his musket on that sash from a hundred yards. I would take it off if I were you."

"Nonsense. If anything, it will bring me luck."

"I understand, sir. I have recently begun to carry my own luck myself." He patted his left breast pocket and then pulled out the bible.

General Brock laughed. "Now that is one talisman I have yet to adopt," he mused. "I have gathered information, studied the land, given my orders, and, now, been ridiculed for my wardrobe choices. But I have yet to ask God to watch over me."

"It is never too late."

"Come, Fitzwilliam, you have seen enough battles to know that is not true. There may someday come a time when I am struck down in battle. But I dare not ask a blessing on this bloody work. God does not draw my sword. Nor does He help me spot the enemy. He may have blessed me with intelligence and bravery, but when it comes down to it, I am confident that God turns His head so as to avoid seeing the battles between His children."

"I suspect any good father would have a hard time watching his children kill each other," Colonel Fitzwilliam admitted. "But that does not mean He cannot speak to us. This is something that I have learned of late. You and I both have a tendency to act instead of waiting. We are good soldiers, and we trust in our own strength, rightly so. I can see this in the very orders you just gave. But there will come a time when men will fail us and the only one left at our flank will be God. Ultimately, we must put our trust in Him.

The general considered his words as Fitzwilliam continued, "My aim with a pistol or the swiftness of my sword is nothing compared to God's inspiration that reveals the enemy's plan before it happens. Whether or not you wish to admit it, that gut feeling you spoke of—call it experience, instinct, intuition, or what you will—that is God speaking to you. There is no louder voice on a battlefield than God's voice when I suddenly feel prompted to move and discover I have just thwarted a direct hit from behind."

General Brock reached his hand out to Fitzwilliam's shoulder. "And that is why I want you there with me, Colonel. If God gives you the power to see behind you, I want to be one step in front of you so that you can watch my back. I, for one, have never been gifted from on high with *hind*sight."

"That is nothing short of humorous!"

"I am not known for my shyness." Both men laughed and gave each other energetic handshakes and then Colonel Fitzwilliam left.

\*\*\*\*\*

Colonel Fitzwilliam penned letters to his mother, to Georgiana, to Isaac Collins, and to Darcy. It was good form to write one's family whenever battle was imminent. None of the letters took long. He informed them of his safe arrival in the Canadian colonies and gave directions so they could write to him. As he folded the last one, he was interrupted by Mr. Lisscord and Mr. Heather, both looking a little mischievous.

"What are you two up to?"

"We just were wondering how you are doing, regarding Mrs. Collins, that is." Fitzwilliam took a good long look at the duo. Mr. Lisscord's beard was not as neatly trimmed as usual. The poor man looked like he hadn't quite recovered from the seasickness. Of all his men, Lisscord had suffered the worst. And once they had hit land, Colonel Fitzwilliam had been forced to take the regiment inland as quickly as possible, marching through the night, to reach camp. The elderly chaplain looked nearly hammered.

"I should be asking you how you are doing, Lisscord. Have you been able to keep anything down yet?"

"I fare well enough with gruel, but beans and cornbread still seem to settle like bricks."

"I am sorry to hear that. Have you been able to give him anything for the nausea, Mr. Heather?"

"No, for he despises all my powders. Although he has helped himself quite liberally to the herbal teas I brought with me from London. Can you believe his nerve? He must have mistaken me for some sort of dear friend. Either that or his manservant."

Mr. Lisscord laughed. "Ah, but a *dear friend* would think nothing of letting me steal a cot from the infirmary. I had hoped we would have better barracks. But do not deflect the question, Colonel. You have said very little about Mrs. Collins since Liverpool. I wondered if your passion had cooled a bit."

"You know me better than that," Colonel Fitzwilliam sighed. "But every time I think of her, my duties as a soldier become foggy. You know how it is. When a man is longing for home, home is what fills his mind. And right now my head needs to be filled with our current situation.

"On the other side of the river are three thousand enemy soldiers, like a ticking clock. Tick tock. I ask myself, will they come today? Or tomorrow? Or next week? At any given moment, I could be using this sword at my hip or the pistol at my side. No doubt even the knife in my boot will be unsheathed at some point. If I let my heart flutter, daydreaming about Mrs. Collins, my senses may be distracted when the time comes. And you know a soldier depends on his senses."

"A wise course of action, Colonel," Mr. Lisscord agreed. Colonel Fitzwilliam moved the letters he had just finished off his cot and motioned for the old man to sit down. The chaplain gratefully walked to the cot, looking more fatigued than ever. "Thank you."

"Other than the seasickness, how are you faring, Lisscord?" Heather asked.

"Fine, fine. I admit I struggle a bit with the life of a soldier now that I am older. But how could I leave these young men? I may not be wielding a sword or loading their pistols, but I feel responsible for them. A heavy weight rests on my shoulders as I watch them write home before battle. I see you are doing the same thing."

"Yes, I am. I intend to address the regiment after dinner, but from the hustle and bustle outside, it seems the word has already spread. How are the men? They have had only a day to recover from the voyage and our march. I know it was rough on them and on you."

Mr. Lisscord sighed. "Ah, do not mind me. I have always had a weak stomach, which is why I never became a doctor. But I would much rather care for souls than anything else. That is why the good doctor and I make such a great pair. He binds their wounds while I pray for their recovery and offer them hope. Speaking of hope, how are you doing with your hopeless case? Have you figured out the parable of the seed?"

Colonel Fitzwilliam frowned. "Yes and no," he answered. He pulled out the bible from his left breast pocket. "Darcy told me it is called the parable of the sower, not the parable of seed. Why do you keep calling it that?"

Mr. Heather looked at Mr. Lisscord, and they both smiled slightly. "Well, let me ask you something first. What does the sower represent in the bible?"

"It is a parable about missionary work, so I would say it represents a disciple or follower of Jesus."

"And what makes you think the story is about missionary work?"

"Well, if the seed is the word of God, and the sower is spreading the seed, then he is spreading the word of God. He is preaching the gospel."

"Exactly. But if the sower is already a disciple, or follower of Christ, why tell a parable about him? What can we learn from him?"

Colonel Fitzwilliam paused to consider the question. "I suppose because how we sow is sometimes more important than what we sow."

"Yes," Heather told him. "Can you really not see how the parable applies to you, Fitzwilliam?"

Fitzwilliam considered the story again, the vultures, the seed, the thorns, all of it. "Wait!" he nearly shouted, "I think I do! I have literally lived out the parable!"

"Yes, you certainly have," Lisscord chuckled.

"First, I showed her my love in front of the vultures of society. Eventually I realized that she accepted my kind deeds better when I was more myself. I foolishly showed my love for her at the wrong time and place before I understood what she might have gone through. But her ground was not fertile, and the seeds were choked out by her thorn of a previous husband."

Mr. Lisscord interrupted and said, "You used an interesting word just now. Consider what word you used in replace of the seed."

Fitzwilliam reviewed what he had just said. *I foolishly showed my love for her at the wrong time.* "'Love'? I meant to say 'seed'. I meant to say, I sowed my *seed* at the wrong time."

"Go on," Mr. Heather encouraged.

"And if I am the sower, then that means that the seed is not the bible. It is . . . love. It is a parable about missionary work because missionary work is love. If a man is a disciple, then that means he loves something so much that he is devoted and committed to it. And the thing he would most like to do is share what he loves. Missionary work is the love of Christ, the love of His gospel, the love of His people. I think I am starting to see it now. You knew I was already in love. I was already converted. But somehow you knew that she was not. How? How did you know she did not love me?"

"We never said she did not love you. Be careful," Mr. Heather replied. Mr. Lisscord nodded his agreement.

Colonel Fitzwilliam rubbed his fingers against his forehead as if massaging it would clear his mind. "No, you knew she was not *aware* of my love. You knew I thought it was hopeless, that I was too discouraged to show her my love. This is starting to spin in my head. I think I am onto something. You knew I needed help sowing the seeds of love. And I did need help. I sowed my love at all the wrong times and in all the wrong places.

"You told me the parable to teach me how to express my love. That is why you referred to it as the parable of the seed rather than the parable of the sower. I needed to pay attention to the seeds, where they fell and which ones grew."

He felt the energy build in his chest as he continued. "It is simply a parable about love. I was already committed to loving her. I was already a disciple of love. You saw my devotion to her affect my sleep, affect my every waking moment, and you knew I needed to express that love instead of hold it in. But first I needed to prepare the ground for her to accept my love. Because it is not so much how the sower spreads the seeds, it is more about sowing them at the right time and place; in fertile ground. That is why you called it the parable of the seed. Goodness, I feel like my mother's rug beaten clean! Tell me I am on the right path."

Mr. Lisscord put his hand on the colonel's shoulder and said, "Indeed you are correct. We called it the parable of the seed because we knew, deep down, that the seed was good. The sower just needed a little help expressing his deep love; a love that was so deep that he could not sleep. But that has changed now, has it not?"

"I have not once administered the sleeping powders for you since we first talked about the parable in East Sussex," Heather added. "Did you realize that?"

The colonel nodded. "I think there is finally some hope for Fitzwilliam now. If I ever return to England, I will not repeat the mistakes of the past. I may be trained to see strategy in war, but I have certainly bumbled my way through love. I may very well have to wave the white flag at some point. In some ways, I already have, I suppose. I have let her go so that she can heal."

Mr. Heather said, "Do not be so hasty as to assume love is not war. Sometimes you win, and sometimes you surrender to its demands. Sometimes it is like taking a cannonball to the gut. But love is worth it. Sometimes it is so fragile it only takes a feather's touch to create a ripple of waves. You may not even notice any specific thing you do, but it is reaching her. Two weeks ago when we were riding out the raging ocean storm, do you remember what we said about it?"

Colonel Fitzwilliam thought back to that day. "Yes," he replied. "You said that each storm starts small; a heavy cloud leaks a drop or two. But eventually those tiny drops can swell into giant waves that can take a man's life. And even though sometimes the storm clouds sail past us without giving up so much as a drizzle, they sometimes pour buckets of water on a faraway land. I think I see now what you meant. You two are very clever. You want me to see that my small acts of kindness and love might have huge ripple effects while I am away."

"I told you he would figure it out."

Mr. Heather chuckled and said, "I never doubted it. Now we should let him prepare to talk to the regiment."

*****

Colonel Fitzwilliam stood in front of his men and felt a wave of compassion for each one. He could name them, one by one. There was not a single man whom he would wish to part from. The sight of them gave him courage for the fight ahead. He slowly raised his hands, ushering a peculiar calm among them. They were ready, and he knew it.

"Men," he began, "we have come all this way to stand for England. And why have we come? Because it is important to stand for what you believe in. If a man does not stand for something, then he will fall for anything at the slightest of pressure. We did not come here intending to merely lie on our bedrolls and miss our wives and children. We came to ensure their chance to walk freely down the street. We came to defend the innate human right to be free, and freedom has never been free.

"You may see brothers fall. But you, as a whole, must not fall. Stand firm in your course; solid and unmoving. Your very breath could be numbered, but let this be the first of an infinite number of breaths that, if combined, moves the mountains that lie in our path. A single man can do little, but an army of men, whose passions are joined in purpose, can do miracles. That is what I expect from you. I expect a united front. No man will be left behind, and every man will be pushed to the brink. But there is great power in the breath of many. Wind of that magnitude can topple the tallest tree. It is true, we are outnumbered. But we have something they do not have. We have each other. So lock arms with the man to your left and watch what forms."

He paused to watch them link arms. "As I see you linked together, I see a solid, unified chain of camaraderie and devotion.

There will not be a one of you that is not vital to our survival. If one man does not do his job out there, then our forces are weakened and our chain is broken. You will need more than the man on your left to be at your side. You will need the man to the right as well. Memorize these faces now. We have spent the last month in close quarters on the ship, and I commend you for enduring the little eccentricities we each have, but now we can use that to our advantage. What we need is leverage. We may not have the numbers in body, but we make up for it in spirit. There is not a man here that I would not give my life for. I know this because your loyalty to this regiment has spread like a wildfire. It has branded my very heart. You are my family now.

"Men, fight for something bigger than yourselves. Fight for England. Fight for the right to not live in fear for our future. Fight so that those at home will never know the horrors we see on the battlefield. But do this as a united front. Every man is vital to our success. Make the passion and pride you feel now fill your heart and guide your aim."

It was time to wrap up his thoughts. "I have recently learned something about love. I speak of love in any form. Love of family, love of country, love of home, and most certainly love of brotherhood. No matter what love we speak of, love can be war." He pulled out his sword and raised it into the air and said, "So fight for what we love—together—as one great magnificent force of nature. Be that united force that can move mountains! Make the last breath you just took be the first that moves this enemy and sends them retreating to the knees of their mothers! The only thing to fear is that we fight for naught! Do not falter in your resolve. Do not falter in your courage. And do not falter in the passion I see in your eyes! Simply put, DO NOT FALTER!"

Cheers erupted, and Colonel Fitzwilliam stepped back and placed his sword back into its sheath. There was a wide range of gestures and words shouted, but one man yelled out, "We will not falter!" Suddenly ten men started chanting it, which turned into the entire regiment.

A quieter voice next to him said, "Well done, Colonel Fitzwilliam."

"Thank you, General Brock. Does this get any easier? I know that if the Americans attack, not every man will survive. I could not pick a single man that I could do without."

"They know that too. It is very clear. Come, it is time. We must head up the mountain."

As they turned to lead the way, the men settled into a quiet calm before the storm, and he knew that, without needing the command, his men were following them. Within a few paces, Everett had caught up to them. He and Colonel Fitzwilliam flanked the general—just like they would in battle. The sun had set while he gave his speech, and they now had the cover of darkness to hide the positions that they took on the mountain. They were as ready as they could possibly be.

*****

It was just after 4:00 a.m., the skies just barely lighting the world around them. It had been a frigid night up on the mountain with no fires to keep warm. Colonel Fitzwilliam had begun to feel the lack of sleep sedate his senses when he heard Captain James Dennis of the 49th Regiment breathlessly ask a man to his right where General Brock was.

"I am right here," General Brock replied from behind Fitzwilliam. "What is it?"

"The Americans are crossing, sir! Three of the boats were swept downstream, but the remaining ones will land at the village any minute now. Ten boats altogether. I was just notified by the sentry. I have instructed my troops to fire as soon as they reach shore."

"I knew it. Colonel Fitzwilliam, mount up! Let us go to the village. Leave a few men here to man the guns. Then follow me with the rest of your regiment. Captain Dennis? Bring up your regiment and fire at will. Blow them out of the water." General Isaac Brock's eyes were steel black with determination as he quickly mounted his own horse.

Orders were sent to the men running the 18-pounder while the rest of the men raced to the village of Queenston. Soon the British cannons began firing.

In the dark gray of dawn, Fitzwilliam could only see shapes and blurred shadows down below. But as he and his men neared the shore, the sun offered just enough light to make the 18-pounder's aim deadly accurate. The massive cannons on Queenston Heights scattered the surprised Americans, but a second wave of boats was just about to reach shore. Colonel Fitzwilliam and Everett flanked General Brock, and he felt his heart race as he spotted the first enemy. Suddenly a boat exploded on the water, a direct hit from the cannons.

Colonel Fitzwilliam heard the cheers of the 49th regiment and turned to see their former leader, General Brock, galloping in. The general quickly dismounted, fully preparing for the fight. The men formed up and readied to run to the beach.

"Charge!" the general called out. Colonel Fitzwilliam struggled to keep up with him. Together the two regiments raced headfirst into battle.

Shots and gunpowder filled the air, and the sound of metal against metal clanged through the early morning as the men fought with muskets and swords in hand-to-hand combat. All the colonel's senses were piqued. He heard the drums in the background directing the regiment. It was as if everyone else was moving in slow motion. Only he possessed the speed necessary to protect the general and his men.

Dawn gradually gave way to morning, and the fighting continued. He shot two men directly in front of him, both falling to the ground before they could pull out their pistols. He took one of their loaded pistols and searched out the next threat.

A large American charged, his musket positioned against his broad shoulder, and he aimed at the general. Colonel Fitzwilliam did not hesitate and shot the man, his aim a direct hit.

General Brock was managing his sword masterfully. His ghastly yellow sash fluttered in the wind with every lunge. Smoke was filling the air so thickly that it was difficult to assess where the most imminent threat was, but there was no doubt that the man was holding his own, despite his age of more than forty years.

They could see the men fighting with every ounce they had. Everett had his sword out and was losing ground against an American when General Brock pulled out his knife and hurled it into the soldier's neck.

Shouts of anguish were heard as men began dropping on both sides. The Americans began to make some headway, and men of the 49th started to falter. Guns were firing heavily on them from every direction. Fitzwilliam saw a few unwounded men falling back in retreat.

The colonel cursed under his breath pointing to the weakening flank and called out, "General!"

General Brock lunged and felled his opponent. Then he raised his sword and shouted, "This is the first time I have ever seen the 49th turn their backs! Surely the heroes of Egmont will not tarnish their record!" He immediately pushed onward and soon it was not just Colonel Fitzwilliam's regiment fighting as the men quickly regrouped. A few minutes later they were flanked with the rest of the 49th and what looked like two more regiments.

General Brock called out, "Colonel Fitzwilliam, have your men follow me to the right. We are making progress here." He yelled out one more encouragement. "Push on, York Volunteers!"

Colonel Fitzwilliam ordered his men to follow. But just as the general raised his arm to motion the men over, his right hand was hit with a musket ball. Although Brock dropped his sword, he barely flinched. The great man took off his wildly flying yellow sash and wrapped it around his bleeding right arm without a word.

Suddenly an American stepped out from a bush. Colonel Fitzwilliam had not a second to move before the soldier took aim at the general's chest. The colonel raised his pistol and aimed at the assassin, but the firearm he had stolen off a dead soldier failed to fire. The American musket boomed, and Brock collapsed onto the icy ground.

Fitzwilliam could hear General Brock spurting and coughing blood. Even so, his last words were undeniable: "Push on, brave York Volunteers."

Knowing that his hero had just died fired something akin to unbridled passion inside Colonel Fitzwilliam. He hurled the pistol that had failed to fire, hitting the American in the head. Then he plunged his sword into the man's chest. As he was attempting to pull out the sword from the man's body, he heard Everett call his name.

"Colonel! Behind you!"

On instinct, he left the sword where it was and reached for the knife in his boot and whirled around to find three American soldiers, each with a weapon in his hand. The one to the left held the most imminent threat. The colonel threw the knife at the man, causing him to drop his musket but not before he fired. Colonel Fitzwilliam felt a sharp pain in his left arm, just above the elbow. He realized that he now faced two soldiers unarmed. He once again reached for the sword, but it still held firmly in the chest of the man that had killed General Brock. With a strength he did not know he had, he pulled it out just in time to thwart a lunge from the second American. But his footing was off, and the pain in his left arm stung terribly. It felt like an eternity before Everett rushed to his side.

His comrade took on the larger of the two Americans, fighting masterfully and advancing against him. Colonel Fitzwilliam lunged and retreated in a dance that was as old as war itself. Men all around him were caught up in their own personal battles. Everett quickly felled his opponent and rushed back to the colonel.

The lone American facing Fitzwilliam saw it was not a fair fight anymore and retreated. Everett followed after him. The colonel ordered a few men to carry General Brock from the battlefield, but just as he turned to see how Everett had faired, he heard a gun go off. It was no ordinary sound; it seemed to speak his name.

They say that in the chaos of war, a soldier can hear and see his death before it happens. Fitzwilliam's vision tunneled, focusing on an American soldier who was dropping to one knee to take aim. Colonel Fitzwilliam knew instinctively that he was the target. Although it felt like time was standing still, there was no time to dodge. He turned to the right just as the smoke puffed from the man's gun.

Colonel Fitzwilliam was thrown back with a force he had never felt. He landed on his back and saw the sky above him go black with each exaggerated blink of his eyes. Two, three, four seconds elapsed with each blink. He saw Everett above him yelling at him.

"Hang on, Colonel!"

The chaos of war was all around him, but the only sensation the colonel knew was an immense pressure in his chest. He felt heavy, as if something was crushing him. He no longer registered the guns, the smoke, the drums of war, or the cries of his wounded men.

The last thing he saw was the various blood splatters on Everett's face. All he could think about was that Everett was above him, his mouth moving frantically, saying something he could not make out, his wild hair whipping at his face, causing the blood to smear further.

Everything was slipping little by little. Then, suddenly, Everett's face was gone.

# CHAPTER 15

Elizabeth was exhausted. She collapsed into the chair, not caring one jot about what still needed to be done. Every part of her body screamed at her in protest, ready to give way at the strain that was placed on her shoulders. She could not place the reason for her pain, but everything—from her hair that felt pulled too tightly against her scalp to the sharp pains in her abdomen that threatened to empty its contents—told her that she was doing too much.

But she could not back down now. There was a room full of friends and family downstairs begging for more from her. She had handled two weeks of the house party; she could last one more.

Suddenly the thought of returning to the room of guests downstairs made her stomach lurch, and she ran to the basin in her dressing room and let it finish in earnest what it had begun that morning. Every last drop was expelled, so quickly that she hardly had time to catch her breath. Her vomiting made a horrid sound, and she wished there had been enough warning this time to at least close her dressing room door. She did not wish to raise anyone's alarm.

She retched one last time, but nothing came out, just as she knew it wouldn't. The force of her convulsion over the basin made her eyes water until she was nearly blind. With a very unfeminine trail of saliva forcing her to hover over the basin, she blindly reached for the cloth that she hoped was beside it. A gentle hand guided her fingers in the right direction, and she prayed it was her maid. In as dignified manner as possible, she wiped her eyes and mouth. Then she looked up to see who her savior had been.

Charlotte's sweet smile and open arms brought new blindness as the tears formed. "It gets better," Charlotte assured her.

"I think I have a touch of something. I would not embrace me if I were you."

"Oh, I do not think it is catching," Charlotte said with a smile. "I suspect you will be fine in a few months."

Horrified, she said, "A few months?"

"Yes. The first few weeks are the worst, but the majority of the nausea goes away after the third month."

Elizabeth stared blankly at her friend until the pieces fell into place in her mind. "You think I am with child?" she asked.

"I should think I would not have to tell you that. Lizzy, dear, you have shown all the signs the last few days. Are you too exhausted to sleep? Do stairs now taunt you because you get light-headed just looking at them? Does that roast beef that used to elicit hunger pains now turn your stomach? Are you sore all over and wonder who seems to be burning you with a branding iron in areas that you never knew existed?"

"Oh, dear."

Charlotte pulled her into an embrace and said, "Like I said, you shall be fine in a few months. But for now, you need to decide when you will tell Mr. Darcy."

"I do not know. What if it is not a baby? He has been hoping for a child for several months now. I do not want to raise his hopes for nothing. And besides which, we are hosting a ball in two days. There is still so much planning to be done." Elizabeth went and stood in front of the mirror and pressed her hand to her belly and smiled.

*A baby? Will's baby is growing inside me at this very moment?* Joy filled her heart, and suddenly she was not quite so fatigued and the strain in her shoulders seemed easier to bear.

"Well, you must get some rest, my dear. You have taken a great deal on your shoulders with this house party. I think I can concoct a satisfactory excuse for you to miss tomorrow's picnic. A good nap in the middle of the day will help a great deal. And no one will question if you take a nap before the ball, for everyone in the house will be doing the same thing. I think it is simply a matter of getting through the dinner tonight without excusing yourself for the third night in a row."

Elizabeth sighed. "Poor Will! What a time to desert him! My mother hangs on his every word and follows him around like a new puppy. And my father has been too preoccupied with the library to offer anything in the way of intelligent conversation."

"Indeed!" Charlotte laughed. "But he has other guests to retreat to when he needs respite."

"And how is Georgiana doing? I confess I have been too preoccupied of late to pay her much heed."

"Do not fret over her. She seems to be enjoying herself with your sisters and Lady Jane. Whenever she visits the General in the nursery she gives me a detailed accounting of all the young people's happenings. Apparently Captain Jersey's eldest, Spencer, is quite taken with her. I have been observing him closely, and he seems quite genuine in his attentions. Whereas Frank Birmingham has filled his entire dance card—first with Lydia, then Georgiana, then Mary, Catherine, Georgiana again, Lady Jane, and Lydia again for the supper set, Catherine, Mary, and Anne for the last two sets. He seems quite determined to secure an entire night of dances with all the most eligible debutants. He is quite charming, but I gather that Lydia fancies him the most."

"Truly?" Elizabeth was surprised, and yet, not surprised.

"Yes. Lady Jane seems to be keeping her distance from him. She confided to Georgiana that she does not trust him. I must agree with her opinion. And Mr. Darcy certainly does not hide his disapproval."

Elizabeth laughed. "Yes, but that is not saying much, as Mr. Darcy disapproves of *all* young men who take an interest in Georgiana. His good opinion of Conrad Jersey certainly does not extend to the captain's sons. Have you talked to him much?"

"Captain Jersey? No, I have not, for his attention seems to be quite occupied with Anne."

Elizabeth had noticed it as well. "Indeed. He seems quite sincere in his attentions to her."

"But he strikes me as a good man. I know at first I resisted the idea of adding more guests, but now that I have met him, I am delighted that you included him," Charlotte added. "I am very happy for my friend Anne."

"Yes. I am glad Lady Catherine is allowing her more opportunities for social interaction here at Pemberley," Elizabeth replied.

Charlotte asked, "How has Lady Catherine been to you?"

"The better question is how has she been to *you*. After hearing the disparaging remark she made to you after our wedding, I am surprised that you have even talked with her."

Charlotte seemed to ponder Elizabeth's words for a moment. "She has not been so bad as all that," she replied tactfully. "Although when Bingley asked Lady Matlock if she had heard from her son since he left for war, I confess I felt Lady Catherine's eyes on me."

Elizabeth squeezed her friend's hand. "I am so sorry, Charlotte. Pay her no heed. She is the type of person who believes everyone else to be subservient, but none of us owe her any allegiance or obedience. She has no power over you now, not anymore."

"Yes, I am aware," Charlotte said.

"How are you fairing when Colonel Fitzwilliam's name comes up? I know you must worry about him a great deal."

"We have talked a great deal about the colonel, have we not? There is really nothing else to say on that subject. I have already told you everything that happened between us. You must not assume he is the center of my every waking thought."

Elizabeth tried not to laugh at her friend's stoicism. "Certainly not. I would never presume such a thing."

Charlotte paused. "I did very well *not* thinking about him until the house party began," she admitted. "It is somewhat more difficult to put him from my thoughts now. Perhaps because he has probably arrived in the Canadian colonies, which means he is in harm's way."

Charlotte paused, and put a great deal of effort into her next sentence. "I have never given up hope for Fitzwilliam. The last few days, I admit I have thought about him a great deal. I cannot help but smile at the kindnesses he showed me. The way he helped me with my shawl, or the smirk that came to his lips before his brilliant white smile—it is all quite endearing. Sometimes I think about the words he spoke to me in the bookstore when he bought me my bible. Did I ever tell you that?"

"I do not believe you did."

Charlotte took a deep breath. "It was that terrible day when we went shopping with Georgiana. The entire population of London seemed to be staring at the pregnant widow in a very unflattering mourning dress. I was quite put out with everyone's pity, and had no humor for the teeniest bit more. I was still fuming about Lady Atkinson and her daughter. Anyway, the colonel and I ran into each other at a bookshop. We both sought to buy a bible, and he offered to buy one for me. Considering the emotional state I was in, I thought he felt pity for me. I believe I hissed a warning at him that I did not need his pity."

"What did he say?"

"He replied, 'As your friend, I promise that you shall never see pity in my eyes when I look at you.' Then he took my bible, kissed it, and handed it to me. It was not just his words that I remember. There was something in his eyes as he handed me the bible. I have thought long and hard about that moment. I think he saw something other than Mr. Collins's widow, or Elizabeth's best friend, or his matchmaking accomplice. I think he saw into my soul. He saw the Charlotte that I used to be. But even that is not an accurate description."

Elizabeth put her hand on Charlotte's and whispered, "He saw the Charlotte you *could* be. It was the same for me."

Tears filled her eyes and she nodded. "I believe so. He saw something of value in me that Mr. Collins never did. He saw my potential. Colonel Fitzwilliam saw the woman whom I am just now beginning to know. How is it that he could know me better than I know myself?"

"That is what love does. Trust me, I know. When I walked in the garden towards the sun in my delirium, my eyes were opened, and for the first time I saw Mr. Darcy as the generous, loving, compassionate, and deeply passionate man that he is. I could not put words to my thoughts right away, but I knew that I loved him from that moment. When we open our eyes and see someone's potential, when we really see them as God sees them, there is no way we cannot love them," Elizabeth promised. "Charlotte, this woman that Colonel Fitzwilliam saw—do you see her in yourself yet?"

"Perhaps a little. I see someone who stood on her own two feet through the death of her husband and the birth of her child. Sometimes when I think of those two things, and when I remember that look in Colonel Fitzwilliam's eyes—I believe I could do anything."

Elizabeth wondered if now was a good opportunity to ask what she never dared ask before. "Did Mr. Collins not see your worth?" she probed.

A cloud of darkness emerged, and Elizabeth knew she had been wrong to bring it up. Charlotte was clearly not ready to talk about the abuse she endured. "Forgive me. That was entirely impertinent."

Charlotte looked away and seemed to be deliberating for an excruciatingly long moment. She finally said, "I do not think you have ever heard me speak one word against Mr. Collins." There was a pause after her words. Elizabeth knew what Charlotte would say next, and her words rang loudly in her ears: *"Nor shall you ever."* But Charlotte surprised her and did not say anything more.

The bruises may have long since faded, but the wounds had not healed. She prayed that Colonel Fitzwilliam's love would ensure they did not leave permanent scars.

*****

Colonel Fitzwilliam could feel something, but he could not formulate complete thoughts. Everything was distant and garbled. Yet occasionally he would hear bits and pieces of familiar voices saying things that just did not make sense.

*". . . too much blood."*

*"We should write his family."*

It all faded away again, but the voices returned unbidden.

*"Dear Lord, take this good man's pain from him . . ."*

*". . . right or wrong, it is what he would want."*

*"How is he?"*

Who are they referring to?

*****

Sometimes he left the voices to return to more pleasant thoughts. *Charlotte, my Charlotte*. She filled his thoughts with daydreams. He remembered sitting next to her at the wedding and giving her that rose in the garden and that night in the nursery.

But eventually, the anxious voices always returned.

*"Life or limb? Is it really that bad?"*

*". . . may be the only option we have. He is succumbing to the fever as each hour passes."*

*"There has to be another way."*

*"Fight, man, fight! I did not save your life so you could give up."*

The voice was familiar, but he could not place it. He did not like being confused. He left again to think of Charlotte.

\*\*\*\*\*

He did not appreciate the interruption when the other voices returned.

*"Death is closer than ever."*

*". . . white as a ghost."*

Colonel Fitzwilliam drifted in and out but always returned to her. At least she made sense. She was brighter than he remembered her. He knew it was just a memory, but the memory of her was more pleasant than the world around him, clouded over in confusing conversation. Her eyes sparkled and her smile, that beautiful smile, brought him peace away from the strange world he was only grasping minute pieces of.

He looked around for the smile, but there only the smell of burning flesh. He gasped, but then was seized with an excruciatingly crippling pain in his chest.

"Breathe!" she said.

Did he just think that? Or was someone yelling at him? His chest burned, and he felt like he had dived into the deepest part of the ocean. He suddenly was acutely aware that his lungs were begging for air. He heard her again, and gasped; the relief was immediate, but by gads, how it hurt to breathe!

*"Surgery went well, but he struggles to breathe."*

*"Maybe we should tell the men."*

*What men?* He drifted off again, eager to escape the pain.

*"He will make it."*

*"He has to."*

For a brief moment he heard that familiar voice. "I have never given up hope for Fitzwilliam." She was so close he could almost touch her, smell her . . . no, whatever he was smelling was definitely not her!

But other voices began to assault him.

*"Fiend seize it! I don't know a more stubborn man!"*

*"Stubborn can be good. It means he'll fight for what he wants."*

*"Stay with us, Colonel."*

*If I only knew how, I would.*

\*\*\*\*\*

Darcy was contemplating exactly how he was going to make it through a whole night of dancing in two days' time when, just before dinner, Mr. Reynolds entered his study and handed him a calling card.

"A Mr. Benjamin Pastel is here to see you and Mrs. Collins, sir," Franklin announced.

"Now?" Darcy asked. Franklin nodded. *Of all times, he comes now?* "Very well. Please fetch my wife and Mrs. Collins and have them meet me in my study. Show Mr. Pastel into the library."

Mr. Darcy sat back in his chair. It was the 29th of October. Benjamin Pastel had said he planned to call on Mrs. Collins at some point, but to arrive unannounced like this was rather presumptive of him. Charlotte had officially been mourning for six months. At this point, it was appropriate for her to start wearing lavender dresses with black accents, but she still insisted on all black. He had offered to send out for a dressmaker from Lambton, to make something new for the ball, but Charlotte had only dug in her heels even stronger. None of the dresses she had worn before Mr. Collins's death had made their reappearance yet. Not even the lavender dress she had worn only once at his wedding.

Elizabeth came in looking a little pale. "Is there something wrong, dear?" she asked. Charlotte was right behind her with a worried look on her face.

"Have you heard something from the colonel?" Charlotte queried.

"No, nothing of that sort. Actually, Charlotte, there is a gentleman here to see you."

"A gentleman? Who?" Charlotte asked.

"A former business associate of Mr. Collins. To be more specific, Mr. Collins's solicitor. I do not know exactly why he has come to see you. I wish I could prepare you better. But we have little time. He is in the library right now waiting for us. Richard and I both believe this man to be a good man, an honest man—"

"Colonel Fitzwilliam knows Mr. Collins's solicitor? And you do as well? I do not understand. What is going on?"

He wasn't prepared to explain the details nor did not have enough time. Luckily, Elizabeth answered for him. "Do not be distressed, Charlotte. Mr. Darcy only met with Mr. Pastel because his name came up in the parish ledgers you asked Darcy and Colonel Fitzwilliam to review. He seems to be a respectable man; however, it seems that his brother, Clyde Pastel, with whom Mr. Collins usually worked, was not."

Mr. Darcy continued, "I can only guess that Mr. Pastel is here to deliver news and to gather information."

Charlotte couldn't have looked more confused. "Information? What about? Is this about Longbourn? I know my son is technically the next heir, as Mrs. Bennet seemed too eager to point out."

"Forgive my mother for that," Elizabeth apologized. The first day of the party, Mrs. Bennet had awkwardly confided in Darcy and Elizabeth that she was actually quite relieved that Isaac Collins was to inherit the Bennet family home. As she tactlessly exalted in the middle of a crowded rooms of listening ears, 'Oh, it is a shame about Mr. Collins to be sure, but I must say, it has all worked out extraordinarily well for me and your sisters! The child cannot inherit for one-and-twenty years, which will give us plenty of time to live a long life at Longbourn, even if Mr. Bennet should die this very night!'

Elizabeth cringed at the memory. She was sure Mrs. Bennet's declaration had been overheard by at least half the room, including Charlotte.

Charlotte turned back to Darcy. "What kind of information is he looking for?"

Mr. Darcy had to say this carefully. "I do not know. It may just be questions about Mr. Collins's death or about the General's birth. I can only advise you to answer his questions as truthfully and simply as possible. I know you are naturally discreet, but now is not the time for concealment. I wish I could tell you more, but I cannot." It was true. If he disclosed what little he knew about the ledger and the ships, he could endanger her chance to inherit. The risk was too great. He would say no more.

Charlotte stood and announced, "Very well. I trust you, Mr. Darcy. And if you and the colonel believe him to be a good man, I shall answer whatever questions he has."

# CHAPTER 16

Charlotte knew there was more to the story than Mr. Darcy and Elizabeth were not telling her, but she also saw the concern in their eyes. Whatever they were holding back, they had good reason for doing so.

She took a moment to gather her thoughts before entering the library. *Be yourself. Speak to him as you would speak to Elizabeth and Mr. Darcy. They love you and would not put you in harm's way. Colonel Fitzwilliam trusts this man.* And although the colonel, thousand miles across the sea, was unlikely to be able to offer any assistance, the last thought brought her more comfort than she was willing to admit.

Mr. Darcy shook the man's hand and introduced them. "You know my wife, Elizabeth Darcy. This is Mrs. Charlotte Collins, Mr. Collins's widow."

The man had kind eyes but was stiffly formal. He dressed very fine. He had not even taken his gloves off yet before he reached out for her hand, and so she offered it to him, whereupon he placed the smallest of kisses. She curtsied and replied, "It is a pleasure to meet you, Mr. Pastel. I wish I could say I have heard much about you, but I was only just informed that you were Mr. Collins's former solicitor."

"The pleasure is all mine. And I still *am* Mr. Collins's solicitor. He set up a small fund in the event of his death so that I could still perform various duties for him posthumously."

Elizabeth motioned for them to all take a seat. "Please sit down."

There was a moment where everyone seemed to be expecting someone else to speak first. Charlotte finally broke the silence and asked, "What can I do for you, Mr. Pastel?"

He cleared his throat and seemed to examine her for a moment. "I must preface this conversation by clarifying that for reasons I am unable to explain at this time, I must ask some indelicate questions. These questions are not easy, nor in my character to ask, however my profession requires it. I see you are still wearing black," he responded. "I am sorry for your loss. How long has it been?"

"Six months and one day, sir."

He arched an eyebrow slightly, but it was only for a moment. "Many widows start to wear lavender around this time, or resume wearing their regular wardrobe, simply accented with black lace or ribbons. May I ask why you are still in all black?"

*What an odd question!* She reminded herself to be honest. "I am more traditional than most widows I suppose. I am not eager to secure my next husband. Therefore I see no need to advertise that I will be out of mourning soon."

"But do you not have a baby to feed and provide for?"

"I do. He is two months old now."

"A son? That is wonderful. What have you named him?"

"Isaac Byron Collins."

"You did not name him after his father?"

"Indeed I did, sir. Isaac was my grandfather's name, and Byron was the first name of my late husband, although fewknew that. But something tells me that *you* knew that. You are his solicitor, after all."

A small smile came to his lips, and he looked down. "I was aware of that, yes."

"Then what prompted you to ask?"

"Mr. Collins, I believe, went by William, rather than his first name, Byron. I find it odd that you did not name his son William."

Elizabeth started to protest, but Charlotte held up her hand and answered him. "As the child and I are currently living as dependents in the home of Fitzwilliam Darcy, who is often called William, Isaac Byron seemed more appropriate. I certainly do not wish to send a message that might taint the names of myself, my late husband, or Mr. Darcy. It is very important to me, as a widow, to preserve whatever little respect I can garner from people."

Mr. Pastel smiled politely at her and said, "My apologies, madam. I commend you for your loyalty to your late husband and to Mr. Darcy. I truly am sorry for your loss. I admit I did not know him well. Since he lived closer to the firm's London office, your husband worked almost entirely with my brother, Clyde. Tell me, what kind of man was Mr. Collins?"

Charlotte felt a little uneasy with this question. What characterization of the man, short of an outright lie, could pass as acceptable? She could not say he was a devoted husband. That would be a lie. Nor could she could say that he was not the blabbering idiot he pretended to be in society. Although that was the truth, it would elicit follow-up questions she did not wish to answer. She certainly could not say that he felt an irrational commitment to control the world around them. And she most definitely could not say that he was the kind of man who raised his hand to his wife every night.

She felt her heart start to race as flashes of memories came flooding in. She looked down at her hands to give herself a minute before she proceeded. She could not lose herself now, not like she had done with Colonel Fitzwilliam in the garden. With a calming breath, she imagined herself sitting in the window seat at the parsonage, while Mr. Collins was away on business, talking with Elizabeth. With this image in place, she began describing her husband, as she had so often done, in the best possible light.

"Mr. Collins was often misunderstood." *Be honest*, she reminded herself. "Many saw a man who was somewhat silly or ridiculous. He was actually very intelligent and well read. Some saw a man who rode on the coattails of his benefactor, Lady Catherine de Bourgh, but he actually spent his money very wisely. We never once had to ask for better remuneration. Some saw a man who was judgmental of those who were in a different rank or station, however, it was simply important to him to present himself in the best light possible, because he understood that so many people judge on appearances. No one could doubt that he was a hard worker. There were some weeks when he sequestered himself in his bookroom for days on end until his sermon was perfect.

"People respected him as a rector. He actually was really quite talented in directing the parish. He had many loyal parishioners, some of which still write to me and ask me for advice as if he were still alive. However, he had his flaws, for he was, nonetheless, just a man."

She let out a sigh and looked at Elizabeth for reassurance. Elizabeth's eyes were full of unshed tears, and she had a most comforting smile on her face. They were not eyes of pity, they were eyes of compassion and kindness and love. Charlotte turned her gaze back to Mr. Pastel. "Do you have any other questions?"

Mr. Darcy stepped in and said, "Mr. Pastel, we are currently hosting a house party of friends and family, and I believe you are acquainted with one of my guests. Captain Jersey told me that he met you in Liverpool and that you offered him command of one of your ships."

*How odd that Captain Jersey has a connection to both Mr. Darcy and Mr. Pastel*, Charlotte mused. *Is that why the captain made the long journey to Liverpool so soon after arriving here for the party?*

Mr. Pastel seemed genuinely surprised. "Captain Jersey is here? Well, I would love to say hello."

Charlotte noticed Mr. Darcy look at Elizabeth pointedly. Elizabeth seemed to understand the nonverbal communication. "You have surely had a long day's journey, Mr. Pastel," she added. "Are you planning to stay in Lambton tonight?"

"Yes," he replied warily. "At the Rose and Crown Inn."

"Then please accept my invitation to stay here instead. We are having an All Hallow's Eve Masquerade the night after tomorrow and would be delighted to add you to the party. The masquerade is actually quite informal, as many of our tenants will be there, so do not be distressed on that account. And by staying here as our guest, you will be able to spend more time getting to know Captain Jersey and Mrs. Collins. I simply must insist. You really would be doing us a favor for we are long on ladies and short on gentlemen for our ball."

Charlotte knew Elizabeth's condition well enough to know that the idea of adding one more guest was a daunting task, which made her invitation all the more interesting, even peculiar. Charlotte had half expected Mr. Darcy to step in and send Mr. Pastel away along with his intrusive questions. But instead, he was inviting him to be a guest! And Elizabeth was going along with it, even though she is had just begun the journey to produce the first

Darcy heir in the next generation. It felt rather incongruent. The only thing she could surmise was that Darcy must have believed the interrogation was somehow warranted, or at least important enough not to warrant his intervention.

It seemed clear that she had to prove something to Mr. Pastel. But what could it possibly be?

She reviewed the questions he had asked. All of them seemed to focus on her opinion of and respect for Mr. Collins.

*It is as if Mr. Collins's ghost hired Mr. Pastel to check up on me.* If there were such things as ghosts, it was hardly surprising that Mr. Collins's ghost would want to ensure that Charlotte was not sullying his name. She was not daft; she knew how much he craved respect. And an appropriately mournful widow would surely be among his dying wishes. With this thought, the last piece of the puzzle seemed to fit into place.

*Mr. Pastel is not a mystic who can communicate with ghosts; he is a solicitor who is executing posthumous wishes for Mr. Collins! What else can that possibly mean beside a will? Mr. Collins must have had a will!*

She tried not to let her jaw drop as she realized this. All these questions about her behavior could only mean the will included stipulations regarding her behavior! It was hardly surprising that he, of all people, would have schemed a way to control her even from beyond grave. She realized Collins must have had kept some assets hidden from her, and she would only inherit them if she passed Mr. Pastel's inspection. Without a second's hesitation, she added, "I would love to have you join our party, Mr. Pastel."

Mr. Darcy seemed pleased with her statement, and so did Mr. Pastel. "I would love to stay, if it is no bother," he confessed. "Though I admit I did not bring my dancing shoes."

Elizabeth smiled brightly. "No dancing shoes required, Mr. Pastel," she assured him. "Will, dear, please inform Mrs. Reynolds that there will be another guest for dinner and have her prepare a room in the west wing near Captain Jersey and his sons. I think our guest would appreciate that. Mr. Pastel, if you could write out a note for the Rose and Crown, we will send a man for your trunks while we are dining."

"Certainly. Thank you. I must ask, Mr. Darcy, is your first name truly Fitzwilliam?"

"Yes, it is my mother's maiden name."

Mr. Pastel asked, "Then are you acquainted with a Richard Fitzwilliam?"

Charlotte's senses were piqued at the colonel's name.

"I know him quite well," Darcy replied. "He is my cousin. You shall also have a chance to meet his parents, Lord and Lady Matlock, as they are staying here with us as well." Mr. Darcy looked a little uncomfortable for a moment and in a strained voice he added, "And how do you know him?"

Charlotte noted Elizabeth seemed uncomfortable too. It was obvious that they were hiding something, because only a moment ago in the study, Mr. Darcy had assured Charlotte that Colonel Fitzwilliam knew Mr. Pastel quite well and considered him a respectable man. Now Darcy was feigning ignorance of their acquaintance.

"I really only met him a few months ago while his regiment was stationed in Liverpool. He seemed genuinely interested in the shipping business. But I did not place the connection until just now. How odd that I randomly meet two cousins, neither of whom live in Liverpool, with the name Fitzwilliam."

Charlotte couldn't help but think, *Yes, how very odd.*

\*\*\*\*\*

After the typical post-dinner separation of sexes, Elizabeth found her husband leaning over more than a few papers in his study. He was so engrossed in them that he did not hear her enter. She watched him for a moment as he turned page after page before slowly walking towards him. Only when she was directly at his side did he finally look up.

Elizabeth asked, "Is that what I think it is?"

"It is."

"So your man was able to find Mr. Collins's will in Mr. Pastel's belongings while we were at dinner?"

"He did."

"And have you read it?"

"Only half of it," he sighed. "Captain Jersey agreed to occupy Mr. Pastel with my finest brandy for a half hour, and I was hoping to read it quickly before I, or the will, was missed. But this document is so complicated. So many rules and stipulations and deadlines! I must admit that Charlotte was correct; her husband was a very intelligent man. He thought of everything. Even so far as to his name on the tombstone and the color of his wife's dresses. Mr. Collins died very soon after Charlotte became with child; but it seems that he did not waste any time directing his solicitor to add stipulations about the child as well. Based on Mr. Pastel's line of questioning, I fear I will come across an addendum near the end regarding what the child is to be named. But I am out of time."

"Then I will try to buy you some. But do not let yourself be caught returning it. Where did you say the captain was?"

"Occupying Mr. Pastel in the billiard room."

"Then I shall take him on a very long tour of the first and third floors, followed by a thorough study of the east wing. Come find us as soon as you finish. And be careful, dear. I know Charlotte has a right to know of the will, but this feels dangerous."

"Yes, it is. But we owe her this and much more. She risked corresponding with Colonel Fitzwilliam, a bachelor of no relation, so that we could come to an understanding. Have you ever considered how dangerous an act that was, now that we know what kind of man her husband was? No doubt she would have suffered a great deal if Mr. Collins had discovered it."

"I know. I know. Let us pray you get some answers quickly."

*****

Georgiana knew she had to talk to someone. She knocked on Elizabeth's door and heard her say enter. She opened the door and saw that William was just leaving. He leaned in to quickly kiss Elizabeth then walked over to the door where Georgiana stood.

"Have a delightful time at the picnic, Georgie," he told her with a kiss. "I have several matters of business to attend to, so please make sure the guests enjoy themselves."

"I will, thank you." The door closed behind her. "Elizabeth, you are so beautiful. No wonder William fell in love with you. I wish I had half of your good looks."

"Thank you, but you have more than half, my dear. You look lovely today. Georgiana, what is disturbing you? I can see the worry in your eyes." Elizabeth stood and walked her over to the chaise and held her hand. "You can tell me."

Georgiana frowned. "It is about Mr. Pastel. I think I said something wrong at dinner last night. He sat across from me, next to Avelina. She was telling me about a butterfly she had drawn to give to the General when he suddenly interrupted her and asked who the General was. Avelina stated it was Charlotte's son, and he got very curious about the nickname. Avelina tried to explain that he had no name for a full day and so Colonel Fitzwilliam had started to call him the General. Then he asked a direct question that held too much importance for Avelina to answer on her own."

"What did he ask?"

"He asked if Colonel Fitzwilliam knew Charlotte well and would Avelina call them close."

Worry danced across Elizabeth's face, only confirming to Georgiana that she had been right to be concerned. "Then I very plainly said, 'Mr. Pastel, Mrs. Collins is very nearly his cousin. I know of no improper behavior between the two. I cannot even think of a time she has ever been alone with him.' Then I felt embarrassed because I had been so direct. I looked down at my plate and nearly began to cry.

"I just get so protective of those I love! It seemed like he was fishing for evidence that Charlotte was being improper! When I looked up at him, he smiled and said, 'I had not meant to imply anything improper.' But Elizabeth, he did! I know it! I know you mentioned he was Mr. Collins's business friend, but I do not think that he is a friend to Charlotte."

Elizabeth squeezed her hand and said, "I know this will be hard to understand, but he is a good man. He would not intentionally harm Charlotte."

"Then why was he asking questions that might taint her reputation?"

"I wish I could say. For now, just know that you were right not to disclose Colonel Fitzwilliam's tender feelings for Charlotte.

In fact, I think what you said very well might have helped Charlotte. Now, if you will excuse me, I need to tell Will." Elizabeth stood and left.

Georgiana sat and watched Elizabeth leave while she pondered it all. How did what she say help Charlotte? All she was doing was stating the truth. The world around her was getting more confusing. She wished she were better at reading people, like Colonel Fitzwilliam was. She suddenly missed him a great deal. She knew it would be several more weeks before they heard anything at all from him. The strain of this thought was crippling. Then she thought about how hard it must for Colonel Fitzwilliam to be so far away from Charlotte, whom he obviously loved a great deal.

*But even if he were here, Charlotte would still be out of reach, wouldn't she?* She realized for the first time that her cousin loved someone he could not have. For even when Charlotte's mourning period ended, Georgiana knew her friend would never sacrifice her independence to marry again. Oh, this would not do in the slightest! Georgiana had to do something to help Richard! But what could she do? How could she change a mind as stubborn as Charlotte's?

# CHAPTER 17

At breakfast, the morning after the All Hallow's Eve masquerade, Mr. Darcy declared, "I cannot think of a single ball held at Pemberley, or anywhere else, for that matter, that I have enjoyed so well. Would you not agree, darling?"

Georgiana and Elizabeth were the only ones at the breakfast table. Elizabeth looked as if she wanted to return to bed, but she responded lightly, "It does help to have tolerable partners. Did you enjoy yourself, Georgiana?"

Georgiana smiled back. "Oh yes! It was the finest ball I have ever seen at Pemberley! Not being marched to bed at half-past-seven with the nursery maid improved the experience remarkably."

Elizabeth and Will laughed. "You did a marvelous job, Elizabeth," Georgiana added. "Really. I think everyone enjoyed themselves."

"I hope very much that you are correct. I believe even Mr. Pastel had a pleasant time," Elizabeth replied. "I danced a set with him, and it was very enlightening."

William knew his face turned stern as he said, "Yes, I know. I had to give up my supper set to allow him to dance with you."

Georgiana looked like she was trying not to laugh, but a small giggle escaped. "William, do try to calm yourself. It must be a Darcy curse to be overly protective of those you love."

"Actually, it is a Fitzwilliam trait from our mother," Darcy replied, "so be careful where you fling those accusations, Georgie. Your temper, I believe, was once aimed at Richard. He told me about the fire in your eyes when Charlotte fainted in London."

Georgiana blushed. "It is true; I rang him a peel something fierce before I realized how much he cared for her."

The door to the breakfast room opened, and Mr. Pastel entered with a peculiar look on his face. The room went entirely silent.

Mr. Darcy then stood and said, "I hope you are finding everything to your liking, Mr. Pastel. Please break your fast with anything that appeals to you on the sideboard."

Mr. Pastel seemed to be eyeing Georgiana. Darcy suddenly realized what she had said just prior to him coming in. *Fiend, seize it!* She might as well have sung from the rooftops that Colonel Fitzwilliam admired Charlotte.

Will had only been able to get through three-fourths of the will while Mr. Pastel's things were moved from the Rose and Crown Inn to Pemberley. And from what he had read, it was important that Mr. Pastel believe Charlotte was honoring the traditional full year of mourning.

William was still riddled with guilt over doing something as devious as having his man search Mr. Pastel's belongings; but his mind was eased a bit by reasoning that if Colonel Fitzwilliam were here, then he would have done the exact same thing. Darcy had promised him he would take care of Charlotte, as if she were his own wife. And Darcy would do anything, literally anything, for Elizabeth. He owed Colonel Fitzwilliam so much already for offering him the hope when he was so sure there was no hope left for him and Miss Elizabeth Bennet. For a brief moment, he knew that he had done the right thing in stealing the will. If only he had the chance to read the entire document!

For all the ingrained morals and integrity that were at Darcy's core, there was also a very large, and often overpowering, passion to protect those he loved. At times, those two traits were in conflict. And for one of the first times in his life, he had sided with the protective side over his strict sense of right and wrong. He would risk it all to protect those he loved—and that included Charlotte and Colonel Fitzwilliam.

Mr. Pastel silently took a plate and began filling it. He then sat down next to Elizabeth and asked, "Are you feeling well, Mrs. Darcy? You seem pale."

"I shall be fine—just an upset breadbasket from not enough sleep. Did you enjoy yourself last night?"

"I did, thank you. I met many fine ladies and gentlemen. Mr. Darcy, you have some very loyal friends and family, but I admit I was most impressed by the loyalty of your tenants. Every single one of them sang your praises. And Mrs. Collins was kind enough to sit with me at dinner."

Knowing how significant this was, Darcy said, "You are very lucky indeed then, for she told me that she intended to take dinner in her room."

"One could say I am . . . very persuasive. I had not seen her since that morning we met in your library, because she has been so preoccupied with young Isaac. We spoke for a great length of time and, with enough begging, she agreed to join me."

Elizabeth stood and said, "If you will excuse me, I just recalled something I need to attend to." She hurried out of the room.

Mr. Pastel stood as she left and then said, "If you will excuse me for a moment." And with that, he followed Elizabeth out the door.

Mr. Pastel's leaving without eating was too smoky by half. It was clear that the solicitor intended to accost his wife with further questions. As soon as Mr. Pastel was out of sight, Darcy quickly stood up and hid behind the doorway, listening in on their conversation.

"Mrs. Darcy," Mr. Pastel called out, "if you have a moment, I have just a few more questions for you."

Mr. Pastel may have been pleasant enough last night, but there was determination in his voice this morning. He must have heard Georgiana talking about Colonel Fitzwilliam and Charlotte. Darcy thought back to the moment of Pastel's entrance and remembered Georgiana's words, *before I realized how much he cared for her.* With a cringe, Darcy remembered the sight of Pastel's eyebrows rising in surprise as he entered. He very well could have been listening at the door.

Darcy heard Elizabeth walk over to Pastel. "Forgive my new sister," she explained. "Georgiana is very young."

"I have found that the young are often the ones who observe the most."

"Mr. Pastel, I apologize, but I do not feel well. Is there something specific you need?"

"Just one last question, Mrs. Darcy. Has Mrs. Collins ever said anything negative about her late husband?" Darcy recognized it as another stipulation of the will; if Charlotte spread any rumors that cast Mr. Collins in a bad light, she would forfeit the money. The term used in the will was "defamation of character". He froze behind the doorway.

Elizabeth took a deep breath that even Darcy could hear. "Mr. Pastel, I know Mr. Collins was a business associate of yours, and, therefore, your client. I, however, did not enjoy his company before he married my friend nor afterwards. I did not like the man nor respect him.

"On the other hand, Mrs. Collins is a friend, one who I confide most everything in. I have had many months of living with her since her husband's death, and I can very confidently report that she has never, not once, spoken one word that would disgrace his name. She has not even so much as validated my poor opinion of the man. Now if you will excuse me, I feel this moment has left me ill equipped to keep my breakfast down. I hope I have answered your questions in a satisfactory manner."

"Indeed you have. I am sorry to have held you up and that you are not feeling well."

Mr. Darcy exhaled slowly. Hopefully the finality of Elizabeth's words would put to rest any lingering concerns of Mr. Pastel. He was grateful Elizabeth had been able to tell the truth without a moment's hesitation.

It seemed that part of the will could be checked off just like all the others; must wear black for the entire year; must not defame Mr. Collins's name; must name her child after him (what a godsend the child had been a boy!—Wilhelmina was a terrible name); and, of course, the required voluntary visit to the gravesite. There had been a few more ridiculous stipulations and deadlines outlined in the will, but these four were the most important. So long as Charlotte made a voluntary visit to his gravesite before next April, everything seemed to look favorable for her to receive the two ships and the money.

He saw Georgiana's distressed faced as he re-entered the dining room and leaned down and kissed her forehead. Just before Mr. Pastel entered, he whispered, "No harm done, Georgie. But let us be more careful; we still have a few more hours with Mr. Pastel."

But one thing kept nagging at him. He couldn't help but wonder why his wife hadn't told him she was ill. He pondered this problem quite deliberately, rolling it around in his mind and ignoring the conversation around him. His voluntary isolation was partially assisted by two facts—firstly, that he did not wish to speak with Mr. Pastel any more than necessary, and secondly, because the other guests were trickling in to break their fast. He opened the newspaper and pretended to read.

There was an article about a trend of estates not requiring a male heir and that sparked his interest. It was written by a solicitor that said that most estates that were entailed away from the female line had been so for hundreds of years. The main requirement to break an entailment was to have the current estate owner as well as the adult male heir both agree in writing to change the contract. Both had to be willing and both had to be of sound mind.

Since many men who stood to inherit estates did not wish to relinquish their inheritance, the system was nearly always gridlocked. Many fathers with no sons, like Mr. Bennet, found their entire fortune tied up in the estate, destined for some distant male relative. Attempting to break an entailment usually cost thousands of pounds.

He was suddenly very grateful that when Elizabeth became with child, it would not matter whether the babe was a son or daughter. Their firstborn, of either sex, would be the heir. Currently, the country estate in the north was set aside for an inheritance for his firstborn daughter, if a son arrived later. And if they never had a son, their daughter would have the sole rights to Pemberley. If Elizabeth were to get pregnant . . .

*If Elizabeth were to get pregnant . . .*

He put down the paper. "Good God!" Darcy cried out.

Everyone in the room looked at him as he stood up, nearly knocking over his chair. "Excuse me. I must find my wife."

He heard Lydia mumble something like, "Someone seems dicked in the nob this morning."

He very nearly ran up to her chambers and did not even knock. He burst in just as Charlotte was handing her a towel. Her breakfast lay undigested in the basin. Elizabeth looked up at him, and she gave a half smile.

"Is it true?" he cried. "Are you with child?"

She slowly stood up and he approached her. He placed one hand on her abdomen and one on her face. She smiled wider. "I suspect so," she admitted. "At least I hope so. I will not know for sure until the quickening."

He felt like picking her up and twirling her around in the air, but her pallor made him reconsider. He lowered his voice and brushed her curls from her face. "Oh, Elizabeth, this is such wonderful news! I am so sorry you are ill. Is it too terribly bad? Do you need to rest? My mother was always so ill in her first months. And it made my father so anxious." Darcy remembered the months his mother had lain helpless in bed, too sick with child to leave her chambers, and sadness in her eyes when she had twice lost the baby.

"Lie down, dearest," he told her. "You shall not lift a single finger during the rest of the house party, if I have any say in it—"

Elizabeth interrupted him, "Which you do not." She then turned to Charlotte and said, "I told you he would be beside himself. Will, I intend to keep doing everything I am capable of doing. And you will need to let me. I have always been an independent soul. If you plan on imprisoning me in my bed for the next nine months, then you might just find your nights *considerably* chilly this winter," she warned him.

"But Elizabeth, my dear, you must be careful," he urged.

"Yes, but *you* must remember that you fell in love with my independent spirit and my impertinent ways. So do try to keep those characteristics in mind as you escort me back to the breakfast room to greet our guests."

He ignored that Charlotte was even in the room. "How can I help you? I just want to be of assistance."

Elizabeth voice softened, and she cupped his jaw and said, "I know, Will. I know. For now I would just like a cup of peppermint tea to settle my stomach. Charlotte says it is helpful."

"Of course. Are you chilled? Would you enjoy a warm bath? Can I get you—"

"I will tell you when I need something," she promised. "Now please try to calm down. Or this may be a *very* long confinement."

Darcy smiled widely at her. She was just as she had ever been, and he loved that about her. "Forgive me. Over-protectiveness runs in my family, you might say. One peppermint tea."

*****

Charlotte couldn't help but marvel how well the two communicated. Darcy had gingerly escorted his wife out of her chambers, leaving Charlotte alone to contemplate what she just witnessed. Darcy had expressed his fears, and Elizabeth had reassured him with a single touch. It was so tender, so very tender. Unintentionally, Charlotte sighed.

She wanted that. She wanted it desperately for herself.

*****

Colonel Fitzwilliam was cold. His frozen arms and legs felt as if they were strapped to the most uncomfortable bed in England. Every joint protested. He attempted to relieve the pain by turning over onto his side but was shocked to discover he was too weak to move. He heard a crackling fire, and he could smell it burning, but he did not feel its heat. Each gasp of air burned his lungs and throat. He was not sure what was worse, the pain of breathing or his insatiable thirst.

He needed to drink something. Soon.

As he tried to make sense of the things around him, he heard a familiar voice next to him. It was Mr. Lisscord. He was praying. Fitzwilliam tried to focus on the chaplain's words.

". . . must thank you, dearest Father in Heaven, that he has made it this far. Give him the strength to pull through this. Help him to remember there is a lady waiting for him . . ."

*Charlotte!* His eyes burst open, and he was struck by the dimness of the room. He looked around and saw that he was in the infirmary, and not in England. An almost immeasurable amount of light came from the fire, and Mr. Lisscord was backlit by a single candle. It was barely bright enough for Fitzwilliam to recognize the neatly trimmed beard along Lisscord's jaw.

Colonel Fitzwilliam tried to move his left arm, to let Lisscord know that he was awake, but the chaplain seemed not to have noticed. There was a deep ache in his arm that he could not describe. It was a burning sensation combined with the feeling of pins and needles.

He tried to reach out to the man, the old friend he had never really understood until their last days together in East Sussex. Fitzwilliam had once assumed Chaplain Lisscord to be judgmental and proud. Now he knew the old man had a very keen sense of right and wrong. His entire life was motivated by his faith. His passions were in harmony with God. But it was more than that.

The colonel had once been disturbed by Lisscord's ability to see into men's souls. But there was a great deal of comfort in knowing that there was someone who really knew you. Someone who knew you so well that he could counsel you in matters of the spirit or heart. More than ever before, Fitzwilliam felt relieved that there was a man of God in front of him.

But why was the chaplain praying for him? He tried to think back, but his memory was cloudy, and the energy it took to search his brain was intense and overwhelming.

The last thing he remembered was the battle at Queenston. Smoke so thick that a man could not see the enemy at all until they were right up top of you. Guns firing and drums beating in the distance, announcing that more boats were landing on the right. The right was where General Brock had boldly gone. Suddenly a cloud of horror struck him so hard that he sucked in a painful breath. His hero had fallen. He remembered.

He must have been injured too, for why else would he wake up in the infirmary? He did a mental assessment of his body. There were pins and needles in his left arm as well as a strange burning that radiated down to his hand. It hurt a great deal to breathe. He felt quite heavy and . . . was he strapped down? He tried once again to move his legs, and this time he managed a nearly imperceptible tremor.

Mr. Lisscord's prayer paused momentarily, and then Fitzwilliam heard him say, "Doctor! He is moving! His eyes are open!"

Fitzwilliam continued to try to move his legs; they must truly be strapped down, he was sure of it.

Mr. Heather came rushing to his side and immediately put one hand to Colonel Fitzwilliam's head and the other hand against his desperately straining legs. "There now, my friend. Stop fighting it. Relax. You are very ill."

Colonel Fitzwilliam tried to speak again. The thirst that burned his throat was excruciating. He could barely smack his lips together. With the driest tongue he had ever had, he licked his lips.

The doctor called out to someone, "Bring some water! And have the cook heat some broth!"

Slowly, the room brightened as candles were lit. He could see from one of the windows that it was quite dark outside. He heard the enticing, seductive sound of water being poured from one container to another and suddenly there was no other need than to drink. Water was placed to his lips, and someone propped up his head. He was overcome with a powerful relief, but too soon the water was removed.

"More." His own voice was hardly recognizable. It was hoarse and weak and trembled a great deal.

The water returned and Mr. Heather cautioned, "There now, go slowly. The last thing you need is to toss up your accounts. You have come too far to lose ground now."

The colonel drank for a full minute and drained the glass. He rested his head back and sighed.

"How are you?" the doctor asked.

"Cold."

"I imagine so. Your fever just broke, and you are drenched in sweat." He directed a man to his right to get another blanket and to add more wood to the fire.

Colonel Fitzwilliam turned his head and watched the medic from his regiment start to place the blanket on him. "Thank you, Adrian," Fitzwilliam whispered.

"There now, Colonel, no need to thank me, just doing my job. Just like you did yours. Everyone knows how you avenged the general's killer."

"Did I?"

"Yes, sir. Would you like more water?"

He nodded. He drank all that was offered again. His tongue was at least wet now; it felt thick and coated. He chose his questions carefully; what did he want to know first? "My men? How many?" Each word was painful.

The chaplain answered him. "Two-and-twenty perished."

The sadness this brought was overwhelming but he had to ask. "Names . . ." they all knew it was more of a command, than a question.

The chaplain pulled out a list from his bible and said, "I knew you would wish to know." Lisscord began solemnly reading the names aloud. Each one felt like a bullet to his chest. He could feel the sorrow these families would be facing. At one name in particular, the colonel reacted vehemently.

In a croak, he said, "Not Leavitt! He has a new baby!"

"I am afraid so. I am terribly sorry, Colonel. Do you wish me to stop?"

"No. Resume, please . . ." If he thought he had something in his throat before, he most definitely did now.

Mr. Heather stepped in. "I need to examine you, Fitzwilliam. Perhaps Lisscord can finish this another time."

"No. This is more important." His voice cracked for an entirely different reason as tears started to form in his eyes. The chaplain continued reading out the names. The colonel counted each one of them. ". . . only one-and-twenty. You said . . . two-and-twenty casualties."

"And General Isaac Brock," Lisscord replied. The room fell silent for a moment. "Along with casualties in other regiments."

Fitzwilliam closed his eyes. If he weren't so parched, tears would have begun to spill over his cheeks. He was supposed to be General Brock's right flank, and he had failed him. His hero had fallen. There was nothing he could have done to stop it. "And Everett?"

"He saved your life. Stood and fought off at least a dozen men until we could get to you," Mr. Heather said.

Colonel Fitzwilliam pondered this as gratitude surged inside him. It gave him enough strength to form a full sentence. "Please thank him for me and tell him I would like to speak with him."

The cabin door opened, and snowy wind flew in. And there stood Everett. He took off his hat and held it in his hands and walked purposefully to Colonel Fitzwilliam's cot. "I heard the hero had woken. Welcome back, Colonel. I knew you would not leave us for good, but there were several days, weeks even, when I questioned it."

He asked for more water and when he had drank it all again he tried to clarify, "Weeks?" disbelief in his tones. How could a man stay alive, unconscious, for weeks?

"Yes," Mr. Heather answered. "You were severely injured." There was something else in his words that Heather was trying very hard not to say. Colonel Fitzwilliam gave him a look that said to continue. "When you were carried in, there was more dirt on you than blood, and that was saying something. You were shot in the arm, just above the elbow."

Colonel Fitzwilliam looked down at his arm, which was under the blanket. That would explain the burning and pins and needles. "Go on."

"Yes, well, initially the most pressing concern was the bullet to your chest." He bent over and reached under the cot and pulled out a tattered blood-stained bible that had a hole through the middle of it. "Your bible slowed the ball. It still managed to puncture the lung and nick a blood vessel. But without this book, the ball would surely have hit your heart. I had to rush you to surgery to retrieve the ball and cauterize and suture the bleeding vessel. It was a very tumultuous few days. You drifted in and out, your ability to drink waxed and waned." Again it seemed like Heather was not telling him the whole story.

Mr. Lisscord added, "Your situation was incredibly precarious, Colonel."

"I am sure. But what are you not telling me? Why are my legs strapped down?"

"Oh, forgive me." Mr. Heather and Adrian worked to unfasten the straps. Once his legs were free, he found he had only a bit of strength left, hardly enough to move them at all.

The conversation was draining him both emotionally and physically. Mr. Heather continued, "You were having convulsions because your fever was so high. We strapped you down so you would not fall off the cot."

"May I have more water?"

Everett spoke up and held up a kettle, "How about some broth?"

"Perfect." They all watched him drink until he felt waterlogged. The warmth it brought was short lived. Every eye was on him. The look in their eyes was full of pity, and suddenly his thirst was not so important, and the chill returned. "What are you not telling me?"

They all looked to Mr. Heather, who was running a hand through his blond hair. "I did what I could for the most important injury. If I had not focused on the chest wound and cauterized it, you would have bled to death. I hardly looked at the arm until I was sure you could breathe. Your respirations were so labored that I figured air had to be the most important issue. Unfortunately, by the time I undressed the wound on the arm, the infection had spread. I could see streaks running up and down the arm. It was swollen and finding leeches this time of year was nearly impossible. The few I had brought with me were not enough to help."

Colonel Fitzwilliam was usually very quick at figuring out what people were hiding. And Mr. Heather was still far too nervous. Something didn't make sense. The colonel tried to reach his hand out to try to comfort his friend, and when he did, he was shocked to see that his arm was a bundle of bandages that extended only to his elbow. He looked down at the place that should have been his lower arm and hand.

It was gone. It had been amputated.

He looked up at Mr. Heather and saw the deepest sorrow. The colonel could feel his friend's pain. Fitzwilliam may have lost an arm, but the doctor had clearly lost a great deal too in this battle. Colonel Fitzwilliam asked, "May I see the wound?"

Mr. Heather silently started to unwrap the arm. As each layer came off, the arm got shorter and shorter. He could tell it had been amputated above the elbow, but as the last layer came off, it was nothing more than a stump that extended about five inches below his underarm.

The colonel grimaced through the pain as he held it up and inspected it. It was a clean wound; the sutures were precise and even. There was no doubt they were surely painstakingly placed.

Colonel Fitzwilliam consciously controlled his reaction. He showed none of it.

When he couldn't find anything to say, Mr. Heather apologized. "I am so sorry. I did what I could, but there came a moment where the infection forced my hand. It was either take your arm or let it take your life. I took off as little as possible."

Mr. Heather looked at him with sorrow and a great deal of pity. That look was more disturbing than any news so far, and he had to admit he no longer could restrain his reaction.

He suddenly was reminded of what Charlotte said in the bookstore, and he repeated her words out loud. "As a friend, I will tell you this only once. I do not need your pity nor your sympathy."

# CHAPTER 18

The month of November had come and gone. It was nearly the third week of December, and the Gardiners and their daughter, Avelina, were due to arrive anytime.

Charlotte took the opportunity to take the General for a walk in the gardens. The air was chilly, but no snow had fallen yet. The brisk air seemed to calm her a great deal. Her son was now almost four months old. He had just learned to roll over. If he hadn't been so well fed and chubby, he likely would have discovered that trick a few weeks earlier.

Isaac brought her more joy and peace then she had ever known. Anytime someone called him the General, it brought to mind the colonel's sweet words and his kindnesses. He was a good man. She had received another letter for the General a month ago, which was so short that she nearly had it memorized.

> *"I am stationed at Queenston and have told General Isaac Brock all about the General back at home. He was pleased to hear your mother has given you the name Isaac, as he is understandably quite partial to it."*

Charlotte had to laugh at his effort to be humorous. He also tried to be encouraging and to relieve everyone's fears.

> *"You will not find more ready men. General Brock suspects that the Americans will make a push at any moment. You keep pushing your mother too, understood? That is an order."*

Then there was the mixed message that held a little of both. She never had any doubt that the letters to her son were most definitely intended for her.

> *"By now, enough time has passed that you can show your genuine handsome smile. Help her to weed out the unworthy, for I cannot stomach the thought of any other man smiling at your mother. If anyone attempts it, I am counting on you to let out a scream loud enough to be heard across the Atlantic. You have more control over the situation than you think. We must not let anyone break down that fortress we talked about. Until I return, remember that I am praying for you."*

And then he signed it. He was praying for her. The comfort this brought was nearly palpable.

After a few turns in the garden, Isaac started to protest at the chill in the air, and she headed back to the house. There was a familiar carriage in front. She could not place its owner until she got closer. It was Lord and Lady Matlock's livery. Why were they here? Did they have word of their son? Her fingers turned cold as she hurried inside. She went from room to room until she found Lord and Lady Matlock. They were handing Mr. Darcy a newspaper.

Charlotte did not hesitate to ask, "Have you heard from your son?"

Elizabeth and Georgiana both walked over to her and sat her down. The General sensed the fear in her voice and began to fuss a bit. Feeling the blood drain from her face, she was grateful when Georgiana took the babe from her arms.

"Yes," Elizabeth said gently. "The regiment's doctor wrote to Lord and Lady Matlock. I will let them explain."

"Lady Matlock? Is he well?" There was more than a little anxiety in her voice. Lady Matlock had taken time to get to know Charlotte at the house party, and although it was never spoken aloud, Charlotte was sure that Colonel Fitzwilliam's mother was aware of the feelings that had developed between them.

Did she just think "between *them*"? She was blissfully aware of the colonel's attachment, but . . . now was not the time to examine her admiration for a man who very well may be dead.

She looked toward his father. Lord Matlock was the kind of man who got to the point, and Charlotte appreciated that now.

"He was injured in the battle of Queenston Heights on October 13$^{th}$ while avenging the death of General Isaac Brock. There is even an article about what happened in the *London Times*. He is quite the war hero. Everyone in town is talking about him."

"But he is injured?"

"Yes. Mr. Heather, the doctor, wrote as soon as he had a good idea of how he fared. Richard was shot in the left arm and in the chest. He was in and out of conscious for a full three weeks due to the loss of blood, and the lung sustained serious injury, which appeared to be the most pressing concern until it became obvious that the arm had become infected."

"But he is awake now?"

"Yes, as far as we know. It takes a full month for letters to reach England, of course. So what we know is probably old news. But the doctor did not want to write until he had a firm prognosis. So, yes, as of last month, he was upright and walking short distances. The infection is gone, and the lung is making slow progress. He is still quite short of breath sometimes, but the doctor expects him to make a full recovery. In fact, he has already started to administer to the needs of his men."

Relief spilled in her heart, and she couldn't help but let her tears drop. "What will he do now?"

"He would like to return home," Lady Matlock told her, "but he never did like me mothering him. And now . . . now I fear I am more likely than ever to over-mother him. I just cannot imagine my baby with only one . . ."

Charlotte looked around the room, and the looks on their faces said more than they meant to. "What do you mean? With only one what?"

Mr. Darcy stood and walked over to Charlotte and handed her the newspaper. On the lower right of the front page was the title, "Victory over Queenston Heights due to local London hero!"

She thanked him, took the paper and began to read.

## *VICTORY OVER QUEENSTON HEIGHTS DUE TO LOCAL LONDON HERO!*

*Early on the morning of October 13, the Americans, still bitter over the loss of Detroit, crossed the Niagara River only to find the British troops ready and waiting. The battle dealt great losses on both sides, but the Americans eventually retreated and the battle was declared a victory for the British army, thanks to the heroic efforts of Colonel Richard Fitzwilliam, second son of Lord Matlock, the earl of Matlock.*

*According to reports, Colonel Fitzwilliam overpowered the very American soldier who had fired the lethal shot at General Brock. (More on General Brock's role of the battle can be found in the article above.)*

*The colonel reportedly struck the American with a pistol that failed to fire, throwing it and hitting the man squarely on the head, then killed the assassin with a single blade to the chest. With his sword thus occupied, he was threatened by three armed Americans. No gentleman wishes those odds, and seizing the unique opportunity, the colonel threw his knife from his boot and took out one adversary. With no small effort, he retrieved his sword and continued fighting the two remaining soldiers until help arrived.*

*Unfortunately our hero did not escape unharmed. He suffered a shot to the left arm as well as one to the upper left chest. It is reported that the colonel required two surgeries, the latter of which left him with an amputated arm. He is recovering and is reportedly in good spirits. As soon as he can safely make the voyage, he will be returning to a hero's welcome. For without his quick mind and unwavering courage, the battle of Queenston Heights could not have been declared a victory. The rest of his regiment suffered relatively minor casualties.*

*Rumors are that he is devastated by the death of his hero, General Brock. To lose both a friend and an arm could be devastating to any man, but I am sure that those of you who know Colonel Fitzwilliam can attest that he will be back on his feet in no time! As if his charming personality and the chance at a title as a second son was not enough enticement for the young ladies, now he carries the status of hero!*

*How will we mere mortals compete? Congratulations, Colonel Richard Fitzwilliam! If we but had a hundred more of you, England would conquer the world.*

Charlotte felt every word as if it was punctuated with a blow to her spirit. He had been shot *twice*. He had lost his hero. She felt queasy and was glad she was sitting down. Reading about the details of battle made the risk he took seem all too real. She had tried not to think about how dangerous soldiering was, but there it was as plain as could be. He had risked his life and limb for God and country. She handed the newspaper back to Darcy with shaking hands and took a deep breath.

She remembered a conversation from long ago, at the Huntsford parsonage, before Elizabeth and Mr. Collins took ill. She and the colonel were standing in front of the fireplace discussing random topics. The wine had been plentiful, and Colonel Fitzwilliam had been buoyant and lively. Mr. Collins had been preoccupied with Lady Catherine, and Darcy had garnered Elizabeth's attention.

*Colonel Fitzwilliam stood by the fire and poked the embers. "I might never marry, in fact! For unless great harm were to come to my eldest brother, I have no title or estate to entice a lady. My father has bequeathed me a country home, which he is willing to hand over as soon as I find a wife, but I see no need to rush to the altar. If there comes a time when my heart is ensnared by a* woman, it will be because she is intelligent, independent, and has successfully outsmarted me! Nothing less could trap my heart!"

"But do you not want a family, Colonel?" Charlotte had asked.

"Oh, to be sure. I am a bit of a softy for little children. But do not tell the regiment my weakness! No, this soldier will probably never marry, for not only do I need to find an intelligent, independent woman who can outsmart me, but she must bring with her enough wealth to support me! How can a man live with himself if he brings nothing to the marriage?"

"But you earn a decent living in the Royal Army, sir."

"That I do, but I only live like a gentleman off the generosity of my cousin, Darcy. No man can be proud of himself when he cannot live off his own merit. So, I am likely to remain a bachelor soldier forever, or at least until I win enough prize money to be independent myself. And with my expensive tastes, it would have to be a very large prize indeed."

Charlotte then replied, "Well, when you do win that prize money, and you will, be prepared to have every debutant chasing you to the altar. There is nothing better than a rich war hero to start the ladies swooning. With that added to your current status of charming gentleman, you will have to fight the ladies off with a stick. You will be the catch of the season."

He chuckled deeply. "I really am quite particular with my admiration," he confessed. "Not just anyone could earn my regard. There are plenty of ladies out there interested in a title or riches, and perhaps, someday, if I am very lucky I may have both of those things. But there are only a handful that would love me for who I truly am."

"Well then, Colonel, I hope for your sake, and for the sake of your future happiness, that you keep your eyes open. For you never know where or when someone might catch your fancy."

The colonel smiled. "I shall take your advice, Mrs. Collins. I truly am not opposed to marriage; it is simply that I wish to bring something to the altar besides a possible title and my family's connections. But if I win prize money, I shall be free to marry any woman that I set my cap on."

She laughed, "If the woman will have you."

"Of course."

Charlotte couldn't help but smile at this memory. It calmed her heart. She knew deep down that the admiration he felt for her was genuine and could be trusted. He had admitted that not just any woman could catch his eye; only an intelligent, independent woman who could outsmart him could. That woman might very well be herself!

She looked around the room after recalling this memory and saw perplexed looks on Darcy and Elizabeth's faces. She realized that she was smiling far too much for the current circumstance and tried to explain. "I am glad he will be returning to England in reasonably good health. Where will he recuperate?"

"Pemberley," Mr. Darcy insisted, "if that is acceptable to you, Aunt. I know London has the best doctors and surgeons, but I think Richard will soon grow tired of a hero's welcome. And it might be a good idea to help him adjust to having one arm without society watching his every move."

"I admit that was my design in coming here, Fitzwilliam," Lady Matlock confessed. "I have taken the liberty of putting an advertisement in the *London Times* for a doctor to come here to Derbyshire to help with his recovery. I shall keep you informed. I am sure we will have quite a bit of time to find the right match."

Charlotte blushed at the thought of him returning to Pemberley but tried to keep a stoic composure. "I am relieved that he is in good spirits and ministering to his men's needs," she said. "That says a great deal. He may not need a doctor by the time he sails. Surely they would not put him on board a ship when he is not ready."

"You are probably right," Darcy agreed.

Lord Matlock once again spoke the harsh truth. "Perhaps. But it would be unwise to expect him to be in full health when he returns. His recovery will be harder on him than he thinks. Society loves a war hero during war, but once the war is over, he will simply be a one-armed man whom many in society will shun. And he will still need to find a way to earn his living. The army is out of the question now."

"Will," Elizabeth whispered, "perhaps now is the time to make good on your promise to Richard. Even though it was made in jest."

Charlotte saw the confusion on everyone's faces, but it was Georgiana who spoke first. "What promise? Did you make a promise to Richard?"

Mr. Darcy looked at Elizabeth and smiled. "Back in April, during those two weeks after I returned from Rosings, Richard was playing mind games with me," he explained. "He was trying to get me to look for Elizabeth in London, but I was acting a little high in the instep. I was in high dudgeon and had little patience for any and all efforts to change my mood. My injured pride was keeping me quite blind. I was sure that Elizabeth loathed me, wanted nothing to do with me, and I would not listen to him in the slightest. He finally bet me my annual income that the boot was on the other leg."

Georgiana sucked in a breath, and her hand flew to her mouth. It was the same reaction that Charlotte had inside. *Who needed prize money when he had ten thousand pounds?* Any man could live off that, and, with his father's country estate bequeathed to him, Colonel Fitzwilliam could be quite happily situated.

Georgiana smiled mischievously. "Well, it seems a simple question, William. Are you a man of your word or are you not? Will you give him the money?"

Darcy took his wife's hand and kissed it tenderly. "Of course I will. I owe him so much more than that."

# CHAPTER 19

Colonel Fitzwilliam looked out at the cold, turbulent, late-winter ocean that spoke so much of what his heart was feeling. The wild wind pierced his soul. Captain Marcus had finally stopped asking him to step away from the edge. They had argued that subject one too many times. Even as a one-armed man, the colonel was perfectly capable of holding on as the waves threw their weight against the ship.

It had been four months since the battle at Queenston Heights. He had been basically unconscious for nearly three weeks, and when he awoke, he had found himself weak and, quite literally, only half the man he had been before. It took several weeks to simply rehydrate himself. Soon he had been able to tolerate short excursions away from the infirmary. Luckily, Mr. Heather knew him well enough to understand that being around his men would do him more good than resting on a cot under constant watch.

But he was watched, nonetheless, by Mr. Heather and by Mr. Lisscord and by his men. They had watched from behind as if he didn't notice. They watched him carefully as they tried to make him talk about how he felt about the loss of his arm or the death of General Brock. But he gave no indication of the storms that were raging inside. He knew how to behave. He jested about how at least he could still stare a man down at dawn. But he knew his battlefield days were over. Much of his life was over.

Which was why he was sailing back home. He felt the anxiety building in his stomach as he watched the shore grow ever closer. Even if he had fooled some of his regiment, he didn't know if he would be able to fool Darcy. His cousin had written instructions to send word when he arrived in Liverpool so he could come meet him and bring him back to Pemberley. The sounds of happy passengers bustling around him—all anxious to end their month-long voyage and return to normal life—filled him with dread. His arm began to ache.

He waited as the boat docked, and he patiently let those with young children walk past him to depart first. One young boy, Paul, had become a good little friend. The colonel waved goodbye as he passed by with his mother.

An inquisitive eleven-year-old from Manchester, Paul hadn't held back his curious gaze in any way. For three straight days, the colonel had attempted to stare him down, but finally the lad came up and offered to shake hands. He introduced himself as Paul S. Muff. He never once asked about his arm. Instead, he wanted to know who he was and where he was going.

The boy's innocent questions shocked the colonel. It would have been less disturbing if Paul had just asked about the arm.

Who was he? That was a hard question to answer. He was certainly no longer a colonel in the army. He knew many men kept their military titles when they retired, but he wasn't sure he wanted to do that. Although *Mr. Fitzwilliam* definitely had an odd sound to it. He had a second cousin named Mr. Fitzwilliam who was arrogant and conceited. No, *Mr. Fitzwilliam* wouldn't do.

Technically he could call himself The Honorable Richard Fitzwilliam. He was the second son of an earl after all. But that didn't quite suit him either. And it still didn't answer the question.

Where was he going? In the short term, he would go to Derbyshire. But where to after that? During three months of recuperation and another month trapped on this ship, he had pondered his future a great deal. But the only conclusion he had reached was that he had very little future to hope for. There was no hope for Fitzwilliam, colonel or not.

He had no money, no way to sustain himself, and no livelihood. His career in the army had defined him. *I was a colonel. I was Colonel Fitzwilliam. But now who am I? And where am I going?* Paul's questions panged loudly in his heart.

The sorrow was building as he saw that it was his time to depart the ship. He slung his satchel over his head and pushed the cold fingers of his right hand into his greatcoat pocket. As he reached the dock, he placed his feet on solid ground for the first time in a month. The spring flowers had not yet started to bloom at the inn across the street. It was only the middle of February after all. Even his left arm felt cool, and that was rare. Usually it burned and tingled. At the moment, it was a mixture of fire and ice, mirroring the exact torment of his heart.

He started to walk down the street, taking in all that was going on around him. Several post-chaises and carriages were lined up with families embracing loved ones. There was a man sweeping off the porch of a butcher's shop and, with the familiar pang of dejection, he realized that was one more thing he could not do.

Yet. The pain in his stump lessened each day. And each night, he secretly pushed himself to improve. His current task was learning to create sufficient counter pressure in his stump to hold something against his side. He had discovered papers could be shuffled easily enough if they were on a desk in front of him. Writing was not as difficult as he had thought it would be. Which reminded him he needed to send off a letter to Darcy letting him know that he had arrived.

"Colonel Fitzwilliam!"

The sound of his name surprised him since he had not let anyone know when he would be arriving. He turned around and saw Benjamin Pastel taking off his hat and reaching out his hand.

"Mr. Pastel, how are you? Is it Friday?"

"Indeed it is. The *Winter's Night*'s cargo just finished being loaded. Come look at the sister ship to the *Eastern Challenge* you saw last autumn. She is a very fine ship." They shook hands.

"I would be happy to," Fitzwilliam replied. It was odd that the man hadn't noticed the absent arm yet.

But the young solicitor seemed genuinely happy to spend the next few minutes of his time showing the colonel around the ship. They chatted for some time about how he had just returned from war.

Still Mr. Pastel did not ask a single question about his arm. For a moment, Colonel Fitzwilliam forgot about it too as he was shown the ship's captain's quarters and the galley, both of which were so spotless that he could have eaten off the floor. Even the cutlery sparkled.

Remembering the unkempt *Eastern Challenge* he had seen five months ago, Fitzwilliam was surprised. "Pastel, this ship is remarkably well kept. You may call her a sister ship if you like, but I think it is clear she far surpasses the *Eastern Challenge*."

"Not anymore, sir. The *Eastern Challenge* glistens and gleams like this from stem to stern these days. It is all thanks to her new captain, Captain Conrad Jersey. In fact, it was your cousin, Mr. Darcy, who recommended him. The captain is right over there if you want to say hello."

"I would indeed. And you said Mr. Darcy recommended him?"

Mr. Pastel called out to an older man on the dock, and the captain walked in their direction. "Colonel Fitzwilliam, this is Captain Conrad Jersey. He has been commanding the *Eastern Challenge* since you left last fall."

"How do you do?" Fitzwilliam asked.

"I am well, thank you," Captain Jersey replied. "Mr. Darcy will be happy to hear you are well, Colonel. You look a little weather beaten about the face but no worse for wear. You could pass as one of my shipmen now. You must have been on deck a great deal."

*Does no one notice the absent arm?*

"Indeed I was. It was very calming to be outside of my cabin." He thought he would try to investigate how Captain Jersey knew Darcy. "I understand you know my cousin."

"Yes, I do. Miss Anne de Bourgh is beyond words."

Colonel Fitzwilliam raised his eyebrows at him and clarified, "I was referring to Darcy. Am I under the impression that you also know Anne?"

Captain Jersey smiled broadly. "Yes. In fact, I suppose you could say I know her quite well, as she is my intended. We are to be married the Thursday before Eastertide. As soon as I finish these last few runs from Liverpool to London, you and I will be cousins!"

The first genuine smile came to Colonel Fitzwilliam's face in many months. "I am so pleased to hear it! It seems a great deal can happen when a man goes to war."

"Indeed. Did you just make port?" Captain Jersey asked. "Where are you staying?"

"I do not know. Finding an inn is my first task. The second is to write to Darcy to let him know I have arrived."

Mr. Pastel added, "And I imagine that after a month at sea, your third task is to get some civilized food."

The colonel chuckled and said, "I admit I am ready for real food, perhaps something that once grazed on grass."

Mr. Pastel reached out his hand and shook it one more time and declared, "Then it is settled—we will dine at my house. It is Friday, and my cook always makes a leg of lamb on Fridays after I return from the docks."

"And then you shall stay at my house until Darcy arrives," Jersey concluded.

Colonel Fitzwilliam hesitated and finally said, "I imagine that will be much nicer than mutton at an inn. My thanks to you both."

*****

Colonel Fitzwilliam was delighted with the creamed turnip soup placed before him. It was the best food he had had in over five months. "Mr. Pastel, I must say that this is a wonderful treat! Battlefield cooks never attempt to impress, only to satisfy hunger. I admit I thought I was anticipating the leg of lamb, but I think I might have to take a second helping of the soup."

The servant stepped in and started to reach for the ladle, but Mr. Pastel directed him elsewhere. "Joseph, please check when the lamb will be ready. In fact, just inform them to bring it now." The servant left immediately.

Colonel Fitzwilliam was grateful for the tactful way Mr. Pastel had kept the servant from dishing the soup. For some reason, it was easier to forget his ache when people did not hover. Soup he could do. He was hoping the lamb would be quite tender, because he had not yet figured out how to cut meat. He spooned the soup into his bowl. There was not a drop outside of the bowl. He reminded himself to celebrate the little successes.

They ate in silence for a few minutes, and then Colonel Fitzwilliam could smell the lamb as it approached the table. It made him forget everything he had been worried about. He unconsciously pushed the bowl away from him. A very healthy piece of lamb was placed on a plate in front of him. Its pepper and herbs were still sizzling in the juices.

Now was the moment of truth. He picked up his fork and, although not necessarily proper, used the side of it to slice a portion. The meat protested for a moment but gave way under the strain, forcing the fork to clink loudly against the plate. *Too much force.*

He placed the delicious bite into his mouth and tried again with a little less muscle. The fork did a fine job of cutting it. This brought a small smile to his face. He ate the bite he had cut, savoring it like it was the first pheasant that he downed with his rifle when he was twelve.

Feeling proud of himself, he asked Captain Jersey, "So, how did you meet Anne?"

"At a house party in October at Pemberley. I was asked to befriend her by Darcy, but as soon as we were introduced, I saw her for the jewel that she is. I admit it was no chore to be in her company for the duration of the party. I have only been able to spend a week or two at Rosings, but she has journeyed to her London home several times when I put into port."

"And how has my aunt taken the news of the engagement? I imagine she has made her opinions known."

Both Mr. Pastel and Captain Jersey laughed. Mr. Pastel grinned and replied, "Yes, she has. But from what I saw, she was quite pleased with Jersey's attentions."

"You met Lady Catherine? When?"

"In October, at the Pemberley house party with Captain Jersey. You may not be aware, but I am Mrs. Collins's late husband's solicitor. I am managing his assets and fulfilling his wishes."

Of course the colonel knew this, but before he could remember to feign surprise at Pastel's disclosure, he was overwhelmed with memories of *her*. The mere mention of her name brought into his mind her beautiful face, her high cheekbones, and her deep chestnut-brown locks that never had a stray hair out of place. And that smile. He felt his heart lurch slightly. She was most the courageous, smart, and beautiful person he had ever met. His heart picked up speed, and he tried to distract himself by drinking his wine, but his heart rate increased with such fervor that he could feel it in his ears.

He had tried so hard *not* to think about her. He had even gone as far as telling Mr. Heather to not bring her name up anymore.

The wine tasted as bitter as the thoughts in his head. He could never offer for her now. Not when he didn't have a way to support her.

Not when he didn't know who he was. Not when he didn't know where he was going.

But no matter how hard he tried not to *think* about her, it did not stop his heart from loving her, and he knew it never would.

$$*****$$

Colonel Fitzwilliam woke with a start. He smelled smoke. He jumped out of bed and pulled on his breeches before he realized he wasn't at Queenston. He had been dreaming of the battle again. All he could remember was that this time, for some reason, there had been a baby playing at his feet while he fought the Americans—a chubby baby topped with brown curls that covered his ears. The baby looked up at him and smiled. He knew that smile. It was her smile.

It had been three days since the ship had docked. Captain Jersey had insisted Fitzwilliam stay until Darcy arrived from Derbyshire, however the captain had set sail yesterday. It was clear that he was quite alone at the moment.

He was mostly dressed anyway, so he singlehandedly buttoned his breeches. It was a skill that took a great deal of effort and time and guidance from his military valet until he mastered it.

Everything took effort, and all he had was time.

He let his mind wander, but he soon regretted it. The General would be six months old now. The perfect age to smile at his environment and notice people.

Too young to pity Fitzwilliam for having only one arm, but probably too large to be cradled with just one hand. The last thought did not bother him any in the slightest. If Fitzwilliam had been able to stand at the bow of a tossing ship crossing the Atlantic, he knew he could figure out a way to safely hold an infant. The only difficulty would be in readjusting if the child squirmed.

It was a game that he seemed to play with himself. He would ask himself, what could he do with one arm? What could he attempt and eventually master? He had just eaten lamb a few nights ago with one hand. He had learned to button his breeches with one hand.

He had learned that there were only certain requirements in doing certain things. For example, writing was no chore—at first, he had been baffled by sliding papers. Now he simply rolled up his shirtsleeve and held the paper in place with his well-healed stump.

He learned that reading was best done by placing the book on a desk or laying it across his legs, with his feet propped up on an ottoman, thereby leaving his hand free to turn the page.

He had learned that in order to get his coat on, he needed to slide the stump in first and then quickly reach behind him with the good arm to catch the other side.

There were times he really rather liked the challenges in front of him every day.

And then there were days like today.

\*\*\*\*\*

Darcy knocked a third time on the door of Captain Jersey's home, but no one answered. He decided to try Mr. Pastel's office instead since Colonel Fitzwilliam had said in his letter that they had met up the night he arrived. Darcy had come to Liverpool a few times to meet with Mr. Pastel and found he really did like the man. It was difficult *not* to like him. In his office, he adamantly maintained his businesslike persona, but when you took tea with him at the Chipped Kettle he warped into a pleasant man with stimulating conversation. He clearly took his job very seriously, but Darcy could not fault him for that.

As Darcy walked down to Dale Street, he pondered Richard's note. It had been very short, only informing him that he was staying at Captain Jersey's home and not to hurry. But Darcy did hurry. When Charlotte had seen the express come, her eyes had lit up and Georgiana had giggled. He was very glad that Richard would be recovering with friends and family.

By now the man at the front desk knew him. "Good morning, Mr. Darcy. I will show you in."

He followed after him and found Mr. Pastel sitting back, relaxed, and talking to a long-haired gentleman whom Darcy did not recognize immediately until he heard his deep chuckle.

Mr. Pastel stood and said, "Mr. Darcy! Come in!"

Colonel Fitzwilliam stood, and for the briefest of moments, it seemed that he felt a stranger.

Darcy would have none of that. The emotion that flooded him . . . there were no words to describe the relief at seeing Richard standing in front of him. He took three long strides over to him and embraced his closest friend and cousin. They pounded each other on the back and both stepped back afterwards and realized that they had an audience for their long-awaited welcome home. They would have to catch up when Mr. Pastel was not watching.

"The colonel was just telling me all of Miss Darcy's secrets." Mr. Pastel confessed. "I had no idea that she had a white rabbit named Red."

"Yes," Colonel Fitzwilliam laughed, "and she saved it from being served up as stew several times. Mrs. Reynolds almost wrung its neck when it started chewing on the curtains. But Darcy insisted Georgiana be allowed to keep it. When Georgiana found it, it had almost been killed by some animal, so it was red all over. Hence the name. She protected that thing for over a year. Who would ever think to train a wild rabbit to be a pet? Only Georgiana could love that fiercely."

Mr. Pastel smiled warmly and said, "I remember her protective nature well. I fear I was the target of it a few times."

Colonel Fitzwilliam chuckled and said, "Let me guess, she defended Mrs. Collins, Mr. Darcy, and, from the expectant look in your eyes there must be one more . . . Ah ha! Mrs. Darcy!"

"And yourself, sir."

Confused, Colonel Fitzwilliam said, "Me? What reason did she have to defend me?"

"It seemed there was a miscommunication. Miss Darcy was under the impression that you held strong feelings for Mrs. Collins."

Darcy noted that Colonel Fitzwilliam stiffened slightly. He didn't fail to notice that Mr. Pastel was watching Colonel Fitzwilliam very closely. Darcy wished he could step in. But as usual, Colonel Fitzwilliam did a marvelous job of talking himself out of trouble.

"There was no miscommunication. I did admire Mrs. Collins. But she never gave me so much as a flirtatious smile in return for all my efforts to garner her attention. She is the most loyal lady I know. The perfect mixture of respect, intelligence, and independence. And a woman like that is far too smart to fall for a poor solider. And, now I am not even that!"

"I have seen Mrs. Collins's spirit for myself," Pastel replied. "Miss Darcy was correct then? You admire Mrs. Collins?"

With finality, leaving no doubt that the conversation about Charlotte was over, Colonel Fitzwilliam retorted, "I used to."

Mr. Darcy's heart dropped at the words. "Cousin," he said, "we have an appointment we need to keep. We must be on our way."

Farewells were spoken, and Mr. Pastel shook their hands. "Will I be seeing you two again at Miss Anne de Bourgh's wedding?" Pastel inquired. "I do not think I can pass up the opportunity to support my dear friend and his betrothed. And I have been in Liverpool far too long."

Colonel Fitzwilliam looked to Darcy to answer for them. "Yes, it is customary for the colonel and me to spend Easter with our aunt Catherine," Darcy replied. "And, Mrs. Collins has requested the chance to see her husband's gravesite as well. We shall see you there."

Mr. Pastel seemed pleased by the news that Charlotte wanted to see the gravesite, and Darcy felt some small relief regarding the solicitor's investigation into Charlotte's mourning procedures.

But what Colonel Fitzwilliam had said disturbed him greatly.

As they left the office Mr. Darcy advised, "You need a haircut, Fitzwilliam. And it looks like you have been sleeping in the same uniform for five months. Let us stop in at the tailor's before we leave. I would offer you some of the clothes I brought with me, but you seem to be thinner. Are you not sleeping well again?"

"I am fine. I am thinner because I cannot do much of anything anymore. I lost my arm, remember?" There was a distinct bitter tone to his words.

They walked along the streets until they came across Mr. Tabbott's tailor shop and Darcy motioned for him to go in. Colonel Fitzwilliam took a few steps inside and then froze. "Darcy, I cannot do this," he whispered. "I cannot bear to have someone measure and inspect my arm."

Darcy took a deep breath. He hadn't been sure what to expect from his cousin, but there was obviously more to his injury than an amputated arm. He took Colonel Fitzwilliam's right arm and ushered him over to a display of waistcoats. The tailor came towards them, but Darcy dismissed him.

"I am sure the tailor can accommodate—" Darcy whispered.

"No, Darcy. Just let me be. You do not understand—"

"It will be all right, Richard—"

"No, it is not all right!" Fitzwilliam yelled back at him. "It will never be all right! And I will not stand here listening to you pretend that nothing has changed. My whole life, Darcy! Everything I have ever worked towards, is gone!" Fitzwilliam slammed the tailor's door on his way out.

The tailor and two customers looked on in amazement, too stunned to move.

Darcy followed after his cousin into the street, grabbing hold of his coat. "Richard Allen Fitzwilliam, do you think you are the only man who has had their pride injured? Do you think you are the only one that has ever felt the absence of hope? Men have had limbs injured and hearts broken since Adam and Eve!"

Fitzwilliam roughly shook off Darcy's grasp and shoved him with his one good hand. "Go hang yourself, Darcy," Fitzwilliam cursed. "I said leave me be!"

The two cousins glared at one another, breathing heavily. Darcy took a deep breath, resisting the urge to shove his cousin back. "Many things happen to us that we cannot control, Fitzwilliam, but our reactions to those circumstances are entirely within our control. Our attitude is the one thing that no one else can dictate. You may look in the mirror and see half a man, and you can let that define who you are. Or you can start the day looking at what options are in front of you. You can ask yourself 'why me' or you can thank God that it was you and not one of your men."

Fitzwilliam lowered his gaze, and in it the angry fire dissolved too. Darcy was not sure what to expect next. He watched his cousin have an internal struggle between an instinct to yell back and become defensive, or humbling himself and facing the hard truth. Darcy did not know which would win.

His shoulders sagged. "Darcy, I am trying. But you have no idea what this feels like. You have no idea what it feels like to be only half a man. To wake up in an infirmary and feel pain day in and day out with no relief."

Darcy took a few steps toward his cousin. "You are right. I do not. But I am trying to understand." He put his arm on Fitzwilliam's shoulder. "Trust me, Richard. It will be all right."

His cousin scoffed. "I think we must agree to disagree on that point, Cousin." Fitzwilliam sighed, "But I am sorry I was intemperate." The two men sat down on a nearby bench and looked out at the harbor. "What am I going to do? I must leave the army. I am only two-and-thirty, and I feel like my life is over already."

Darcy considered the question. "I do not know," he admitted. "But you will find something. You have a special skillset that few have. You see the world's inner beauty. You are able to lighten the room with your jokes and your ready smile, and you can ease the most troubled spirit. You have never worried before about how you look to others. Do not let that be a new precedent."

Richard scoffed again. "I suppose at least I can console myself in the fact that I will be the center of attention in every room now."

"Yes, that is true. And if you look for prejudice against you in every room, you will surely find it. But I counsel you to learn from my mistake. My pride nearly lost me the chance to marry Elizabeth. Do not let yours ruin a single ounce of your future happiness, no matter what road you take or who you end up taking it with." He said the next words distinctly as if each word was a sentence of its own. "Let. Go. Of. The. Pride."

Colonel Fitzwilliam looked over at his cousin. "Very well. If I must be fitted for new clothes, perhaps we can negotiate a discount at the tailor's. As you said yourself, I am only half the man I used to be."

"That is a bag of moonshine and you know it."

The corner of Colonel Fitzwilliam's mouth went up slightly and he said, "Since when does the master of Pemberley speak cant?"

"I will speak in Greek if it is the only way to get through that thick skull of yours," Darcy retorted. "Do you remember that wrestling brawl we had in my room after Elizabeth first woke up after her convulsion and said I had compromised her? Do you remember what you said to me?"

"I called you a coward."

"Yes, more precisely, you called me a cowardly, proud man. And I was. Do not make me turn it back on you. Do I make myself clear?"

A genuine smile came to Colonel Fitzwilliam's face ever so slowly. "Perfectly. Now, regarding the tailor's bill. Even at a significant discount, I am afraid—"

"It is on me. I owe you a few pounds anyway."

"Whatever do you mean?"

"We will talk about it later, maybe when you and your injured pride come down from that high horse of yours. I admit I am looking forward to a good old-fashioned row with my cousin."

Colonel Fitzwilliam raised his amputated left arm and laughed openly saying, "For once you might have the upper hand!"

As soon as he heard his laugh, Darcy was put at ease.

"That is more like it." They returned to the tailor's and spent the next few hours measuring Fitzwilliam for a new wardrobe fit for a war hero. The tailor, who turned out to be quite experienced in fitting soldier amputees, recommended that the sleeve fall exactly at the end of the amputation. That way the stump could be functional, but not in the way. The shopkeeper was professional and acted as if it was no different than adjusting the length of a tailcoat.

As each hour passed, with Colonel Fitzwilliam trying on and being measured for four new coats as well as shirtsleeves, Darcy saw the old Colonel Fitzwilliam slowly emerge. Simply taking off the old dirty uniform brought something to life in him that must have been a heavy burden to carry.

Darcy knew Richard was right. He didn't know how it felt to lose an arm, but he did know what it felt like to have hope ripped from him, and he knew what it felt like to believe that you would never win the heart and hand of the one you love. Elizabeth's rejection had taught him that. Darcy said a prayer of gratitude for having that heartache, a pain he never ever wanted to feel again, because now it gave him a better understanding of Fitzwilliam's pain. Darcy was determined to help Richard as the colonel had once helped him.

And when Darcy paid him the ten thousand pounds on his wedding day and saw the utter bliss in his eyes as he kissed Charlotte, then, and only then, would his debt truly be paid.

# CHAPTER 20

Charlotte felt an urge to pace, but she restrained herself. Mr. Darcy had been gone over a week, and there was still no word on when they would return. "Elizabeth, I think I will check on the General. He has been sleeping for quite some time. If the men return, please send someone for me."

"Of course."

Charlotte paused. "Do you miss him?"

"Terribly," Elizabeth admitted. "This is the longest separation we have ever had. His usual trips to Liverpool are normally less than five days, there and back. I wonder what has taken so long."

For a moment, Charlotte wondered what that would be like, to miss someone as well as to be missed by them. Then she turned her thoughts back to the present. "Yes, I think I can imagine how that would feel. Well, if you need me, I will be in the nursery. I am sure the General will be hungry soon."

Charlotte stood and walked upstairs to the nursery, and sure enough Sally was changing him preparing to be fed. "You know you do not have to change him, Sally. I am perfectly capable."

"Aye, but I was ready and willin' myself. Ain't nobody gonna' say that Miss Sally don't love this little boy! Here you go, Mrs. Collins, he is all ready and wantin' his mum." She handed the General to his mother and said, "I best be checkin' on the crib linens I was havin' laundered and pressed."

Charlotte thanked her again and gave her son several kisses on his cheeks. His eyes were always so bright after sleeping. They were getting darker in color with each passing month. She tried to play with him and talk with him for a little while, but he was having none of it. He was hungry and new exactly what to do.

She let her mind drift to the colonel and what he must be feeling. He was a confident man, but even a confident man could lose his footing after sustaining such injuries. She thought about his broad shoulders and how they would look after he had been so ill. Would he still carry himself erect and would his smile be as welcoming, or would his spirit be crushed? Such thoughts were not new; she had pondered them many times. She found the best time to think was when she fed her son. It was a calming moment where worries seemed to magically find answers and fears dissolved away.

Today she let her mind drift to that morning when she had overheard him while he held her day-old nameless son. She smiled at his commanding tones as he directed her son in his heartfelt speech. *Desertion. Yes. I know that is a big word for a little man like you. It means having a change of heart, but let me assure you that will not happen to me; I am not leaving for good. I will be back.*

Isaac was done feeding, and so she put her dress back together and played with him. It was a favorite time to play with her son. One thing she had learned during her brief marriage was that a man, no matter his age, was happier with a full stomach.

Suddenly she had a sense that someone was watching her and knew it was the colonel. She continued to play for a few minutes even though she could now smell his scent—it was masculine, with a touch of cloves to it. She took a few breaths through her nose and let it calm her.

*He is home.*

He had come to see her and her son. The peace this brought made her breath catch in her throat. She had missed him deeply. After six months without him, her heart ached to see him again.

She slowly turned around and saw Colonel Fitzwilliam standing just outside the nursery door, hiding the left side of his body outside the door. He was looking at her with gray-blue eyes, eyes that hinted at a novel's worth of conversation ready to erupt. He said nothing but just looked at her as she approached.

Charlotte smiled at him, walked over to the colonel, and said to her son, "General, you remember your colonel. He has returned like he said he would." Then Charlotte looked at Colonel

Fitzwilliam and murmured, "He is a man of his word. Colonel, would you like to hold General Isaac Byron Collins?"

The colonel seemed to hesitate momentarily but then he reached his right arm out. Charlotte placed her son in his arm and watched him look down at him with admiration. Isaac looked up at him.

He spoke to her son in a silly playful voice, "Well, General, it looks like you have kept things calm on the home front. Any casualties I need to be aware of?" Isaac giggled and reached for his face and pulled at it. Colonel Fitzwilliam smiled widely and reached out with his left arm, which he had obviously been hiding behind the doorframe, and tapped the General's nose with the end of his stump. Almost immediately, he returned his left arm to his side. Then he took a noticeably deeper breath.

Charlotte said, "Colonel, the General enjoys playing blocks on the floor. He is able to sit up now. Why do you not come in and play with him?"

"Thank you. But I must decline."

She couldn't believe how disappointed she was. "May I ask why?"

Colonel Fitzwilliam stepped forward and said, "Because I want to play with the wooden horses and soldiers instead. I never did like to play with blocks. More of a combat man myself."

A broad smile appeared on his chiseled face, and Charlotte let a giggle escape. *He is even more handsome than I remembered!* Her heart seemed to pick up the pace, but then he broke their gaze, allowing her to take in a deep breath and try to control the color that was rising in her face.

Colonel Fitzwilliam was already adjusting her son in his arms, ready to kneel down with him. She watched him masterfully and very gracefully use his left arm to gently place him on the floor. "Well then," Charlotte stammered, "do not let me disturb your action time."

"Do not leave. Please. I have not been around too many people lately. It would help me a great deal if you stayed."

Charlotte started to blush again. "I am your humble servant," she replied.

Colonel Fitzwilliam laughed. "Plagiarism is not allowed in the nursery, dear Mrs. Collins," he teased her. "We must each use our own imagination. I hope you have been teaching Isaac to outwit his playmates. It is a very useful skill. And I can think of no greater teacher."

"We usually do not call him Isaac. I am afraid that he is more familiar with being called the General, thanks to you."

Colonel Fitzwilliam combed his fingers through her son's curls and said, "A mighty fine name for such a handsome boy. He has grown up fast. Has he said anything yet?"

"Not anything discernable. He makes a great deal of noise and sounds, but it is still early."

Colonel Fitzwilliam had set down the baby with relative ease and placed the toys in front of him. Charlotte knelt down across from them.

He picked up a drummer and placed it in front of Isaac. "Drummer," he instructed. "This is a drummer. Can you say *drummer*? This man is very important. He is the key to communicating with the entire regiment. He stays back, usually on a hill, and drums messages—secret codes—to the troops so that they know where the enemy is. Even though he may never fire a shot in battle, he saves more lives than anyone else because he is able to get people with two different perspectives to be able to unify their forces. I still hear drummers when I go to sleep sometimes."

Isaac put the drummer soldier in his mouth. Colonel Fitzwilliam chuckled. "No, no, General, the drummer is too valuable. Here, eat a lowly infantryman instead."

There was a bit of silence for a while. Charlotte and Colonel Fitzwilliam took turns stealing glances at each other until Charlotte said, "You look well. But are you well, Colonel Fitzwilliam?"

*****

Colonel Fitzwilliam thought the nursery seemed to shrink in size. The noises made by Isaac seemed to fade away.

*Am I well?*

Colonel Fitzwilliam kept his gaze averted. "I will be," he declared. "There is a great deal of uncertainty to my future. I have retired from the army, you know. I am not even sure if I should continue calling myself 'colonel'."

"Even if you do resign the title, you will always be Colonel Fitzwilliam to me."

He looked up and saw her kind eyes. Her hair seemed to be a little more relaxed than usual. She even had a few ringlets on the side of her face. Had she taken extra care because he would be coming home? "Then you have just settled my fate. I shall not resign the title. I admit I did not wish to change it."

Charlotte reached out and touched his left shoulder. He flinched at the touch. "Oh, I am sorry, did I hurt you?" she asked.

"No, forgive me. Few people touch that arm. I simply was unprepared for it."

Her next words shocked him. "May I see it?"

*She wants to see it?* His deformity? The scars were still pink. His heart battled his fear and his pride fiercely. Darcy's words reminded him not to be a proud, cowardly man. Her courage to be direct in her curiosity and bold enough to ask was one of the things he so loved about her. "Most people just pretend I still have two arms."

"I am not most people."

"No, you are not."

Without a word, he rolled up his custom-made jacket and shirtsleeves and watched her closely for her reaction. She tilted her head to the side inquisitively and reached to touch him. He braced for the touch. But instead of fire and ice, he felt a soothing warmth spread as her fingers explored the wound. She scooted a little closer. "It is really rather striking," she said admiringly. "Whoever amputated it did a beautiful job."

"Beautiful? It is a stump."

"It *is* beautiful. It is so smooth and rounded. A little ink-smeared though."

"What?" Colonel Fitzwilliam was shocked out of the deep pleasure he felt from her touch. He rotated the stump up towards his face and sure enough there was an ink smear on the end. He laughed out loud. "Lands alive! That must have been there since yesterday when I wrote my mother and father a letter."

Charlotte stood. "Let me get that for you," she offered.

She came back with a wet cloth, knelt down, and, with gentle strokes, rubbed the end; her tender touch nearly driving him to Bedlam. His insides were aching, and he could smell her fresh rosewater scent. He closed his eyes for a brief second and savored the moment. It was so foreign to have anyone touch his arm to begin with, but to do it so tenderly, with no hint of disgust or revulsion, was soothing inside and out. He opened his eyes and watched her as she concentrated on cleaning off the ink. He could see the porcelain ivory tones of her skin this close. Her cheeks seemed to be slightly flushed, and he wondered if she too felt the intimacy between them. She glanced at him, and he smiled at her and was rewarded with the glorious smile that said so much about her.

"You really are beautiful, Charlotte." *Did I just say that out loud?*

Charlotte slowly dropped the washrag and put her hands on her knees. She knelt there for some time and then finally said, "You are the first man to ever tell me that."

"I am sorry Mr. Collins did not see your value. But I do. I am glad to call you my friend." He wanted to say more and then he noticed a slight pain in her eyes. Had he gone too far? Had he said too much?

Her next words clarified his worry. He had said too *little*.

"I was under the impression that you wished to call me more than a friend."

He reached his hand up to her face and moved one of the ringlets. His voice cracked as he said, "I have nothing to offer you. I cannot . . . excuse me."

He quickly stood and left the room. His throat seemed to have swollen to three times its size. He could hardly breathe. In his hurry, he descended the stairs faster than his lungs could handle, and he had to pause at the bottom to catch his breath. He was still too weak to handle his heart racing like this. Each breath sent sharp pains through his left side, and the air hunger made his anxiety worse.

He looked for a seat nearby, but the nearest one was across the hall by the front entrance. Collapsing on the stairs instead, he propped himself against the banister and tried to slow his breathing.

*Now what?* The hurt on her face as he said that to her was heartbreaking. But it was true. He had nothing to offer her. Slowly, the pain of breathing lessened, and he closed his eyes tightly only to find that tears escaped. He swallowed hard and told himself that it was the right thing to do. He had to let Charlotte go. She deserved someone who could take care of her and provide for her and her son. Until he knew where he was going, he simply could not encourage her.

*****

Georgiana had had enough! For three weeks she had watched Charlotte and Richard tiptoe around each other making small talk about how warm the weather was in Derbyshire for the middle of March. It seemed the only time the two were together was when the General was in the room. They played for hours with the boy, yet the two adults seemed to have little to say to each other. The silence between them was painful, even for her.

Today it would end. Charlotte and Richard were sitting on opposite sides of the sofa in the library. Charlotte was doing needlework, and Richard had a book propped open in his lap. Although Georgiana was sure he wasn't reading.

She walked over to them and sat down with a dramatic sigh. It had its intended effect, and they both looked in her direction.

Richard said, "Is there something wrong, Poppet?"

Charlotte asked, "You do look distressed. Is there something on your mind?"

"I admit I am getting rather nervous about my coming out. It is unnerving to think about all the rules of what you can do and what you cannot do."

"It is not as hard as you might think," Richard assured her. "Be honest and open."

Charlotte added, "And do not say anything you do not mean. Words have a great deal of weight in the matters of the heart."

"What if I say the wrong thing?"

"Poppet, we all say the wrong thing sometimes," Richard assured her. "Even I do."

216

"But will it ruin my chances of finding love?"

"Certainly not," Richard answered. "When someone really loves another person, it does not matter what they say."

Charlotte interjected, "I disagree, Colonel. In my experience, both ladies and gentlemen need a little encouragement."

Richard closed his book, turned towards Charlotte, and replied, "But encouragement should only be offered when there is an actual opportunity for a successful union."

Georgiana saw Charlotte turn as well. Looking directly at Richard she asked, "And what exactly is a successful union?"

"Marriage, of course. And for that, a gentleman must have the means to provide for the lady."

The battle between the two had begun, and Georgiana just listened as the argument went on.

"And what about love, Colonel?"

"What about it?"

"Money and wealth can be lost, but love, as I understand it—true love—can stand the test of time."

"I agree that true love will never die. But it cannot put bread on the table."

"Men are not the only ones who are required to put bread on the table. I have young Isaac to feed. It is a worry that plagues me daily, but does that stop me from loving him?"

"You are his mother."

"And that is not because I gave birth to him. It is because I love him. I would not abandon him the moment I could not give him what he needs."

"I am not saying you would."

"Then what are you saying? That a man should abandon his wife if he suddenly loses the ability to work?"

"I am saying nothing of the sort. I am just saying that starting a courtship or union without the means to see to your wife's needs is very unwise."

"Then it seems some hearts can easily succumb to deflection."

"Certainly not. True love never deflects. Give me one example of a heart, truly touched, that deflected from love."

Silence fell between them for a moment. Charlotte finally said, "Contrary to your opinion of ladies in general, I have known ladies who love very deeply—who care nothing for titles, connections, or wealth. And I have known gentlemen who claim to be of the same opinion yet seem to think of nothing *but* wealth when the decision presents itself. If that is not love deflected, what is?"

"A smart lady should at least think about her future with the man she hopes to marry."

"Then an intelligent lady would have to outsmart the man and somehow show him that she actually cares for the man he has always been and always will be."

Fitzwilliam paused. "People change."

"Not at their core. Men will stumble on their weaknesses until they choose to correct them."

"What kind of weaknesses? Like missing an arm?"

"That is not what I meant. I was referring to pride and self-pity."

"No honorable man would wallow in pity. A man wants to be respected and honored. Why else do you think gentlemen still duel?"

"And how is a man supposed to be respected when he does not respect himself?"

"You are stubborn."

"And you are proud."

"A man needs a bit of pride in himself. Trust me, I know."

"I did."

There was a prolonged second of silence.

"Pardon?" Colonel Fitzwilliam asked.

"I *did* trust you."

Georgiana was shocked at Charlotte's bold statement and turned to see how her cousin would respond. Richard opened his mouth, as if to retort, but was silent for a prolonged moment.

When he did finally respond, his tone was soft and tender, speaking her name humbly and reverently. "Charlotte—forgive me, Mrs. Collins—what have I done to make you distrust me?"

"It does not matter."

"It matters to me. I value our friendship."

"As do I."

"I have to find a way to provide for myself before I can follow my heart."

"—your heart?"

"Yes," He said confidently, and persuasively. "I want desperately to follow my heart. But I cannot."

"You are sure it has not deflected?"

"Heavens no. It could never be more loyal than it is now. Is that why you have been so distant?"

"I have not been distant. It is you who has hardly looked in my direction."

Georgiana tried not to smile outwardly, but she could see they were finally talking it out.

"Mrs. Collins, why do you suppose I spend my every waking moment with you and the General? It is torturing me, but I cannot help myself. I am drawn to you."

"I thought that was because you wanted to play with the General."

"I love the General, but he is not the one who has secured my most sincere regard."

"Truly?"

"Indeed."

"Then why have you ignored me? Why have you not spoken more than two sentences to me at a time? I thought you had changed your mind."

"I could never change my mind about that any more than I could sew on a new arm. Charlotte, you have to believe me, I want to provide for you and Isaac. But I simply do not see a way. I am sorry I have led you to believe I did not love you. My heart has never been more invested, but love is not enough."

"Truly? I was worried that you—"

Richard slapped his hand on his thigh. "Rocks! I sowed among the rocks!"

Georgiana didn't understand much of what they had been arguing about but this new element really threw her. "Rocks?"

"'And the seeds withered away without moisture.' Fiend, seize it!" Colonel Fitzwilliam stood and bowed to Charlotte, "Do not mistake my meaning in leaving, Mrs. Collins. I need to speak with Darcy. But before I go, let me just say that I have never battled such a worthy opponent. And you, Georgiana! You have been the best little drummer in the regiment! You directed the troops nicely and saved many lives today."

Georgiana watched Richard leave and turned to Charlotte. "What did he mean by calling me a drummer?"

Charlotte smiled. "I think he meant that you did a fine job on directing today's battle."

Georgiana smiled back. "Then it worked?"

"I hope so. I truly hope so."

# CHAPTER 21

Colonel Fitzwilliam rushed into Darcy's study without knocking. "Darcy! I need a job." Fitzwilliam suddenly noticed that his cousin was with his steward. "Sorry, Kelsey. Do you mind giving us a moment?"

"Not at all," Mr. Kelsey replied, and with a bow, he left.

Mr. Darcy looked up at him. "Pray tell," he said, "what kind of work are you looking for?"

"Anything that pays honest money. I mean it. If I can do it, I will."

Darcy was relieved that they could finally discuss the topics Colonel Fitzwilliam had so consistently avoided ever since his return. But he tried to keep a straight face. "That is a bold statement," he told his cousin. "I have horse stalls that need cleaning."

Colonel Fitzwilliam paused for a moment. Darcy just waited. *Will he take the bait?*

"Very well. When can I start?"

"Oh, I never hire anyone without a proper interview," Darcy replied. "Sit down, this could take a while." It took all of Darcy's willpower not to smile.

Richard looked a little puzzled, but sat down. It seemed that he was fairly desperate. "Very well, I will play your game," Richard announced. "Go on. Interview me."

Darcy took up his pencil and leaned back in the chair and asked, "Why do you need the work?"

Richard squirmed a little. "It is either find a profession or follow in Phillip Astley's footsteps and apply for a position in the circus at the Royal Amphitheatre. I suppose I could share the stage with the world's largest bearded lady."

"I see. Those are your only options?"

"More or less."

"You seem a little undecided. I prefer to hire men with firm convictions; men who know what they want and are willing to work for it. Would you say this describes you?"

"Absolutely."

Darcy started passing the pencil from finger to finger and back again to stall his next question. "How so?"

Richard cleared his throat. "I am passionate and loyal. This has led me to build strong lifelong friendships with those that are important to me." Richard winked at him.

He was pleased to see his cousin's mood, which had been even more taciturn than his own in Hertfordshire, almost visibly lift with the playacting that was going on.

"I see. And these friends, how would they describe you?"

"As you know I was a colonel in the army. My men looked at me with respect. They often told me they would die for me. Many did. But I no longer can fight on the battlefield. I am retired, for obvious reasons." He held up his left arm.

He was confident that Richard was ready to be pressed like this. Darcy replied, "Yes, I did notice the arm. I wonder if having only one arm will be a problem."

With a touch of seriousness, and perhaps it was really more of the determination that was so classic of his cousin, Richard said, "It will not be a problem. I can do most anything you can do. You yourself have seen me mount a horse one handed without a mounting block. It does not hold me back physically."

"I would agree that you have seemed to grasp the mechanics of what is physically demanded of you. What about emotionally? Are there battle scars that might interfere with your ability to work?"

"I can do anything I set my mind to."

"I respect any man who shows that kind of determination. What exactly has made you so determined?"

The colonel paused, and with a smirk that was minimally noticeable, he replied, "Rocks."

Darcy smiled slightly. "Yes, rocks can get in the way," he responded. "How does granite and marble pertain to this drive for employment?"

"It would appear that certain friends were under the misconception that my loyalties have wavered, even withered away. I will admit that it is most likely due to my own negligence. It seems a drought is upon us."

Darcy wanted to make sure Richard was saying what he thought he was saying. Darcy held his serious tone. "It is spring, Richard. We are not in a drought."

"I thought we were speaking in riddles."

"No, only you seem to be doing that. So far you have mentioned joining the circus, rocks, and a nonexistent drought. Might you take a moment and explain yourself? Feel free to speak plainly."

Richard seemed to be weighing his options, no doubt that if he chose to be direct and honest, it would be costly to his pride.

After a moment, Richard stood and started pacing. Darcy continued to sit patiently, and finally Richard started to speak. "I love Charlotte. I love the General as if he was my own son. Although she is in mourning, and although she has not actually declared her feelings for me, I believe she feels the same for me. If fact, I would bet money that she does."

Darcy sat up a bit and leaned forward, leaning on his elbows. "You would bet money, money that you do not have, on this belief?" It was perhaps indelicate to manipulate his cousin this way, but Richard had just inadvertently opened his own opportunities by using such a common expression.

Worry etched into Richard's brow momentarily. Then he firmly declared, "Indeed I would."

"And what makes you think a wager of that sort would be wise?" The idea of letting Colonel Fitzwilliam make a bet on his gentleman's honor had not crossed his mind. In fact, it may very well be the only way he would accept any help from Darcy at all. Pride was a foe that even the colonel had to battle.

Richard took a deep breath and raked his hand through his hair. "There have been signs. She smiled at me at your wedding. And again before I left for war. And I am fairly certain she overheard me praise her while speaking to her son that morning I left. She did name him *Isaac*, after all."

Darcy sat up. "Isaac was her grandfather's name," he parried.

"Yes, but it is also the name of my hero, General Isaac Brock. She heard me talking to the General about it. And she calls him the General!"

"But we all call him the General. I believe you specifically asked me to continue the nickname."

"I know I did."

"So far you have given little evidence for your belief other than the fact that she smiled at you six months ago. A lot can happen in six months. If I was a betting man, I would want to bet against you."

Richard looked genuinely dismayed and Darcy questioned his tactics slightly. "Come, Darcy, you would not crush my hopes now that I might have a chance with her, would you?"

"I am sorry, Richard." And he truly was, but only partially, because Richard's hole he was digging would simply be his escape to freedom. "But I would urge you to be cautious. In fact, I am willing to bet you my entire annual income that Charlotte does not feel the same way about you as she did the week you left."

Fear flashed across his cousin's face. Compassion swelled in Darcy's breast for the pain that sentence must have caused Richard, but he had to do this.

The fear on Richard's face was replaced with determination. "Very well. I accept."

Darcy tried to act surprised. "Pardon me?"

"I accept the wager. On my gentleman's honor, I bet you that Charlotte *does* love me. In fact, I bet she will accept my hand in marriage within a month of coming out of mourning."

"I do not know about that. Are you so confident that you can win her when you yourself said she still carried wounds from her previous husband? A woman who has been married to a man like that will not trust easily."

"I am aware of that. Do you accept the terms or not?" Richard seemed to fidget with excitement.

Darcy tried to sound dubious. "Ten thousand pounds?"

"You and I both know that is just the rumors of your annual income. Do not try to cheat me."

"Very well, give me a moment." Darcy stood and walked past Richard. He couldn't help but smile to himself as he opened his study door and asked Reynolds to have his steward, Mr. Kelsey, attend him in his study.

Moments later Kelsey returned. "What can I do for you, Mr. Darcy?" he asked.

"Please inform my cousin as to my annual income last year. Be completely honest."

"I believe it was just over fourteen thousand, sir."

"That is all, thank you." Kelsey left and Darcy said, "So, let us clarify the precise terms of this wager. You say she already returns your admiration. You are also confident enough to state that she will accept your hand in marriage within a month of the anniversary of Mr. Collins's death. If she does accept your offer of marriage, then I owe you fourteen thousand pounds. If she does not, I propose that you clean my horse stalls for a month, personally brush down my stallion after every ride, and oil every saddle I own. Do you accept?"

Richard stood up and offered his hand. "It is a deal."

"I would practice shoveling with only one arm if I were you," Darcy teased.

Richard smiled and declared, "Just you wait and see, Darcy. If she does not love me now, she will."

"Her mourning will be over in five weeks. That gives you just over two months to win her hand."

Richard seemed to smile slightly and if Darcy didn't know his cousin as well as he did, he would have missed the smile melt into a genuine look of gratitude. Darcy had offered Richard a way to "earn" his living in the true manners of a gentleman. Darcy would never know for sure—for unquestionably, it would never be discussed openly—but he knew the Colonel well enough to know he saw Darcy's ulterior motives. For in Darcy's heart, he had not been playing any sort of game; no, instead, he had found a way to furnish hope for Fitzwilliam, just as the man had once done for Mr. Darcy.

Although no words were said, Darcy nodded almost imperceptibly and the short flash of gratitude that was on his cousin's face was swiftly replaced with the stoic man Darcy had always known.

*It is indeed good to see him back.*

"Start writing that bank note, Darcy. There is one thing my men understood about me; I never back down from a fight. And you, my dear friend, will simply be another casualty of war."

\*\*\*\*\*

Colonel Fitzwilliam left Darcy's study and grinned at himself. He wasn't sure who had played whom in there. But he now had something to work for. Maybe Darcy had planned it all along, but at least he hadn't exhibited that blasted pity Fitzwilliam saw in so many people's eyes.

Now the colonel had a job to do. It may take a great deal of work, but wasn't that what he wanted?

*There is no time like the present*, Colonel Fitzwilliam thought. He went back into the library, and finding her alone, asked, "Mrs. Collins, would you and the General like to take in the fresh air?"

"We would love to, Colonel. How delightful! Perhaps Georgiana would like to go with us."

*Remember, fertile ground. She needs to be ready.* "Of course. I will go collect Georgiana."

Colonel Fitzwilliam bowed and turned. *"Delightful."* *"Love to."* And he still had two more months.

He found Georgiana in the music room, and, without any hesitation, she accepted.

He stopped by Darcy's study, leaned his head in and said, "You might want to pull out your bank note now and practice your signature. Will you need help spelling my name? F-I-T-Z . . ." He chuckled to himself and left without seeing Darcy's reaction.

Seeing the ladies and the General outside the front entrance, ready and waiting for him, lifted his spirits even more. The General was in his pram, and Georgiana had taken the prerogative of pushing it, so Colonel Fitzwilliam offered his arm to Charlotte.

She finished tying her bonnet and put a gentle hand around his arm. "I heard you have begun riding again," she remarked. "Is it difficult?"

"No, not really," Fitzwilliam replied. "My father always taught me that a good rider uses his knees and legs to guide the horse as much as the reins. And riding is in my blood. I have done it since I was a lad. Do you ride much?"

"I used to, when I was a little girl, but I have not ridden in many years now. Without the proper attire, there is little opportunity."

"Charlotte," Georgiana piped in, "Elizabeth is going to have a few gowns made when we go to London next week. Why not have some made for you as well? And a riding habit?"

"Oh, my black dresses will last a few more weeks. Perhaps I can order some new ones, something less dark, when we travel to Rosings for Easter. Speaking of which, Colonel Fitzwilliam, will you be ready for your hero's welcome?"

"My hero's welcome?"

"Shhhh!" Georgiana whispered. "You were not supposed to tell him!"

"Tell me what?" Fitzwilliam asked.

Georgiana made no reply.

"Georgiana Marie Darcy, what are you talking about?" Fitzwilliam demanded.

Georgiana sheepishly admitted, "Oh, do not be mad! Everyone is expecting to see you. They are calling you the hero of Queenston Heights! Your mother may be planning a *small* ball for you in London on our return from Rosings . . . "

He furrowed his brow slightly. "How does everyone know about the battle? And why are they calling me a hero?"

"Your success avenging the death of General Brock was published in the *London Times*," Charlotte explained. "The detail of your battle was impressive. At great persuasion from the *ton*, your parents and Mr. Darcy have agreed to throw a ball in your honor after Anne's wedding. They have been under a great deal of pressure from all the ladies. It seems everyone wants a chance to become Mrs. Colonel Fitzwilliam."

Colonel Fitzwilliam laughed. "Perhaps, but when they see how difficult it is to dance a quadrille with only one arm, they will leave me without a partner on the dance floor!"

In her typical protective manner, Georgiana declared, "Certainly not! I will trip any lady who tries it. I will dance with you. Your arm does not bother me."

Colonel Fitzwilliam turned to Charlotte. "And what about you, Mrs. Collins? Would you care to dance with a man with only one arm?"

She smirked at him slightly. "I admit I would decline any dance partner with only one arm," she teased. "But fortunately, you have *one-and-a-half* arms."

"Yes, of course," he replied with a grin. "Anything less would be unthinkable."

"Indeed it would." Charlotte flashed him a smile. He would not push her to dance a set with him. After all, he still had a few weeks until her mourning was over.

"Georgiana," he asked, "when did you say this ball was going to be? Do I have any say on it?"

"Well, Anne's wedding is the fourteenth of April. I imagine we will have the ball when we return through London. What date would you suggest?"

Colonel Fitzwilliam couldn't be more pleased. "It is just that I would like a few weeks to settle in before my hero's welcome ball. What if we had it the first day of May?"

"I imagine that would be fine," Georgiana replied. "Will you dance a set with me, Richard?"

"Georgiana, generally a lady waits for the gentleman to ask. But I suppose I will be obliged to dance with any lady who will have me now." He then felt the slightest squeeze on his arm, and he couldn't help but smile. Charlotte had just told him in her own way that she would dance with him. Now all he had to do was make it past April 28th so that he could truly pursue her. Until then, he would continue preparing the ground for the planting.

They walked in silence for a while until Charlotte announced, "Colonel Fitzwilliam, as a friend, I must warn you that Georgiana has quite slandered you in your absence. She has spoken to me about little else but the misdeeds and escapades of your youth."

Georgiana giggled. "Charlotte!" she squealed. "Do you wish to see me crucified?"

Colonel Fitzwilliam cleared his throat and said, "I have nothing to be ashamed of. Unless you told her about sledding down Freestone Hills."

"Oh, she told me about that."

"And she probably made it sound as if I meant to have my breeches rip down the center seam in front of everyone."

"I assumed that on my own."

He laughed at Charlotte's comment. Georgiana whispered, "I may have told her about your first kiss too."

"I was seven!"

"But your mother still tells it like you were old enough to know better."

Charlotte agreed, "I am afraid I side with your mother on this one, Colonel. Seven is old enough to know right from wrong. Did you learn your lesson?"

"Hmm, her stinging slap to my face was certainly *instructive*. And I can honestly say that I have not tried to kiss her since." Charlotte and Georgiana giggled. "But, in my defense," he continued, "she did say she would kiss me if I caught her a butterfly, and I caught a butterfly. It seemed a fairly straightforward arrangement. She just underestimated my determination. What other unflattering stories did Georgiana reveal to you?"

By now they were making the final bend of the path around the pond. The day was coming to a close. Colonel Fitzwilliam would have been delighted to keep talking with Charlotte like this all night. He had received more of her brilliant smiles than ever before. It was very comforting.

"She claims that you are a horrid speller," Charlotte continued. "So much so that you carry a dictionary with you when you travel. This surprises me since you read so often. I should think that one who reads would naturally be a good speller."

"It is true, I read a great deal. However, do not think I use a dictionary because I cannot spell. I take great care composing letters, and a dictionary is very helpful in that regard. After all, once something is written down, it is as good as fact. My words are how people see me. I am simply fastidious in how I wish to permanently portray myself."

"Really?" Charlotte teased. "Such as how you pretend to be a man about town? Or a jester?"

"Now, I only do that because it provides distraction from my duties as a colonel. My regiment is entirely made up of men, the cooks included. And in order to keep from speaking and behaving like a man's man, I must work hard on the performance of the opposite. And I only tell jokes because I am so observant."

"How so?" Georgiana queried.

"Well, for example, I once saw a woman loudly arguing with her son in a bookstore. The child had to have been about ten years old, and the mother looked ready to box his ears right then and there, for the entire shop to see. They were the rudest pair I have ever had the misfortune of shopping with. Finally the mother turned to the bookkeeper and asked, in a tone of exasperation, if he had any books that would teach her son how to behave in public. The irony of seeing her behave so poorly one minute and yet ask for a book on proper manners made it nearly impossible to keep from laughing. Amusing things happen all around us every day. We just have to keep our eyes open and let ourselves be entertained. People can be quite diverting."

Charlotte replied, "Well, Colonel, I shall take that as my first lesson. I shall try to be as observant as possible." The way she said it seemed to have more meanings than one. It made his heart speed up in excitement.

"I would have it no other way. One can learn a great deal about the true character of those around us if we simply listen. I always tell my men that our ears may be on the sides of our face, but they tell us more about what is in front of us than our eyes."

Georgiana said, "I told you, Charlotte."

"I believe you are right. He is a man with more depth of character than most people give him credit for." And at that moment, she wrapped another hand around his arm and clung to him perhaps a bit tighter. He couldn't help but smile.

Poor Darcy was going to be fourteen thousand pounds poorer in just a few short weeks.

# CHAPTER 22

The next few weeks, Charlotte could not think of much else besides Colonel Fitzwilliam. Things seemed so natural between them now that she nearly forgot that she still had two more weeks of mourning to go.

Every day she would rise to check on her son, and every day she found Colonel Fitzwilliam already there, playing with the General and telling him stories. The first day it happened, she had stood outside the door and listened, but the urge to be in his presence and talk with him soon became overpowering. On the rare morning when her son had not woken yet, she found him whispering little stories to the General. She began to rise earlier and earlier each day, eager to meet him again.

Each morning, while everyone else was still asleep, they would sit together for an hour or so, playing with the General and talking about all sorts of things. She had never felt such devotion from a man, yet never once did she feel like he was trying to woo her or pressure her. Their private meetings in the nursery continued when they traveled to Darcy House and, later, to Rosings Park.

Anne and Captain Jersey were to be married in a few days. Today, as Charlotte woke in her bed, she felt even more anxious than usual to see the colonel again. There was nothing she looked forward to more, no activity more enjoyable, than listening to him tell stories to her son. He was animated and jovial, which always made Isaac giggle. Her son would even try to talk back with the random noises that babies like to make. The colonel would pretend he understood what the General had said and carry on the conversation in such seriousness that she often found herself laughing outright. She was somewhat surprised one morning to realize that was just one of the many things she loved about him.

One morning she asked him how he prepared men for battle. He had obliged her by sharing the speech he had given his men at the battle of Queenston Heights. It was very moving to hear his fire and passion in defense of their country. This led to more detailed stories of what happened in war. He voiced his concern that perhaps war stories were an inappropriate conversation topic for a lady, but Charlotte had insisted.

If she was being honest, it was not just the stories that enthralled her; it was his smooth, deep, velvety voice. Listening to him was like hearing a lullaby. That was another thing she loved about him.

Charlotte had known, in the deepest part of her heart, that she was developing strong feelings for him. But it was not until yesterday morning that she found the words to describe what she felt. They had been talking about how fear can be crippling on the battlefield. It could literally cost you your life. Remembering his words filled her heart again with her newfound conclusion, confirming once more that she was entirely correct.

She loved him.

She let her mind review that moment.

*"But surely your men were scared."*

*"Undoubtedly," he nodded. "I was scared too."*

*"But how did you reassure them? How did they face it?"*

*"Oh, I made a fine speech, but I do not know how much I reassured them," he replied. "A wise soldier once told me that courage is not the absence of fear. It is learning to go on in spite of it. There comes a time when each of us must face our deepest fears. It is not always on the battlefield." The colonel looked up at her and paused. "There are many battles within us, personal fights against foes that no one knows about. Those enemies can be far more dangerous."*

Charlotte remembered the sensation of icy fear filling her veins. She remembered the way it made her limbs freeze, the way she flustered and fidgeted in its tight grip, and feeling of sharp prickling of hairs on the back of her neck. It had been a familiar companion for many months. But although it had been many months now since she had felt that kind of crippling fear, she had never talked to anyone about it.

*"Yes," she added hesitatingly. "I think that is true. We each must face our own fear, not just soldiers." When she dared to look over at him, she was nearly overwhelmed by the kindness in his eyes. She took a deep breath and looked away.*

*"It requires a great deal of courage to overcome our fears," the colonel replied. "Which is why I admire so much those who are able to do so."*

*Charlotte blushed but made no reply.*

*After a moment or two of silence, the colonel continued, "In my experience, there are only two things that help one face one's fears. The first is our attitude. We must determine that fear will not direct us anymore. Take my rather-lacking-left hand for instance," he continued, adopting a more lighthearted tone. "I can look at myself in the mirror and fear its absence or I can see a devilishly handsome fellow who has learnt to untie a cravat singlehandedly. It is all in one's attitude."*

*Charlotte laughed. "And what is the second tactic, Colonel?"*

*"Well, that is one that this soldier has learned quite acutely as of late—to turn command over to God. For He is the only one capable of healing wounds that others cannot see. He is at our flank during those wars within us. And He can never be defeated or overpowered."*

*And at that moment, Charlotte suddenly realized that she didn't just love the colonel because she appreciated his friendship. It wasn't simply because she had missed him or worried about him while he was at war. And it wasn't because he loved her son so much—although he obviously loved Isaac as if he were his own.*

*She loved him because her heart had finally healed from the abuse she had suffered at the hand of Mr. Collins. That war inside her, that inner foe that he spoke of, which had once driven her to crave independence above all else, was now replaced with an unbreakable bond to him. Her soul was inexorably connected with Colonel Fitzwilliam now. And it had altered her in such a beautiful way that she felt whole for the first time. She felt hope inside her soul, instead of fear. And Colonel Fitzwilliam's unwavering devotion no longer felt undeserved. For the first time, she felt valued, respected, and appreciated by a man.*

*No. It was more than that.*

*She felt cherished.*

*And all of this had happened without a single flirtatious wink or an unsolicited compliment. It had happened because he saw her potential. He saw her as more than Mr. Collins's widow. More than the hardly noticed friend of the great Elizabeth Darcy. She was important enough for him to spend hours in silent companionship while they played with the General. It was clear by his behavior that, no matter what they talked about or what room they were in, being in her presence was priceless to him.*

*As all these thoughts tumbled into her mind, she spied her reflection in the nursery's windows. For the first time, she saw herself as the woman she had wanted so much to become. She was a respectable, confident woman; a woman who was worthy of the love of an honorable gentleman. And she did not mean gentleman as in a landowner. She meant she deserved the love of a gentle man. And there was no longer any doubt that Colonel Fitzwilliam, even with all his ability to be a fearful foe on the battlefield, was a gentle man. He was the man who had somehow captured her heart in the nursery as he rocked her baby and whispered soothing tales.*

*"Colonel Fitzwilliam," she whispered, "even with only one arm, you are ten times the man Mr. Collins ever was."*

*Charlotte found herself looking into his gray-blue orbs, and in that silent moment as he reached for her hand, she knew she had lost her independence.*

*And she no longer cared.*

*She loved him. Every brick of her fortress had been crushed by his gentle, loving ways.*

*She was very happy to relinquish her heart to the colonel.*

As she looked over to the clock on the mantel, she saw that it was time to meet him again in the nursery. She quickly dressed and left her room. She found him standing with his back to her, looking out the window. This particular gray-blue great coat, tailored for his broad shoulders and his arm, accented his eyes so dramatically that she sucked in her breath when he turned and looked at her. She would never get used to seeing his regal frame and sculpted chest. It was perhaps less defined than before the war, but it did not detract from her attraction to him.

Colonel Fitzwilliam smiled warmly at her and whispered, "He is still sleeping. It seems the entire house is still asleep. Would you like to take a stroll in the gardens with me?"

Charlotte did not think twice about accepting, even though there would be no chaperone. "I would like that very much."

He offered his arm, and they headed out towards the front entrance. He very skillfully assisted her with her pelisse, leaving her nearly breathless as his hand reached down to adjust her neck collar, which had folded under itself. His feather-light touch sent her heart racing. She offered her gratitude, and he held the door open for her.

The day before had been wet, and the smell of the cherry blossoms was in the air. An unexpected thought suddenly flew into her mind. "Colonel, do you mind if we visit Mr. Collins's grave?"

"I am *your* humble servant," he answered with a kind smile.

They spoke of all sorts of things as they walked the distance to the parsonage cemetery. As he opened the iron gate that led to the grounds, Charlotte began to feel something that she had not anticipated. She had expected to be assaulted with feelings of anger, or even fear. She had worried that she might relive those painful memories and be forced to hold in her anxious tears. But fear and anger did not come. An entirely different feeling came.

She could see from here that the curate, Mr. Cress, was raking around the many graves near Mr. Collins's headstone. Colonel Fitzwilliam allowed her to proceed without him, somehow knowing that she needed to do this alone.

The short ten yards to the stone that held his name seemed longer than it should have been. She half expected to hear his angry voice shouting at her once again. She walked slowly, ready to flinch at any sudden noise, but none of that happened. Minutes went by as she read and reread the words and dates on the headstone.

William Collins had not been a good man. He had possessed an exaggerated view of his own importance in the world. He had been a vile, abusive, angry, and controlling man who never learned to love anyone other than himself.

But, for the first time, she felt sorry for him. She truly pitied him. To be chained to society's view of one's self seemed like such a sad way to live. Being motivated by the approval of the rich and connected, had brought him no joy. She could not say he had led a happy life. Yes, she pitied him. He had been weak enough to need others opinions to dictate his importance and value. For the first time, she felt the need to tell someone about it.

She turned as Mr. Cress and Colonel Fitzwilliam came up to her. They both had taken their hats off in respect for the hallowed ground.

Mr. Cress said, "It is so nice to see you, Mrs. Collins."

"Thank you, Mr. Cress," she replied.

"I am sorry that we meet again under these circumstances," the old curate apologized. Just then, two ladies appeared in the church door and waved Mr. Cress over. "I am so sorry, Mrs. Collins. I am afraid I must go back inside. If you need anything, please have the colonel come and retrieve me."

"Of course. Thank you," she said. She watched Mr. Cress leave, then turned to Colonel Fitzwilliam, whose eyes were full with emotion. She knew what to call it now. It had never been pity she had seen in his eyes, nor merely compassion. It had been love and respect. That was what he saw when he looked at her.

"Are you well, Mrs. Collins?" Colonel Fitzwilliam asked her. "You seem to be holding up remarkably well."

"I am well. I have shed many tears over the last year, but for some reason I find myself brimming with peace right now. That peace is ready to show itself and drop from my eyes, but do not mistake my tears. Colonel, I need to tell you something about Mr. Collins. I have not shared this with anyone, because I feared what they would think of me. But I realize now that I do not care what people think of me anymore. Living our lives looking for acceptance will only bring us unrest. Mr. Collins never understood that fact." Charlotte took a deep breath before continuing.

"My husband was a cruel man," she stated. "He was motivated only by power and his desire to control others—those whom he considered less important than himself, which included nearly everyone. To him, I was just Charlotte. He told me that frequently. 'You were nothing more than a simple country girl named Charlotte when you married me. Now you are my wife. I have given you everything that is worth having.'"

Colonel Fitzwilliam patiently waited for her to continue. Her tears dropped, and the colonel offered her a handkerchief.

"Thank you. But what he gave me or what he did to me . . . it does not matter anymore. I forgive him. And I feel sorry for him. I truly do. Love is the only thing that matters, and he had none. He could have loved me if he wanted to, but he did not. No one ever loved him the way I am loved now. I *am* just Charlotte. And I am more now than he will ever be."

She looked into the colonel's eyes. "He will never know how gentle love can be," she said. "He will never know the peace that comes from surrendering one's heart. He will never know what a beautiful gift it is to offer someone kindness, love, mercy, and hope. He will never know the passion of a long-awaited reunion. And he will never know the power of a loyal friend's heart."

Colonel Fitzwilliam put his hand on her shoulder, brushing his thumb on the exposed skin near her neck. "You finally see your worth, Mrs. Collins," he whispered.

She smiled at him and nodded. The realization of her own worth was flooding through her veins, and she felt empowered to take another step. "I have asked you to call me Mrs. Collins many times. And I have refused to call you anything other than Colonel Fitzwilliam. But would you do me the great honor of calling me just Charlotte from now on?"

He seemed to be on the verge of speaking. After a moment's hesitation, he cleared his throat and said, "Well, 'Just Charlotte', I can honestly say that you have done me a great service."

"How so?"

"I have been fighting my own battle for many months now, reminding myself to call you Mrs. Collins because that is what you have asked. I am very relieved that I do not have to resist my heart's wishes any longer."

She boldly asked, "And what are your heart's wishes?"

"To call you something far more dear," he replied. He looked at her intently before continuing. "I have learned this last year that there is a right time and place to say and do something. I am well aware that you have eleven more days of mourning left, but there is a burning in my chest that has nothing to do with my war injury. It is threatening to engulf my every sense. You must allow me to tell you that no matter how long it will take, whether it is eleven days or eleven years, I will wait for you, Charlotte. I will never love anyone as much as I love 'Just Charlotte'. I want so badly to do this . . ." He reached over to her face, and with the back of his fingers, he brushed her cheek.

The tenderness was powerful. Who knew that a single touch could elicit an acute acceleration of her heart so dramatically? Who knew that hope could flood her so quickly that her very lips burned with desire?

He continued, "I want so badly to ask permission to taste your pink lips, but I will not."

Charlotte was shocked by the disappointment she felt. She silently listened to him continue.

"I will not allow you, now that you have seen how valuable a person you are, to sacrifice what I love most about you. Charlotte, I love you so very deeply. My love for you is the very thing that puts me to sleep at night and the very first thing that I feel when I wake. It has been my constant companion this last year. I have always loved your loyalty, and I will not allow you to sacrifice it a mere eleven days early. I love that you are loyal to Mr. Collins, despite his unconscionable treatment of you. For if he had only opened his eyes—truly opened them—and seen the Charlotte that I see, he would have treated you the way a lady deserves to be treated."

He then lifted her hand and kissed it and brought it to his face. "I will be patient," he promised, "I must confess there is nothing I want more than to spend every day of the rest of my life with 'Just Charlotte'. She is the strongest, most courageous, and most loyal lady I have ever known. I respect that you have fought battles that are far more dangerous than I ever did. You are the real war hero, Charlotte."

Charlotte had new tears forming in her eyes as he spoke such kind words. "You know I will be out of mourning at your hero's welcome ball."

"I do."

She smiled and said, "I am stronger than you may think, but even I know my limitations. I do not think I will be able to bear seeing you open the ball without a fellow war hero at your side."

His chiseled jaw broke into a grin that made his entire face soften. "Then please do me the honor of standing up with this one-and-a-half armed man for the opening set. There is no one I would rather have at my flank."

"I shall be delighted to."

"I should warn you, Charlotte, it might be quite scandalous. For we will nearly be in each other's embrace as we turn, and I do believe the quadrille says we must dance an arm's length apart."

She smiled. "And are you prepared for what others might say?" she asked him.

"Oh, I am very willing to spread the rumors myself," he teased. "Darcy claims I have no scruples whatsoever in bending the truth to meets my needs. I am telling you, one cannot trust a one-armed man."

"On the contrary, I trust one-armed men completely."

"How so?"

"Because I can always see what they have up their sleeves!"

Laughing out loud, he pulled her into an embrace. She felt his chest vibrate as he chuckled. "Oh, Charlotte, I thought I was supposed to be the funny one!"

His fresh masculine scent engulfed her, and she felt his arms wrap around her as best they could. She did not flinch from this man's touch. It was the first embrace she had ever received from a man who knew how to be kind and gentle and loving. It was the first time she had ever welcomed a physical touch that brought hope rather than fear.

*So this is what love feels like.*

She had won. She had won the battle. She was a war hero. She wanted nothing more than to be at his flank for the rest of her life.

# CHAPTER 23

"I am terribly sorry," Fitzwilliam whispered, withdrawing his arms from around her. "I am afraid you must think that I have no patience at all and feel I can do whatever I please."

Charlotte pushed back her curls and said, "Well, at least I welcomed it better than the kiss in Pemberley's rose garden. But we should probably return to Rosings."

"Yes, of course. The General is probably awake now." Colonel Fitzwilliam offered his arm and tried with all his might to chastise himself for holding her like that, but no matter how hard he tried to berate himself, the memory of it simply brought a smile to his face.

*Poor Darcy. Literally poor, poor, Darcy. He, of all people, should never have bet against love.*

Fitzwilliam felt proud to have earned Charlotte's love. It didn't even require concentration; he could still feel her soft form against him. She had definitely rested her head against his chest.

As they entered Rosings, Charlotte excused herself to check on the General, which meant that she needed to feed him. Therefore he sought out other company.

He found Georgiana and Mr. Pastel, who had indeed come for the wedding, at the piano, deep in discussion. They seemed strangely preoccupied with each other as of late. Mr. Pastel was asking questions about her training and her tastes in music, topics that the colonel did not necessarily want to participate in.

Anne was sitting quietly with Captain Jersey. Their body language alone was proof that he would be an intruder.

He continued walking and found Elizabeth and Darcy whispering quietly. He watched Darcy reach his hand out to touch Elizabeth's growing abdomen, and Fitzwilliam found himself, once again, driven to seek other company.

He exited the room and heard Aunt Catherine speaking to his parents. "My Anne has never been so happy. Even though Captain Jersey is a second son, he has made a fortune in shipping. You know, I was instrumental in selecting him as a match for her myself, Brother."

Colonel Fitzwilliam rolled his eyes and passed on participating in that conversation as well. He finally resorted to go to the library to find a good book to read as a distraction. He had approximately half an hour to himself before it would be appropriate to reappear in the nursery. With all this talk of matches and couples huddling together in every room, perhaps it was only natural that Colonel Fitzwilliam had spent the majority of these last few days and weeks with Charlotte and the General.

He checked his pocket watch. Twenty-four more minutes.

He examined the books around him, but Lady Catherine's library was not nearly as well stocked as Pemberley's. He silently cursed himself for not remembering that.

Nineteen minutes.

He came across an old bible and realized that he had not read the parable of the seed for some time. In fact, it had been several months. He took it out and sat on the chaise and opened up the book. He read the last part of the parable, the only part that hadn't been fulfilled yet.

The power of the words this time pierced his soul. So much so that he began to read it out loud.

"And other fell on good ground, and sprang up, and bare fruit an hundredfold. And when he has said these things, he cried, 'He that hath ears to hear, let him hear.'"

He heard someone come in the room and looked up to see Charlotte and the General staring at him. "Who are you speaking to?" she asked.

"I was reading aloud. Forgive me. Well, hello, General! Come here!" He set the Bible aside, and Charlotte handed the General over to him.

Without any notice, the General reached for his face and very distinctly said, "Da-da!" Surprise must have shown on the colonel's face, but it sounded so right that he kissed the General soundly.

"As my commanding officer, you can address me however you like, General."

"Da-da." the General patted Colonel Fitzwilliam's cheeks and looked to his mother and said while patting his face again. "Da-Da!"

Charlotte knelt beside them and said, "Forgive him. I do not mean to make you uneasy."

"I am in no way uneasy," Fitzwilliam replied. "Quite the opposite in fact. Sit down, Charlotte."

She sat down and patted her son's head. "What were you reading?"

"The parable of the sower. Have you heard of it?"

"Yes, the one on missionary work. Why were you reading it aloud?"

"It is nothing really. I was counseled by Mr. Heather and Mr. Lisscord, my friends from my regiment, to read and study it. Line upon line, I have come to understand its true meaning."

"What meaning is that?" Charlotte asked.

"It is a story about love," the colonel explained. "The sower wants to spread God's love. Sometimes people are not yet ready to receive love, but this story encourages us to keep trying, even when our efforts appear unsuccessful. Charlotte, I cannot let you go one more day without making sure that you know my intentions. I want to marry you. I want to be the only father the General will ever know."

"Colonel—"

"Will you please call me Richard?"

"Richard . . ." Her face was soft as she said it, and an adorable blush infused her cheeks. She paused for a moment, for which he was grateful for. To hear her finally speak his name was indescribable. "Richard, I want to marry you too. And I think we could live quite well on the money from Mr. Darcy's bet. I know you—"

"Pardon me, Charlotte, but how do you know about the bet?"

"Mr. Darcy told us about it when we heard you were injured."

He adjusted the General a bit and turned more fully to Charlotte. "But I had not even made the bet yet."

She looked confused. "What bet are you talking about?"

"The one where he bet me his annual income."

"Yes, it is one in the same. He told me that you bet him almost a year ago exactly that Elizabeth did not feel about him the way he thought she did. It was said in jest, but he plans on paying you, Richard. Has he not spoken of this to you?"

Now Colonel Fitzwilliam started putting the pieces together. He remembered the pain in Darcy's eyes when Elizabeth accused Darcy of compromising her. It had been Colonel Fitzwilliam who carried her to her bed after he stormed out. And it had been Colonel Fitzwilliam who had heard Elizabeth tearfully ask why Darcy had gone away after promising to never leave her. It was clear to Fitzwilliam that Elizabeth still loved his cousin very much, but Darcy had insisted on an immediate departure from Rosings. Colonel Fitzwilliam hadn't known what to do other than pray.

And pray he did, until two weeks later when he received a letter from Charlotte informing him that Elizabeth had returned to London. Knowing Darcy's competitive nature, Fitzwilliam had bet his cousin a year's income that there was still some hope for Mr. Darcy.

It was much clearer now. "He thinks he *already* owes me his annual income? And he plans on paying me?"

"I believe so. He said he owed you that and so much more. If you had not reunited them, they would never have known the happiness they share now. What bet were you referring to?"

Colonel Fitzwilliam then said with a grin, "I would rather not say. It might be eleven days premature. But why did he make a second bet?" Richard mused. "Did he doubt my ability to woo?"

"Excuse me," Charlotte interrupted, "your ability to do what?"

"Charlotte, I could never divulge the details of a gentleman's wager," he teased. "And in all fairness, Georgiana did warn you back at Darcy House that I am an accomplished ladies' man."

"Yes, that fact must have slipped my mind." Her sweet laughter put him a little more at ease. "Do all men bet on winning ladies' hearts?" she asked.

"It seems those named Fitzwilliam do. I am sorry Georgiana gave you such a terrible impression of me. Am I really as bad as that?"

"Most definitely not. You are skilled at conversation, that much is true, but it is always very clear when you place full meaning in what you say."

"Is that so? And if I said that you were the most courageous woman that I have ever met, one who found peace in an environment of war, what would you say?"

She smiled sweetly at him. "I would say that perhaps you have had a bit too much brandy."

"I have not had any brandy in nearly a year. I find there is only one thing that calms me now—the sweet smile you have on your face at this very moment. It is captivating and intoxicating. I must admit I am quite foxed right now because of it."

Her cheeks flushed brightly, and she tapped the General's nose with her finger. "General, what will we do with your colonel?"

"I will tell you what you can do," he replied. "Tell me that I will be *your* colonel soon. Claim one more victory, Charlotte. I would be quite happy to surrender. All my hopes are entirely in your power."

She blushed even deeper and looked away. "I often thought to myself how much I hoped for Fitzwilliam to return safely," she said. "It occupied many nights."

"And in my unconscious world, I think I may have heard you even say it to me.'"

"What do you mean?" Charlotte asked.

"When I was in and out of consciousness those three weeks after the battle, I often heard people speaking to me. Sometimes it was the voice of Mr. Heather. Sometimes, the chaplain, Mr. Lisscord. Sometimes, my men. But there were several times when it was you. Sometimes when the pain was too intense, I would drift off into a world where I could think about you. It was your smile that kept me going, Charlotte.

"One time near the end, I was struggling to breathe. My lungs were too weak. I felt like I was at the bottom of the deepest part of the ocean with a house full of bricks on my chest. I very distinctly heard a voice telling me to breathe, and somehow I managed to take one more breath. It was not the voice of Mr. Heather, or Mr. Lisscord, or any of my men. It was your voice."

"What did I say?" Charlotte asked.

"You said, 'I have never given up hope for Fitzwilliam.'"

"Oh, Richard! I never did! I do not want to wait eleven more days. Ask me now."

He suddenly saw just how serious she was. She was ready, he was ready, and even though it was eleven days early, he had to ask that ever-important question. He wanted to do this right. He placed the General on the floor and handed him his pocket watch to play with. It was enough to distract him sufficiently. He took Charlotte's hand and kissed it. There were no words to describe what it felt like to offer oneself, but he took comfort in her smile.

However, just as he opened his mouth to speak, he heard Darcy outside the library door employing an exaggerated, overly loud tone, clearly meant to warn Fitzwilliam of his imminent entrance. "Hold that thought," Richard whispered. "It seems we have company." He sat upright and dropped Charlotte's hand.

Darcy could be heard saying, "I believe I saw Mrs. Collins enter the library, Mr. Pastel. She is so diligent in the General's learning." Colonel Fitzwilliam scooted away from Charlotte and picked up the nearest book. He had done it so quickly that he hadn't realized that the book was upside down, but it was too late to change it now. He simply pretended to read.

*****

Mr. Darcy was relieved to find Richard and Charlotte not together in the nursery and not directly interacting. It was more important than ever that Richard maintained propriety, and from the looks that were exchanged between the two of them over the last few days, it was a rare occurrence indeed that they would be in the same room and not completely engrossed in each other.

Mr. Pastel followed him in and announced, "Mrs. Collins, I was hoping to catch you yesterday, but it seems our paths have not crossed. I understand you rose early this morning."

"Yes," Charlotte replied. "Colonel Fitzwilliam was kind enough to escort me to Mr. Collins's grave."

"Wonderful. How was it?"

Charlotte's face flashed a momentary look that could only have been picked up by those who knew her well. The look was brief, but clearly it was one of trepidation. Mr. Darcy said a silent prayer that Charlotte would say the right thing.

"I admit the experience was somewhat different than I expected. Instead of anxiety and fear over the reminder of my late husband's death, I was relieved to feel nothing but peace."

Mr. Pastel seemed to accept this answer. "I am very glad to hear so, Mrs. Collins," he replied. "For now I can finally conclude the business that has plagued me for so long. As you know, I was Mr. Collins's solicitor. I am here to inform you that your late husband created a secret will."

Darcy feigned a gasp of astonishment at this revelation. Colonel Fitzwilliam, however, dropped his book entirely and nearly knocked over a vase on the side table.

"Really?" the colonel asked Mr. Pastel as he returned the vase to its original location.

Mr. Pastel glanced briefly at each man then back to Charlotte and said, "I will share it with you now, with your permission."

The lady nodded with obvious trepidation.

"I apologize for the secrecy, but I was bound by the will to keep the matter strictly confidential. Mrs. Collins, this may take a bit of time, may I still proceed?"

"Yes, of course," Charlotte replied. "Let me ring for Sally to take Isaac." After she rang the servant's bell, an odd silence enveloped the room.

"Is there a place we can speak privately, Mrs. Collins?" Pastel asked.

Again a subtle look of trepidation crossed her features. Mr. Darcy was relieved to hear her say, "Both Mr. Darcy and Colonel Fitzwilliam helped me balance the ledgers when Mr. Collins died. They are, I daresay, even more familiar with matters of his estate than I am. I would prefer it if they stayed."

Mr. Pastel sent a fleeting look to Colonel Fitzwilliam, who by this time had stepped closer to Charlotte. "Very well," Pastel replied.

The maid came in, and Charlotte directed her to take her son to Sally. Mr. Darcy closed the door after them, and they all settled into chairs. Richard sat down next to Charlotte, but Mr. Pastel remained standing.

"Mrs. Collins," Mr. Pastel began, "I never worked directly with your late husband, but judging from his will, I gather that he was obsessive and meticulous. Let me say that I worried a great deal this day might never come. But it has come, and I admit I am quite relieved to inform you that you are not a penniless widow. At least it appears that way."

Mr. Darcy asked, "What do you mean it appears that way?"

"Either she is or she is not," Colonel Fitzwilliam asserted. "Do not toy with her emotions."

"If it were entirely up to me, then I would gladly hand over all that should rightfully be hers," Mr. Pastel explained, "but there were several stipulations in the will that must be satisfied."

"What did my late husband demand of me?" Charlotte asked.

Mr. Darcy heard the pain in her voice. Even Mr. Pastel seemed moved by it. "Let me start by telling you about the stipulations you have already fulfilled," he said gently. "You have worn black, not any other color, for the entire year. You have praised him to his parishioners, his business associates, and Lady Catherine de Burgh. You have not defamed his name in any way. You have voluntarily visited his gravesite within the year of his death. You had an expensive gravestone engraved within the allotted time, with his name as William Nathaniel Collins, not Byron William Nathaniel Collins, and said gravestone specified his position as rector. And you have named your child after him—in a way."

Darcy interjected, "Pardon me, Mr. Pastel, but Mrs. Collins named the child after his father. There can be no question on that matter. Byron was his first given name—was it not?—despite Mr. Collin's preference for William."

"Yes," Mr. Pastel agreed, turning to Darcy, "of course." He then returned to Charlotte. "Also, you did not attend any social events unsuitable for a widow in mourning. You have not disclosed, not even to your closest friends, any unsuitable behavior on the part of Mr. Collins as a husband."

Mr. Pastel paused before continuing. "As to that last part, Mrs. Collins, I can only imagine what that stipulation might refer to, and you have my sincere condolences. Please allow me to say that, for a long time now, I have wanted nothing to do with executing your late husband's will."

"Thank you," Charlotte said. Her voice cracked slightly with those words, and yet she held her head high. Colonel Fitzwilliam's face exhibited a mixture of a desire to attack Mr. Pastel and a resounding pride in how well Charlotte was taking the news.

"But there is still one more stipulation that I need to address before I can award you what Mr. Collins bequeathed to you."

Mr. Darcy was unaware of any other stipulations. He felt anxiety start to build in his stomach. Without realizing it, he and Colonel Fitzwilliam scooted forward in their seats. Darcy did not like surprises. He wished once again there had been time to read the entirety of the will that had become the definitive factor on Charlotte's financial future.

"Forgive me, but I must ask a question that might make you uncomfortable," Mr. Pastel explained.

"Proceed. You may ask me anything in front of these gentlemen. I trust them completely."

Pastel sighed. "I was afraid that might be the case."

Mr. Darcy did not like the tone of his voice. "Mr. Pastel, is there something in the will that has not been adhered to?"

Pastel turned to Mr. Darcy and said, "I am a business man, an *honest* business man. People have come to request my services because they know that I will be thorough and diligent in handling their affairs. It has not escaped my notice these last few days while at Rosings that Mrs. Collins and Colonel Fitzwilliam have been in each other's company a great deal. One of the requirements of the will demands that I ensure that there have been no clandestine relationships during her year of mourning." He turned to Charlotte and asked, "So, I must ask you, Mrs. Collins, has Colonel Fitzwilliam ever offered marriage to you?"

Darcy winced at the question, because he did not know the answer. He knew that Colonel Fitzwilliam had kissed her in Pemberley's garden before the war, and he also knew that Richard intended to offer her his hand in marriage. They had even bet on it. He waited to hear Charlotte answer.

"I can honestly say that he has never asked me to marry him."

Mr. Pastel looked relieved. "Then I am happy to tell you that you are now the proud owner of two very fine ships, the *Eastern Challenge* and the *Winter's Night*, as well as," Mr. Pastel pulled out a piece of paper and read, "Thirteen thousand, seven hundred, and sixty pounds, give or take. There is still one more shipment to be made in his name before you can claim it."

Charlotte gasped and covered her open mouth with her hand. She seemed to be so shocked that she was insensible of the fact that everyone in the room was watching her.

After a few minutes of silence, Mr. Pastel said, "Congratulations, Mrs. Collins. I will have ownership signed over into your name as soon as the year of mourning is up. As long as you keep doing what you are doing, you will become a wealthy widow in eleven days. Having enjoyed your acquaintance over the last year, it brings me great pleasure to award this to you. You most definitely deserve it."

Charlotte, still too shocked to make a reply, nodded but said nothing. Mr. Darcy stated, "I do not understand how a rector could have amassed enough money to buy two cargo ships. Do you know when he purchased them?"

"Mr. Collins was a very frugal man," Mr. Pastel explained. "Mrs. Collins told me as much herself last October. When his father died, he was left with a large sum of money. I am told by my brother, Clyde, that he had a few good hands at the card table which nearly doubled it. He then immediately invested in the two ships and has made large profits since then. This year alone he made nearly a thousand-pound profit, even after expenses. Some years, when his cargo was slightly less honest, he was able to earn over four thousand pounds."

Charlotte's head perked up at that comment. "What do you mean 'less honest'?"

"Mrs. Collins, I do not think you wish me to go into the particulars."

"I believe she does," Mr. Darcy asserted.

"I know I do," Colonel Fitzwilliam said.

Mr. Pastel took a seat. "My brother, Clyde, managed the ships until Mr. Collins's death last spring," Pastel stated. He paused. "I cannot be certain, but I am afraid the two of them were involved in trafficking children." Charlotte audibly gasped for a second time. "The term my brother used on the paperwork was 'providing transportation and apprentice arrangements for urban orphans'. He claimed he had a contact in London who would find and take in street orphans and arrange apprenticeships for them. Supposedly, it was an opportunity to learn a trade and become an honest, hard-working member of society."

Mr. Darcy said, "But you do not fully accept this . . . ."

Mr. Pastel cleared his throat, "Ah, no, I do not. There were too many secrets. He refused to show me the details of where the children went once they arrived from London. I was even denied the chance to see the children myself. The few times I managed to watch the loading or unloading of the ships, I saw many boxes and crates, but nothing that looked like food or clothes for orphans. And I never saw a single child on the deck. So, if he did have children on board, they must have been kept below deck. I cannot imagine any child would do so willingly."

"What do you think happened to the children?" Charlotte asked, "Were they sold?"

"I really do not know. I am somewhat grateful to not know the particulars. For if I did, I might be forced to turn my brother in to the authorities. I think Clyde knew this as well. That is why he kept it from me. All the paperwork simply said they were transporting orphans to apprenticeships in London, which is a perfectly legitimate business transaction. Clyde is very good at details. I tried the best I could to find out what they were doing, but all I hit were dead ends. I doubt there is much trail to go on now.

"As soon as I heard of Mr. Collins's death, I took over management of the ships, arguing that as executor of Mr. Collins's will, it was only right that I assume control. Clyde begrudgingly relinquished control. There was nothing left on board by then, but I knew from my previous investigations that the cargo was always chained and locked tight. If fact, Captain Jersey told me at the time of his interview that he was specifically prohibited from opening the crates for any reason."

"What do you think they were transporting on the return trip?" Fitzwilliam asked.

"What do I think? Most likely stolen goods. Or perhaps, contraband from France. But what can I prove? Nothing. However, you have an honest crew and captain now, Mrs. Collins. I can personally attest to the fact that the ships' current cargo is nothing but Italian fabrics and the occasional piece of artwork. You will have nothing to worry about."

"But if the money was earned by trafficking children, I am sure I do not want it."

The room fell entirely silent.

"Is there any proof at all that there was something illegal going on?" Darcy asked.

"No, nothing more than the hefty profits and the suspicions of Captain Jersey and myself. Perhaps I should not have even told you. I can assure you that if there was any evidence of illegal activity, I would have put a stop to it immediately. You should feel confident that the money and the ships are now yours. What happens from this point on can be entirely up to you. Do you wish to sell the ships or to have me continue the management of them for you?"

Charlotte still remained silent.

Colonel Fitzwilliam spoke up, "I think she needs some time. Thank you, Mr. Pastel. If that is all, we shall discuss this matter further with Mrs. Collins and let you know of her decision."

Mr. Pastel bowed and left after congratulating her once again.

*****

Charlotte could not stop repeating it in her head. *Two ships, £13,760.* That was a fortune! It would certainly put bread on the table for the General. For the rest of his life. As much as he needed.

She had done it. Somehow she had found a way to provide for her son. And she had done it without even knowing it! She had done it by being true to herself. She had done it by being 'Just Charlotte'.

She was sufficiently distracted that she did not hear her name being called until Colonel Fitzwilliam put his hand on her shoulder. "Charlotte? I asked if you were well. Would you like some wine?"

She looked at him. He was kneeling down in front of her with such depth and compassion in his tone and words that she reached her hand up and swept back the curls that covered his forehead. "Richard, we did it."

"No, Charlotte, *you* did it. This was entirely your success. I very nearly ruined it for you just moments ago." He reached up and grasped her hand and held it against his cheek. "You should be very proud of yourself. The *Winter's Night* and *Eastern Horizon* are sister ships to each other and I have seen both of them. There are no finer ships in England."

"You have seen them? Tell me about them."

"They are mid-sized ships, very well taken care of. In fact, you know the captain of the *Eastern Challenge*: Captain Jersey."

Mr. Darcy said, "Do you have any thoughts about what you want to do, Charlotte? If you keep the ships, they will provide plenty of income. But if you sell them, you could live reasonably well on the interest."

"Nearly fourteen thousand pounds will provide plenty of interest by itself," Charlotte marveled. "I could never have imagined such a sum!"

Colonel Fitzwilliam turned to Darcy. "Speaking of which," he said, "I believe you have some explaining to do, Cousin. If I am not mistaken, it seems you have duped me into making not one, but two wagers with you this year. I am afraid to tell you your bank account will be twenty-eight thousand pounds poorer when Charlotte and I marry."

Darcy let out a laugh. "I am just as surprised as you that I had the skill to manipulate you, the master of conversation, into a second wager. Although I do not think my annual income quite compares to a clean horse stable. But you were so assured of yourself. And what is it you always say? A confident man is always the one who slips on the ice."

The gentlemen laughed knowingly.

Charlotte was amused to hear the details of the bet. "Wait, you would have to have to clean horse stalls if I do not marry you? That bet seems rather lopsided."

Darcy laughed and replied, "Do not be too hasty, Charlotte. According to your answer to the last stipulation in your late husband's will, he has not won the wager yet. You must accept his hand within a month of the end of your mourning. I may very well still have the cleanest stables in all of Derbyshire!"

Charlotte looked at Colonel Fitzwilliam kneeling in front of her and smiled at him warmly. The realization of how her life had changed over the last year simply brightened her smile even further.

Colonel Fitzwilliam whispered, "Completely foxed, I say. That smile is intoxicating." He took her hand and kissed it gently, sending goose bumps from her hand all the way to her toes. His handsome gray eyes winked. "Not a trifle disguised or bosky. Not tap-hackled. Not even properly shot in the neck. I am one-hundred percent ape-drunk."

# CHAPTER 24

Charlotte thought that Anne and Captain Jersey's wedding had been very nearly perfect, especially since Richard had sat with her for the ceremony, their fingers caressing discretely throughout their vows. It made her hopeful for her own upcoming union.

Mr. Pastel had made all the final arrangements, and the paperwork was now official, even though there were still two days until the full year of mourning was over. The ships and money were in Charlotte's name.

They had spent a week at Rosings before travelling to London for Fitzwilliam's ball. Georgiana and Elizabeth rode in the carriage with Charlotte and the General while the men rode alongside on horseback. It offered them several hours to talk as dear friends do. She finally gathered her courage and told them about her newfound wealth.

Georgiana could not have been happier. However, Elizabeth did not seem all that surprised, which led to questions about her involvement. The whole story of Elizabeth discovering the mysterious ledger last April, and meeting Mr. Pastel on their wedding trip, as well as everything Richard had discovered in his investigations, was explained.

She found it very curious how easily Richard had extracted information from Benjamin Pastel while simultaneously developing a sincere regard for the man. The colonel had certainly accomplished a great deal during the few short weeks he spent in Liverpool. Charlotte and Georgiana were shocked and amused to hear that Mr. Darcy had pinched the will from Pastel's luggage in order to read as much of it as possible.

After a moment of silence, Elizabeth exclaimed, "Just think of it, Charlotte! It is just a few days away from the anniversary of

Mr. Collins's death, and you have done so well for yourself! Look at how far you have come since last April!"

"Yes, it is hard to believe how much my life has changed since then," Charlotte said with a smile. "You two have been so kind to me. I must confess I am excited for my mourning period to come to an end." She hesitated to share her good news prematurely, but found that she was unable to resist any longer: "In fact, I have it on good report that the colonel will formally ask for my hand in the next few days."

"That is so wonderful!" Georgiana squealed. "I am so happy for you!"

"Thank you. You two are both so dear to me!" Charlotte squeezed Elizabeth's hand and took a deep breath. There was one more thing to say. She knew the time had come. "And as my dear friends, there is something I should have told you both a long time ago, something that I have never told anyone. You both know that Mr. Collins and I did not have a love match. But the truth of the matter was much worse than that. My husband was cruel and hateful. Some nights he would . . ." she sighed and briefly lowered her head.

*No, you need not be ashamed of another man's sins. You have fought this battle already*, she told herself.

She confidently looked up and spoke words she never had admitted to another soul. "Well, the truth is that nearly every night I fell asleep hurting . . . because of him. Sometimes it was a sore cheek and the pain would be gone by morning. But often it was much worse. Sometimes the pain lasted much longer.

"In fact, there are days where the pain still affects me," she put her hand over her heart and continued, ". . . right here." Then she touched her brow. "And here."

Georgiana gasped and tears started forming in her eyes.

Charlotte continued, "Please do not cry for me, Georgiana," Charlotte whispered, trying to comfort her young friend. She knew Georgiana's innocent, trusting heart would take the news badly.

"That is why . . . that is why you did not wish to marry again?" Georgiana guessed.

"That was part of it," Charlotte admitted. "But now I have a future ahead of me that Mr. Collins will never be a part of. Richard is as kind and gentle as any man could be. He has helped heal my distrustful heart. For the first time . . .”

Georgiana finished for her, “For the first time, you are in love!”

“Yes, exactly. I told you once that I valued my independence more than anything else. But I was wrong. Now I value love above all else. For love has given me everything I ever wanted and all that I did not know I needed. I never imagined it possible, but little by little as my bruises faded, my fear and anxiety and distrust disappeared as well. It might surprise you that those scars took a great deal longer to fade than the broken ribs.”

Charlotte turned to her oldest friend. She couldn't help but notice that Elizabeth was considerably less surprised by the news. It was as she had suspected. “Elizabeth, I know you have known the truth for a long time—at least since that night you comforted me in Pemberley's rose garden. Please tell me, how did you find out? I tried so hard to hide it from everyone.”

Elizabeth then told Charlotte about how she had overheard the parsonage servants whispering at Mr. Collins's funeral about Charlotte's bruises. “I am sorry I did not tell you,” Elizabeth apologized, “but I knew you were not ready to share. At times, I confess I was afraid that the scars left by Mr. Collins might never completely fade. I have been so worried about you this past year. And now I am so happy for you, my dear.”

Charlotte found it strange that she could not stop smiling. The subject that she had once dreaded disclosing, even to Elizabeth, now brought her only peace. Even the memories of Mr. Collins's cruelty had faded. It seemed that her heart was filled to the brim and overflowing with pleasant memories of the last year—precious moments spent with her son, Elizabeth, Georgiana, and Darcy, and, of course, Richard. She was overwhelmed by a feeling of forgiveness and love that settled on her.

She looked from Elizabeth to Georgiana and back again. “I cannot tell you how much your friendship has meant to me this past year. Thank you for showing me that there was still hope for Fitzwilliam—and for me.”

The three friends embraced, sharing several more tears and extending their warmest wishes. Georgiana and Elizabeth soon steered the conversation to Charlotte's wedding plans. Although

Charlotte denied she had gone so far as to imagine which of her newly ordered dresses she would wear, she did confess, with a blush, that she would like a summer wedding.

"Oh, I have so much to look forward to in a few months when I enter society!" Georgiana exclaimed. "I want so badly to find my own love match. But how will I know it when I find it?"

Charlotte considered the question carefully. "We each need different things to feel loved," she replied. "I, for instance, never knew how much I needed to be respected until Richard offered me his respect. His faith in me makes me want to be the best Charlotte I can be."

"And I never imagined myself with a man like your brother," Elizabeth confessed. "I did not know how much I needed his quiet strength. Keep your eyes open, Georgiana. Look for someone you trust, someone whose actions reveal an honest nature. Many people pretend to be good, but fewer are truly good at heart."

"Thank you, Elizabeth and Charlotte. There might be hope for me yet."

"Of course there is!" Charlotte exclaimed. "In a few more months, we shall all hope for Georgiana!"

\*\*\*\*\*

It was Saturday, the morning of Colonel Fitzwilliam's ball, and three days past the anniversary of Mr. Collins's death. Charlotte hadn't seen Richard at all since Thursday, and she was getting rather nervous. It seemed she had taken living with him under the same roof for granted. For some mysterious reason, he had chosen to stay at his bachelor's flat when they returned to London.

Rumors of the ball's guest list were circulating, and Elizabeth had multiple visitors paying calls, all hoping to hear the latest news on Colonel Fitzwilliam. Charlotte had sat in on a few. Most of the ladies tried to mask their curiosity by covertly asking about Richard's condition. Charlotte was sick to death of their veiled comments:

"I have not seen the colonel since his return. How is he faring?"

"Is he much altered since the war?"

"How very lucky you are to have had him with you at Pemberley!"

"We have not seen him since he returned to London. Where could he be hiding?"

Then again, other times the press for gossip was more direct, and often quite offensive. They would say things that no one would consider saying, yet they did.

"I hear his arm prevents him from doing most things."

"What will Colonel Fitzwilliam do now that he is unfit for duty?"

Lady Atkinson and her daughter dared to show their faces the day before the ball and posed the question most directly, beating out all other visitors in their complete lack of tact: "War can be quite disfiguring. Do you fear Colonel Fitzwilliam will struggle with being accepted again by the *ton*?"

Charlotte was not disappointed to see the visitors leave. But as the morning began to turn into afternoon, she became slightly disappointed that the colonel didn't appear. Worry began to seep into her countenance.

Elizabeth rested her hand on her arm. "How are you, Charlotte?" she asked.

Charlotte sighed. "I am sorry, Elizabeth. I fear I have been acting like a spoiled child! It is just that I miss him terribly. Why has he not come to see me these last few days? I have never seen him act so mysteriously!"

"I hope you do not think he is having second thoughts about you."

"Oh, no. I have no doubt that we will come to an understanding, but every day when I put on one of the new gowns I had made, I wonder if today will be the first day since your wedding that he will see me in anything other than black."

"Try not to worry, Charlotte. You will have a whole lifetime to show him your pretty dresses," she teased. Charlotte struggled not to laugh. "Although, that yellow dress is very becoming on you. I think the neckline is particularly beautiful. How does your ball gown fit?"

"Very nicely. Perhaps that will be the first colored dress he sees me in." She looked out the sitting room window and sighed again. "I should probably rest while the General is sleeping. It will be a late night tonight."

"Charlotte," Elizabeth reassured, "do not worry about why Richard has not visited. I have been sworn to secrecy on the memory of Princess Le Grande Fiona, but I can assure you there is nothing the matter. He and Will have been attending to . . . some business that has occupied a great deal of time these last few days."

"Very well. I shall just have to content myself with seeing him at the ball."

\*\*\*\*\*

Charlotte stepped out of the carriage and into the night. Matlock house was brightly lit with torches and red-and-white silk ribbon bows. It was so well lit that one was hard pressed to claim the sun had gone down.

Mr. Darcy had insisted that Georgiana stay home. It was improper for her to attend any of society's balls until her coming out. But to soften the blow, he had promised her that they would host a private ball with all of their closest friends and family at Darcy House very soon.

As Charlotte exited the carriage, Mr. Darcy offered one arm to her and his other arm to Elizabeth, and the three of them walked to the front door. They could hear the musicians warming up, and the smell of fresh flowers permeated the foyer. The hustle and bustle of people arriving was overwhelming. They were all warmly welcomed by Lord and Lady Matlock. The ball was so well attended that Charlotte feared that she would never find the colonel in the crowded house. But that did not keep her from trying.

The uniformed men were so thick that the ballroom appeared as an ocean of red, with other colors merely bobbing among the waves. Charlotte looked down again at her deep-rose, two-toned, floral silk fabric. Although a modest style, she still felt a little uncomfortable in anything other than the high-necked black mourning dresses she was so used to. She clung to Mr. Darcy's arm, and the three of them started making the rounds of the ballroom.

She searched and searched for the one man her heart ached to see. Every one they met inquired about the man of honor. She was introduced to Mr. Frenton, who asked for a set, which Charlotte accepted. His sister, Miss Frenton, was a beautiful blonde young lady who seemed genuinely concerned about Colonel Fitzwilliam.

"I do hope he will not feel uncomfortable in society," Miss Frenton remarked. "Look how many people are here to welcome him! Will he be arriving shortly?"

"I am not sure, but knowing Richard, no doubt he will make as grand an entrance as possible," Darcy chuckled. "His mother would never start the ball without him." Then he whispered to Charlotte, "Do not fret. He will be here."

The ballroom became more and more crowded, and still there was no sign of him. She heard Elizabeth say, "Excuse me, Will, I just saw a friend. I shall be back shortly."

Then Mr. Darcy released Charlotte's arm to shake the hand of a Captain Wellington, whom he apparently knew quite well. Charlotte continued walking around the room. She felt the eyes of a few people, but the majority of the crowd seemed to take no notice of her. The anticipation of seeing Richard was beginning to get overwhelming. The ball had not officially opened yet, and already the room was heating up. If guests continued to arrive at this rate, they would soon run out of space for dancing.

She saw a balcony that seemed to be less crowded and started to make her way there when a silence fell over the room. It was clear that something—or, she prayed, someone—had just garnered the attention of every guest. Her eyes searched frantically, and she followed everyone's gazes until she saw him.

He was in fine-fitting, regal dress regimentals, and with his height, he stood almost a full head above most of the men. A flock of ladies swished their skirts to be the first to receive that charming smile. Charlotte watched the crowd around him build and marveled at his ease in the middle of it. She could tell he had just had his hair trimmed. The natural waves seemed more bold and dramatic, mirroring his handsome countenance. It made her think of the General's head full of curls. She desperately wanted to go claim his every attention but, at the moment, she enjoyed observing him from afar.

Slowly the crowd huddled around him made progress in her direction, but yet he still had not made eye contact. The opening notes of a song alerted the guests that the first set was about to start.

He then looked directly at her, as if he had known she was there all along. The look in his eyes was breathtaking. He smiled broadly, and every conversation in the room stopped as he pardoned himself and politely pushed through the group. Soon all but the most oblivious guests took notice of his determined approach. The crowd started to part as he made his way toward her. A moment ago she had been uncomfortable with a few pairs of eyes on her, but now it was very clear, with his gaze fixed on her, that the entire room was watching.

The crowd completely parted, and Colonel Fitzwilliam took those last few steps away from the group. She gasped. He had two arms that gracefully swung at his sides. Her gaze followed the left shoulder down. His shoulder seemed a little bulky, and the fabric on the elbow seemed too loose. She could not tell how it was done, but his left hand filled his dancing glove perfectly. She looked up at him as he took the last step towards her and smiled.

"I remember that you said you would not dance with a one-armed man. And it would not do to have your first ball out of mourning break with propriety." He stretched forth his left arm, and she could see that it moved forward as an entire unit. She looked back up at him and truly tried to say something. When her words failed her, he said, "Mrs. Collins, I believe it is our dance. I cannot imagine opening my hero's welcome ball with anyone less worthy. Shall we?"

She smiled at him and took his offered left hand. She could feel the firm cool device under the glove. She wrapped her arm around his and again the crowd parted so that the man of honor could escort his chosen dance partner up to the front of the ballroom. The room started to fill with whispers. No doubt everyone wanted to know who she was. And, they all wanted to know the same thing she wanted to know: what did Colonel Fitzwilliam have up his sleeve?

The couples hurried to take their place in line, and Colonel Fitzwilliam nodded to the orchestra, and the music began. The men and women bowed and curtsied. As each step of the dance progressed, her heart began to speed up. They had only been dancing for a few minutes when she concluded most decidedly that he was magnificent on the dance floor. He had a way of parading her as if she were a prized jewel in need of proper display. His enthusiasm for dancing with her infiltrated her every thought, and soon she couldn't help but smile just as joyously as he did.

As they were about to turn, he whispered, "There it is! I have missed your smile these last few days." She felt her cheeks flush with his compliment, and momentarily they were separated.

When they returned, she reached for both his hands, and they promenaded down the rows of couples, everyone watching them intensely, but she felt surprisingly comfortable. In fact, nothing felt more natural than dancing at his side with his regimental buttons reflecting the candlelight from the room. "You look wonderful, Colonel."

He smiled at her and gave a subtle wink. "Is that so?" he asked. "You like my new look?"

"Yes. Although I must confess, I had gotten rather used to the old new you. Is this what kept you away for the last several days?"

"It is. The blacksmith had me in his shop from nearly dawn until dusk making a contraption that straps to my shoulder. I am unable to bend much, but it serves its purpose, because now I am able to do this—" They had reached the end of the row, and he used his left arm to lead her into a twirl under his new arm. He then reached both arms out to take her hands. "But I am limited in sensation. How I wish I could feel your hand in mine! All I can tell is that you have added weight to the shoulder. But I always say the subtlest of touches can be the most passionate."

She giggled, "Is that so? You *always* say that? I fail to see how such an odd adage could be used at any other time than in this precise situation."

He chuckled and gracefully led her to the next step where they separated again as partners were temporarily exchanged. When he returned, he confessed, "I see my ability to sway you with my superior conversational skills has led me into trouble. I suppose I must concede that I invented that saying just now on the impulse of the moment. However, I do not retract it; it is entirely true. Being able to hold you with both hands is a feeling that ignites no small amount of passion."

She wanted to chastise him for being so bold when there were so many people watching—and most likely listening—but all she could do was laugh outright. The moment was entirely too enjoyable. "I am afraid that feeling is mutual," she admitted.

"I am glad to hear it!" He was so proud of his ability to guide her around, and turn with her gracefully, that the rest of the dance was performed with poise and meaningful silence. Every touch and stolen glance sent tingles up her spine. His gentle hands, as they guided her gracefully, affected her so entirely that she was no longer aware of anyone else in the ballroom. It was just Richard and her, promenading and twirling. It was not possible for her smile to widen, her blush to deepen, or her heart to speed up. Every part of her body felt a deep and abiding love for the man who had captured her heart. Nay, her heart had fully surrendered.

But all too soon, the music ended, and he bowed to her. She smiled once more to him and curtsied. Their time had ended. He offered his right arm to her, she welcomed it eagerly, and he escorted her to the side of the ballroom.

"Mrs. Collins, I do hope you enjoyed dancing with me, for I fully intend to impose upon you for the final dance. May I be so bold as to assume your acceptance?"

"If you ask the right question, I might just say yes."

He smiled broadly. "Hmmm," he replied. "That sounds like an answer that could be understood in more than one way."

"Yes, I believe it could."

"Well then, I shall have to think of just the right question." Colonel Fitzwilliam kissed her hand, and warmth filled her entire bosom.

# CHAPTER 25

His dance with Charlotte could not have been more thrilling. She looked stunning in her rose silk gown. Her hair was tastefully elegant, as always. But now, her smile never left her face. Indeed, she had never looked more beautiful.

Dozens of gentlemen pulled him aside to inquire after her. Who was she? Did he admire her? How well did he know her? He dismissed their questions, replying only that they should wait and see. At the end of the ball, he planned to make a very special announcement. He had mentally rehearsed a thousand times. "He that hath ears to hear, let him hear: Charlotte Collins has accepted my hand in marriage!" The prospect nearly made him giddy.

In the meantime, his hero's ball seemed to progress at a snail's pace. He continued to make the rounds between sets, and he was in no want for partners, but whenever possible, he was right at her side. Though he felt hundreds of curious eyes on them, he introduced her only to those guests worthy of her. That omitted the Atkinsons. It was unclear how they had even received an invitation after his direct cut last August. His close friends were all sufficiently impressed—and sufficiently curious—to request a set with her, which pleased him greatly.

It was rather amusing to see her surprise at each request. *Charlotte still has no idea how beautiful she is. That will change.*

He was selective enough in the ladies he danced with to leave no doubt that Colonel Fitzwilliam was not the same man he used to be—the flirt who had once so persistently pursued the most sought-after ladies. Tonight he only asked the ladies who seemed to stand by themselves or who appeared to be in need of a bit of joy.

It was finally time. Halfway through with the second dinner course, Colonel Fitzwilliam reached his hand under the table and pressed Charlotte's hand. She looked at him curiously, then he leaned into her and whispered, "I have a great desire to see my grandparents' swing, and you look quite flushed. Might you accompany me?"

He was rewarded with her amazing smile. "Certainly."

He smiled back at her and instructed, "Wait a few minutes. When Darcy and Elizabeth rise, follow them. They will show you the way."

He stood and set his napkin on the table and went to the lemonade bowl. There he singlehandedly ladled the drink into his cup. Then he turned back to Darcy, still seated at the dinner table, signaling him with a nod. Darcy cleared his throat and invited Charlotte and Elizabeth to take a turn with him in the garden. Charlotte blushed and stammered her agreement. The colonel winked at her as the trio left, which deepened Charlotte's blush several more shades.

Colonel Fitzwilliam sipped his lemonade and meticulously counted the minutes that passed. Sure enough, Darcy and Elizabeth returned to their seats a few minutes later. Elizabeth was in her sixth month of pregnancy now and looked somewhat uncomfortable, but her face glowed brightly with a warm smile. Darcy discreetly made eye contact with him, and the colonel knew he had his sign.

His heart started marching to a strange, new rhythm. Without taking his leave of anyone, he left the dining room and anxiously went to the west sitting room, near the back of the house. Pushing aside the closed curtain, he opened the door that led to the private terrace and garden.

His grandparents had built the terrace after an apoplexy paralyzed the right side of his grandfather's body. It had been their daily pleasure to sit together on the bench swing and watch the sun set. The last few years of his life, they had cherished each other and seen the end of each day's close right here on this terrace.

He saw that everything was just right. The servant had set up a small table with enough candles to light the small, enclosed garden in a soft glow. His eyes searched for her; he found her seated on the bench swing with her back to him, gently using her foot to propel the swing's motion.

He waited a moment more, simply taking in the moment. He had learned that there are certain moments that you want to permanently etch into your memory. This was one of them. He could see the feminine curve of her elegant long neck and the glimmer of her dress in the candlelight. Suddenly the urge was too strong to resist. He came up from behind and placed his right hand on her neck and leaned down and whispered in her ear, "You are irresistible."

She leaned into his touch, and he could smell the rosewater scent that was never overwhelming but always noticeable. Her encouragement was stirring and therefore he indulged himself for a moment. He lightly brushed his fingers along the curve of her neck and then down to her collarbone. She paused momentarily in her swinging, and he heard her let out a sound similar to a kitten purring. That evidence, that she welcomed his touch, elicited an intense pleasure inside him. He walked around to the front.

"Good evening, Richard."

He sat down and let the moment fill him again. "Fancy meeting you here, Charlotte." She smiled. "You know, this is quite an exclusive area of the Fitzwilliam estate. You should feel quite honored to be here," he teased.

She giggled. "Really?"

"Oh yes. My grandfather built all this—the terrace and the garden and this swing. He suffered an apoplexy when he was one-and-fifty. But Grandmother stood by him, undeterred in the slightest. They used to sit here together every evening. Grandfather's manservant would place him on the swing, and my grandmother would place his arm around her like this." He stretched his arm around her shoulders and gently pulled her to him. She gave no resistance. The swing rocked forward and backwards.

"Every night they would swing here together," he continued. "Time would come and go, the sun would set, and they would just swing. This was their private sanctuary. All the servants knew not to interrupt them for any reason. Sometimes they would talk, other times they would just hold each other. I remember watching them from the upstairs window, and I thought to myself that someday I would like to grow old with someone like that. To swing with them, here, on this swing."

Charlotte finally broke her silence. "I missed you," she declared. "Not just the last few days when you were at the blacksmith, but while you were at war. It was the little things. I missed the sweet way you bowed slightly deeper to me than to anyone else. Yes, I noticed that. And how you flashed smiles in my direction from across a room. And that I could ask you to rearrange the nursery a hundred times, and you still responded every time with a pleasant and rather selfless 'I am *your* humble servant'. I missed how I could talk to you about anything. I missed our friendship."

Colonel Fitzwilliam nodded. "Yes, that friendship will get us through anything. Who knew that an Easter visit to my aunt's parsonage could change my life forever?" he marveled.

"I certainly was not prepared to fall in love. But I have, Charlotte. You have captured every part of my heart and body. I had no idea that love could be so overpowering that my every thought—nay, my every word and action—is dictated by my love for you. I am so permanently altered that I will never be the same again. I have been to war many times. I have faced enemies who have shot at me and wielded their swords at my throat. My courage never faltered. The only thing I have ever feared is the thought of not having you by my side forever."

She laid her head on his shoulder, and he heard her take in a deep breath. "And I was so fearful of everything. You do not understand how healing your tenderness has been to me. You are my medicine. I never imagined a gentle word or touch could send a cannonball into the fortress around my hardened, distrustful heart, but it did. I too, am forever changed because of you."

"Let us make a promise to each other."

"Anything," she vowed.

"Promise me that we will never lose this moment. Promise me that even after I ask you to marry me, and even after I hear your precious answer, that we will always find moments like this. No matter what trials come our way, promise me that we will create these moments—these tender mercies from God."

"I promise. And in return, you must promise me to always look at me the way you do tonight, for I shall never tire of seeing how much you love and respect me."

"I shall do better than that, I promise to love you the way you deserve to be loved. You are a precious commodity, Charlotte. You are so much more than 'Just Charlotte'. You are a mother, a friend, a sister, a daughter, and if you will do me the great honor of accepting my hand, you will be a wife."

She lifted her head off his shoulder and looked up at him. Her eyes were wet, and joyful tears dropped as she said, "Only if it is comes with your heart. For that is the only thing that matters to me. I do not care about your hand."

Unable to let the joke pass by, he raised his prosthetic arm and replied, "Well good, because my surgeon has already claimed my hand—which is odd because I cannot recall offering it! This fake arm does not make you swoon?"

She giggled, "I admit it is rather *interesting*. Why did you have it made? Were you worried that society would not accept a one-armed man?"

"Excuse me, but I am a *one-and-a-half* armed man. There is a vast difference." Charlotte laughed out loud. "But to answer your question, no, it had nothing to do with what others think. I simply wanted to be your devilishly handsome *hand* ornament so that others could see how beautiful you are." She bowed her head momentarily and then looked back up at him. "Charlotte, you really are beautiful. I am not talking about just tonight—although tonight you take my breath away. I am talking about your very spirit. I have never known someone so courageous or so forgiving."

"Thank you, Richard. I never knew a man could be so tender with his words."

He was looking down at her face, and he rotated himself slightly so he was facing her too. He reached his hand around the curve of her neck and slowly, painstakingly inched closer to her face. He saw anticipation in her eyes, and he inched even closer. Their faces were a mere inch away, and he felt her sweet breath on his lips. With the last ounce of self-control left, he asked, "Will you allow me to show you that a man can be gentle not only with his words, but with his lips as well?"

"I knew you would finally get around to asking the right question."

He smiled at her and said, "Am I to take that as an affirmative answer?"

"Indeed, sir," she whispered almost imperceptivity.

He closed the small gap between their lips, and he brushed them together ever so lightly, but that feathered touch was enough to ignite a fire that had been longing to start for the last year. He wrapped his right arm around her a little further, and she responded by reaching her hands up to his shoulders. He continued to barely touch her lips with his. He could tell she had begun to smile slightly. He guided his kisses to each corner of her smile that he loved so much, and then he returned to the center and pressed his mouth to hers with slightly more pressure.

Her every movement was begging for more, but did he dare? She had now moved her hands from his shoulders to his hair and was pulling longingly. He wanted so badly to show her what tenderness could do. It was of the utmost importance that she knew how a man should kiss a woman. He felt his heart begin to race.

*She needs to know what a loving kiss really feels like. In reality, this is her very first kiss.* He felt her hunger for more in every movement, and so he did what a loving man would do. He kissed her with all the passion he felt for her, moving his lips with hers as if they were one unit.

He knew by her response that it had been the right thing to do. Ever so carefully, he pulled away just enough to make a trail of kisses up to her ear. Moving his hand to the curve of her neck, he tilted her head just enough to engulf his mouth around that tender spot just under the lobe where he spent a meaningful amount of time exploring with his lips. And as he did so, he felt her moan vibrate on his lips before the sound escaped her lips. It was a sound that came from deep inside, and he knew that she understood that a man could love passionately and selflessly without the use of power or control.

His desires were not, however, stronger than his respect for her. She had accepted his hand, and that was all he needed from her at the moment. When they were married, it would be a different story, but for now he was more than satisfied.

He pulled away, placed one more gentle kiss on her lips, and said, "That is how a man should love a woman."

Her eyes slowly opened, and she looked as if she were foxed herself. He couldn't help but chuckle, which must have reoriented her to the situation. "Were my inexperienced kisses that humorous?" she asked.

"Oh, Charlotte!" He laughed, "If only you could see how desperately in love I am with you!"

"I can only imagine what *I* look like, as *you*, sir, are completely unpresentable with that satisfied grin on your face. There will not be a soul in the room who will not know that you have just loved a woman to the point of no return." They giggled together, both giddy and intoxicated by their kisses. She reached up to his face again. "Richard, I cannot describe how that felt. All I can say is that I never dreamed that fire could permeate my soul with such gentleness. If Mr. Collins only knew that gentleness possessed far more power than force."

"Then I will consider your first kiss to be a success. Have I finally sown my seeds in fertile ground?"

"Pardon me! I believe my reputation is still intact!" she teased.

"Forgive me," he laughed. "That sounded very ungentlemanly. I was merely referring to the parable of the seed. I confess I pray that kiss will bear fruit an hundred fold. I will tell you about it sometime, but for now, we need to return to the ball."

She reached for his hand, squeezed it, and said, "Wait! Promise me that we shall have many tender mercies like that every day."

"With all my heart. And I promise to kiss you until your eyes glaze over and you successfully have driven me to passionate madness." He squeezed her hand. "You know, Charlotte, they say no kiss can be better than your first kiss. And you may be surprised to hear it, but aside from the time when I was seven, it was my first kiss too."

"And so the union begins. Both on equal ground."

"Oh no, my dear, I will always look up to you. You will be my commanding officer from now on." He leaned in and kissed her tenderly for emphasis. She would never again doubt her value or his love for her, and he made sure that this kiss left her entirely convinced of the fact that she was the most loved woman on the face of the Earth.

---

*THE END*

---

Final book in the Hope Series Trilogy:

# *Hope for Georgiana*

Miss Georgiana Darcy's deepest hope is to find love with a good man who sees her inner value—and doesn't care a whit about her dowry. But as she prepares to enter her first London season, the pressure to find a good match builds. Her brother, Mr. Darcy, hopes to help her along by inviting the devilishly handsome and charming Henry Darcy, a distant cousin from America, to stay with them.

But Henry Darcy will not be the only eligible bachelor watching this young lady blossom into the catch of the season. Benjamin Pastel wasn't raised as a titled, wealthy gentleman. He has nothing but his integrity and work ethic to recommend him. But he carries a secret hope for Georgiana to see him as *more* than a friend. Will his efforts be enough, or will he remain unnoticed in Henry Darcy's charismatic shadow?

*In this conclusion of the Regency "Hope Series Trilogy", Georgiana learns that hope is more than merely a flimsy feeling. Just like it did for her brother, Mr. Darcy, and her cousin, Colonel Fitzwilliam, hope provides vision and strength for Georgiana at a critical time in her life. And it teaches her to never relinquish her future to anything other than her own dreams—especially when it comes to love.*

**Coming November 2016**

# About the Author

Jeanna Ellsworth Lake entered a new era in her life in December 2015. Through all her single years, she kept searching for a Mr. Darcy, but didn't realize that what she *needed* was a Colonel Fitzwilliam! And she found him: a second son with a passionate heart, who never fails to make her laugh. She is so proud of her three daughters, who have supported her through her writing, and have always been her inspiration.

She also proudly states she is the eighth of thirteen children. When she isn't writing, blogging, gardening, cooking, or raising chickens, she is thoroughly ignoring her house for a few hours at a time in order to read yet another romance novel, and does not feel the least bit guilty in doing so. She absolutely loves her chance to influence lives as a Registered Nurse in a Neurological ICU. She finds great joy in her many roles she juggles, but writing especially has been her therapy. She claims she has never been happier.

Jeanna fell in love again with Jane Austen when she was introduced to the incredible world of Jane Austen-inspired fiction. She can never adequately thank the fellow authors who mentored her and encouraged her to write her first novel.

She is a member of Austen Authors and regularly blogs at www.austenauthors.net. She loves hearing from her readers and cherishes the chance to interact with them. For more information on her books and writing, please visit her website:
www.HeyLadyPublications.com.

# Other books by Jeanna Ellsworth

## Pride and Prejudice variations

### Mr. Darcy's Promise
How can an honorable promise become so vexing?

### Pride and Persistence
At some point, a good memory is a bad thing.

### To Refine Like Silver
Our trials do not define us; rather they refine us.

## The Hope Series Trilogy:

### Hope for Mr. Darcy
Hope is all they have left, will it be enough?

### Hope for Fitzwilliam
For two destined to be together, hope is their only defense.

### Hope for Georgiana (Coming November 2016)
Hope has become vital—*especially* when it comes to love.

## Regency Romance

### Inspired by Grace
What started as friendship has evolved into something quite tangible.

### Buying the Duke's Silence
(Sequel to *Inspired by Grace*—Coming September 2017)
Eventually Evelyn learns that Silence is golden.

Made in the USA
Monee, IL
02 March 2021